War in Sorcery's Shadow

I0639311

Elise Carlson

Faraway Fiction Press

First published in Australia by Faraway Fiction Press

The font used for chapter headings is called Unzilash and was designed by Manfred Klein.

ISBN 978-0-6454633-6-1 Ebook

ISBN P 978-0-6454633-8-5 Print

By Elise Carlson

LAND
Tira
Tarz's Castle
Galvation Farmland
Fang Mountain Prison
Mountain Flow
Galvatia
City of the Guard
The Trine
Deserted Farmland
Wineya Forest
Rocky Plains
Forest Prison
The Ancient Valley

Dramatis Personae

Tarlahns

Heir Ruarnon (they/them)

King Urmillian (Ruarnon's father)

Queen Corina (Ruarnon's mother)

Prince Omah ((Ruarnon's uncle)

Princess Telena (Ruarnon's aunt)

Lenaris, Ruarnon's best friend (she/her)

Companion Pamoran (Lenaris' father)

Companion Tor, Ruarnon's tutor (he/him)

Advisor Monin (Pamoran's father)

Captain Arleath, of Ruarnon's bodyguard (he/him)

Aza, First General (he/him)

Takanis, Second General (she/her)

Zaldeaans

King Kyura (deceased)

Companion Karmarn (Ruarnon's Uncle)

Merlah (Ruarnon's aunt)

Captain Coroth, Ruarnon's cousin (he/him)

Governor Syenne (Kyura's sister)

Governor Iomar (he/him)

Governor Iagl, Iomar's twin, (he/him)

Governor Derlan, the twins father, deceased traitor.

AUSTRALIANS

Linh, Year 10 student, (she/her)
Fiona, Linh's best friend, (she/her)
Troy, becoming Linh's friend, (he/him)
Michael, new friend, (he/him)

URAI

Mocco, apprentice elder, (he/him)
Mawana, Mocco's cousin, (he/him)

Prophetess Lylah (also a Guardian?)

CAULDRON ISLAND

Flariah, Lylah's sister (& Guardian?)
Selenia, Tiran refugee (she/her)

ISLAND OF THE GUARDIANS

Lylah's sisters (and Guardians?) Desriah and Sryah

TIMBALENS

Emperor Yarath (he/ him)
First Captain Rilmar (she/her)
Commander Octharl (he/him)

GALVATIONS

Prince Maharl, Rebel (he/him)
Joharlen, Rebel & Maharl's brother
False Priestess Amina, Maharl's cousin (she/her)
Shella, rebel (she/her)

AZULANS

King Narz

Keeper Captain Melroth (he/him)

Jaygoff, Keeper (Captain Melroth's brother)

FOREST REALM

Queen Ziliene

CREATOR GODS

(Absent since creation.)

Mijora (earth goddess)

Esira (sun god)

Esla (sea goddess)

Chaos (god of sorcerery)

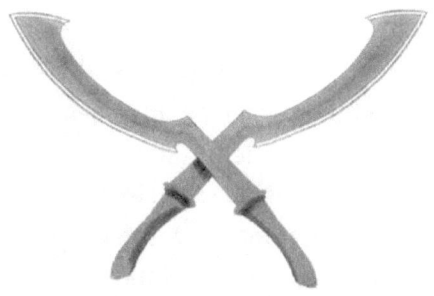

A CHAPTER 1

THE WESTERN VOYAGE – RUARNON

Sunlight glinted off the silver busts of former advisors on Regent Ruarnon's right, in stark contrast to the grave faces of people gathered around the meeting table before them.

Battle scarred, former general Monin eyed Ruarnon with concern. "Benevolence, what could the soldiers possibly have learnt in the east that would equip them to recover seven thousand men from sorcerers in the west?"

"And can it withstand enormous strain on morale?" Companion Noma asked, slumped in her chair beside him, her young face pale after a prolonged, almost fruitless information gathering voyage west. "The soldiers who sailed home with me do not wish to assist the recovery expedition, not even to free the king and queen."

"What I learnt in the east would have made me appear to have misplaced my mind, had I put it in writing," Ruarnon replied. Their shoulders tensed, because their advisors questioning their grip on rational thought was still very much an option.

Ruarnon braced themself to utter truths Tarlahns had never known, even immediately after the Sorcery War, and made themself speak before their jangling nerves put them off.

"I learned that the only thing separating sorcerers from ordinary people is sorcerer's extraordinary ability to overcome their fear and doubt about magic craft. The difference is their determination, motivation and persistence with it. Over generations, parents have taught children, which has led to younger generations crafting more magic to greater effect.

"We all doubted any of us could wield magic, because those rare times we survived in battle when we ought to have died were passed off as battle rush. Or divine intervention from the Ancestors. But it was magic. That is what we learnt in the east. How to craft defensive magic. And we have been practicing it for our entire homeward voyage, to prepare us for the western recovery expedition."

Monin's critical gaze sought his granddaughter, Companion Lenaris across the table, his brows scrunched in confusion. Lenaris merely sighed at his scrutiny. Monin turned to Companion Tor sitting calmly beside her and his eyes widened.

"That is an extraordinary claim," said Companion Noma. "The soldiers who sailed west with me were terrified of the men we saw start the forest fire with sorcery. Those soldiers may be more frightened by the claim they too can wield magic."

On her other side, General Aza surprised Ruarnon, smiling slowly across the table at General Takanis' nod. He trusted Takanis' judgement, and he alone seemed to have accepted magic was the only possible reason for Ruarnon's change of heart and confidence about how many they could free from sorcerer-king Narz's captivity in the west.

"Show us Benevolence," Aza said.

Monin shook his head. "I have lived too long. First midlun heir of Tarlah, and you occupy the Zaldeaan Realm, win the co-operation of the Zaldeaan royal family and governors, re-establish relations with the reclusive Urai, then go racing off to the east to learn magic. You need to recover your father. I cannot spend my final days as advisor, the twilight of my years sprinting to keep up with you!"

Ruarnon smiled at the mix of exasperation in his gruff tone, the frown of his silver brows, and the spark of adventure in his wise old eyes, much like his son Companion Pamoran's eyes, whom Ruarnon also hoped to rescue in the east.

Ruarnon inclined their head. They focused on the air above the table, mentally projecting. A mist-like, oval shaped shield appeared. Monin flinched back, silently staring. General Aza's mouth opened in wonder and his eyes shone with hope. He reached forward carefully, until his deft fingers pressed against the shield. Ruarnon sensed the pressure of his touch, like a mental push, as Aza's knuckles turned white. But Ruarnon easily held the shield in place, the magic within and without them tingling with power.

"As strong as iron," General Aza declared, his smile broadening. "Are the soldiers as strong as you?"

Ruarnon hesitated.

"Few are as capable as their Benevolence," General Takanis answered. "Though my skills, Tor and Lenaris's are not far behind. And in numbers, for say, storming the cell in which Narz holds our king and queen prisoner, I like our soldiers' chances, even against a few sorcerers. Our soldiers' bronze shields and ordinary weapons, in numbers and force, proved effective against magic in the Timbalen Empire."

Monin's lips twitched. "So this is why your youngest companions sat this meeting out, so they didn't see us gaping like fools." Monin shook his head. "You are far too wise for your years Ruarnon."

Lenaris beamed at her grandfather's praise, but Ruarnon was bemused by their most senior advisor calling them 'wise'. They had to push the thought away, much like they resisted Aza's pressure on their shield, so they could update Advisor Monin, General Aza and Companion Noma.

"Lylah wanted us to meet her sisters," they continued, "so Flariah could teach us to craft shield magic and Sryah could teach us sleep magic. It was just as well they did. When we reached our allies' waters, they were under attack by sorcery wielding damars."

Monin's mouth fell open. Aza shook his head. "Those murderous fiends can craft magic? Ancestors preserve us!"

Ruarnon ignored their racing heart and the tension in the room, longing to be finished with unpleasant surprises. "They aren't the only ones. The Elite Guards 'special abilities' were always magic. They *all* wield it as capably as sorcerers."

Monin was staring into the distance.

"And they agreed to help us?" Aza asked. "The Timbalens are sending Elite Guard to help us free our royal family from Narz's sorcerers?"

Ruarnon nodded.

Monin shook his head. "So our chances of successfully freeing your Benevolence's family from under Narz and his sorcery-wielding underlings noses may be as possible as it was becoming impossible? I presume your Benevolence intends to proceed with intelligence gathering, raids and stealth operations in the west, to prepare the expedition?"

Ruarnon released their magical shield and nodded. "King Narz's sorcerers are as powerful as the empire's Elite Guard. We should engage them only if stealth fails us. But my plans have changed. I will not sit idle while all my friends and the bravest of my soldiers sail west to confront sorcery, free my parents, uncle, aunt, cousin and seven thousand of my subjects.

"I may not be as restless and energetic as Pamoran, but while the western expedition is under way, it will be my highest priority, and having dedicated everything to Tarlah and the Realm these past eleven months, now I would dedicate everything to recovering my parents, king, queen, family and subjects."

Ruarnon paused. Even Aza's mouth opened in surprise at the reversal of their decision. Companion Noma was staring blankly at them, but she had missed much while she was sailing west.

"The advisors when I was your great uncle's companion," said Monin, "lifetimes ago, would have called me a fool and had my hide if they suspected I would one day let the sole heir to the throne wander off into the west, pursuing their hearts desire, and leaving rule of Tarlah to someone else. Not even to royalty.

"But they did not witness Kyura standing in what he found to be an impossible situation, his father's legacy of peace on one side, warmongers and mutinying soldiers on the other. They did not see him struggle to take control, betray his father's peace and fail to protect his subjects from damars while he waged war with us. They did not see circumstances break him to such a point he felt his only way out was to claim his own life.

"The Zaldeaans would say a leader who admits they cannot do something is weak. That a ruler should do whatever they must, even if they are terrible at it, or if it destroys them or others. The Zaldeaans are wrong and ultimately self-destructive. Avoiding a situation that puts your feelings and desires at war with yourself, that could destroy you, is not weak. It allows you to preserve your strength. It is wise. To be clear, you suspect you will rule as effectively in peacetime as my son would have?"

Ruarnon blinked, then remembered Pamoran had defended Tarlah City during the siege from *on* the city walls, and *that* was how he had got himself captured. Getting that man to sit still and govern during a lengthy peace would probably require weighting his legs down with stone.

But Ruarnon remembered how helpless they felt sitting in safety while their friends' battled sorcerers in the sewers of Imperial City. While those same friends risked their lives recovering Lenaris's father and Ruarnon's parents in the west, Ruarnon would hate the unimportant by contrast day-to-day rule of Tarlah at peace. They may even become as reckless as Pamoran.

Ruarnon inclined their head to Monin.

"If you are to stand aside during the expedition, how would you place us?" Monin asked.

"I would take Tor west as advisor, and my young Companions west. Leaving Companion Noma as Regent in Tarlah, and Advisor Monin as Regent in the Zaldeaan Realm. Should I not return, should my parents not return and my line end, I would have Companion Tor as regent if he were alive, and Companion Noma adopt Tor's son Drake if he is not. Either way, I would have Drake as Heir, and co-regency begin once our deaths were known."

Monin nodded slowly. "Drake is no war-time leader, but he is clever and sensible and would be good in peace. And with at least his aunt, uncle and mother to guide him, his chances are good. Better if his father makes it home. But we all know the best option is you dance with Chaos himself like you did in the Zaldeaan Realm, then finish what you started here."

Monin didn't smile, but there was fierce joy in those grey, wizened eyes.

"What of us?" General Aza asked.

"It is a long time since a general was abroad for an extended period," said Ruarnon. "But I want one of you to accompany me west, while the other remains here to advise and support Regent's Noma and Monin."

Generals Takanis and Aza exchanged looks and each bowed their head.

"I would like to volunteer," said General Takanis.

Ruarnon smiled. General Aza was an excellent leader and manager of soldiers, but General Takanis thought outside the box, and had proven against the damars the value of that. She had also sailed east with Ruarnon and was competent at shield magic and had experience managing soldiers wielding it.

Ruarnon, the Companions, Generals and Monin all inclined their heads in agreement.

"You may need to brief me on how Tarlah and this Council functions under Regent Ruarnon," Companion Noma said to Monin. "It appears much has changed."

"It would be my honour," Monin replied.

"I would have all of this written up, and everyone at this table sign it," Ruarnon added. "Should anyone go against it, the penalty will be banishment to the Timbalen Empire."

Monin inclined his head. "I doubt we will bicker amongst ourselves like the Zaldeaans, but measures against it are wise."

Ruarnon exhaled with relief. They had doubted Tarlahn logic would allow their advisors to accept such a drastic departure from traditions governing Tarlah since its birth, but apparently they underestimated the council members who hadn't sailed east.

Ruarnon summoned Drake to the Golden Meeting Hall, while a scribe laid the conditional succession documents on the table beside a stylus and ink. Ruarnon grit their teeth. This wasn't the first time they had set sail away from Tarlah, but from this voyage, they may not return. Their expedition would contend with sorcerers. If it went wrong, their attempt to free the Zaldeaan army could enslave their expeditionary soldiers, while their attempt to free their parents could land them in a cell beside their parents.

To risk all that, Ruarnon would walk away from duties that had shaped their life so far, placing both their kingdoms in their advisors' hands, without knowing whether they or their father would return to take those duties back. It was daunting, yet Ruarnon's four Australian Companions had faced uncertainty since they stepped from Australia to the Timbalen Empire over a year ago. Ruarnon smiled at memory of their friends' resilience, stepped towards the greatest deviation from tradition in Tarlahn history, took a deep breath, and signed their name to it.

With a bow of his head, Tor took the stylus from Ruarnon's hand. Monin followed, then Companion Noma. The generals signed swiftly, Lenaris following their lead. Then, with a reluctant bow showing acceptance of the future that awaited him if the worst should happen, Tor's adopted son Drake signed. Ruarnon exhaled deeply. After eleven months of fulfilling other duties, it was time to pursue the desires of their heart.

A day later, Ruarnon entered the castle courtyard in their iron armour and leather kilt, with their enchanted, bronze-iron sheened sword buckled at their waist. Before them, captains issued orders. Line upon line of elite soldiers in full bronze armour formed up. They carried swords at their right hips or quivers at their left, bronze round shields and spears, or bows in hand. Most were veterans of the Damarian Wars,

15

and all were volunteers. These were the bravest, most capable soldiers Tarlah had ever known and Ruarnon was proud to lead them.

Ruarnon's friends and bodyguards rode into the courtyard, led by Lenaris, whose pale face was confident and proud, her blue eyes sparkling, her long blonde hair in a Tarlahn braid. Mawana rode beside her, tall and powerfully built, his dark, finely braided hair concealed by his bronze helmet. Both wore a gold chain at their right wrist, a symbol Lenaris had pledged to protect Mawana with her spear and Mawana had pledged to protect her with his, while each pledged their heart to the other's keeping. The ceremony had taken place only a week ago, but the time to fulfil those vowels was near at hand.

Behind the couple rode Mawana's cousin Mocco and their four youngest companions from a distant land called Australia. Mocco's mouth was pulled into a tight line, probably the closest he came to showing nerves. Stocky, broad-shouldered Troy was talking to his smiling Australian friends, his brown curls bouncing as he walked.

Freckled faced Fiona wasn't saying much, but dark-haired Linh had plenty to say and dark featured, serious faced Michael chipped in, both likely tempering Troy's wilder predictions of what would happen on the voyage. They were louder than usual and there was a nervous edge to their smiles. Because after many delays and so much preparation; it was time.

Ruarnon descended the steps, mounted the horse Captain Arleath brought them, and greeted their guards and friends. Then they healed their horse and led their friends around the expeditionary soldiers to broadly built Generals Aza and Takanis, who sat their horses in full bronze armour, and iron general's helmets. Both generals bowed, as captains behind them raised their spears in salute, sunlight glinting off iron signalling each unit was ready.

With a clatter of hooves, and the soft tread of hundreds of leather sandals, Ruarnon led the column through Tarlah Castle's outer walls down to North Road. Tarlahns with blonde and brown braided hair threw poppies on the road, showing support for the royal family. Solemn gazes met Ruarnon, some eyes wide with concern, others' features pinched tight with nerves. Some men, women and midluns smiled sadly, accepting the danger, and knowing some soldiers who walked or rode before them today would not return.

Children wriggled to the front of the crowd, and a small boy saluted as Ruarnon passed. In their mind's eye, a boy saluted from the back of an evacuating wagon before the siege. Ruarnon had ultimately commanded this city's defence, ensuring it still stood for these children to return to, but now, Ruarnon was leaving both. They returned the salute with a sense of loss.

They rode on towards a gap in the crowd, around a large group of bearded men, Zaldeaans. Tarlahns around them shifted uncomfortably, at the obvious reminder Ruarnon also sought to recover the Zaldeaan army.

"I am Arogar," a man called loudly, "Speaker for the People. What says the King?"

Ruarnon smiled, halting the column.

"I go West, seeking a king, a queen, a princess, two companions and an army, seeking my people, who I would restore to their proper homes."

"The army should be proud to have such a king," Arogar replied with a bow.

"Long live the king! Long live the king!" the Zaldeaans began to chant, as Ruarnon acknowledged them with a smile and led the expeditionary soldiers on, not provoking the Tarlahns by dismissing Zaldeaans with a double salute.

The Tarlahn crowd looked on uncertainly, then several young men called, "Long live the Regent!" and more Tarlahns took it up, drowning out the Zaldeaans, who smiled smugly. Both disliked that Ruarnon was the other's leader, but their feelings mostly manifested as competition, and the fact Ruarnon ruled both would be easier to overlook in Ruarnon's absence.

They turned down Middle Road towards East Gate. The road was lined by farmers in kilts and straw hats or linen dresses, throwing more poppies onto the road. Soldiers at East Gate saluted as Ruarnon approached, and Ruarnon returned their salute. Then they rode through the thick stone walls of Tarlah City, and exhaled deeply, as a great weight lifted off their shoulders. Companion Noma and Advisor Monin were regents now. Ruarnon was just Heir Ruarnon, Tarlahn Commander of the Western Expedition. They smiled and led the column through dappled sunlight, under forest trees, towards the eastern coast.

When the trees thinned, Ruarnon gazed over a band of golden sand to sailors' and soldiers' families lining the docks of Tarlah Harbour. Officials in silk tunics gathered on the decks of private ships around the Iylena, Uria, Meera and newly completed Saeron. The Iylena's familiar decks shone in the sunlight, newly polished, while masts rising from fore, main and aft decks flew a red flag above their top sails. Her supplies had been loaded, the crew stood ready, and tanned, weathered Captain Dargeth stood by the helm.

Ruarnon led their column across the sand, and crowds on wooden docks parted for the column to move through. Ruarnon's gaze was drawn over their heads, across the water to the east. The Timbalen fleet approached. Its ship's generous decks rose high above the water line, each with three masts with main and top sails set, yellow flags flapping above them. Each prow was overshadowed by an intricately carved sea serpent's head with open jaws, while serpents' tails rose from each stern.

Ruarnon, their friends and guards dismounted at the end of the docks, leaving the horses with grooms. A small party of familiar faces awaited them, beyond which a horn signalled the approach of two Zaldeaan ships from the north, under Governor Iagl's command. Behind Ruarnon, General Aza directed soldiers to begin boarding their ships. It was time to say goodbye.

Regent Noma, Aunt Telena, Advisor Monin and Drake all stood waiting for Ruarnon, while Mawana said goodbye to his parents and the Australians and Lenaris talked to Selenia and Mocco.

"Good luck with your regency," Ruarnon said to Noma. "Ensure you treat Tarlahns and Zaldeaans equally to reduce tension."

Noma bowed her head, wishing Ruarnon well.

"You have grown so much Ruarnon," Aunt Telena said softly. "You have proven that you can put your people first, but you deserve your parents. You will have to take risks to retrieve them. It will cost lives. I advise you to assess the risks and determine which ones you are willing to take, and to assess possible prices and determine what you are willing to pay, before you act."

Something in Ruarnon longed to turn away from those stark realities, but she was right.

"Thank you," they replied.

She embraced them and whispered in their ear, "I love you. Good luck sweetheart."

Ruarnon held her tightly, aware she was the only living relative whose safety they were sure of. They took a steadying breath, composing themself as they let her go.

"Come back to us," Monin added sincerely.

"I shall do my best," Ruarnon replied.

"Please watch over my father and Lenaris," Drake said, from beside his aunt Noma. "May fortune go with you."

"And remain with you," said Ruarnon.

Then they turned to Selenia.

"I will miss you," she said with a smile. "Do not put yourself under additional strain by expecting too much of yourself."

How had she seen that in such a short visit to Tarlah? Ruarnon smiled and replied, "Thank you. Whatever you decide about Flariah's task, take care, and send word of your safety if you can."

"I will sail with Urai merchants to make enquiries," she said. "I want to understand who King Narz is in his homeland, before I make my final decision, because Flariah's task could end his reign."

Ruarnon bowed their head in acknowledgement.

She stepped forwards and held them tightly. It was difficult to accept she was sailing alone, while most of Ruarnon's friends accompanied them. But an Urai ship sailing solo would be more neutral and hopefully safer.

Ruarnon turned to Mocco. The voyage west would not be the same without his calm and steady presence.

Mocco smiled sadly. "I can only spend so much time galivanting around the world fancy-free, unlike my reckless cousin."

He smiled at Mawana, who attempted to frown, but Mawana's mouth was smiling, and his eyes looked sad.

"I missed the quiet and peace of the jungle too much to leave it so soon. And my studies. I don't have our friends reckless, ceaseless love of adventure. And as much as I would like to support you all, this voyage won't help my people make allies or involve trade agreements. It would be a private venture."

Ruarnon bowed their head. "Mawana is a wild cat, but you are more a creature of habit and routine. All those times you were so quiet... for me, it means I am thinking, but for you, it was stress?"

Mocco turned away and nodded.

Their Australian friends had taken the news more easily than Ruarnon anticipated. Even Linh and Michael's postures were relaxed as they waited beside Mawana, content to have his company on the voyage.

Mocco looked up again. "Keep everyone safe," he asked quietly. "And keep Mawana out of trouble, and his wife," he whispered.

Ruarnon smiled. "I shall do my best. I wish you well with your studies, my friend," they added, hugging Mocco goodbye.

"We expect you to be sworn in as a full Elder by the time we get back," Mawana added, maintaining a serious expression long enough that Lenaris quirked an eyebrow. Then Mawana seized Mocco in a bear hug. Ruarnon wondered if their own parents would hold them like that, sometime in coming weeks or months.

Then they took a deep breath, set their posture upright to show confidence to soldiers and crew, and led their friends, Companion Tor and General Takanis up the Iylena's boarding ramp, to her foredeck. The sea breeze ruffled the tunic under their iron armour, and salt filled their nostrils. Adventure, the unknown and the opportunity to be reunited with their parents all beckoned from across the sea, as the Iylena's sails were set, and Ruarnon's recovery expedition sailed out of Tarlah Harbour, towards the Western Ocean and the perils on its far side.

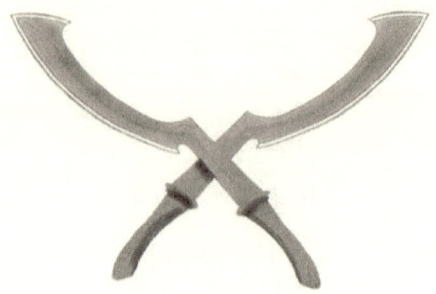

CHAPTER 2

ACROSS THE WESTERN OCEAN~RUARNON

R uarnon sat at the wooden table in their cabin, only partially managing to ignore the rapid beating of their heart, as they opened a letter from the Timbalen Commander. Emperor Yarath's determination to wipe out Narz's armies had made them nervous for weeks. General Aza had assured them Commander Octharl was level-headed and would not take unnecessary risks, but with both rulers controlling sorcerer armies, great risks were inevitable.

The letter on Ruarnon's table contained Octharl's immediate intentions when they reached Galvatia. Those intentions would signal when war between the Timbalens and Azulans may start, and the continent would likely become too dangerous for Ruarnon to carry out their expedition. It would likely dictate the timing of Ruarnon's schedule to recover their parents, aunt, uncle, cousin and Lenaris's father, and to free as many Zaldeaan soldiers as they could.

Each thing Ruarnon had waited so long for may be about to happen hard on the heels of the next. They steadied themself, leaning on the table with their spare hand and unrolled the letter.

To Their Benevolence Ruarnon, Regent of Tarlah,

If fishing has truly ceased, trade is banned, and we are unlikely to be sighted, as King Narz's sorcerers suggested, we will land on the Galvation coast soon. When they find somewhere to accommodate us, my friends will conceal us.

Ruarnon sighed, relaxing into their chair at confirmation the Elite Guard would use magic to conceal the fleet from Narz. The two armies hiding from each other ought to prevent immediate, ill-prepared-for conflict.

The longer we remain, the greater the risk he shall find us. We will learn his terrain, numbers and outposts as swiftly as we may, and launch before we are noticed.

Ruaron bit their lip. So the Timbalen army was still keen to invade Azula as soon as possible. Narz's calculated, pre-emptive attack by fire magic crafting damars on the Timbalen Empire had made his terrible fear of Elite Guard clear. If Narz thought those magic crafters were coming for him, he'd tighten his castle's security to such a degree that recovering Ruarnon's parents would be impossible. Ruarnon's best chance to free anyone was before Narz learned of the Elite Guard presence in Galvatia. But it may be difficult, if not impossible, for Ruarnon to know when Narz became aware of their presence.

I will lend you my friends, when we are nearly ready, so they do not give us away.

Ruarnon's shoulders tensed. Elite Guard could protect and guide their friends and help recover Ruarnon's family and Lenaris's father safely. But waiting for Elite Guard aid could mean trying to free everyone on the eve of war. It could be terribly dangerous.

As soon as they have identified a good place, I will send my friends ahead to bring me word.

May Esira shine upon you, and Mijora hasten your errands upon Her lands.

The race to plan and conduct Ruarnon's recovery expedition before the war would begin as soon as Elite Guard scouts set foot on Narz's continent.

Ruarnon stood and stepped out of their cabin, onto the main deck. Spears clashed atop the rear deck, where soldiers trained. Sailors stood alertly at strategic points across the main deck or sat in the rigging, awaiting the captains' orders.

Women, midluns and men appeared focused and determined as they maintained the ship, kept watch, or trained over the first few days of the voyage. But as weeks passed, spear slashes missed opponents altogether, ropes sailors were supposed to be securing fell to the deck, and soldiers and sailors alike snapped at each other.

Everyone felt the same tension that knotted Ruarnon's stomach, and the weight of anticipation and the unknown began to weigh everyone down. The decks quieted as the western continent drew nearer.

After seven weeks at sea, a warning bell tolled from a Timbalen fighting top. The prospect of land being sighted quickened Ruarnon's steps up the foredeck stairs to the railing. Their Australian companions talked and frowned at the cloudbank, beside Lenaris and Mawana. Companion Tor and General Takanis also studied the sky.

Ruarnon's brows furrowed. Beyond the bulky Timbalen ships, grey clouds barred the horizon. There was no sign of land, but the fleet was on course to meet a gargantuan storm front.

Warning bells sounded from fighting tops nearby.

"I'll not sail into that Benevolence," Captain Dargeth yelled from the aft deck. "It's as likely to set us afire with lightning as to capsize us. I assume the Commander has called a halt, to see which way it's moving."

Ruarnon acknowledged him with a wave, then scanned the dense black cloudbank. No misty rain sheeted beneath it. The storm hadn't broken yet. But compared to it, the slowing fleet was an insect in the path of an eagle. A storm that size could unleash wind and waves powerful enough to batter their ships to pieces. And judging by the darkness of the sky, the winds heralding its outbreak should lash the decks at any moment.

Ruarnon's shoulders tightened, and they resisted the urge to bite their lip. Everyone on deck stood still, holding their breathes, except sailors standing by to adjust the sails. Perhaps others were ignoring the way their hearts pounded against their chests, like Ruarnon's. Ruarnon had to take a breath. Then another. Because the storm didn't break fast enough.

They waited tensely. More moments passed. Ruarnon's brows furrowed. The wind didn't seem to be picking up and the clouds didn't appear to be moving. The stormfront didn't seem any closer. But nor did it appear to be moving away. Perhaps it was too monstrously large to gauge its distance accurately with the naked eye...

Michael's black eyebrows furrowed beside Ruarnon, his green eyes inscrutable and dark brown face unreadable. "It should be raining," he said, his gazed fixed on the charcoal-coloured cloudbank. "And there should an electrical storm and thunder, if those clouds are moving at all."

But the ocean was calm around the fleet's ships, and the water ahead seemed calm, until it disappeared beneath the storm clouds. There was no sign of winds whipping up waves, as would usually herald a storm. It was as if the storm *wasn't* moving...

Ruarnon waited, but no headwind came and the water remained calm. They sensed something in the stillness ahead, a kind of tingling... magic. It came from the direction of the stormfront. And as the fleet advanced, the tingling of magic craft became clearer, stronger, unmistakable.

Sweat trickled down Ruaron's back. Magic tingled near Mawana's fingertips, as he sensed the magic craft ahead. The others didn't seem able to detect vast amounts of formed magic yet, but postures were tensing across the foredeck.

Linh's black eyes narrowed beside Michael, her long black hair hanging limply down her back, testifying how still the air was.

"How much magic would it take to craft an illusion that size?" she asked tightly, speaking the truth none of the adults seemed to wish to contemplate.

Mawana gripped the railing, his brown knuckles paling. "An army of Jandar's."

Ruarnon swayed. Surely even the entire Elite Guard army couldn't contend with *that*?

"It's flawless," Mawana added, shaking his head. "I haven't seen a single ripple of illusion. I don't know how it is maintained without killing sorcerers."

Troy shifted uneasily. "An enchantment?" he suggested, his tan face paling.

"North Landers can't perform them," Mawana objected.

"The knowledge may have survived in the West, with the sorcerers who survived the war," Linh suggested, and Ruarnon wondered how many other dread things survived there.

Sailors behind Ruarnon whispered prayers to the Ancestors. Soldiers gripped sword hilts firmly, as they stared at the awesome stormfront from the main deck. Ruarnon needed to reassure them.

"General Takanis," they called to the main deck, "have our soldiers assemble."

Takanis bowed her head and passed on the order to the captains on Ruarnon's three other ships.

"The Timbalens are sending a scout ship," said Lenaris, pointing towards the sea before the dense wall of impossibly dark clouds.

Ruarnon fetched their looking glass and surveyed the horizon beyond the small vessel. "There is a low-lying island before the clouds," they told their friends. "But the island is grey, with black lines rising from it. Like the whole island has been burned."

"I doubt it was a natural fire," said Michael. "If the whole thing's burnt coast to coast."

Tor straightened beside him. The golden-brown hair in his Tarlahn braid was equally mixed with grey now, his beige skin more care lined, his blue-eyed gaze as penetrating and figure as robust and battle ready as ever.

"The island may be a training ground for combat magic," Tor said grimly. "It is far from the mainland, a good location to train sorcerers in secret."

Ruarnon tensed, wondering if it was where the sorcerers who controlled the forest fires Companion Noma had witnessed had trained. Sight of it was hardly going to calm the soldiers they were about to speak to. But the Timbalen scout ship was on course to sail right past the island, into the storm front. That may help.

Ruarnon walked to the back of the foredeck, eyeing lines of bronze armoured soldiers, men, women and midluns, old and young peering up at them from the mid deck. Every face seemed paler than its usual colour. Some younger soldiers shivered or bit their lips. Veterans gripped sword hilts tightly, but stood up straight, putting brave faces on the most awesome display of sorcery any of them had encountered.

"We have anchored before what appears to be a mighty storm front," Ruarnon began, forcing themself to take measured breaths and project calm into their tone. "The apparent storm front is a magically crafted illusion. Our allies fear it not. Their scout ship sails into it. Narz seeks to frighten us, instead of attacking. Like a viper in the jungle, he fears those who oppose him. Remember that and take this opportunity to accept the power of his magic. We will see more of it. It will not deter us."

It wasn't hard to project determination into their expression, because Ruarnon was sure they were the only person onboard who was utterly undeterred by the awesome display of power barring sea and sky alike before them.

Some soldiers' gazes lowered at Ruarnon's determination. At knowing the fleet would not turn around or sail wide of the magic curtain hanging before them. But the bravest soldiers and stalwart veterans were already turning to stare down the storm front illusion. They knew the best way to overcome something that terrified you was to confront it, until the fearful compunction to turn away left you.

Ruarnon did the same, watching at the corner of their eye as one by one, hesitant faces looked up, expressions firmed and gazes fixed on the clouds. Some soldiers turned away again. Ruarnon waited for the number staring steadily ahead to grow.

"Alas, I have other duties to attend to," Ruarnon broke the silence. "But I suggest you remain, until the desire to turn away leaves you.

Achieve that, and nothing you face in service of your king, queen or of me will phase you."

Ruarnon dismissed them with a double salute. Soldiers turned on both sides of the deck, as if they'd forgotten three other Tarlahn ships, two Zaldeaan ships and an entire Timbalen fleet sailed around them. The double salute reminded them they would not undertake the recovery expedition alone, and as Ruarnon's soldiers moved off, veterans and some newer soldiers relaxed their shoulders and seemed to breathe more easily.

Ruarnon sighed, more aware than ever that this expedition wasn't defending Tarlah. It wasn't about survival either, because fleeing would ensure that. These soldiers were here to aid the royal family and they would have to overcome their worst fears about magic to have any hope of success. It would be the greatest test of Tarlahn morale. Having occupied the Zaldeaan Realm and purged it of damars, having fought damars and learnt magic across the eastern ocean, had Ruarnon finally asked too much of their army?

Blue flags raised on Timbalen aft decks ahead. Sailors scuttled in response to the signal, setting the Iylena's sails, and she glided forwards in the wake of the Timbalen ships, flanked by the Uria and Meera, followed by the Saeron and the Zaldeaan ships. Overhead, the Iylena's sails rippled, but great spans of fabric slackened.

"Why are we stopping?" Linh asked.

"We are becalmed," said Ruarnon.

The wind had failed just as it became clear the storm front illusion hadn't deterred the fleet…

"Magic cannot abolish the wind," Mawana asserted calmly. "No one could be powerful enough to use magic to overcome the forces of nature. The strain would kill them. This must be a natural calm."

Ruarnon sighed. The air ahead thrummed with magic now. As if it were a living creature, and its entire being pulsed with the beat of its heart. Fiona clutched the railing as she stared and Lenaris was unusually quiet. Linh's brows furrowed in a deep, continuous frown. They sensed it too. The vast airy plain of pulsing magic, maintaining form, not even flickering the illusion once, was hair raising.

Thankfully, Ruarnon sensed nothing from the sky above, or immediately before the Iylena. But the coincidence of a frighteningly large storm front teaming with magic lying ahead, and the wind dying when the stormfront didn't deter the fleet's advance, sat uneasily on Ruarnon's shoulders.

The unfaltering, dizzying sense of power around the storm front heightened Ruarnon's alertness to the same level as when they hunted damars in the Zaldeaan Realm, alert to a screech, a hiss, the merest sign murder on legs was approaching. It tightened Ruarnon's shoulders.

Sight of the scout ship sailing into that vast field of crafted magic no one knew the nature of made Ruarnon want to shout at them to turn back. But the Elite Guard scouts, dwarfed by the black cloudbank they were approaching, must sense the magic more clearly than anyone. They alone could calculate its power and the number of magic crafters required to keep it stirring. They must think they had the power to confront it. Ruarnon wasn't sure whether they should fear for the Elite Guard or fear them.

Cries of surprise went up across surrounding decks. The scout ship's prow had vanished. The main and rear decks were still, advancing, but the planks of the main deck cut off into open air... and the main deck was shrinking. With every stroke of oars protruding from its sides, more main deck disappeared, as if the whole vessel was sailing into nothingness.

More cries went up as the main deck disappeared. For a moment, the rear deck moved on its own, shrinking. Then it too vanished.

Ruarnon gripped the railing, struggling to breathe.

"He's concealing how close we are to the mainland," said Mawana, frowning. "The vessel appears to have vanished because it's passed through the illusion."

Mawana shook his head. "It didn't even *ripple* when the ship passed through."

"But the ship *did* pass through a curtain of magic," said Ruarnon. "I sensed it too."

Several people shivered.

"Does he know we're here, or is that illusion a precaution he threw up in advance, for when we get here?" Michael asked.

"Judging by how paranoid he is," said Linh, her gaze downcast, "It might be a precaution he took when his Timbalen invasion failed. He's probably been expecting Guardians for weeks."

Ruarnon sighed, noting the discomfort in their chest from not breathing in enough air, as they contained their emotional response in front of their soldiers. The magic they sensed was greater than the magic craft which shielded the Iylena when fire magic-crafting damars attacked her in Timbalen Waters. It was greater than the entire row of Elite Guard shields all four hundred Elite Guard had sheltered behind, as they faced off against fire-magic crafting damars on the shores of Timbala City. And that power may stand between Ruarnon and the captive members of their family.

The Iylena's timbers groaned as a drumbeat began below deck, the rhythm pulsing across the fleet as sweeps assisted lateen sails to manoeuvre the ships beside the burnt island, where it anchored.

Sometime later, the scout ship reappeared, and its archer shot a report via arrow into the target board on the Iylena's foremast. Ruarnon summarized the report to their companions and General Takanis.

"There's a league of sea ahead, then a continent bordered by sheer cliffs, surrounded by fire blackened forest. There's no animal life, humans or damars nearby. The clouded sky extends beyond sight. An archway in the cliffs opens to fertile, green land extending to mountains with clear sky, animal and birdlife and fresh water. The scouts suggest it is the best path for my scouts to enter Galvatia and seek out the resistance."

"The cloud illusion spans the sky?" Mawana asked.

Ruarnon's heart skipped a beat. If the stormfront illusion was to deter the fleet, why would the sky above Galvatia appear cloudy too?

Ruarnon wrestled with frustration over the next few days. The whole point of sailing west was evading the helplessness they'd felt while their friends' fought sorcerers in the sewers of Timbala City, while Ruarnon sat in safety. But their first few days in Galvation waters were spent waiting, with crafted magic pulsing on the edge of their awareness so strongly that Ruarnon felt they could have reached towards the sky and touched the field of magic in the air. Facing it was one thing, but focusing on it alone could destroy a person's mind.

Ruarnon developed a training schedule with the generals and captains. They rotated soldiers on and off deck, and had soldiers sharpen weapons and polish armour when they weren't training. But they kept some soldiers staring at the storm, on brief rotations. Veterans tried to best each other, making light of the situation and calming younger soldiers. Ruarnon gave daily awards of extra rations for taming fears and teamwork. The winners tended to share their prizes, which also helped morale.

Ruarnon was so focused on the soldiers that a splash one day caught them off guard. It was Troy, who'd climbed overboard and was swimming in his under garments. Ruarnon raised their eyebrows at Mawana, who shrugged.

"He needed space," said Mawana. "I told him there's plenty of room overboard."

Mawana grinned. Michael was smiling too. Soon they, Linh and Fiona were splashing each other in the sea beside the ship, while soldiers shook their heads at the peace-time activity, and Lenaris and Tor watched them carefully.

"Benevolence, there is another matter we ought to discuss," General Takanis called as she approached across the deck.

Ruarnon pulled themself back from the welcome distraction of their friends' enjoyment and turned to the general.

"Given the extent of Narz's magical capabilities, and our soldiers discomfort over the last two days," General Takanis added in an undertone, "we may need to reconsider who will seek out the Galvation resistance and how. I suspect the Galvations will be less trusting and more fearful than we thought."

Ruarnon sighed. The mass of dark clouds blotting out the horizon must be far more frightening to live with for days, even months, if Narz had ordered that enchantment cast when his attack on the Timbalen Empire had failed. It would remind the Galvation resistance of the power they were defying every time they set foot outdoors or gazed out of a window.

"I'll call a council meeting soon," Ruarnon said, taking time to think while their friends finished swimming and changed into dry clothes.

Then Ruarnon called their companions and the general into their cabin. General Takanis and Companion Tor sat at the table with Ruarnon and Lenaris, while Mawana leant against the wall and the four Australians raised Takanis' brows by sitting on the edge of Ruarnon's bed.

"Given the fear Narz's magic must inspire," said General Takanis, "I suspect the resistance will be wary of anyone travelling in Galvatia and will assume they are Narz's spies and avoid them. Contacting the resistance may be a matter of gaining their trust. They may observe us at first, trying to determine our identity. And when contact is established, if it goes poorly, we may scare them back into hiding."

"You believe we may only get one chance to establish contact?" Tor asked and the general nodded.

"Do you advise we send people who look non-threatening?" Ruarnon asked. "Younger, newer soldiers, who remind them less of the battle-hardened Zaldeaans patrolling their lands?"

"*We're* less threatening than that," said Troy.

Everyone turned to him and he shrugged. "Me, Mic, Linh and Fi have got less military skill than anyone else on this fleet. Even the sailors have done more arms training than us."

"And we're among the youngest," Linh added. "And Zaldeaans don't let women fight, so they won't have any female soldiers patrolling Galvatia. You could send women soldiers. And Narz only sent men against the Timbalen Empire, which suggests sending women will show we're not Azulan either."

Ruarnon grimaced. It was extremely dangerous. But they were right. Troy and Fiona were probably the least threatening people in the entire fleet. With her quiet, considerate manner, Fiona could put anyone at ease, and with his sense of humour, so could Troy. They would have to part with the fleet sooner or later, to seek their way home, but it was too soon, far too soon for Ruarnon. They weren't ready to say goodbye to their Australian friends just yet.

"They raise excellent points Benevolence," said Tor.

Ruarnon sighed. "Galvation fear of magic suggests they are unlikely to know about sorcerers. It's very unlikely they can help you get home."

"No one on this fleet can help us get home either," said Michael. "We'll have to leave sooner or later."

Fiona looked up, her kind blue eyes falling on Ruarnon. "At least this way we can help you, and the Galvations."

"If you are going anywhere," Lenaris said sternly, "you are not going without me."

Mawana smiled and crossed his arms. He would go too…

"No trained Galvation soldiers will fail to recognise a scout, or another soldier on sight," General Takanis warned. "Women soldiers will suggest the people we send are not known enemies, but it will still make the Galvations suspicious."

"So don't send soldiers," said Michael. "Send us, Lenaris and Mawana, with one or two scouts to guide us."

Troy smiled slowly. "Into occupied territory, to make contact with an underground resistance. I've wanted to do that all my life!" he finished, excitement shining in his eyes, his inspired smile tight with fear.

"Try not to get us killed," Michael replied, his lips curling in the hint of a smile. Troy flashed a nervous grin.

"Do you understand what you risk?" Tor asked.

"Capture by Zaldeaans, being sent to Narz for questioning, imprisonment, torture, etc," Michael replied, with a hard edge to his tone.

From their postures, Linh and Michael were resolved to go, while Troy shifted in what Ruarnon suspected was restless anticipation. Only Fiona bit her lip. If they wanted to find Red Cloak, or sorcerers who controlled Gateways of Umarinaris, they were more likely to find them by wandering alone, instead of presenting as Timbalen allies and Narz's enemies. The status of neutral foreigners would serve them best in finding their way back to Australia.

"I'm guessing Galvation soldiers could be mostly men too," Linh added. "Won't the presence of women make the Galvations curious?"

"Of course it will," General Takanis replied. "Men do not like you putting yourselves at risk."

They exchanged smiles, but Tor looked concerned.

"I don't like it, but this is our best chance to help you, and to find sorcerers and our way home," said Fiona.

Ruarnon exhaled deeply.

"I am sorry Ruarnon," said Lenaris, "but I cannot stay here if we are letting them loose in Galvatia."

Troy grinned. He didn't object to her wanting to come to boss him around, he seemed grateful for it.

"Do the Elite Guard employ East Islanders?" Lenaris asked, and Mawana straightened, following the conversation more alertly.

Ruarnon grimaced, resting their head in their hands. All of their friends would go. And the duty of leadership would keep Ruarnon here.

"Few," Tor replied. "Elite Guard have been used to stem rebellion in the East Islands. The emperors were always nervous of training East Islanders in magic."

"So I can go without my appearance giving away the presence of the Elite Guard?" Mawana asked.

"From the prisoners we saw on Cauldron Island and in the empire, it seems inhabitants of this part of the First Land are generally lighter skinned," Tor replied. "Dark-skinned people may also spark Galvation curiosity. The Zaldeaans may recognise you as Urai, but they are unaware the Unspoken Agreement is ended, so your presence will not expose Tarlah's. But you may draw Narz's attention to your people if you are captured."

"I doubt he will worry much about one man far from home while he fears a Guardian invasion," said General Takanis.

"Unless he associates you with his 'Guardian prophetess'," Ruarnon warned.

"But Narz doesn't know my people exist," Mawana objected.

"But the Zaldeaans can tell him where you live, and if he knows or guesses the 'Guardian' prophetess lives there too, he can mistake you for her servant," Ruarnon explained.

"Then we cannot be captured," Mawana insisted.

The tension in Ruarnon's shoulders said that wasn't the only risk. Narz's behaviour towards the Zaldeaan army, creature armies and Timbalen Empire suggested he saw every powerful and unknown group as a threat. And tried to annihilate them.

"You *cannot* craft magic," Ruarnon warned. "If you fight off a Zaldeaan patrol with magic, Narz will assume you are Guardian spies. Your lives could depend upon abstaining from magic, let alone preserving the secrecy of the Elite Guard invasion."

"We have other skills," said Mawana.

"If you resist a Zaldeaan patrol with force of arms, you will be mistaken for Galvation rebels," Tor warned. "If a patrol approaches, your best chance of safety and ensuring the expedition's secrecy is to submit. Hopefully, you would be sent to Companion Karmarn, who will recognise Lenaris, and conceal you from Narz. Can you agree not to resist, if you are surrounded?"

Mawana and Troy tensed, but Michael nodded, and the others slowly agreed. Ruarnon doubted they would agree so willingly in the spur of the moment. They knew their friends too well. And last time they had had to make a choice under pressure, everyone had responded instinctively and foolishly, when Ruarnon hadn't been there to stop them. Would that hold true this time?

"The sensible thing is for me to stay here," Ruarnon said, thinking aloud. "But what if we only get one chance to negotiate with the

Galvation resistance? They will recognise me as a soldier, but my education and upbringing will also be obvious. The curiosity that will stir will give me all the opening I need to put them at their ease."

Tor frowned. "Even common Zaldeaan soldiers may recognise you. Many saw you when you visited the Realm with your uncle. Your midlun appearance likely had the remaining soldiers gossiping."

"Making me an excellent candidate to contact my uncle and find out what binds him and his army here. If I am captured by a Zaldeaan patrol, I am the most likely person to be taken to him, because I *am* likely to be recognised."

"That might be our best plan, if everything goes pear shaped," said Michael. "I mean wrong," he added, when Ruarnon's older advisors, less used to Australian expressions, frowned.

"Narz hasn't deemed Galvations worthy of pitting sorcerers —or his own soldiers— against," said General Takanis. "And the rebels have hidden from him and resisted the Zaldeaans for months. The safest place on this continent may be in a rebel bunker, while Narz's focus is on other, more powerful enemies. The danger is getting your Benevolence to that bunker."

"Then we are agreed I am the best candidate to negotiate with both the Galvations and my uncle?" Ruarnon asked.

"Your negotiations with the Zaldeaan governors went extremely well. There is no question of that," said Tor

General Takanis smiled. "In any other context it would be irrational to send the last of the royal line wandering into an occupied kingdom, seeking people who may take them for an enemy and at risk of capture by people who know them as an enemy. But should Narz take this fleet by surprise… the fleet is ultimately an illusion of safety, that may hold right up until it explodes or burns down to the water line. We cannot be sure we will have warning of that moment, or time to evacuate your Benevolence. Seeking Galvations could be your Benevolence safest course of action."

Tor sighed and bowed his head in agreement. "I am conspicuously recognisable as a soldier. I assume you intend me to command your ships, in your Benevolence's absence?"

Ruarnon inclined their head. This would be the first time they wandered off towards danger without Tor. But someone had to stay in command, and Tor knew Ruarnon's mind and will better than Takanis.

"There is little you could do," Ruarnon replied, "especially if my capture proves the only way to contact the Zaldeaans."

Tor was slow in inclining his head.

Lenaris looked on silently, her mouth slightly open at Ruarnon's two senior advisors agreeing for Ruarnon to take a huge risk. But the logic of it was undeniable. And in accompanying their friends, Ruarnon could keep their promise to Mocco to keep everyone safe...

Ruarnon smiled slowly. Decisive times called for decisive action, and they were finally in a position to do so personally.

"I will find women soldiers who are also farmer's daughters to accompany us, and we shall dress as farmers," Ruarnon added. "If Mawana and Michael's skin is concealed, that will hide your identities from afar, but you must avoid being seen up close."

Ruarnon's friends met their gaze. All of them smiled, to a lesser or greater extent. The thrill of challenge beckoned, and they were glad Ruarnon would accompany them to meet it.

CHAPTER 3

ANCIENT VALLEY-LINH

L inh took a deep breath and eyed the hammocks hanging from the ceiling of her cabin one last time. The first time she'd entered a cabin on Umarinaris, she'd worried about storms and the risk of capsizing. But this cabin had become a space where in shutting the door, she and her Australian friends shut out the dangers of the west, and recalled loved ones and favourite places, books, shows and songs they missed from home. This room had been a refuge on the shores of a continent as safe as Pandora's about to be opened Box.

But Linh knew their best chance of getting home was blundering onto the western continent, as lost and clueless as they'd been when they first set foot in Umarinaris. There was no chance of meeting someone as helpful and intrigued by their presence as Nuard this time, but not being mistaken for Guardians, Elite Guard, Azulans or Zaldeaans seemed a better option than travelling with the army.

Her nerves had been unhappy from the moment General Takanis explained the fleet was an 'illusion of safety.' It was time to leave the illusion of comfort and safety these bare plank walls provided, to face the little-known dangers of the mainland.

Linh sighed, bidding her hammock goodbye, and followed her Australian friends up a ladder. The cool of the bronze iron sheened key from Myleth Island hung from its necklace against her chest, and her pack weighed her down. But when she stepped on deck, following

Ruarnon, Lenaris, and Mawana through pools of lantern light and darkness, the absence of the weight of her armour on her shoulders, and her bronze-iron sheened sword at her hip made her feel exposed. Unfortunately neither would let her pass as a lost innocent.

Ahead of her friends, a rope ladder was slung over the side, and a boat waited to take them ashore. Knowing her wits were her only defence against the dangers ahead made Linh shiver, despite the mild night air. She exhaled, trying to ignore the tension in her shoulders.

It was over a year since they had persuaded Ruarnon to occupy the Zaldeaan Realm. She, Fiona, Troy and Michael had all turned seventeen since arriving in Umarinaris. Her eighteenth birthday wasn't far off now, and she was keen to celebrate at home. But that didn't make leaving the deceptive safety of the fleet and rowing to the most dangerous continent on Umarinaris less daunting.

Fiona knelt before the rope ladder and began her climb over the side. Linh took a deep breath and backed up between a gap in the railing. She gripped the upper rungs tensely with both hands, probed lower ones with her feet, and reluctantly shifted her grip as she climbed down through darkness.

Slowly, she descended into the grey light of the rowboat's dark lamps, then took her seat in the bow, last to board a rowboat containing her three Australian friends, Ruarnon, Lenaris, Mawana and women soldiers seated on either side. The soldiers rowed them forwards.

Beyond the shadowy decks of Timbalen ships lit by dark lamps, their masts fading up into blackness, the cloudbank illusion caused utter darkness. Silence stretched beyond the rhythmic splash of paddles in the hands of their guards.

Linh turned back to the dull glow on the Iylena's decks. She waved to Companion Tor, then turned towards darkness and a Timbalen boat rowing into it. The boat carried General Imphin, who would survey Galvation terrain for battle planning. They would travel through the fertile valley and mountains with General Imphin and his guards, another illusion of safety. But after that, she and her friends would travel with only a handful of Tarlahn guards.

The gentle rocking of the boat as the guards rowed gradually eased Linh's tension, until waves foamed noisily ashore and the Timbalens disembarked, carrying grey islands of dark lantern with them. Moments later, Linh and her friends climbed out into cold shallow water. She shivered as the chill water lapped against her knees, then waded towards dark grey sand. The Timbalen dark lanterns shone against a nearby vertical cliff, which extended until it faded into darkness either side and high overhead. Beyond the dark lamps was eerie pitch black, as if the world ended abruptly.

Linh jumped at a strange sound beyond breaking waves, but it was just a horse snorting. Six horses stood on an approaching barge, the first of two rowing towards them.

"I see fate has called you to danger once more," General Imphin greeted them, as they approached the dry sand on which he waited.

"It's likely our way home," Troy replied. "This being a land of sorcerers."

"True enough," Imphin replied. "I hope you find what you are looking for, but you must be exceedingly careful. If I am discovered, it may commence war, and the repercussions of your discovery may be no less serious."

"They will have my guidance," Ruarnon replied. "I am Tarlahn Ambassador Drake."

Linh checked Troy's gaze was averted and not giving away that Ruarnon was using an alias. General Takanis' final word of advice had been to keep Ruarnon's presence secret from the Timbalens roaming the continent, in case they were captured.

General Imphin introduced himself to Ruarnon, Lenaris and Mawana, then waved at a patch of grey along the cliff.

"Our scouts," he explained. "Akhtar will remain with me, but Mayrun will accompany you. They know a safe passage into Galvatia, and their comrades scouting further ahead will leave them signs of safe passage, or danger."

General Imphin led everyone along the cliff towards the scouts. But as they walked nearer, another source of light lit up the night ahead. A pale, rectangular patch of light shone through a rectangular archway in the base of the cliff. When Linh reached the archway, the land behind it was lighter. There was a grassy clearing beyond the arch. Beyond it, trees were silhouetted against a deep blue sky scattered with stars, and two moons. An owl hooted among the trees.

Linh blinked. The scout report said the forest was burned along the coast. How could trees, branches and leaves be silhouetted against the moons ahead?

Fiona stopped beside her, staring up at a statue above the archway. Torchlight rimmed the underside of the woman's windblown hair, and her rippled skirts, carved from the rock of the cliff. Her chin was held high, and her shadowed face appeared solemn.

"She looks like statues in the City of Peaks," Fiona said quietly.

"And these cliffs are as natural as Tava's Gap at Cauldron Island," Michael added. "I bet they used to be part of a Guardian fortress."

As she stepped under the stone arch, Linh looked up. The sky was star studded ahead, but behind her, the stars gave way to straight-edged darkness. She shivered. Her sense of wonder and confusion had dimmed it, but magic tingled along the cliffs and over the arch. It was like the buildings in Timbala City, only this sense of tingling was stronger. And the cliff walls seemed to be resisting Narz's storm cloud illusion, completely.

"Is no one maintaining this?" Troy asked, gesturing up at the clear, starry sky. "You can't sense anyone cutting off the cloud illusion above the walls? Even while we stand next to them?"

Akhtar, the male scout, shook his head. "It is enchanted," he replied. "The cliffs team with protective magic and the air hums with it."

Linh shivered. *She* could sense what the Elite Guard could sense?

"Shame the Galvations hate magic," said Michael. "This place would be a perfect base for Galvation resistance headquarters."

"And much easier for us to find," Ruarnon added. "I doubt our task will be that easy."

The tingling of magic remained at the edge of Linh's awareness as they erected their tents, unrolled their bedding and she lay down next to Fiona. Every time tiredness made her want to drift off, she noticed the tingle of magic and became fully aware of the dark fabric hanging above, and the grass and bedroll padded ground beneath her. She lay awake, struggling to relax when a powerful substance operated seemingly of its own accord, a short distance away.

"At least there's no sign of Narz's sorcerers yet," Fiona said into the dark. "I know the idea of enchantments is scary, but at least no one is threatening us with magic."

Linh sighed. "You're right. I just wish that made me feel better. I'd like to sleep anywhere else."

"Maybe you need to picture anywhere else?" Fiona suggested.

Linh slowly smiled, suspecting the place Fiona was suggesting. She thanked her friend, lay on her back and tried to picture golden sands radiating the sun's heat, a bright blue sky and the splashing fountains at the end of Desriah's Palace path. Bit by bit she relaxed and eventually drifted off to sleep.

In the morning, Linh stepped out into bright sunlight and a grassy clearing. Her friends ate breakfast ahead. Beyond them, a leafy green forest spread beneath a clear blue sky. On her left, sunlight beamed onto weathered cliff so narrow it had to be an ancient wall, towering over the forest. Directly above the wall, clear blue sky turned cloudy. Further on, clouds thickened to grey, then black. Linh shivered. That didn't look like a cloud illusion. Of all the places on Umarinaris, why did this one have to be the most likely place to contain a functioning gateway and sorcerers capable of opening it to Australia?

"Come on Linh, we'll be ready to march soon," Fiona called, and Linh hurried to breakfast, where she bit absently into her fruit.

As they ate, Fiona eyed the sky apprehensively. Michael frowned at it.

"It's *not* possible," Michael said, his gaze fixed on the thickening clouds just beyond the wall, and the denser clouds beyond. "Trying to halt clouds passing through the sky or dropping the immense volume of rain those dark ones must carry involves resisting atmospheric pressure endlessly. I don't see how *any* human could have that power."

"If it's a weather enchantment," said Fiona, "what's it for?"

"Drought," Lenaris replied. "If the Galvations do not have canals and rivers fed by snow melt as we do, then stopping the rain will kill their crops and livestock. In time, drought will force the resistance to surrender or abandon Galvatia. Its magic as warfare."

Lenaris shivered and Mawana squeezed her hand.

"Using magic to attack the land itself?" Mawana asked. "I like Narz even less."

Ruarnon shook their head. "I can scarcely believe withholding the rain, let alone on such a scale, is magically possible."

"Even the secret histories of our Elite Guard suggest is it not," said General Imphin from his breakfast on a picnic blanket further right. "Our people have not encountered anything like a vast cloud illusion since the Sorcery War itself. But the Elite Guard only had to pool their magic craft as one when the damars invaded us. It may be that sorcerers in this land are more practiced at crafting magic together, and that such a practice allows them to achieve more than we thought possible."

Linh's shoulders tightened at the idea. His logic set her teeth on edge.

"Unless this is what remains of a Guardian fortress," said Ruarnon. "Everyone's stories seem to agree their magic craft outstripped that of the sorcerers, and anyone but the faeron, from whom they likely learnt magic craft."

"I hope," Imphin replied, "for all our sakes and the entire fleet, that you are right. The sky enchantment ought to be occupying the best of Narz's sorcerers. But if others here have the power to counter such an enchantment, and they join our war against him, the scale of its destruction may rival that of the first Sorcery War."

Linh squeezed her wooden cup so hard she suspected it would have broken if it was made of glass. The only thing more reckless than wandering into a country with its sky blanketed by a possible enchantment that prevented rain from falling, was staying in this place where clear sky gave way abruptly to dense, dark clouds. The point where two incomprehensively powerful enchantments contested each other's wills would likely put cracks in your sanity, if you stared at it for too long.

"Let's go," she said to her friends, standing, a half-eaten fruit lying at her feet, her appetite lost.

Troy stood, stuffed a couple of fruits in his pocket and then everyone packed up their bedrolls and tents. They saddled their horses so quickly they were ready at the same time as the guards and General Imphin.

A woman wearing a finely woven tunic and leggings stepped forward. Linh assumed she was Mayrun, the female Elite Guard scout.

"We do not think there are any other magics in these trees, or in this place, but I suggest we stay close together," Mayrun told them. "And if you hear anything that sounds louder than a bird, like a twig snapping, please tell me or Akhtar, quietly. Narz may have scouts spread along this coastline, keeping watch for the retaliatory attack of the Timbalen Empire we believe he anticipates."

Linh's jaw clenched at the idea of someone watching them. It was a slight relief to mount their horses and follow Akhtar out of the clearing, but anyone could be hiding behind the trees or among the bushes surrounding her companions. The dense, wild green tangles offered excellent cover for spies.

"Try to focus on the view," Fiona whispered.

Fiona's gaze was on Linh's whitening knuckles, which clutched her reins too tightly. Linh grit her teeth. This ride wouldn't be short, and that grip would make her fingers ach before the end. She sighed, slowed her breathing, and tried to relax her fingers. Michael had told her ages ago that railing against things she couldn't change would just make her miserable. Here, it would make her tense, and anxious. Over time, that would wear her down.

This was no place to be exhausted. She needed to be alert and capable of defending herself physically and magically. That meant finding peace with her surroundings, no matter how dangerous they seemed or how much actively shifting magic they contained. But how did she do that?

Fiona wasn't riding calmly either. She was eyeing the scenery with a pale face, and from the sounds of it, breathing more shallowly than normal. She was nervous too. But at least she was trying to do something about it. And she and Michael were right. They couldn't change their surroundings. The only thing they could change was how they responded to them. Linh was going to have to figure out how to do that. No matter what she saw here. Now seemed a good time to start.

She sighed and followed Fiona's gaze into the trees. Leaves rustled in the wind and lifted the end of her tunic. She shivered. The air here was *moving*. But the fleet, not so far away, was becalmed. Her shoulders tightened, as she fought the idea the enchanted clouds weren't an illusion.

She swore under her breath. Why did the first thing she noticed have to put her more on edge? But getting angry wouldn't do any good. She'd have to notice something else, something distracting and calming.

Linh fidgeted with her reins, took a deep breath, and stared into the wilderness. Brown cracked-bark trunks rose around her. A mild wind blew against her face. Leaves rustled overhead and birds called from the treetops. The scent of wildflowers blew on the wind.

This place was alive, and normal, like somewhere back home. Best enjoy it while she could. That became her aim, for the rest of the day, the night and the next morning, as they continued their ride through the wilderness, until they reached a cave on the edge of the mountains.

Linh halted her horse behind her older friends, as the Timbalen and Tarlahn guards lit torches.

"You are sure the horses will manage being underground?" General Imphin asked.

"The non-scout ones may be uneasy, but it is only for two days, scarce long enough for them to know it isn't just night-time," Mayrun assured him.

"And Narz's spies won't hear us coming?"

Ahktar pointed to a small strip of green, tied beneath a strip of brown to a low-lying branch near the opening. "The bottom rag signals the tunnel," he replied. "The top one signals it is clear."

General Imphin nodded, then everyone dismounted, leading their horses into the tunnel one by one, following Mayrun's lead. Linh surveyed the walls by the flickering light of torches the soldiers lit. The floor seemed to curve down naturally, but the ceiling was uneven, and bore chisel marks.

"It looks like a mine entrance," said Lenaris. "We dig shafts down to the gold mines in Tarlah. This seems fancier."

"Or dug for larger loads to be carried out," Ruarnon added. "I see no sign of pulleys to lift the diggings out."

Linh followed Ruarnon's horse down the ramp. Her horse snorted at the dark open space yawning before it, but followed her lead. The cavern bellow was wide enough that her horse could walk beside Ruarnon. The walls stretched further on either side, but the roof was too low for the horses at the edges.

"Through here," Mayrun called, from the far side of the cavern.

An archway was cut through the far wall, and the trickle of water echoed from it.

Fiona stepped into the cavern behind Linh, biting her lip.

"Any Balrog's down there?" Troy called from behind, "If not, this place is fine with me!"

Linh shook her head. "As if Umarinaris doesn't have enough scary things to worry about!"

Mayrun led them through the archway on the far side. In the chamber beyond, the soldiers' torchlight reflected off water running down creamy cones gleaming from the ceiling. More water dripped onto creamy cones rising up, from which it ran down the smooth, pale rock to the wet cavern floor. On Linh's left, a white ledge rose to a wall, beyond which stalagmites rose thickly.

There was something odd about the wall, jutting out from the rest of the cavern, and about the placement of the largest stalactites, which hung around the walls. Linh couldn't put her finger on it.

Mayrun led them along a smooth section of rocky ground, a former streambed. Water trickled through the darkness further to their right.

Mawana walked up to the ledge and knocked on it with his fist. He moved along, until he hit a section that sounded hollow. He shoved at the stone.

"That wall doesn't look like it's in any hurry to move mate," said Troy.

"It was a door, a long time ago," Mawana explained, walking back to where Lenaris held his horse's reins.

"But stalactites and stalagmites take thousands of years to form," Linh objected.

"Maybe it was a door when the Faeron lived here, and this was once a Faeron building," Fiona suggested.

Linh surveyed the cavern. That's what was odd. The stalactites around its outer walls all hung from the same height. They were very similar in size and shape, and evenly spaced. Were those torch-brackets once? Had Faeron architecture survived here?

She followed the Timbalens through a roughly cut tunnel to another ledge, on the edge of a cavern so vast that everyone mounted their horses through it. The ledge curved, hugging the cavern wall on the right. On the left, the guards' torches shone into darkness.

They followed the rocky ledge, spiralling down the walls and skirting the cavern's black interior. The ledge ended on flat ground beside a ragged wall of quartz, where torchlight shone on a pickaxe. Further down lay half a dozen pickaxes before piles of quartz chippings and dust.

"Looks like they downed tools and ran for it," Troy commented.

"If they lived anywhere near the forest fires Narz's sorcerers spread," Michael added, "then they probably rushed home to help their families evacuate."

Linh's horse followed the others' horses past more tools and rocky debris. Michael pointed beyond a chunk of quartz lying on the floor to the small gold vein it exposed.

"No one would leave that if they noticed it," he said, "and they must have been very frightened not to."

The image of a wall of flame spreading rapidly over a field, towards a town of thatched roofs and wooden walls came to Linh's mind unbidden. She shivered and fervently hoped the miners had been safely reunited with their families.

It was bad luck the cavern floor was the best place to camp for the night, with thought of the spreading fire and the last people to set foot here fleeing fresh on her mind. Was that how Narz crafted magic in his war with Galvatia? Using it to frighten them? A psychological war of intimidation?

But Darius, whom the Timbalens had captured in the sewers of Timbala Island, said the Galvations hadn't been afraid. That they'd rallied to fight the enslaved Zaldeaan army, and even damars. That the Galvation soldiers who escaped that battle still resisted Narz from the wilderness of their sorcerous-sky clouded home.

Linh respected and admired their will to do that, especially so close to obvious signs of Narz's power. But there was something odd about that power. Narz wielded so much of it, yet for months it sounded like he'd refused to wield it against the Galvations directly. Despite how much Darius and even Poran insisted Galvations hated sorcerers, Narz hadn't attacked them directly with magic.

It didn't make any sense, a grand show of magic across the sky, when more direct magical attacks could have instantly achieved his goals. Especially when it sounded like it took months of drought, a great fire and days of fighting to conquer Galvatia. Was Narz holding back?

The next day Linh, her companions and their guards entered a cavern with a clear space along the left, bordered by strange brown vines growing from floor to ceiling on the right. Imphin's guards rode with their swords drawn, scanning the tangled mass, but their torchlight dimmed into shadows and darkness.

"Halt!" Mawana called, and everyone reined in.

Wood creaked and something shifted at the edge of the torchlight.

"It's a child," said Fiona. "Can you lower your swords?" she asked Imphin's guards. "She looked frightened."

Imphin nodded to his guards.

"There must be Galvations hiding in tunnels linked to this chamber," Lenaris guessed. "I doubt it could be anyone else."

"We will only frighten them away if we wander into their hiding places uninvited," said Ruarnon. "If we leave the child alone, word of us may spread and the resistance might seek us out."

Linh pursed her lips. Just how deep into hiding were the Galvations?

She rode on, eventually following the Timbalens into a cavern where a vast ledge stretched before them, vanishing into darkness on the left. The rush of a river rose up from the darkness and a stone bridge arched off the ledge ahead.

Linh tensed in her saddle. The bridge was wide, but had no railing, and ended at a much higher point in the cavern on its far side. Her stomach roiled at the sight of it. She grimaced in distaste.

Imphin advanced with the scouts, and his guards followed him in rows of three, leaving gaps between themselves and the edge.

"We can ride either side of you," Mawana offered Linh, and she smiled with relief.

"I'll take your left and Fiona can take your right," Michael said behind her and she turned to see Troy's eyes widen in surprise. Then his face split in a shy grin. Fiona smiled and Michael winked.

Ruarnon advanced with a pair of Tarlahn guards, sitting calmly upright. Linh tried not to envy them. She grit her teeth and healed her horse forwards. Lenaris and Mawana kept pace either side of Linh. She kept her gaze firmly on the stone ahead, trying not to think how far below the rush of water echoed up from and to focus on the ledge she was approaching.

The tightness in her shoulders eased when she, Lenaris and Mawana reached the highest point of the bridge. She exhaled with relief as their horses rode onto the platform beyond, then crossed it into another dull tunnel. Fiona caught her up, smiling, probably because the tunnel rose steeply upwards, and bright light shone at its far end.

Linh smiled too, grateful to leave the dark heights of the cavern behind. Her shoulders relaxed as they rode after the Timbalens, out through an archway. It led to a wide ledge, beyond which small plants clung to dry mountainside, which fell steeply away.

Linh drew a nervous breath, wondering what altitude they were riding out onto. She gazed down a rocky slope across flat, barren plains, scattered haphazardly with boulders and rock formations. Rocky hills rose in the distance, giving rise to mountains beyond. The sight reminded her of the barren wasteland of Lava Island, without signs of volcanism, or the dramatic fault lines of an earthquake. What had broken up the rocks?

"It goes as far as the eye can see," Michael said as he rode beside her, staring at the sky.

Linh froze in her saddle. Clouds barred the sky above the plains, hills and mountains lining the plains on the left. Clouds dominated the sky over the river and the edge of a forest on her right. Dark grey or blackened clouds hung over all Galvatia, and there wasn't a bush or living tree in sight.

"I thought you said it was impossible to stop the wind," Troy said faintly, as their guards reined in, staring at the sky.

"It shouldn't be possible," Michael replied. "For those clouds to be that dense and dark, Narz's enchantment must be defying the water cycle. Water evaporates and becomes clouds, but he's suspended the wind, and forces the ever-denser clouds to withhold their rain, over tens of square kilometres of sky, every inch defying the laws of nature every second those clouds exist. Whatever power brought us from Earth could pale in comparison to the power preserving that enchantment."

"Narz most definitely knows the secret of enchantment crafting," Mayrun said quietly, her patient expression exposing carelines Linh hadn't noticed on her tan, weathered face. "And he has mastered the art of joint crafting, wielded by many sorcerers, to put such an enchantment in place over such a vast area."

"Mijora preserve us," said General Imphin.

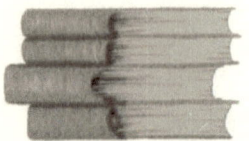

Chapter 4

Beneath the Clouds- Linh

Linh wasn't the only person with bags under her eyes at breakfast on the mountain ledge the next morning. The ominous sky hung over them like a shroud, visible in all directions unless she kept her gaze on the ground. Timbalens, Tarlahns and her friends ate their meal in a circle, and uneasy silence, until Mayrun returned.

"We have an update on scout reports," she told everyone. "Beyond the mountains barring the south lies a city occupied by damars. There is a castle in the south-western mountain range occupied by Zaldeaans, in which two sorcerers have been detected wielding magic. We presume the city and castle mark the Azulan-Galvation border.

"North of the plains before us, over the river lies unburnt forest, densely populated with savage damars. An armed Zaldeaan supply convoy was sighted travelling through it, so we think there is a Zaldeaan outpost there."

Ruarnon sighed. "So Narz has sorcerers keeping an eye on my uncle."

Linh tensed. She heard their unspoken words, "If we're captured, deceiving Narz into thinking we're no one important or of preventing word of our capture from reaching Narz could be more difficult than we thought."

She assumed they held those words back in General Imphin's presence. Something told her the Timbalens weren't aware that Ruarnon being captured by Zaldeaans could become part of their plan to contact Commander Karmarn.

General Imphin nodded to Mayrun to continue.

"Our path lies west," Mayrun added, turning to Linh and her companions, "through the rocky plains before us, between the southern and northern Zaldeaan outposts. West of the plains lies a city the scouts believe is Galvatia. They sighted two men in the wilderness and suspect there is an underground tunnel system beneath the city. The rocky plains and barren farmland ahead are uninhabited, leaving nothing for us to blend in with."

Ruarnon bowed their head. "So we must not be seen or heard by patrols. We will still dress as farmers, travel quietly, and rely on you and Mawana's tracking abilities to give us warning of approaching patrols, hiding until they pass."

"We will part ways here," General Imphin said to Ruarnon. "I wish to explore the plains nearer the Zaldeaan outposts as potential battlegrounds and scout the edge of Azula. But should you succeed in contacting Galvations further west, please offer them an alliance on our behalf. Any tunnels they have dug may help our scouting efforts, and we would like to use their geographic knowledge to plan our march on Azula."

Ruarnon bowed their head.

"When do we leave?" Mawana asked Ruarnon.

"As soon as you are ready."

"Not under cover of darkness?" Lenaris asked.

Ruarnon sighed. "Beneath the clouds will be near total darkness at night. There's too much risk of injuring our horses and getting lost."

Linh's shoulders began to ache as she rolled up her bedroll and helped Fiona pack up the tent. With a grey and black sky dominating the horizon, the air perfectly still, not a drop of rain on the parched soil beneath her feet, and a violent thunderstorm seeming only moments ahead, riding out under that sky felt like crossing a mine field. She shuddered and tried to focus on something else, but there was no vegetation to distract her this time, just stark rocky plains and the bleak sky overhead.

By the time they sat on worn saddles, wearing coarsely woven tunics, pants and cloaks, and worn leather boots, their packs on their backs, presenting as farmers, Linh's jaw was firmly clenched. Mawana and Michael wore straw brimmed hats angled to conceal their skin colour, and by extension Mawana's people's presence in Narz's lands, but if anyone was seen by a Zaldeaan patrol... Linh gripped her reins tightly, nudging her horse between Fiona and Troy's. Troy nodded to her, but Fiona bit her lip and eyed the ground.

Linh suspected everyone was keeping their thoughts and tension to themselves, in an attempt not to heighten others stress levels. Or at least, that was what she was doing

Ruarnon and Mayrun led them past dried up bushes and spindly plants along a trail which zig-zagged down the mountainside. Vegetation soon became sparse, and the slope grew rockier near the boulder strewn plains. At the bottom, a row of rocky mountains faded into the horizon on Linh's left, screening the damarian city. Rocky plains on her right stretched to a distant river, with the greenery of damar infested forest beyond.

The reddish-brown soil of the plains was hard and cracked, the rocks eroded by the elements. But the rocky formation ahead of her wasn't cracked, except at the edge, where part of it had fallen, and lay in weathered shards scattered across the ground.

Linh frowned. There were cracks on the edge of the rock formation before the erosion. But the cracks weren't vertical. They rose from the side in multiple directions, up, sideways and down. As if they radiated from a single point. As if some extremely powerful force had struck the side of the rock formation, blasting into shards the rocks scattered beside it.

Linh struggled to keep her breathing steady as she scanned more rock formations. The rocks were reddish brown, but some had darker areas, erratic in shape, blackened. The earth showed no signs of fire. Could these plains a battlefield the Sorcery War was fought on?

Shivers travelled down Linh's spine. Hearing the odd reference to a mythical war, even as an explanation to present-day Umarinaris had been uncomfortable enough, but riding through possibly sorcery ravaged plains, with a general scouting an invasion route behind, had her breathing heavily and shoving the idea forcefully aside.

At home and school, they always said don't go to dangerous places and don't do dangerous things. Those choices were luxury goods Galvation rebels couldn't afford, and if she ever wanted to get home, neither could she.

"We're only likely to meet Zaldeaans on these plains, and they can't wield magic," Michael said softly, as if detecting the tension boiling silently in the air.

Troy sighed and nodded, and Linh gaped at Michael reassuring Troy, whose face had turned almost as pale as Fiona's normal skin colour.

"We'll keep a careful eye and ear out for patrols," Mawana added. "If Mayrun and I do well enough, you won't even see them."

Linh remembered how Mawana had tracked an abducted girl through Timbala City by sound, despite noisy celebrations and panicked parents seeking their daughters in the streets. They were lucky to have Mawana with them, though she sincerely hoped they had no need of his shield magic, especially when Mocco wasn't here to help.

Mayrun led them around boulders and rocky hills, and Linh's eyes flitted to shadows, as did their guards', sweeping every crevice.

"Can you tell us more about this city with damars in it?" Michael asked Mayrun. "The ones we've met tend to run wild if not enchanted to stick together. So how are they living in a city?"

"Its walls are high, and the gates closed," she replied. "The savage kind are virtual prisoners. We are unlikely to meet any roaming these plains."

"The savage kind?" Lenaris asked.

Mayrun's lips pulled into a taught line. "Some of them move more slowly, more purposefully. They seem to be keeping an eye on the others."

She paused, then added, "And we saw one damar repairing damage to a building in its city, without human assistance or supervision."

"Sky Gods preserve us!" Mawana exclaimed.

Linh gaped. The first damars they'd met had trampled the bodies of their own dead. They'd shown no awareness for their own kind.

"The damars that attacked Cauldron Island were trained to fight," said Michael.

"And the damars that attacked the Timbalen Empire could craft magic," Linh added. "But how do you train a damar to mend a building? That's not just an extension of survival reflexes, like fighting."

Michael frowned, but didn't answer.

As for supervising anyone, surely that required conscious thought?

They rode in uneasy silence.

"Halt!" Mayrun said softly.

Linh and the others reigned in.

"A group approaches from the south," Mayrun warned.

Linh blinked, but only rock formations lay ahead, and she heard nothing.

"This way," Lenaris whispered. She led everyone north of a rocky hill and they reined in behind it. Mawana dismounted, and crept to the edge of the hillside, peering around it.

"They are just within sight," he reported. "A mounted patrol heading west across the plains, parallel to us."

The patrol was *behind* everyone when Mayrun noticed it?

"How many?" Ruarnon asked.

"Twenty, at least," Mawana replied. "They are staying south-east of us. If we let them get far enough ahead, we should be able to travel parallel and behind them, far back enough they won't see us."

"I advise keeping our distance as much as possible," said Mayrun. "They may loop back towards us, and we want to keep hills and boulders between us no matter which way they turn."

"You don't detect sorcerers?" Lenaris asked.

Mayrun shook her head. When she was satisfied the patrol had moved far enough ahead, they continued west across the plains. The guards and Mawana kept a careful eye on the patrol, while Linh wondered how long they could tail it without being noticed.

Blackened hills loomed in the distance beyond the boulders, burnt looking hills.

"There are more people," Mayrun reported, "approaching in front of us, heading towards the first patrol."

Ruarnon motioned everyone to dismount. Linh led her horse after Fiona's, behind a large boulder. The others moved behind two more nearby boulders and waited silently. Linh strained her ears but heard only the rapid beating of her heart.

"Both patrols are within hailing distance," Mayrun reported from a crack between two boulders. "And still approaching. They have stopped."

"Can she sense them?" Fiona mouthed. "Surely she can't see all that?"

Linh's mouth dropped open. She nodded slowly.

"They are separating again," said Mayrun. "I think…yes, one is coming closer and the other is moving further away."

Mawana crept around the boulders with the elegant silence of a cat. "They are retracing their steps," he reported, "Moving back along the plain."

"Well that's silly," said Troy. "Neither patrol is going to catch any rebels they didn't see earlier."

"The patrols may be for show," Ruarnon suggested, "a message to rebels that King Narz is watching, and they cannot move freely. If that's the case, we still need to be vigilant, but they may be complacent, if they march the same route every day."

After a lengthy wait, Linh and her companions resumed their ride, keeping boulders between them and the plains on her left where the patrols had disappeared. She and her companions drew nearer the burnt landscape ahead, and she made out blackened trunks rising from hills amongst strange towers.

"They're chimneys," said Fiona. "They must have been on the ends of wooden buildings that burnt down in the fire."

"It was an unnatural fire," Michael added, pointing.

Linh followed his gaze to a carpet of ash and charcoal that came to a sudden end at the foot of trees and bushes growing in a solid line of green, untouched forest. The fire looked targeted and carefully controlled. She clenched her fists. More intimidation tactics from Narz's henchmen?

"What's the point of attacking a small town?" Troy asked. "I mean, who lived here? Craftspeople? Shop owners? What harm could they do Narz?"

"Perhaps farmers who sheltered and fed the resistance," said Ruarnon.

"They are only a day's ride from the border with Azula," said Mayrun. "Narz would not take kindly to anyone harbouring his enemies so close to his homeland."

Linh shook her head. "He's afraid of them. Why else would he exert so much magic craft to keep them at bay, and starve them out of their lands? Why waste so much magic trying to drive them further away from his border?"

"When with the Zaldeaan army, he has the numbers to round up the rebels and enslave them all," Ruarnon added. "Unless my uncle isn't co-operating and is hindering Narz's efforts as he attempts to free his soldiers."

"He'd dare do that?" Mawana asked.

"He dared spy on his own nephew for us, out of loyalty to his half-brother's peace," Ruarnon replied. "And he attained his rank as Companion via hard work, like any commoner, as his and Kyomi's father did not acknowledge him as the king's son. I doubt after marrying my aunt, a Tarlahn wife, and dedicating years of his life to peace, he would settle for being trapped here indefinitely.

"He must realise I have united Tarlah and the Realm, and the peace he's dedicated his life to has likely been achieved. Monin was half surprised he hasn't brought the army home of his own accord."

As they crossed the blackened hills, Linh counted at least twenty stone fireplaces rising above piles of charcoal. Ash coated pottery protruded from burnt debris, and not a single wall remained standing. Here and there, large pots rose above piles of ash. There was almost nothing left of a place that must have housed at least a hundred people and no sign of its former inhabitants.

Her companions rode in grim silence, until Mayrun led them down a narrow cart track through the trees.

"What's that?" said Fiona, pointing at something bright on a nearby tree.

"It's a handkerchief," said Linh, snatching it off the branch it was caught on. "It's not burnt."

Linh blinked. "The only pottery I could see back there was the rims of large storage pots too heavy to carry, not smaller containers people could flee with. There might be refugees from this town hiding in this enchantment blasted kingdom somewhere."

Fiona smiled, her eyes shining with hope, but her smile was hesitant. Ruarnon turned inclined their head, a small smile saying they had the same hope.

But there was no sign of people in the forest, just branches that became Zaldeaan patrols or damars in shadows on the edge of Linh's vision. Tired of false sightings, she was glad when the trees thinned and gave way to open country again. But the hills before her were parched and lined with fence posts. As if this was farmland. Yet there was no grass for herds to graze on. No crops to be harvested. Every hillside before her was bare, sections of dry brown soil cracked, suggesting the drought had lasted months, perhaps even years.

Her fists clenched again. Ruarnon was right. Narz was using a cloud enchantment to perpetuate drought, and if all Galvatia's farmland was this hard hit by it, every farmer must have walked off their land by now. But where had those who escaped gone?

Fiona gasped, and Linh reached out to squeeze her teary-eyed friend's hand, while Troy turned with a concerned frown. Linh didn't feel sad. How could Narz do this? How could he claim to care about humans, yet treat some humans like *this*? Her left hand gripped her reins tightly, and she repressed the urge to throttle something.

The river was so far away on her right that she could no longer see it, and the mountain range on her left extended beyond her vision. Everything before her was dry plains, small hills and parched or cracked soil.

In the distance lay white rectangular shapes, with smaller shapes scattered around them. Linh studied the shapes as they rode closer.

"Are those houses?" Fiona asked softly.

"They are strangely spread out," said Mawana.

"Not for farmhouses," said Michael.

"How can they be farms?" asked Troy. "There's no crops, or cattle, just funny white rocks."

"I don't think that's a rock," Michael said, pointing towards something round on their left, with white things sticking out from it. "It's a skeleton."

"A skeleton of what?" Linh asked.

"We believe they are cattle," Mayrun replied.

Judging by its elongated skull and large ribcage, it was a cow skeleton. More were scattered nearby, perhaps a farmer's entire herd. Linh assumed drought had killed them. Her grip on her reins tightened.

Michael's piercing gaze swept the countryside, his eyes burning with quiet anger. Lenaris spoke softly to Mawana, while Ruarnon surveyed the devastated hills in complete silence.

"Are you all right Ruarnon?" Lenaris called.

Ruarnon inclined their head slowly. "However badly I once thought of Zaldeaans, even they wouldn't do this. Yet Poran judged the

Zaldeaans ruthless killers and felt morally superior to them. I wonder if Narz does the same, and how he can, when he has reduced Galvation countryside to this."

Linh shivered. Another contradiction in Narz. There were too many of those. She didn't like to consider their implications for Narz's mental health.

She rode past many cow skeletons, most looking as though they had collapsed where they stood, from dehydration or starvation. It wasn't one farmer's herd; it was several.

"Why's that door open?" Fiona asked.

They were approaching a white-washed, wattle and daub farmhouse with a thatched roof.

Linh braced herself and dismounted, handing her reins to Fiona. She strode determinedly towards the house, looking for signs someone had escaped. She drew a deep breath and pushed the front door open. The stench of rotten food hit her nostrils.

"Yuck," said Troy, covering his nose with his sleeve as he stepped beside her. "Something's gone off."

A large table set with course pottery lay before them. Several wooden chairs were knocked over, and the bowls were overflowing with mould, some with wooden handles protruding from them, while wooden spoons lay scattered on the floor.

Linh sighed. "They were taken," she said, surveying the fallen furniture. "There was a struggle, and they were forced out of their home. Maybe Narz did try to round up everyone, in the end."

The building was one room, with straw sleeping pallets along the wall and a firepit at one end, with a smoke hole in the roof. Many hooks lined the ceiling beams, with dried plants, a cloak, pottery and odds and ends hanging off them, but many were bare, perhaps plundered by Narz's soldiers.

Troy coughed and left, and Linh followed. Troy was describing what they'd seen when she reached and mounted her horse.

"Why would anyone take farmers prisoner?" Fiona asked. "They're the last people who would threaten Narz's rule."

"To control anyone he believes threatens him," Linh replied. "That's why he seized the Zaldeaans, invaded Cauldron Island, the Island of the Guardians and the Timbalen Empire. I think we were right in the end, Narz is driven by fear, and lashing out against anyone he thinks threatens him."

"Don't forget how effective Mocco and Mawana's charge with conventional weapons was against magic crafting damars in the Timbalen Empire," Ruarnon added. "Farmers are potential levied soldiers, and even levied soldiers can threaten sorcerers, if enough of them attack. His policy against the Galvations is brutal, but its sound strategy in a war that could last as long as our wars with the Zaldeaans."

"But what does he do with the people he's taken?" Troy asked.

"Probably have them farm for him," Linh replied, "like the Romans got some of their rebellious subjects they relocated to do."

"And stop them allying with the kings further south, whom he fears are allying against him," Lenaris added. "That may be what drove him to attack the Galvations first, so he could take control of Galvatia before it became a base for his southern enemies on his doorstep. It's ironic Galvatia may now become exactly that base and invasion route for the Timbalens."

"Now I get why the Timbalens feel they need to take Narz out for their own safety," Troy said, shaking his head. "The Galvations must feel the same way. They'll be thrilled when we offer them an alliance."

"We have to find them first," said Michael.

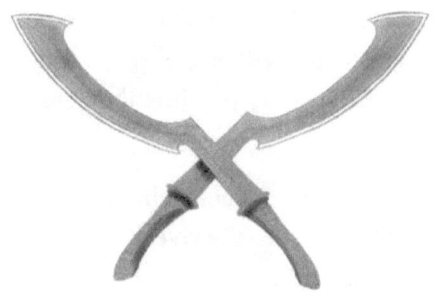

CHAPTER 5

THE DESERTED CITY-RUARNON

Everything Ruarnon had witnessed of Galvatia was worse than they anticipated. It seemed whoever Narz hadn't defeated in battle, he'd driven away, with their children and farm animals. As if he sought not just to conquer Galvatia, but to ensure it offered nothing of sustenance and little of cover to his enemies.

In their heart, Ruarnon feared there may be no one here to make an alliance with. Darius' reports of Zaldeaans patrolling this wasteland for rebels were weeks old now. Surely the Galvations were long gone? Perhaps the Zaldeaans were merely keeping patrols against shadows and flights of their imagination.

Ruarnon was relieved by the distraction of the riverbank coming back into view on their right. Forest greenery rose beyond it, softening the bleak land of lifeless soil. But Narz had poisoned the forest too, letting savage damars roam it…

A rectangular rock formation in the distance slowly resolved into a city, accessed via a bridge over a branch of the river. The city's walls were built of reddish-brown stone, while the bridge looked wide enough for multiple wagons to cross simultaneously, a reflection of prosperous time now past.

"There are no patrols nearby," said Mayrun, as they approached the bridge. "But we shall be visible above the line of the horizon while we cross. And there is a patrol leaving the western end, and another leaving the north. The northern patrol will travel round and enter the eastern gates, while the western patrol will circle round and enter from the south. We shall pass through the city while they are at their furthest points from its centre."

Ruarnon frowned, then shook themself. "Everyone dismount," they instructed. "Lead your horses into the riverbank and bind their hooves with rags. We will walk them across."

As Ruarnon led their horse down a gentle incline of riverbank, they noted that water only flowed through the centre of the riverbed, barely a meter wide, and ankle deep. There must be rain further north or west of Galvatia, but the river flowed from the south.

When their horse's hooves were muffled, Ruarnon had everyone bunch up, the guards forming a tight ring around them. Then Ruarnon led the way onto the bridge. Its interior walls were carved reliefs. Stylised people in veils and flowing clothing marched towards the city along the bridge walls, and tall, bare-chested guards stood at the near end of the wall, in sharp contrast to the abandoned road ahead, leading into a silent city.

Gates rose beyond the bridge, made of thick timber and reinforced with iron bars. They hung open.

"Do you detect anyone inside?" Ruarnon asked Mayrun.

"No," she replied, confirming Ruarnon's suspicion she had a magical sense of what lay ahead.

"I suggest we stay on horseback," said Mawana. "Any patrol that sees us will assume we're Galvation rebels and pursue us, so we need to be ready to move at speed."

Ruarnon sighed. Fleeing could get messy. It was the only way of resisting arrest consistent with their pretence of being Galvation refugees, or rebels. And their companions couldn't contact Galvations stubborn enough to defy the vast power laying waste to their land if the Zaldeaans captured all of them. They may be forced to split up to escape. Ruarnon knew this. Lenaris had argued passionately that it must be part of their plans. Ruarnon had resisted the idea, until now, when the logic of it became undeniable.

"Should we be forced to flee," Ruarnon said, "follow the other branch of the river further west. South leads to the border with Azula so you *do not* want to go that way. We cannot risk leading patrols back to the army by riding east and the forest to the east has damars in it. But so far as we know, the western wilderness is safe, will not give away Timbalen presence and the Zaldeaans won't expect it."

"Use the river to navigate," Lenaris added to the Australians. "There are few landmarks here, and mountains in three different directions. If you get separated and don't know where to go; stick to the river."

Ruarnon inclined their head. "If we get separated, the northern branch of the river will be our regrouping point. Ride as far along it as you need to get beyond sight and sound of patrols, then hide and wait for us to find you."

Everyone mounted and rode through the city gates. Inside, the road was stone paved and lined with tall, multi-storeyed apartments of red-brown stone, with wooden framed windows. Each apartment had steps up to double doors and some were flanked with torch brackets.

The main road and every side street were deserted. Windows in upper stories opened to dark rooms, while front doors hung ajar. Beyond the clack-clack of their horses' hooves was silence.

They passed more red-brown stone buildings, hearing only their horses' muffled hooves on pavement.

"Do you think there could be secret tunnel entrances in the houses?" Lenaris asked.

"It is possible," Mayrun replied.

"Then Zaldeaan patrols moving above ground may not have found the tunnels," said Mawana. "I've seen nothing of rebels these last few days, and I am good at spotting shy and reclusive animals in the jungle by the slightest sound. If I cannot hear the rebels, and they have been near us, it's worth searching houses."

Ruarnon sighed. That was a more optimistic reason for these lands seeming utterly abandoned. And it tallied with the child they'd glimpsed in the tunnels through the mountains a few days ago. It was worth investigating.

"We don't have long," said Ruarnon. "I do not want to risk being sighted by patrols inside the city, where they can block our exit. But if we find any evidence people have been here after the city was abandoned; it may be worth searching it for rebels."

Everyone dismounted, leaving their reins with guards. Ruarnon hesitated as their Australian friends and Mawana rushed into buildings.

Lenaris paused too. "Does it feel like invading privacy?" she asked.

Ruarnon inclined their head. "It feels little happier than watching masonry hurled by power slings smash through the roofs of homes during the siege. All that will lie inside those homes is ghosts of the past. I would rather focus on what can still be."

"You rarely speak of the siege," said Lenaris, eyeing them intently.

Ruarnon slumped in their saddle. "This city feels as lifeless as Tarlah City did then. But this is worse. Tarlah had some life in it, fighting to hold on. But it looks and sounds as if there is nothing here. As if Galvatia City is lost, as dead as the former farmland around it."

Lenaris hand clasped their shoulder. "There are rebels hiding in this Gods forsaken kingdom somewhere. We will find them."

Ruarnon was right to keep their doubts to themself. There was no point discouraging the others, unless it became clear their search beneath the clouds was a waste of the limited time they had before the Timbalens invaded.

Ruarnon shook their head. "I wish I'd thought to ask Poran more about the lands around Galvatia. Aside from the damar infested forest, I know nothing about what lies to the north or west. Only that Auzula and the castle my uncle guards on the Galvation-Azulan border lies further south. That isn't going to help us locate anyone who fled these lands, and they may be easier to find than rebels."

"Perhaps they will find us," Lenaris suggested. "If they see us and realise we are not Zaldeaans, they will be curious."

"Would you indulge that curiosity if the sky above Tarlah looked like this?" Ruarnon asked, gazing up at the dark sky, then fighting the instinct to flee for cover from the violent storm their instincts said would erupt at any moment.

"Would you?" Lenaris asked.

Ruarnon considered it. "Had the Timbalens not answered our call for aid during the siege, and we sighted unknown strangers wandering our farmland... I suppose I would. If the strangers offered hope when Tarlah had none. I hope Galvatia is not so desperate."

It felt too soon to give up on contacting the Galvations, but it had taken almost a week already. And if all that lay beyond this city was more desolate wilderness, then it may be time to revise their plans to contact their uncle instead.

Ruarnon started as Lenaris spoke to Troy, who was exiting a building nearby, followed by Michael, who blew out a candle and left it on a stand by the door.

"Did you find anything?" Lenaris asked.

Troy shook his head. "No sign of anyone."

Linh and Fiona smiled as they excited the house next door. "There isn't much food left either," Linh reported. "All the small containers left in the kitchen were empty, and the big grain pot in the pantry was half empty too. If it was soldiers, wouldn't they have taken all the food?"

Ruarnon considered it. "Most likely. You think the family walked away with what they could carry?"

Fiona smiled and nodded. "There was some clothing, but it was old and worn. And there were no travel cloaks."

So Galvations had fled into the wilderness... But *where* did they *go*?"

Mawana returned a moment later, shaking his head in answer to the anticipation on Ruarnon's face.

They rode on, past row after row of deserted stone apartments and front doors ajar, hearing only the muffled thumps of the horse's rag bound hooves, and the occasional scuttling of birds.

A while later, Mayrun turned down a side street and led them through smaller apartments, towards a pair of open gates in the western city wall. They rode out onto a large stone paved area. Tables with empty pottery vessels, delicate glassware or stone vases, and a few blankets with wicker furniture across them formed isles along pavement. A marketplace, with many vacant stalls.

Ruarnon rode cautiously down a central aisle, scanning the hilltop first, as did Mayrun, but there was no sign of movement. Beyond the bare tables and odd stall mat weighted down with stones lay a hill covered in strange mounds barring the horizon. Burial mounds, Ruarnon suspected. They ought to provide cover to survey the land beyond.

Ruarnon led everyone through the marketplace. Each mound had a stone false door, carved with a life-size relief depicting the deceased. There were stone inscriptions either side, stating a name and rank, and beseeching the reader to pray for the deceased, that their spirit may live on. Reliefs depicted men veiled below their eyes, some showing women on a smaller scale beside them, the women wearing veils over their hair, both wearing loose clothing.

Ruarnon's attention was drawn beyond. They stayed well back from the edge of the hilltop, peering across the plains and their shoulders tightened. It couldn't be. There were hundreds... but it couldn't be anything else.

"Only a disturbing sight awaits you here," Ruarnon cautioned, as their Australian friends' voices drew nearer. "There was little clean up after the battle," they added.

Countless skeletons littered the plains, dull light glinting off battered breast plates, armguards, helmets and blades of various lengths, bronze or leather shields scattered among them. Hundreds must lie there.

Even the Zaldeaans had honoured black and red flags, pausing fighting to let both sides recover their wounded and dead, during the heat of battle. Did the Galvations not know of such a system, or had Narz not honoured it? So many lay where they had fallen, un-cremated, unburied, abandoned without mortuary rites. It was sacrilege. People who died in battle deserved better, no matter who they fought for.

Many skeletons were missing helmets or armour. The dead had been plundered, but not laid to rest. Ruarnon cursed.

"This a new low," Michael said grimly, on Ruarnon's right. "I bet the Galvations buried some, but it would take ages to bury that lot, and they're probably trying to do it without being seen by patrols."

The armour and shields that remained were of a similar style, boiled leather cuirass, leather shin guards, some bronze, and bell-shaped helmets with a nose guard and an outward-curving rim protecting the neck. The Galvation dead, Ruarnon assumed.

Their fists clenched in anger. Few Zaldeaan style helmets were scattered along the edge of the field. The Zaldeaans had buried their dead, but no such courtesy had been afforded the Galvations.

"I will check their devices," said Mawana.

He dismounted and crept downhill on foot.

"Damars fought," Troy said, pointing to one end of the battlefield, where short, unarmoured skeletons lay side by side with leather clad ones.

Ruarnon tensed. Poran and Dargus had sworn damars were never unleashed here. Had this happened after the pair set sail to the Zaldeaan Realm?

"Judging by the lie of the skeletons, the creatures were used to wall the army in," Lenaris observed.

Ruarnon found the notion so abhorrent they didn't register Mawana's words. Troy and Linh's words swept over them, until Troy disappeared over the edge of the hill, Fiona riding with him. Then Ruarnon processed Mawana saying, "Fresh tracks!"

And Troy's reply, "At last! So there are Galvations here somewhere!"

Fiona was disappearing over the edge and Linh was right behind her, whispering urgently.

"All of you back up here!" Ruarnon said quietly, pitching their voice low so it wouldn't carry, and fighting down panic. Their friends would be visible for leagues on the edge of the hilltop, from every direction.

Linh disappeared down the hillside. Ruarnon's fists clenched. If they pitched their voice to carry, anyone might hear it. Like Zaldeaans lying wait in an ambush.

"Mawana will bring them back," Lenaris whispered. "He shouldn't have gone. He may be able to move unseen, but his news distracted the others entirely."

"I hope he realises they're following him soon," Michael added.

Ruarnon's nails dug into their palms, and they bowed their head. "You didn't follow them?"

Michael smiled bitterly. "I was as distracted as you. Long enough to realise they were doing something silly."

Ruarnon stared at the edge of the hilltop, hoping to hear approaching hooves any moment.

Linh stared ahead. At the bottom of the slope before her lay skeletons. *So many*. Troy's gaze was on them too. Mawana stood at the edge of hills beyond the battlefield, flinging up a hand for silence. But he didn't look back, so he couldn't motion Troy to return to the others.

Fiona lunged and poked Troy in the shoulder.

Troy jerked around. Linh gestured violently up the hill, atop which there was no sign of Michael, Ruarnon, Lenaris or the guards and Mayrun, because they were too sensible to ride into the open.

Troy pulled up his reins and his horse halted before Fiona's. Linh halted her horse. Hooves clopped behind Linh. Mayrun appeared atop the burial mound hill.

"Something is wrong," Mayrun warned softly, her eyes wide with panic. She was breathing too fast.

Mawana ran full sprint, leaping onto his horse. Linh turned her mount around. Guards riding along the base of the hill dashed across Linh's peripheral vision towards Troy and Fiona, as their horses clacked up the hill behind Linh.

Linh healed her horse forwards and looked back over her shoulder. Beyond her friends and the guards, riders approached the battlefield. They wore bell shaped helmets, bronze plate armour, presumably carried weapons and outnumbered Linh's companions. Mawana was gaining on Fiona and Troy, but the mounted soldiers were gaining on them all.

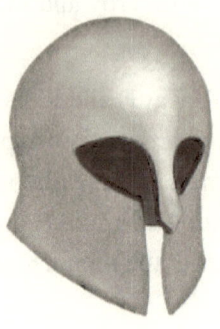

CHApTER 6

FLIGHT- TROY

Guilt broiled in the pit of Troy's stomach. The hope of finding live, free, healthy humans in this enchantment blasted land had made him forget himself. Hadn't anyone realised he was the worst person to follow? He always got so distracted. And his body raced off to explore as quickly as his mind. He'd be halfway through something before he realised he wasn't thinking.

And he'd spent SO MUCH energy restraining himself from doing that for days. But finally a distraction so pleasant his body and mind had literally ran away with the idea had come, and Linh and Fiona had followed to bring him back to safety. And now they were at risk because his impulse control had failed, for the billionth time.

"Sleep magic!" Mawana warned.

Troy gaped. They weren't supposed to craft magic. Zaldeaans couldn't do magic. And Mayrun wouldn't give herself away. Someone else must be doing it. And the only someone else was sorcerers.

Troy's alertness dulled. Adrenaline faded. His vision blurred. He started, as Fiona slapped his arm.

"I'm sorry, but you need to stay awake!" she called.

Guilt about hurting him warred with urgency in her eyes and her mouth remained open in fear. She was terrified, but still felt bad for hurting him. Dear Fi. How had he not seen the beauty of that quiet, gentle spirit for so long?

She shoved him and his adrenaline sparked. He recalled that a mounted patrol assisted by a sleep magic crafting sorcerer was pursuing them.

"Get moving!" a guard hissed as she reached his left.

Three guards moved behind her, between him and Fiona and the rapidly approaching Mawana. No, two guards. The third horse had no rider. The rider lay on the ground, unmoving. Troy sat frozen on his saddle. Had his impulsiveness got her killed?

A second guards' eyes closed and she toppled off her horse.

Fiona and Troy's horses accelerated up the burial mound hill. Troy gripped his reigns in a death grip as he bounced around on the saddle blanket, cursing whoever hadn't thought to invent stirrups in this world yet.

"That's not sleep!" Fiona explained. "They're unconscious!"

The guard's horse on Troy's left halted abruptly. She cried out and flew out of her saddle. Her horse thrashed on the slope behind her.

"INVISIBLE SHIELD BARRIERS!" Mawana's voice bawled. "DON'T RIDE STRAIGHT!"

"Veer right!" said Fiona.

"But Linh and Michael are straight ahead!" Troy objected.

"Right Troy! Please!"

Troy's horse screamed and stumbled. Could it climb this slope with an injured leg? Fiona reached for him. He grit his teeth, fighting the urge to swear repeatedly and crouched atop his saddle. He wobbled, nearly falling off. His heart leapt into his mouth and his stomach sank far below. But if he stayed on his horse, they would catch him.

Troy leapt. He clutched instinctively at Fiona's waste, and by sheer luck got his right leg over the horse. He groaned at the pain of poorly attempted splits over the saddle blanket and grabbed the horses flank with his left leg as he held Fiona, having almost pulled her off the horse. He heaved her back on more securely, gasping for breath.

"Sorry I… panicked," he said.

"It's ok. We just need to get out of here," Fiona whispered.

"Remind me," he panted, "never, to switch horses, mid-ride again. I'm not equipped for this!"

"Are you ok?" Fiona asked.

Troy blinked back tears. The rough ride without stirrups wasn't helping.

"Is my horse ok?" he gasped.

"It's fallen behind," Fiona replied. "The Zaldeaan patrol will get it."

Troy sighed. He liked that horse. It wanted to go faster and further than everyone else, just like he did. It suited him to a tee. But he'd lost it. He groaned in frustration. The animal would be fine if he'd stayed out of sight. Mawana might have dodged the patrol, everyone else could have hid and they wouldn't have lost two guards to capture.

"I can't see Linh," said Fiona, scanning the top of the slope as they neared it. "She rode off as soon as we got moving. But I lost her when our guard fell."

Over Fiona's head, Troy viewed a bare slope and a bare hilltop beyond. Linh must have reached cover and the others had disappeared, probably back into the city to lose their pursuers, or hide. Much better than feeling your back was a target board for sleep magic or fearing your horses' legs breaking against a shield any moment and tossing you back down the slope. Troy grit his teeth as fear bit him and tried not to hold Fiona too tightly.

Their horse crested the hill, and he heaved with relief as they rounded the burial mounds. Their horse rushed towards the marketplace and down a centre aisle. Blankets and tables flashed past. There was no sign of Michael, Ruarnon, Lenaris or Mayrun, but a raggedly dressed woman ran towards the city gates.

"Follow me!" the woman yelled, sprinting through the gates.

"Who are you?" Troy asked, as their horse followed her into the city.

"Galvation," the woman replied. "Friends tracking the sorcerer said to help you."

Red-brown buildings blurred either side as they followed the apparent rebel to the main road.

"Why?" Troy asked.

"They want to know who you are. And why a bewitched sorcerer is after you."

A bewitched sorcerer was hunting Troy and his friends?

"The Zaldeaans *knew* we were here?" Fiona asked.

Troy swore.

The buildings became less of a blur as Fiona's horse slowed.

"We'll hide nearby," the woman said, as she turned left into a side street.

"Why not leave the city?" Fiona asked.

"They're too close –they'll catch us."

A rebel who knew how the patrols behaved, and the city. She led them down another side street. It was a narrow, winding road, with many bends. Troy swore as his toes banged against a wall, then turned his feet in to avoid further injury. He ducked under wooden signs hanging from shop walls, envying Fiona's more comfortable, straight-backed ride at a lower height before him.

The road ended suddenly, in apartments, with a wall towering beyond. The rebel turned to an apartment on the right and opened its doors.

"Where are the others?" Troy asked. "I thought they were ahead. Did we lose them?"

Fiona turned. No-one rode behind them. Troy hadn't heard any other horse's hooves. Now Fiona's horse stilled, there was silence. He gazed around the laneway, but none of his friends appeared. His heart began to pound.

"We need to find them," he insisted.

"Are your friends important?" inquired the rebel.

"Not to Narz."

"Then they will be sent to the Forest Prison. We can break them out later."

"You'll what?"

"It is poorly guarded. We have been breaking them out cell by cell for weeks. And the sorcerer will guard them until they reach the prison. You can do no more for them now."

"My best friend is out there," Fiona said, slumping in the saddle. "With a sorcerer hunting her."

"You have no weapons to defend yourselves," the rebel replied. "Do you have sorcery to combat him?"

Troy growled. He'd be useless against a sorcerer. Fi would stand a better chance but on her own...

"No," said Fiona.

Troy gaped. Galvations hated magic. If this woman was Galvation, telling her they could craft magic was a bad idea. Was that why Fiona was lying and not using her amazing shield craft to help her friends?

"I hear hooves," the rebel warned. "Too many to be friendly."

She stepped into the apartment. There was a pause, in which the world stopped turning. In which Troy fought down the urge to yell at Fiona to turn the horse around. He trusted her judgement. And he had a nagging feeling he'd forgotten something important, *again*.

"Come on Troy," Fiona said, dismounting.

Troy sighed and got off the horse. He scanned the lane, but there was still no sign of anyone. He stomped his foot. If he hadn't ridden off after Mawana... but fighting the restlessness, his tendency towards distraction and the impulsivity, all day, every day, for days of uncertainty on the voyage... if he was honest with himself, it was a wonder he hadn't screwed up sooner.

He hadn't told the others. Hadn't wanted them to worry he couldn't trust his own brain. Hadn't wanted to admit the thing he truly missed about home was the way ADHD medication calmed his mind, and his body, and made it so much easier to remember and actually do what he was supposed to, without rushing off on distracted, impulsive detours, multiple times, before recalling what he *should* be doing.

Too many hooves to be Michael and Linh approached. Troy followed Fiona and the horse into the apartment. The rebel barred the door behind them, silencing the hoof beats. The rebel crossed an empty room and pushed against the far wall, which moved slowly back, revealing a tunnel. She lit a torch and strode into the darkness.

Fiona led the horse into the dark tunnel, and Troy clenched his fists and followed her, fighting the restlessness that made him want to run back into the street to search for his friends. He tried to ignore the ever-present urgency to act and focus on Fiona instead.

The wall rolled and a metallic click sounded, as the rebel pushed it back into place.

"My name is Rila," she said, as she led them down the tunnel. She looked in her thirties, with golden brown hair, blue eyes and a tanned face for someone who lived in hiding. "We'll be under the palace gardens in a moment," she added, as the tunnel slanted steeply downwards, curving in a spiral.

"I'm sorry," Troy burst out to Fiona. "I shouldn't have ridden off. It was thoughtless."

"Hoping lots of Galvations made it to safety and that we could see them at last?" Fiona asked, her beautiful blue eyes brimming with warmth. "That isn't *thoughtless* Troy, it just wasn't the thing we needed to be thinking about at the time."

"I'm always wandering off," he added, his speech keeping pace with his thoughts. "I can't sit still, not even to keep us safe!"

He wrung his hands.

Soft fingers clasped both his hands. "You've got ADHD, haven't you? And you've been fighting it this whole time?"

Troy peered into her eyes like a parched man seeking water. Of course there was no judgement there. Fi didn't judge people. She just accepted everyone as they were. And she'd seen through him ages ago. And probably hadn't told the others, out of consideration for him.

He smiled sadly. "I had medication for *five* years. That's a long time of calm and being able to focus, before adjusting suddenly back to the chaos of a brain that wanders through ten different thoughts in a second and starts and doesn't finish five different things at once, and that wants to rush into umpteen things without even thinking, even though I *KNOW* how dangerous it is here."

Fiona's right hand cupped the side of his face. "All those silly pranks at school. You leant into the distraction of devising clever ways to get back at nasty teachers? And bullies? And sometimes you just did it, impulsively? You leant into the way your brain normally works?"

Troy sighed and his shoulders sagged. "It's a lot less tiring than fighting the restlessness of how bloody boring school is half the time. But it didn't matter back home. And I had medication to calm my brain. But all I've had for months on end is you lot. I know I forget things because I get distracted. And I miss things because I'm too busy racing onto the next thing. But I know you, Linh and Mic are way better at keeping track than I am. That's why I always agree to whatever any of you suggest."

Fiona frowned. "You don't trust your own judgement?"

"I could have got us killed the first day we came here, chasing after Red Cloak, with no idea he's probably a highly trained sorcerer allied with or working for Narz. I don't think things through half the time. I just impulsively act, and then I make up reasons for what I did after the fact."

"Are they good reasons?"

Troy frowned, wondering why that mattered. "Usually."

"So you know what you want and you pursue it. You're not just impulsive Troy, you're more decisive than I am. If it wasn't obvious this lady could take us to safety and we didn't know where else to go, you would have had to steer the horse here because I would have hesitated. There are times when acting swiftly and knowing your mind are strengths. It's not all bad."

Troy sighed heavily. He didn't want to argue with her. But right now, he was having trouble identifying those times when being impulsive was a strength.

Rila was eyeing them strangely, but she didn't comment.

"Who built this tunnel and where does it go?" Fiona asked, probably to distract him, or Rila, as they continued down the steep, spiralling tunnel, Rila lighting the way with a burning torch Troy hadn't noticed her pick up.

Troy sighed and tried to let his torso relax.

Fiona taking his hand and squeezing it helped.

"It was used by spies," Rila replied, "so we weren't noticed coming and going from the palace. Assassins used it once when there was feuding over the throne. It is ancient."

They walked quickly and soon reached a small, torch-lit chamber in which an elderly woman waited.

"Guests," she said, shaking her head. "I almost did not believe it."

The woman was silver-haired, with a lined, stern face and sharp blue eyes, which softened at the sight of Fiona and Troy holding hands. Fiona smiled shyly, but Troy didn't let go of her hand.

"Shella was Chief Steward when things were right in the palace," said Rila. "She stays to help those passing through find their way."

"Come, I will show you to chambers where you we can rest," said Shella. "The patrols will search the city and probably post sentries for a time, so you will need to stay until you can leave without being noticed."

She led them down another tunnel which was straight but continued to slope downwards.

"Why's it so deep?" Troy asked suspiciously.

"Below the ground floor are the cellars," Shella replied, "bellow that the dungeons and bellow them the sewers. These secret passages go below everything."

That sounded true enough. Shella also carried a burning torch. Torchlight shone on walls cut into natural rock and soil, reinforced by timber frames and ceiling supports, like in a mine.

Eventually the tunnel led to a small hall, with heavy fabric draping objects stored haphazardly throughout. At its far end, blankets, bedrolls and a long row of shelves with wooden boxes lined the wall.

"This is where we stay when we must hide in the city," said Shella. "We keep it supplied. You can tether your horses on the hooks at the end of the shelf."

Fiona tethered her horse, while Troy noted shadowy walls on all sides, save the entrance they'd approached by. He shivered and tried to shake off the cabin fever he expected to hit at any moment.

Shella gestured them into seats around a square table. Troy eyed the floor darkly, wondering if the others had made it safely beyond the patrols. Shella offered them dry biscuit, which Troy gratefully accepted, finding he was hungry, as usual. Fiona smiled and gave him her biscuit too. He smiled his gratitude as he accepted.

The rebel worked in the corner, several noises echoing in the confined space, as she raised a bucket of well water. Fiona's brows raised.

Shella smiled. "This was the chamber in which the entire court weathered siege laid by the dreaded God Kings of the Far South for weeks."

"They weathered a siege by the *God Kings*?" Troy asked.

"The God Kings once ruled most of the continent, but Galvatia was built by survivors who fled the Sorcery War, the home of resistance. When the God-king's grand magics failed to uncover the simple means by which our court survived, he abandoned his siege. That was over four centuries ago, and the God-kings have stayed in the Far South ever since."

"Why couldn't he capture this place?" Fiona asked.

"His most powerful spells were destructive, but he did not want to destroy the city. He used magic to question people, but all involved in the tunnel's construction were hiding here, so no-none could tell him how we were supplied or how to access us, and he was too arrogant and impatient to search the palace properly. He abandoned us in disgust. Unfortunately, King Narz is very different."

Troy sighed. The way Narz had tried to starve out Galvation farmers spoke of his patience. It seemed a very slow way to wage war, though it had clearly worked.

"We haven't seen young people in these parts for many months," Shella added, eyeing them both keenly.

Fiona gazed uncertainly at the table.

"As you might have guessed from how we blundered into that trap, we're not from around here," said Troy. "But where are your young people?"

"Safe," Shella replied.

So she'd taken them in, but she didn't trust them yet.

Troy laughed. "I'm sorry, but I'm pretty sure no one intended *me* to be having *this* conversation. It was supposed to be Ruarnon, or Lenaris. They're the highly educated, competent ones. I'm just along for the ride, here to help if I can. Fi and I are two seriously lost teenagers incredibly far from home."

"Why did you come to Galvatia?" Shella asked.

"Our friends seek an alliance with you. Do you realise the Zaldeaans are here under duress? Our friend wants to bring them home."

Shella gaped. "You would have me believe the youthful king who came to power when the Zaldeaans invaded us, has come west to claim them?"

"I'm not full enough of myself to think I can make you believe anything," Troy retorted.

"But that's the truth," said Fiona. "That's why Ruarnon sent people here, to make contact with your people."

"And why are *you* here?" Shella pressed.

Troy sighed. She was *good*. "Because we stumbled through a magic gateway and got stuck here. We've no way of contacting the man we think opened the gateway, and he mostly doesn't seem to give a shit what we do, and apparently the west is the only place on Umarinaris where Gateways of Umarinaris are still operational, assuming we can find a sorcerer willing and able to operate one to send us home."

Fiona bit her lip.

The creases on Shella's forehead deepened. *Shit*, she didn't think he'd lost his grip on reality, did she?

Shella shook her head. "You seem calm, good humoured and reasonable for someone whose mind has gone to Chaos."

Troy couldn't help grinning. "I appreciate your sincerity as much as you appreciate mine."

Shella eyed Fiona keenly.

Fiona sighed. "If you're hoping I can give you a more reasonable explanation, honestly, I'd just be rephrasing what Troy said. It's been over a year and my siblings will be missing me terribly, not to mention we all have parents who probably fear we're dead. I want to ease my family's worry as much as I want to see them again."

"Your story makes me question your capacity for rational thinking, which suggests you are not Karmarn's latest ploy to infiltrate us."

It couldn't hurt her conclusion, asking what Troy and his three Aussie friends most wanted to know, could it?

"Have you heard any stories about magical stone archways?" he asked.

"There is at least one in Azula," Shella replied so quickly that Troy gaped.

She thought he was delusional, but she *had* heard tales like his?

"It *is* in Azula!? Where else would it be?" he added. "We *really might* have to ask Narz's sorcerers to help us get home."

Troy shook his head. Why did Poran and Darius have to get themselves captured? Either one may have helped Troy and his friends get home, if they'd met them here.

"There may be more archways in the Far South, but it is an even more dangerous land," Shella added.

"More dangerous than Narz's territories?" Fiona asked.

Shella sighed. "I think Narz may truly want sorcerers to live in the open, under his strict guidance. His aims may be as good as his propaganda makes them sound. His fault lies in what he is prepared to sacrifice to achieve his aims. The God Kings however, believe themselves superior to all non-magic wielding humans. We are but slaves and playthings to them."

So how *did* Narz see Galvations?

"How many people escaped this city and what the hell happened to the people from the abandoned farms?" Troy thought out loud.

Shella frowned. Her pale blue eyes probed his. "The farmers were taken by surprise, and all who did not flee the drought were abducted. When we learnt Narz's army was coming, the city was evacuated of all non-combatants, in case Narz's sorcerers fought."

"But they didn't, did they?" Fiona asked.

Shella's lips pulled into a grim line. "The forests burned during the field battle. Fortunately, miners and outlying farmers warned most villages, but at least a dozen died, and hundreds of homes were destroyed. The clouds have been this way since before the army came. We were not certain it was sorcery until the forest fires began."

"But they didn't use sorcery in the battle?" Troy pressed, curious.

Shella frowned and replied, "No."

"And your leaders?" Fiona asked. "It sounds like this is an organised rebellion."

"It is. And they are safe."

"Then you should contact them," Troy said, recovered from his surprise at stumbling into the role of improvised ambassador and deciding he'd better do the job properly. "And tell them Tarlah offers them an alliance and is interested in planning to free the Zaldeaan army and captured Galvations with them."

"You offer this on behalf of whom?" Shella asked.

"Regent Ruarnon of Tarlah, Prime Ruler of the Zaldeaan Realm and the North Lands," Fiona replied with proper titles, making Troy smile. He'd forgotten those titles. They probably mattered under these circumstances.

Shella shook her head. "I hadn't put it past Karmarn to set up a fake trap, in hopes we were watching and would take in spies who 'escaped' it. Perhaps he would even employ Azulan youths and women to conceal that you *were* spies. But I can't imagine Karmarn trying to convince us of anything using children's tales and wild stories too fanciful to be anything other than madness or the truth. I still cannot tell which of the two it is, but whoever you are, it seems you are not enemies, and I will send word about you to our commanders."

Troy sighed and slumped in his seat. She didn't seem sure if he was rational or not, but it didn't matter, because they had successfully established contact with the Galvation rebels. Hopefully the rebel leaders would speak to people much better qualified at diplomacy next, someone whose capacity for rational thought they were not inclined to question. But for now, he and Fiona had achieved what no one intended or expected them to on their own. He beamed.

Fiona beamed back at him and gave him a quick peck on the lips.

Rila frowned.

Troy held Fiona's hand. "Are public displays of affection not a thing in your culture?"

"They are not something we expect from people in an uncertain situation, with complete strangers, who only just decided they are probably not spies," Rila replied.

Troy burst out laughing, then found he couldn't stop. Life was absurd. It truly was. And he was glad his inexperience and unconventional character hadn't hampered making contact with Galvation leaders. And he and Fiona seemed safe here. You really couldn't be sure where life would take you, but at least it wasn't all bad.

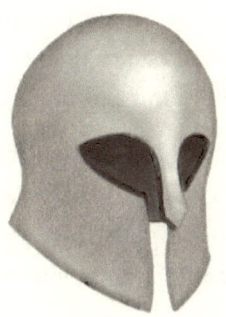

CHAPTER 7

ON BEING RESTLESS: TROY

T roy blinked at a stone ceiling high overhead. A torch-lit table with two women seated at it lay on his right. Fiona slept on a bedroll on his left. His other friends were… he didn't know. His gut twisted.

"…send word to the west when the patrols go. The others might hide in the farmlands," Rila was saying.

Hope flared inside Troy. There was a safe place in the west, where his friends could go… but they didn't know about it. His heart sank.

Shella motioned Troy to the table. It had taken her what, ten seconds to notice he was awake? She was sharp. What did she plan to do with him and Fiona?

Fiona stirred as Troy accepted a biscuit and well water and joined them.

"Do we think Mic and Linh got caught?" Troy asked, as Fiona picked at her breakfast.

"They might have made it back to the riverbed," said Fiona. "Especially if everyone stayed together and Mayrun led them. They might be waiting for us."

Troy's right hand clenched in a fist. The riverbed. The place Ruarnon wanted everyone to fall back to if anything went wrong. He slumped.

"I suppose the others all went there?" he asked.

Fiona sighed and fidgeted with her biscuit. "Linh was on her own, between us and Michael. I'm not sure if she caught up, because I lost sight of her when the sorcerer attacked our guards."

Troy's mouth opened, but he didn't know what to say. He shut it again. Then gripped his fork unnecessarily hard. He hated the idea of Linh out there by herself. She'd get stressed out and scared. She'd probably try to hide, but stealth and navigating foreign territory weren't exactly her skill set.

"When can we look for our friends?" he asked Shella. "Have the patrol finished searching the city for us yet?"

Shella shook her head. "More patrols have been arriving throughout the night. We suspect they are searching thoroughly. You must not leave this chamber until they move on. We cannot risk you being caught. Or these tunnels being exposed."

Troy slumped. The rebels probably used the tunnels for smuggling or spying or whatever it was you did as a rebel organisation when you were occupied by the enemy. And Shella and Rila had taken them in, kept them safe and fed them. Exposing their tunnels to Zaldeaan patrols was a poor way to repay their hosts. Troy knew that. He also didn't care, because Linh would be the most anxious about being stranded in the open. And what if she was about to get caught? He *knew* where safety was. He could offer her that and company, if he could find her.

The trouble was, the more the patrols searched the city, the more likely Linh or any of his friends were to be captured, *if* they were hiding in the city. And it sounded like the rebels didn't want to leave their cover or deliver messages until *after* the patrols moved on, too late to usher friends to safety.

"So we need to sit here, letting any of our friends in the city get caught, even though we could hide them?"

"We do not know where your friends are," Shella countered. "If they are smart, then they used the city as cover to cross the plains, then rode into the open, where it will be very difficult for the patrol to corner them."

Troy's hands balled into fists. "I'd never have thought of that. Neither would Linh. Even Mic wouldn't realise that under pressure."

Fiona sighed. "If Linh or Michael got separated from the others, I think they're hiding in the city."

"Surely there aren't enough soldiers to search *every* house and room?" Troy asked. "Why wouldn't they be safe in the city?"

Shella turned away. "They *will* search every room. They've done it before, when we were patient and waited in hiding, trying to make good our escape when we ran out of food, several days after being sighted. Karmarn learned from that. If anyone is sighted in the city, the entire city is systematically searched by hundreds of Zaldeaans from Fang Mountain Prison. Anyone hiding anywhere but our secret tunnels will most likely be caught."

Troy banged his fist on the table, ignoring the flair of pain it caused.

"If there are secret tunnels," Fiona said tentatively, "is there any way we could eavesdrop on Zaldeaan soldiers from them?"

"It is highly unlikely you will hear the news you seek," Shella replied.

Needle in a haystack, Troy suspected.

They finished their meagre breakfast, rubbed Fiona's horse down and still there was no word from rebels watching the city. Still the search continued.

Linh or Michael could be hiding fearfully, about to be captured any moment. What would a patrol do with them? Question them, or torture *then* question them? How had the latter not seriously occurred to Troy when they decided to take the risk of coming ashore?

Troy's heart sped up. His legs urged to run back up the tunnel to search the city for Linh, Michael and the others.

"Can we please do *something*?" he asked Shella.

She handed him a cloth and asked him to dust leather harnesses and equipment on the shelves. He groaned then took to the task aggressively, knocking over wooden tools and sneezing at the dust clouds he stirred. But he couldn't focus. His brain kept playing him images of soldiers dragging Linh and Michael out of a wooden trunk like those inside the Galvation homes and hitting them every time either Aussie said something the Zaldeaans didn't believe. He couldn't stand it.

He threw down the cloth and started pacing across the floor. But he ran out of floor too soon. The wall got in his way. So he turned, and his rapid, long legged steps carried him towards another offending wall, barring his path. He groaned again.

"Come here Troy," said Shella's voice.

Troy frowned. What highly important distraction did she have to offer now?

"Can you work off enough steam to move through the tunnels without being overheard?"

Troy's mouth dropped open. Was she changing her mind?

Her stern gaze softened ever so slightly. She was.

Troy grinned and fought the urge to punch the air and yell "yes!" in triumph.

"You are not good with staying in one place, or is it staying underground?" Shella asked.

"The former. We've spent far too much time in cabins on a ship, for weeks. And I especially can't stand being cooped up when people I love might be in trouble. If I could just hear something, that they're hiding, or left the city —anything is better than sitting here knowing nothing."

"There is a secret passage to the stables, and it will let you out of this room," Shella said. "You must not under any circumstances leave it to go to the stables, as they are on the other side of a garden and running to them may expose the passage and ultimately this chamber to Zaldeaan guards.

"The Zaldeaans know there are secret passageways in the palace, and they have damaged walls trying to find them," she added levelly. "If you make any noise, we may all be captured. You must go stealthily and freeze every time you think you hear movement in the rooms beyond the walls, even if you just hear a bird, lest soldiers searching the palace hear you.

"I am prepared to let you walk through the secret passages, if you swear by the Gods to do so with utmost caution."

Troy's body sagged with relief. He needed to move, as far as he could, to burn off the restlessness. If he burned off enough, he'd be able to pay attention to how he was moving and do so carefully and not risk bumping his shoulders on doorframes and attracting patrols attention. He *could* do this, in a way that didn't put exposure of the secret tunnels, Shella or Rila at risk.

"Are you coming with me?" he asked Fiona.

Fiona smiled. "Would I like to get out of the hall many stories below ground?"

Her smile twisted in distaste and Troy mentally kicked himself. It wasn't that long ago they'd been riding through underground caverns, and she'd been nervous having so much rock, soil and weight pressing down overhead. He should have remembered.

"Thank you," he said to Shella. "We really appreciate this. I won't enter the tunnels until I've walked off enough steam to move quietly through them."

Shella bowed her head.

Troy wasn't a fan of sit ups, or push ups, but both had aided his restlessness on Myleth Island, and doing twenty of each back-to-back helped steady him, somewhat.

"Follow me," Shella said when he stood again.

She led them to a ladder extending to the ceiling behind blanket covered shelves, while Rila brought them a burning torch.

"There is a series of ladders," she explained, "then secret, narrow passageways inside the palace walls. If you feel restless at the end of the ladders, climb back down and up again to as you call it, 'burn off steam'.

"In the passages, if you hear any sounds beyond the walls, stop until they cease. It is unlikely you will overhear the news you seek, but I understand your need to try. I was young once."

The glimmer in her eye and quirk to her lips hinted at a smile. Troy wondered what sort of young woman Shella had been.

Then both rebels wished them luck, he took the burning torch Rila offered and climbed a solid timber ladder carefully. He leant into it and held on with two fingers when his torch bearing hand was the only one gripping a rung.

Moving out of the dark hall was a relief, until he started wondering how high he was off the floor and how sturdy the ladder was, and was it really best to just stop thinking? Which of course, he failed at, his mind having no pause button nor concept of mental breaks.

Switching ladders looked daunting. He paused where two joined. There was no floor level, no landing like a staircase would open out onto, just another ladder, the end of which was bound behind the top of the first with rope and nailed to the side of the shaft with iron pegs.

Troy paused. "Did they have mines in the Roman Empire?"

"Yes," Fiona called up to him, "though they tended to dig pits and not go very deep compared to early industrial minds like our goldrush ones."

"So can we trust this ladder engineering?" Troy added for clarity.

Fiona laughed. "Are you asking *me* to help *you* be reckless?"

Troy smiled. What was he thinking asking Fiona, of all people, or anyone for that matter, to nudge *him* into being more reckless? If he couldn't climb this thing, no one could! Even's Linh's common sense when it came to danger and her fear of heights wouldn't stop her, if he was lost on the other side. A pang went through him.

Linh wasn't too switched on when it came to romance. Often Troy and Fiona would be getting cosy in the presence of their friends. It made Troy a bit shy, and sometimes he'd wished for a moment or two alone with Fiona. But he'd give anything to have Linh or Michael with him in safety now. Even climb this wooden deathtrap. He smiled grimly, gripped the right ladder for dear life and positioned his right foot on its bottom rung carefully, before pulling his body across and continuing the climb.

Two ladders later, Troy groaned as he heaved himself up with aching arms and shoulders. It was a relief to stand on solid ground. But the passage was so narrow he had to shuffle along it sideways, holding the torch ahead so he didn't risk burning himself. He turned back, and when Fiona nodded she was ok with the confined space, he led their sideways shuffle forwards, straining his ears.

He froze at the first sound beyond a wall, and hardly daring to breath, his heart racing. Was that footsteps? Quiet ones, fading way, until silence fell. He sighed, and continued shuffling.

What if the guards didn't speak? If they learnt nothing? They'd have to go back to the hall and wait for the patrols to finish searching the city, still not knowing where Linh, Michael or anyone else was. But at least then they would have *tried* to do *something* to help.

Troy shuffled on. Occasional footsteps beyond the walls made his heart quicken again, but the only sentence he heard was, "Did you check those cupboards?"

His heart rate took a long time to slow down, as they moved slowly on, and around occasional tight corners. Logic told him this was pointless, but his sense of urgency, or restlessness, wouldn't let him go. It spurred him on until sometime after his muscles cramped in protest at prolonged sideways shuffling. Then, voices finally rose again.

"We're not going to find anything, the rebels are in the wilderness, if there's any left in Galvatia," a man's voice complained.

"Duty needs to be performed regardless," another replied formally.

Troy's breath caught. He turned to Fiona. Could their friends be clear of the city, safe after all? She smiled hopefully and squeezed his hand.

What did 'duty must be performed' mean? Was it like Shella said, the systematic search of the city had to be completed, because Karmarn wanted everything done by the book?

Troy waited until the footsteps faded, then continued creeping sideways, hoping the conversation would continue in the next room and trying to track the soft footsteps. But the soldiers didn't speak again, and their footsteps faded.

As Troy shuffled on through silence, the truthful part of his brain, the part the restlessness hated listening to and often fought, told him that was the opinions of only two soldiers, who hadn't searched the whole city, who may be wrong and that was all he was going to get.

This was a fool's errand. Maybe Shella had only let them attempt it because she hoped it would be good for his mental health and trusted he wouldn't screw it up. But his body was aching, and even lighter, fitter Fiona must be tired. It was past time to turn back. Fiona had probably let him continue because she hoped roaming through the walls would calm him. It had been a nice stretch of the legs and all, but he was at the end of the line.

Light shone beneath a door at the end of the tunnel. Going further meant exposing himself to patrols. But turning back felt like giving up. It meant going back into a deep underground hole to hide, leaving his friends to an uncertain fate, while he waited for it all to be over in safety.

He stopped, repressing the urge to kick the door. He didn't want to worry Fiona by showing how upset he was. Then he noticed a small hole and stepped quietly forwards to peer through it, at a garden bed of dead trees and bushes, with a dried yellow lawn and a wooden building beyond, the stables. On the edge of his vision, a soldier stepped against the railing of a balcony. He sighed.

"Come on Troy," Fiona whispered gently, sympathy writ in the gentle set of her mouth and tilt of her chin.

He took a step forward and she took the lead. But at the corner of his eye the guard on the balcony turned and walked out of sight. And just like that Troy had an opportunity to do something constructive, something of benefit; the chance to get proper feed for the horse that had rescued them from a sorcerer. A familiar restlessness stirred Troy's limbs and sped up his heart.

He pushed the door open and gazed through the dead garden until he spotted a side door in the stables opposite. On his right, the balcony was abandoned. On his left, the gate in the garden wall was closed. And the garden was silent. The coast was clear, and the thrill of achieving things by breaking rules fuelled Troy's adrenaline.

He shut the door carefully behind him, before Fiona had a chance to follow or worry, and crept around brown, dried bushes and branches, trying not to brush against them. It would be a short sprint to the stable door, and the balcony and dried lawns on his right were deserted. He moved swiftly around the dead brown leaves of bushes in the garden bed.

Hooves clacked on the far side of the gate on his left, where a woman's voice said, "It's nice to see you Jormar. I thought you were patrolling today?"

Troy froze.

"We were chasing a rebel towards the north-western branch of the Trine," a man's voice replied, "but my old mount couldn't keep up."

The gate creaked, opening. Troy's heart stopped. He turned back. The tunnel door was too far away and the garden bed too full of dried leaves that would crunch noisily as he crossed it. He couldn't risk exposing the secret passageways…

He turned, looking for a tree or bush with enough dead leaves on it to hide behind. Instead, he looked into the wide eyes of a guard entering the gardens. Keeping the tunnels secret meant not getting caught or questioned. So, get chased around the gardens or make a break for it?

Troy ran towards the opening gates. On the far side, a guard walked beside a pretty woman, leading a horse by its reins. Did Troy run past? But the guard could mount the horse and overtake him…

"Rebel!" the guard behind Troy cried.

Troy dashed towards the surprised couple. He snatched the reins, tugging the horse awkwardly around and then down, so it bent its knees, bringing the saddle blanket closer. He flinched at a blow to his back and flung himself onto the saddle blanket, heeling the horse to a gallop.

"Rebel!" the guard yelled.

A pair of guards beyond the gates drew swords and stepped to block the road. Their eyes widened at the horse's speed and they dived aside. Troy's horse clattered noisily onto paved road and apartments flashed by.

A nervous grin split his face. He wasn't safe by a long shot but this was immensely better than hiding underground.

He glimpsed soldiers in a side street on his left and more on his right. With so many and the loud clack of his new mount's hooves echoing off the walls there was no chance of hiding. He'd have to keep running and hope the main road he was galloping down led out of the city. He smiled, grateful for the first bend putting him out of sight.

"Hey you!" a man yelled ahead.

Troy's heart stopped, as the man sidled onto the road. His horse responded before he could. It reared. Troy flung his arms around its neck and gripped with his knees as he slid backwards on the saddle blanket. The horse kicked, but the man was beyond its reach.

Troy tried to calm the horse by patting it and making soothing noises. The horse settled on all fours. Troy's heart hammered against his ribcage. The leather vested guard eyed him with a frown. The man's posture was awful, and he had practically staggered onto the road.

"Grooms shouldn't be... get off ye..." the man slurred.

Troy dismounted, wondering if he could pose as a groom.

"Naughty boy!" said the man, suddenly angry and he lurched forwards.

Troy responded instinctively, punching him in the nose. The guard staggered and fell, hitting his head on the front steps of an apartment and knocking himself out. Troy massaged his aching wrist. He couldn't hear pursuers behind him, only his pulse echoing in his ears. There might be time to hide the guard and the fact he'd ridden this way.

He seized the guard by the armpits and heaved him up the steps, hoping against hope the man wouldn't regain consciousness. The guard slurred something as Troy paused to open the front door but he didn't wake. Troy dragged him inside and let him slump against a side table.

The table had a bronze helmet on it, beside a half empty jug of wine. Troy smiled, seized the helmet and put it on. Then he looked for armour. A cloak rack stood on his other side, with a worn looking leather vest hanging from it. Troy's smile broadened as he snatched the vest and shoved it over his head. He tightened the belt swiftly, then hurried back outside.

"He went that way!" a voice yelled down the road.

Troy flung himself into the saddle. He healed his stolen horse forwards. Then he gazed over red-brown rooftops, searching until the high walls of the city rose beyond. The gates and his best chance of escape weren't too far away. He smiled and rode on, meeting no more guards on the main road.

A few guards in side streets turned bored gazes towards him as he rode past. Hopefully his helmet disguised his nervous face… but there would be guards at the city gates. He might need to lie his way through.

Apartments flashed past, and the city walls loomed before him. Then the road ended before a pair of open gates blocked by four guards holding wicked looking spears. Troy's chosen lie flit through his mind. He swallowed nervously and reined in.

A guard stepped forwards, saying, "Your orders soldier?"

"I was sent to replace Jormar Sir," Troy replied, "To pursue a rebel fleeing towards the north-west branch of the Trine."

"Was Jormar with a woman?" the man asked.

"Yes Sir," Troy replied.

"I will have his hide," the guard muttered. "Proceed."

The other guards stepped aside.

Troy bowed his head and heeled his horse forwards instinctively. Shock slackened his face as he rode through the gates. They were letting him go. It had *worked*! He grinned, proud at remembering every word the woman and guard whose horse he'd stolen had said.

But where was the north-west branch of the Trine from here? He gazed across dried plains and a wide riverbed, at a large, healthy green forest, the damarian forest. Which meant he was facing north.

Northwest must be left, and Troy had better ride that way in case the guards were still watching.

He turned the horse alongside the riverbank, parallel to the city and grinned, happy to be alive and free. Then he had a sinking feeling. Fiona would have no idea what had happened to him. She would be worried. She was sensible enough to retreat down the secret passage without him. But he hoped the guard who was looking for him hadn't found it, or her...

He sighed. The city walls turned a corner on his left, running atop a hill. There were guards in the marketplace, and the west gate must be guarded. He'd have to keep following the river north until he was out of the guards' sight.

He rode past the battlefield, looking ahead across dry plains. Was that green in the distance? How could –the rebels had mentioned farmland in the west, where his friends could be hiding. Safety! He could ride to safety!

His heart leapt and a smile returned to his face, as the distant green farmlands drew nearer. The river forked ahead. One branch continued west towards the greener land, but the other turned north-west. It couldn't be more than an hour since the guard whose horse he'd stolen had chased a rebel along that branch. What if the 'rebel' was still there? What if it was Michael? Troy smiled broadly at the prospect of finding his friend and leading him to safety.

When he reached the fork in the riverbed, he rode into it, across the trickle of water and down the north-west branch. The light was brighter here. Pale grey clouds blanketed the sky. On his right, the bank was lined with green, healthy tree branches, the damar infested forest. Which reminded him he was unarmed. He rode up the left bank, keeping the riverbed between him and savage damars. On his left spread rocky, hilly plains, open land.

After a while, men yelled beyond a rocky hill. Troy dismounted, tethered the horse to a dead tree and crept up the steep slope on foot to a boulder lined ridge. From there, he peered down between boulders at a rock scattered plain on which two riders stood beside their mounts. Each gesticulated in a different direction, while three riders looked uncertainly from one to the other.

"He went north I say!" one man yelled.

"How do you know he hasn't found another hidey hole? He could still be here!" the other yelled with both fists clenched.

"I'm not going to lose the only stranger of rank we can catch because of your incompetence!" the first man snapped.

"INCOMPETENCE? You're the one who insisted he couldn't be around last night, and we lost him because *you* overlooked his hiding place!"

"Is this insubordination?"

"It's not insubordination when the captain is incompetent!"

The captain strode forwards and punched the soldier in the jaw. The soldier reeled, then hit back and suddenly both were grappling, while the others watched nervously.

Troy shook his head. If these soldiers, who presumably knew about tracking, weren't sure which way a rebel had gone, he didn't stand a chance. And why would his friends go north? Of course, Ruarnon's meeting point. But if the others had come this way too, then Michael was unintentionally leading a patrol towards them.

He crept back down to his horse, untied its reins and mounted.

"THIS WAY RELMAR! WE SEE HIM!"

Troy froze. Would his friends hear that and hide? Or was he needed as a diversion?

Troy healed his horse around the hill. Beyond it, five men on horseback rode away from him, on the trail of four riders further west, and one smaller rider in the distance, too tall to be Linh. It *had* to be Michael.

Troy's heart leapt into his mouth. He heeled his horse ruthlessly, ignoring his aching shoulders and arms. The first patrol was closing in on the rider, who veered around a steep rocky hill, out of sight. Four riders followed.

Adrenaline spiked in Troy's veins when the second patrol neared the hill. Air gusted around him, but his horse wasn't fast enough.

The second patrol rounded the hill. Troy rode alone on the boulder scattered plain, straining his ears for shouts. But beyond the frantic pounding of his horse's hooves was silence.

He rounded the jagged slope. His horse veered right, dodging a large boulder. The ground before him was boulder and rubble strewn, and a chasm loomed beyond. Zaldeaan riders flashed in and out of sight around boulders, as they raced towards the chasm.

Troy rode in amongst boulders, trusting his horse not to hit them, crouching low and keeping his feet turned in. Rock obscured his view constantly, but as he left the largest boulders behind, the first patrol came into view, re-grouping as they entered the chasm. The chasm's right wall was extremely tall, with rocks sticking out at all heights. Those rocks could knock someone's head in. What had driven Michael in there?

The boulder-strewn plain fell behind, and Troy hunched instinctively towards his horse, as he entered the confined chasm. Rapid hoof beats echoed off the walls so chaotically there was no risk of either patrol hearing him. He ducked instinctively aside, wondering how the horse dared move so fast in such a narrow, dangerous space.

Around a bend the chasm forked. It was narrow and dark, and both paths had so many bends he couldn't see which way the patrols had gone. He took the right turn, hoping the rebel picked whichever side didn't lead to a dead end.

The chasm was bearing left, and a confused echo of voices muddled with hoof beats rose ahead. He slowed his horse, and a moment later, the pounding of hooves stopped. Troy reined in. Sweat trickled down his neck, as he strained his ears, willing someone to speak.

"Good thing he fell here," said a man's voice. "Looks like our way joins that other turning. He could've done the loop and disappeared."

"He's dead!"

"Are you sure?"

"Did you see how hard he hit his head? And how much it's bleeding?"

"Check his pulse! We're not leaving him here if he's alive. Those women reckoned they were farmers, but that boy's important."

Troy held his breath, as the guards checked the rebel's pulse.

"We'll have to hope the other patrols were more successful," a voice said gravely

Troy's heart sank. He didn't process that both patrols were riding away until the sound of their horse's hooves faded entirely. Needing to see for himself, he dismounted, his stomach roiling, and stepped hesitantly around the bend.

There was no sign of the rebel's horse, but someone lay on the ground, someone with dark, short hair. Michael. Blood pooled around his head.

"Mic!" Troy gasped, tears filling his eyes as he rushed forwards and dropped to his knees. "Don't be dead!" he pleaded.

Troy leaned closer and something tingled on his left hand, as he stared frantically at Michael's face, hoping to see his eyes pop open, his mouth twitch, some sign of life.

Something tingled his hand again. He reached distractedly for whatever was crawling on him. Something tingled on both hands. His hands were opposite Michael's mouth. Troy stared. Michael's chest rose slightly, then fell again.

"You're alive!" he cried, flinging his arm over Michael and hugging him where he lay. Then he lifted Michael into a sitting position, holding him around the shoulders, and examined the blood on his head, fearing a terrible wound. Michael's skin had split above his right eyebrow, but the cut didn't look deep. Troy frowned. It was still bleeding, so he folded his sleeve and pressed it against the split.

"Can I stop now?" Michael asked dazedly.

"Yeah mate, you've split your head open, so I'd say you deserve a break."

"Troy?" Michael said, smiling. "Why's there four of you?"

"You must have a concussion. *Again*. You need to stop hitting your head Mic. You could lose brain cells and stop being so clever!"

Troy beamed, but tears blurred his vision.

"Banged my head on the ground," Michael replied. "It's harder than concrete."

Troy smiled, but Michael said nothing more. He must be dazed. That was why he wasn't asking about his friends.

"Don't suppose you have any Panadol?" Michael asked. "My head's killing me."

Troy shivered. Did Michael think he was back home? Michael smiled weakly and Troy relaxed and grinned at the joke. But Michael didn't seem to know where they were or what was going on... how severe was his concussion?

"How about food?" Michael asked. "I haven't eaten since yesterday, too busy fleeing."

Troy rummaged through his stolen horse's saddlebags and found a leather canteen and a pastry. He passed both to Michael, who leant heavily against the chasm wall and against Troy's side as he ate and drank his fill, bringing a little colour back into his face.

"Where'd the soldiers go?" Michael asked suddenly.

"They thought you were dead," Troy replied. "Couldn't find your pulse."

Michael smiled. "When we measured our blood pressure at school, the machine said I was dead too."

He looked more alert but had dark circles around his eyes and his face was several shades paler than usual.

"What are you wearing?" Michael asked.

Troy frowned, then remembered the stolen helmet on his head and his stolen vest. He grinned and replied, "Long story mate. It can wait till you're feeling better."

Troy reached for him, and Michael gasped as Troy folded him in a bear hug. "Do me a favour," Troy whispered in his ear, "don't let me think you're dead ever again, ok?"

Michael hugged him tightly back. "I promise."

They were both teary eyed when they let each other go and exchanged a smile. Troy was more fortunate than he deserved with Fiona, but damn Andrew was lucky, having Michael. There was every chance Troy would find a good friend in Andrew too, when they got home. For now, he'd probably better continue playing nursemaid to Andrew's boyfriend.

Troy ducked under Michael's arm and helped him stand. Michael was shaky on his feet, so Troy supported him to walk towards Troy's horse, then heaved him up into the saddle. Troy climbed up behind him, wrapping his left arm around Michael to keep him steady when his friend swayed, taking the reins in his right hand.

"Where are we going?" Michael asked.

Troy remembered the grassy hills and sunlight along the western branch of the river. "Somewhere safe," he replied.

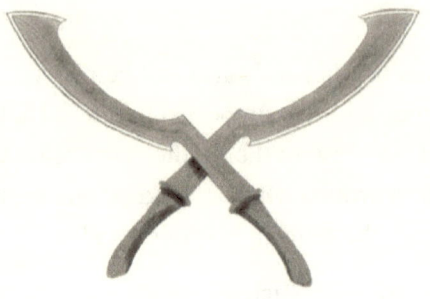

Ruarnon gripped their spear, as Linh rode up the hill towards them.

"We are target practice here," Mayrun said firmly.

"Mawana is in the most danger," said Lenaris, watching her husband grip his horse's flanks hard, as it raced ahead of a sorcerer crafting so much magic that even at this distance Ruarnon sensed its tingle.

"They will think he is our scout," said Ruarnon. "I should love to wait for him and escort our Australian friends to safety, but they will know *we* are in charge of this group. The sorcerer is most likely to target *us*."

Decisive times call for decisive action. Uncle Omah was right again. They couldn't use magic, couldn't fight or draw attention to the Timbalen Army anchored in hiding offshore. Their best option was not getting captured.

The Zaldeaans would seek a leader, but they may misgender Ruarnon at this distance, and think they were looking at three well protected women, in which case they may target Ruarnon, Lenaris *and*

102

Mayrun. The best way to help their Australian friends and Mawana was to split up.

"Michael, ride west around the city and hide in the riverbank. Follow it west, then take the northwest branch."

Michael nodded and healed his horse away.

"Head east around the city," Ruarnon told Mayrun.

"We'll cut through the city itself, split up, and backtrack to the bridge," they added to Lenaris, who nodded. "I hope Mawana follows."

"He will. Mawana *is* our tracker," said Mayrun.

Ruarnon and Lenaris bowed their heads to the Elite Guard, then turned their horses around. Michael was already riding around the marketplace to circle the city walls. Linh was cresting the hill before the marketplace. For a moment, Ruarnon hesitated. But magic tingled on Linh's heels. There was no time to wait for anyone, and if they knew Linh, she would follow Michael to safety.

Ruarnon healed their horse, and market stall tables and blankets blurred either side of them, Lenaris's horses clacking alongside. They didn't like this. Mayrun had proven her ability to track people was excellent. But she had just told them she couldn't track Mawana or the three Australians, despite them being *within* her sight. And Mawana hadn't seen anyone…

Hooves clattered on their right. Ruarnon twisted in their saddle blanket. Linh had reached the top of the hill and was turning round the marketplace, after Michael. But someone was cresting the slope behind her. Mawana?

The figure cleared the hill and turned in their saddle towards Ruarnon. A man. A stranger.

Magic stirred in the air. The sorcerer.

"Faster!" Ruarnon urged Lenaris.

Their senses probed the air. No magic craft stirred towards them. But something stirred ahead. The archway across the end of the marketplace began to crack. The cracks grew larger and small pieces of stone began to fall.

"Duck!" Lenaris yelled.

Larger pieces of stone fell. Lenaris and Ruarnon ducked. Ruarnon flinched, as a chunk of stone glanced off their shoulder. Lenaris cried out. Then they were clear and red stone apartments whizzed past them.

"Where are you hit?" they asked.

"My back," Lenaris groaned. "It's not too serious."

Ruarnon grimaced at a small red patch seeping through her shirt beside her shoulder blade. But she sat upright and didn't seem too seriously injured.

"Let's split when we hit the main road," Ruarnon suggested. "I can find my way out from the left turning. You can ride back the way we entered the city."

Lenaris nodded.

"Fortune be with you," they told Lenaris.

"And with you," she replied.

Ruarnon turned left. Lenaris horse's hooves clacked away in the opposite direction. More hooves approached. Lenaris's hooves faded, but the sorcerers' hooves remained steady. They were following Ruarnon. Just as Ruarnon had hoped.

Ruarnon smiled. Then then leant forward and rested their head on the horse's neck. So heavy. So tired.

Everything went black.

Lenaris hoped Ruarnon managed to shake the man off. They were disciplined enough not to use magic, but Mayrun's ability to detect people had been suppressed… and why had a sorcerer been sent to meet them?

Lenaris rounded a bend, so lost in thought she was slow to notice continuous noise echoing off walls around her. That was hooves. Was it coming from behind? Enemies or friends? But it sounded like it was in front of her as well…

She pulled back on the reins, quieting her horse and straining her ears. It sounded like at least one horse was behind her, but many hooves clacked, the sound echoing down the road ahead. Perhaps enough to be an entire patrol.

Lenaris healed her horse into a laneway on the right, hoping the silence and echoes were making the patrol sound closer than it was.

Houses of this laneway were narrower than on the main street, with simple doors, instead of grand entrance archways she could hide in. And there was no sign of an intersecting road nearby. She surveyed doors, chose a big one on the right, reined in and leapt from the horse. The door opened at her touch, and she led the horse inside, leaving the door open a crack to peer down the street and listen for the patrol.

The hoofbeats got louder and louder.

"Keep an eye out for escapees! The trap ought to be sprung now!"

Lenaris fought the urge to growl. This patrol must have been following them into the city, to cut them off if they doubled back. And Mayrun hadn't detected it either… And the Elite Guard scouts had sent no warning.

"Halt! There's no more strangers entering the city, but four were seen riding this way. Split up and find them!"

That shout came from the left, ahead of the patrol. A soldier who'd ridden behind Lenaris? But if two patrols were now searching the city, would they check buildings yet? Could she get trapped in here?

She peered down the street. There was a road intersecting hers further down, parallel to the main road that intersected the marketplace road. A backroad to the marketplace.

Lenaris tugged the reins. Men were yelling and hooves clacking. She rushed her horse around the corner, hoping the patrols couldn't hear her over their noise.

By sheer luck, the back road was made of dirt, the homes even narrower and less stories high. A poorer street who couldn't afford pavement, a quiet path less likely to echo any noise she made seeking freedom.

Hope and excitement sped her heart and made her smile, but she kept her horse at a walk as she remounted, knowing cockiness and letting their guard down had got many of her sparring partners into trouble when they faced more experienced opponents.

Several men yelled something on the main road and hooves began to clack towards her. Someone was searching the side street she'd fled down.

She healed the horse to a trot, hoping the marketplace road was still clear.

The lane ended ahead. For a moment there was silence.

"There's no one down here!" someone yelled behind, from the laneway intersecting hers.

"Spread out! Bar the main road, one man per lane. I want us to see them when they move. They could still be hiding!"

No-one was stationed on the marketplace road. They seemed to think everyone who had escaped their trap was further into the city.

The marketplace road was cobbled. Lenaris smiled grimly, remembering the rags stowed in her pack and dismounted, binding her horses' hooves again. She made the knots as secure as she could, so stray rags didn't leave a trail, then mounted again, turning the corner.

The odd clack echoing down the marketplace road suggested soldiers were still repositioning to block and keep an eye on inner city roads, but her way was clear. She healed her horse into a trot, heading for the archway ahead, her door to freedom.

The archway looked thinner now and chunks of stone were scattered beneath it. It seemed a single blow from a mallet could bring the rest down.

"Hey, where are you…"

A soldier sat atop a horse at the edge of the marketplace.

"Halt!" the man cried, raising his spear and urging his horse forwards.

Lenaris veered under the right side of the arch, deflecting the spear thrust towards her and rode on.

A figure ran up behind the rider. They seized the saddle blanket and mounted behind him. Then they rode out of Lenaris's sight.

She turned back. The soldier sat limply, head tilted to one side, a pair of dark-skinned hands holding them. Mawana had knocked the soldier out.

She smiled and shook her head as he grinned at her, steering and healing his horse to catch her up. He rode alongside her, off the marketplace and among the burial mound hills.

"Where is your horse?" she asked quietly.

"I hid behind a rock and let the guards chase it into the hills."

Mawana tipped the unconscious soldier sideways off the saddle blanket.

"Where's Ruarnon? And Troy and Fiona?" he asked, reining in behind a burial mound.

Lenaris frowned. "The sorcerer followed Ruarnon when we split up. If Fiona and Troy followed us into the city, I didn't see them and there are soldiers between us now. Michael rode to the river and I think Linh followed."

"Let's follow the city walls north, check Michael and Linh reached the river and see if we can distract soldiers near Troy and Fiona if needed."

Lenaris hadn't heard shouts indicating Fiona and Troy had been sighted, suggesting they'd avoided the patrol arriving from the south. Given they were fleeing a patrol from the west as well, the most logical thing was to ride for the northern gate. But what if Fiona and Troy hid hidden in the city? There was little she or Mawana could do then, other than get captured trying to find them. She sighed and nodded.

Ruarnon should be riding for the river too, to follow it west. If they had escaped the sorcerer…

Mawana angled west down the burial mound hill, keeping close to the hill the western city walls rose from. The sun must be low on the horizon in the east, as it was casting darker shadows than usual, which should make them less obvious to patrols in the west.

Occasional shouts rang out from the city. Lenaris startled on understanding the first. "Keep searching further north! They may have fled that way."

She turned to Mawana, who gaped. "*I* understood that," he whispered. "I don't speak a word of Migryan. How can I understand what any Zaldeaan is saying?"

Lenaris frowned. "The intense tingle at the gates of the Guardian walled forest..." she whispered. "What if they contained an enchantment like the one the Australians encountered when they first arrived here? A faeron enchantment to make you understand other human languages?"

Mawana's gaze became distant.

Lenaris wanted to consider the advantages that offered, like no need for translators to communicate with Galvations... but now wasn't the time.

She nodded to Mawana, and they rode on, the hill behind them descending, the city walls climbing down it to rise beside them. Meanwhile, the already dim light became darker, the closest this sorcery blasted land offered to sunset and twilight.

"Where are the rest of the soldiers that were chasing you?" she asked Mawana, after a long period of silence from the city.

Mawana shivered. "I lost some of them east of here, but some followed Linh. That's why I'm not riding that way. Half the patrol is between us and Linh."

"Which way was Linh riding?"

"South."

Lenaris swore. "Michael was riding north last I saw. I thought she was following him."

"I couldn't see him to know she'd changed directions," Mawana added.

It was too late now. They could reach Linh *and* evade soldiers by continuing to skirt the city, along its northern wall. Michael shouldn't be too far ahead of them, but he was nowhere in sight.

They slowed the horses as they neared the riverbank bordering the battlefield and the northern side of the city. Mayrun and Ruarnon should be here, but there was no sign of them, only a Zaldeaan patrol stationed near the northern gate, on her far right.

She and Mawana steered their horses swiftly down the steep riverbank, out of the patrol's sight. The trickle of the river flowed fairly straight in both directions, but its mostly dry riverbed contained only rocks and open air.

"Do we try and sneak past the patrol along this riverbed?" Mawana asked.

Lenaris sighed. "Michael may be ahead of us, Mayrun too. I don't want to risk leading a patrol to them. But once the patrols finish searching the city, this riverbed is the next logical place to look."

Neither of them wanted to abandon the others, especially when Linh and Michael were outside the city, still riding, and may make it. The problem was, the land beyond the riverbank was bare plains, which would leave them exposed. As would riding down the straight riverbed, the first bend that could conceal them lying far north-west. But the most likely thing to delay their friends was being chased by guards, in which case, Michael and Linh may need guidance. So they waited.

The guards at north gate paced, some gazing across the plains and riverbed further east, but most faced the city, from which Lenaris heard occasional, distant cries.

She sighed. "Surely every gate has guards by now. The only chance of anyone coming to meet us is Linh and Michael successfully riding three quarters of the way around the city."

"Then we wait. And we hope," said Mawana.

Lenaris inclined her head.

But they couldn't wait forever. Soon she could no longer make out the guards, and dark of the city walls began to look similar to the dark of the clouds above. It must be nightfall.

Mawana sighed too, gazing down the riverbed. "If we wait any longer, we risk one of our horses turning an ankle in the small ditch that trickle of water that was once a river has made. And our friends have much worse night vision than I do."

"Which means they are likely camping, if they are still free. We could camp here and wait till morning, but I'd rather move around the bend, where the north gate guards cannot spot us by walking thirty paces nearer the riverbed."

Mawana inclined his head and they rode north-west, along a riverbed she struggled to distinguish from the sky, in the rapidly increasing darkness. It was a welcome concealed roadway across the plains. But to where? Mayrun's combined scout reports hadn't got that far. Which was odd, given Lenaris and her companions had ridden as far as Galvatia.

Small hills lined the western horizon and there was something odd about the land ahead.

"Halt your horse," Mawana said quietly.

Lenaris reined in, curious, given Mawana had deferred to her leadership so far.

In the quiet as both horses stilled, men's voices carried across the plains on their left.

"Hurry up lads! There'll be no one left to round up!"

"Quiet fool! Don't warn them off."

"Surely they know multiple patrols are after them by now?" the first voice added. "They'll notice half Fang Mountain's guards hunting them soon enough."

"Keep an eye out for anyone fleeing within shouting distance," the second voice ordered.

Lenaris and Mawana sat in silence, while other, quieter voices moved away, fading into the distance in the south-east.

"The fools should be searching this riverbed," Mawana said quietly. "It's an obvious concealed road out of Galvatia."

"They might be bored and uncaring about the job," said Lenaris. "Remember they're captives. They have no grudge against Galvations. But if any of them ride around the city instead of into it…"

Mawana sighed. "Linh and Michael could be captured."

Lenaris clenched her reins. "If Fiona and Troy have not yet, they must be hiding in the city. But with Ruarnon not having reached us yet, I fear they have been captured. If they, Michael and Linh are not ahead of us, we may be the only ones riding north-west, unless some of our guards made it."

"Several fell when they came between the sorcerer and Troy," said Mawana. "I fear the rest did too while we scattered."

Lenaris squinted. "Is that starlight ahead?"

"It is!" Mawana exclaimed. "The sky ahead is clear!"

They rode on towards it. It was very difficult to tell in the dark whether they had reached or even ridden past the bend they sought. But sight of glowing white pin pricks of light and the pale grey of the land beneath was too welcoming, too enticing to halt.

"Have we reached the edge of Galvatia?" Mawana wondered.

"It could also be one of the small kingdoms Narz has recently taken control of, for all we know," Lenaris warned. "We'd best be cautious. Do you think this is far enough away enough to stop?"

"Let's stop under the stars," Mawana replied, his gaze fixed on the sparkling, clear sky ahead, a dreamy smile on his face.

That was one way to be sure they *had* ridden beyond the bend and the view of anyone searching the riverbed near north gate.

They rode on until the sky overhead was clear and full of stars twinkling away. Lenaris took first watch, while Mawana lay on his bedroll and surprised her with how swiftly he went to sleep. Faint voices rose, moving in the same direction as the patrol they'd heard earlier. It sounded like a lot of Zaldeaans were stationed at Fang Mountain and could be spared for random mass searches of Galvatia.

Uneasiness weighed her down as she sat. They'd left their friends in danger, not drawing patrols away from them. Ruarnon could hide and play cat and mouse in buildings –if they were still free– that was all part of their military training. But the Australians had fallen off the deep end, and she and Mawana had failed to protect them.

She took the first watch, listening keenly for any sound of her friends. But the night was silent and she took a long time to get to sleep.

CHAPTER 9

REBELS ~LENARIS

Lenaris spent the next morning back tracking along the riverbed, while Mawana scouted ahead. She rode quietly, a knot in her stomach, as she looked for friends who may not be coming. The light dimmed back under the clouds, darkening as they thickened overhead.

The upper sides of the riverbed were bone dry. Thin patches of grass grew either side of the trickle of water, where it ran across soil. But there was no moss on rocks at the edge of the water, regardless of their size. If this was Galvatia's only water supply, the rebels must be rationing water carefully. Could they really be hiding under the clouds, in this virtual desert?

Eventually the riverbed began to curve, and she dismounted, tying her reins to a narrow rock and crept forwards on foot.

"Why would they come this far?" a faint voice asked. "There's no cover out here beyond the river, and they'd have to come through us to get back to the city. Makes no sense."

"Unless they know what's beyond the ambushes in that big forest and are using the river as a highway to it."

"If they know that, why didn't they circle the damar infested part at the eastern end? Why ride all the way up here?"

Lenaris's heart sank. She ducked low and peered around the bend. The soldiers were a good way further back, their voices amplified along the empty bed.

She crept swiftly back, dancing on rocks fixed in place, avoiding wobbly ones in case they made a noise. She mounted swiftly, steering her horse onto a patch of soil less likely to tear the rags muffling her horse's hooves and healed it to a trot.

Mawana was waiting for her. She motioned for him to speak quietly and pointed behind her. He nodded.

"There are people out here," he whispered. "Farmers, tending crops and livestock, and a small village half a bell's walk away. They look free and there's no sign of soldiers."

Lenaris sighed. Had they roamed beyond the lands Narz controlled? But did he still have influence here?

"We should spy on them," she said. "The patrol behind me didn't think anyone would come this far. If they are not Galvation, Narz may have offered them a reward for the capture or news of Galvation rebels. They might not be enemies, but they might not be friends."

Mawana scurried down the riverbank. "Rider!" he said.

"What do they look like?"

"A big man, crossing the plains. He must be in full view of Galvatia. He's following the river east of us."

Lenaris frowned. One lone rider? When every patrol soldier she had seen travelled with company? Was this a messenger? But what was he doing here? Offering to bribe the people ahead if they turned over any strangers who wandered into these parts?

Mawana peered above the riverbank. "Actually, it's two men, riding doubled up. One of them's a bit thin, young maybe. But the other wears a bronze helmet and a leather vest. A soldier."

"Grass," said a distant voice. "Oh how I've missed you!"

Lenaris met Mawana's gaze as her mouth opened. Mawana smiled broadly and stepped head and shoulders out of the riverbank.

"Troy! Where did you get the armour?"

Gentle hoof beats moved closer, then Troy's horse was descending the riverbank. A huge grin split Troy's face, while Michael's face was several shades lighter than usual, looking sickly and he smiled tiredly.

Mawana ran forwards and practically lifted Michael off his horse, giving him a bear hug before setting him down.

"Help him stand!" Troy called as he dismounted. "He's concussed."

Lenaris offered the wobbly Michael an arm, supporting him while Mawana enfolded Troy in a bear hug.

"What happened to your head?" she asked Michael, eyeing the bloody bandage around it.

"Fell off my horse," he replied.

"What in the name of Chaos are you doing riding about when there are guards' all over the place!" Mawana demanded, as he let Troy go.

"Trying to avoid them," Michael replied with a smile.

Mawana flinched at the blood-stained cloth tied around Michael's head. "What happened to you?"

"When we split up, some guards followed me around the city. I tried to lose them by fleeing down the south side, but I kept running into guards and having to change direction, fell asleep in hiding then got chased into the riverbed in the morning. I finally lost a patrol when damars attacked them, but then two patrols chased me into the chasm where I fell and hit my head."

Lenaris shook her head as, Troy explained how the patrols had left Michael for dead. Sheer luck appeared to have spared Michael twice.

"I am sorry," she said. "Ruarnon and I thought you would be safer outside the city, where you couldn't get lost or cornered. The sorcerer pursued Ruarnon and I, so our route wasn't safer, though I suspect I heard you and Fiona pass just after the sorcerer moved out of your sight as you entered the city."

Troy shivered.

"Where is Linh?" Lenaris asked Michael. "She was following you."

Michael's face fell. "She never caught up to me. I didn't see her."

Troy punched the air.

Lenaris sighed. Linh was most likely captured. It could be worse. They might have caught Troy, who might have told them everything, which might have got back to Narz. But Linh was smarter and slower to trust. Lenaris hoped her stubborn streak won out over her fear and helped her stay calm and avoid all mention of both armies anchored off Narz's shores.

Troy surprised Lenaris, explaining that Fiona was safely in hiding with people he was fairly confident were Galvation rebels.

"What did you tell these rebels?" Lenaris asked sharply.

Troy grinned sheepishly. "My ambassadorship is somewhat not as good as yours, but Shella said she'd send word to the Galvation leaders that Ruarnon offers them an alliance."

Lenaris smiled. He was doing well with a spear, but she could never be sure how much of what she said sunk into that wandering, restless mind of his. Apparently more had than she thought. "Then you have done well."

Troy beamed at the praise. From comments the Australians had made, she gathered praise was something most of Troy's teachers rarely gave him at home.

"Why are you riding this way?" Mawana asked Troy.

"Shella told Rila to send word of us to a safe place out here. Apparently the rebels have friends this way. Haven't you found them yet?"

"Perhaps they were not ready to be found."

Lenaris pivoted and her hand went for a short sword she wasn't carrying. But the man who peered at them from the riverbank, having silently approached, stood calmly.

"How did you sneak up like that?" Mawana asked.

"While you were distracted by your friend's arrival," the man replied. "You claim to have met Shella?" he asked Troy.

Troy fidgeted with a loose end on his sleeve. "Rila said she was head steward of the palace, or something like that, before the war."

The man smiled. Was that something only someone he trusted could have told Troy?

"We have not received her message yet," the man replied. "Perhaps you can deliver it yourselves?"

"I am happy to do so," Lenaris replied. "But we need to move. There is a Zaldeaan patrol further back in the riverbed, looking for us."

"Will you join us for lunch?" the man asked.

Mawana inclined his head ever so slightly at the corner of her eye, signalling that he trusted the man.

"It would be our pleasure," Lenaris replied.

She helped Michael back onto his horse, half lifting him into the saddle. When he wobbled, she had Troy mount behind him to keep him steady. Then she and Mawana led their horses out of the riverbank, near a gentle rise in the land the man motioned them too, which she hoped concealed their exit from the soldiers behind her.

"Have we crossed the western border of Galvatia yet?" she asked, as they rode among gentle, grassy hills.

The man smiled but didn't answer her question.

"Do the clouds stop here because it is the edge of Narz's reach?" she tried again.

The man inclined his head, as he led them onto a grassy stretch of riverbank, beneath blissfully clear skies and bright sunshine.

"We believe so," he replied. "He knows Fang Mountain is beyond the clouds because he captured it in a stealth attack, forcing the watchmen to report everything as normal while he marched on our capital. But the area I am taking you to now seems beyond his reach."

"What happened to the people in the city?" Troy asked.

"It was evacuated in haste, while the army assembled. King Narz pit the Zaldeaans against us, and we had success against them at first, but then damars flanked us. The Zaldeaans retreated at night, but damars didn't. The brutes stalled our attempts at retreat until the Zaldeaans moved to engage us early the next morning.

"By the second day we were exhausted and had suffered heavy losses. We questioned whether we should fight to the last soldier or abandon the city. His Majesty insisted on retreat, so our soldiers could continue resisting Narz alongside our elderly, children and non-fighters, and he won us over. Once we breached the damar lines, they were useless against us and that became our retreat route. Roughly two thousand soldiers were captured, but many escaped."

"And your king?" Lenaris asked.

"Our Prince retreated also."

Lenaris studied him. It was hard to tell if he was concealing the king's existence, or perhaps the king had fallen in battle. She decided not to press him.

Troy and Mawana's smiles distracted her. They kept gazing up to the clear blue sky overhead and at grain fields and small hills the dirt road the man led them down wove through. The sight eased tension in Lenaris's torso and somehow let her breathe more freely.

The hills grew bigger further south, on her left, and the outline of what must be Fang Mountain rose sharply, while more bumps dotted the western horizon, a distant mountain range. All of it was lit by sunshine, and the air smelled fresh and of grass. This was more like the fertile Zaldeaan Realm, a land of life.

Thatched roofed, stone cottages lay ahead, the edge of a village with open fields stretching around it. The man led them to a house with a stable, where they left their horses, then into a large room with a table with simple wooden chairs set around it for lunch. A woman served vegetables and cuts of meat onto pottery plates. Their guide greeted her and a second man at the table, who invited them to sit.

Food lay upon the table and familiar styled eating implements, whittled from wood. Lenaris hesitated. Posing as Galvations, drugging rebels then handing them over to Karmarn sounded a good way for these people to collect any reward Karmarn offered.

"It is good to see your hesitation," said the second man. "It reassures me you are genuine outsiders."

"What do you mean?" Mawana asked.

"Some of our people spotted you days ago," the first man replied, "and a friend and I were sent to identify you. We were near enough to hear you trying to make sense of the battle, but we feared another of Commander Karmarn's ruses."

Mawana gaped, probably shocked his tracking abilities hadn't noticed the rebels tailing them. But Mayrun hadn't noticed the rebel pair either. There must have been an enchantment blocking her ability to sense people. But how did whoever set the ambush know to block her abilities? It sounded like the trap Troy had tried to ride into had been days in the making.

"My name is Maharl," said the man who was seated when they entered, "and this is my brother Joharlen," he nodded to the man who had thwarted Mawana's ability to detect his presence at least twice.

Joharlen looked younger than he sounded, and the care lines on his face and grey in his shoulder length hair seemed premature, while his eyes looked wise beyond their years. He reminded Lenaris of Regent Omah.

The resemblance between the brothers was clear in their grey eyes and the set of their long noses. Both had tanned skin dotted with freckles, worn and weathered looking. Both wore their light brown hair half tied back, several thin plaits running into a half ponytail.

"We should dearly like to know what brings you here," said Maharl. "If you are not lost."

"We are here to free the Zaldeaans and bring them home," Lenaris replied, to raised eyebrows. "We understand that would benefit Galvatia. Hence, we offer an alliance."

The two men exchanged a frown. She had decided to be open and honest, and had expected questions, having heard how Shella had questioned Troy and Fiona. But she worried these men would not be easily convinced of the truth.

Yet, she had their attention. As did Mawana's dark skin and braided hairstyle, which from the way Joharlen's gaze kept flicking to them, were unfamiliar to him and marked him as an outsider.

"That would be welcome news. We assumed you were someone important, as Karmarn does not employ sorcerers, yet one was tracking you."

Maharl spoke with a neutral tone. It sounded like Ruarnon's description of their first meeting with Emperor Yarath; polite conversation, casual questions constantly probing, testing. Every word weighed. Maharl was going to take serious convincing this wasn't another of Karmarn's traps.

"How did you know about the sorcerer tracking us?" Lenaris asked.

"When some of my people suspected a sorcerer was moving with a patrol marching an unusual route at an unusual time, I sent scouts to track the patrol."

"What do you think it means, Narz sending a sorcerer?" Lenaris asked.

"I suspect Narz knows there are strangers wandering his lands. Some of my people glimpsed strange riders in the wild. They disappeared. We suspect they were captured and Narz knew to put a sorcerer on the ground because he suspects some of those riders could wield magic."

Lenaris gut clenched. They hadn't even planned to free the Zaldeaans yet, let alone her father and Ruarnon's parents. The Timbalens weren't ready to invade either, and already Narz may know Ruarnon and the Timbalens were at his doorstep.

But now wasn't the time to panic. These men seemed prepared to give her information and they weren't asking questions she didn't want to answer yet. She had to take advantage of that.

"Where will our scouts be taken?" she asked.

"To Fang Mountain Prison, our former watch tower south of here. King Narz keeps his powerful opponents there, where the mountains rise suddenly from flat plains and there is a clear view of anyone approaching in all directions. It is conveniently far from kingdoms he begins to rule and is guarded by sorcerers."

Lenaris's face fell. That sounded like where Poran thought her father was imprisoned.

"What are our chances of breaking anyone out?" Troy asked.

Lenaris's brows rose and both Galvation men turned to Troy wide-eyed.

"Rila said you'd been breaking people out of the Forest Prison for weeks," Troy added. "Can you do the same at Fang Mountain?"

"The sentries have an uncanny ability to detect anyone near their walls," Maharl replied in the same controlled, calm tone. "Several of our spies have been captured, while others have had close escapes. None succeeded in entering the prison."

"You need excellent stealth and skill with magic," Mawana speculated. "That could be a job for me."

"For both of us," Lenaris replied, eyeing him sternly and he smiled.

"Do not judge the sorcerer guards of Fang Mountain Prison by the sorcerer you escaped yesterday," Joharlen cautioned. "From the way he saved his most damaging spells for your horses, I assume he had orders to take you alive. King Narz must want to learn your identity. But he knows everyone sneaking about on Fang Mountain is an enemy, and most scouts we sent who were not captured were killed by sorcery."

Lenaris shivered. Poran had believed Narz wasn't using sorcery oppressively in the lands he ruled, as he tried to use Keepers of the Peace and Healers to placate old and new subjects alike. Apparently Galvatia was an exception.

The way Fang Mountain Prison was being guarded and the skies over Galvatia were enchanted resembled more the man Lenaris and Ruarnon had feared when they first heard Narz's name. It fit a man whose very existence challenged the beliefs of many of his people, who lived in fear that he and everyone like him could be killed, and who responded to opposition with the brutal force he believed that level of threat required to contain it.

"Do your scouts mean so much to you?" Maharl asked.

"My father does," Lenaris replied. "I am told he is imprisoned on Fang Mountain."

"Who are you that your father would be taken as such a serious threat?" Maharl asked.

"Do your people know of the stingers nest Narz has kicked in the east?" Lenaris replied.

Maharl leant forwards at mention of the east.

"The Timbalens?" Joharlen asked. "There are legends from before contact was lost with them, after the Sorcery War. It is said their land was a safe haven. But why should Narz fear them? Unless the Guardians who left our lands went east, to protect the Timbalens?"

He reached the conclusion so naturally and swiftly that it made Lenaris wonder if Narz had done the same.

"We believe that's what Narz believes."

Maharl frowned. "Narz attacked them? And you have come here?"

"The Timbalen Emperor believes the empire will not be safe until Narz is dead," she added. "And from what we have seen of Narz in the east, we agree with him."

Joharlen chewed his lip.

Maharl gazed into space. "I thought you might be southerners. I heard rumours they were suspicious of and rallying against Narz."

He eyed Lenaris critically. He was still testing her.

Lenaris shook her head. "The Elite Guard of the Timbalen Empire have been the greatest power in the eastern seas since the Sorcery War. Narz scared them half to death. We have no reason to believe he could send a fourth damarian army into the east, let alone sorcerers, but emperor Yarath believes his Elite Guard will not be safe until Narz is defeated."

Maharl stood suddenly, then turned to eye Lenaris again. "You are quite serious? You seem calm about all this."

"Ruarnon is the best negotiator we have. If they couldn't dissuad Emperor Yarath, then he cannot be dissuaded. Even Ruarnon doesn't seem to think they can dissuade the Timbalen Commander now."

Maharl sat abruptly. "The *fool*! He has enough enemies at home, even if one counts us as conquered and of little concern! Why would he be so reckless?"

Joharlen remained silent, his face turning deathly pale.

"We concluded Narz's mind is damaged quite some time ago," Lenaris replied. "Irrational fear seems to be the most powerful thing driving him."

Joharlen shook his head. "With all the resources he has… have you seen what he did to our sky? To our country? We call ourselves a resistance, but there is precious little we can do against him! He is a mallet, and we are but a blade of grass. I told you Maharl; Narz has entirely lost his grip on rational thought."

Maharl stood again, shaking his head and began pacing around the kitchen. "But our people could have poisoned the Middle South against him. They are little fonder of sorcerers than we are, living in the shadow of the God Kings, as they do."

"But to hit us so hard," Joharlen argued, "so early on, with so little evidence we would pose a threat? Ideology is too important to him. He seems to value it beyond reason. I know how terrifying the notion is, but the man who broke our kingdom is assuredly delusional."

Now the colour was draining from Maharl's face. He took a deep breath, then turned to Lenaris.

"You have come to ask our help freeing our people, and yours, from the imprisonment of a sorcerer who cannot differentiate between historical figures and real and present enemies?"

"That mad man holds my regent's parents, aunt, uncle, cousin and seven thousand of their subject's captive. Ruarnon will not give up on those people, not until they have done everything they can to free them. Yes, we offer an alliance."

Joharlen slowly shook his head. "Sorcerers offer *us* an alliance?"

Lenaris smiled. "Oh they haven't yet, but they wish to. I am Tarlahn, as is my regent. We wish no part in the Second Sorcery War, but only to recover our people. It is our allies the Timbalens who want Narz dead. If you are willing to work with them too, we can contact them to arrange a meeting for you."

Maharl shook his head continuously. "We fought Narz *alone*. We have resisted for months, alone, and now *two* distant people's from lands of myth beyond the sea offer us an alliance?"

Lenaris smiled sympathetically. "Imagine how my regent feels, in a land where we believed sorcery no longer exists, yet they've been attacked by creatures from the Sorcery War and had half their family abducted by a sorcerer king worthy of myth."

Slowly, Maharl nodded. "The whole of Umarinars seems to be turning up-side-down. I never dared hope anyone in the east would come here seeking retribution. That anyone in their right mind would dare go to war with Narz now, when his sorcerer following grows by the day and his influence spreads ever further south, where people begin to speak of him not just with fear, but with awe, even optimism. It seemed the greatest victory we could attain was our survival. But you would raise our hopes higher?"

Hope began to glow in Joharlen's eyes, while Maharl still seemed to be fighting it.

"We should be more formal," Maharl said in a more official tone. "To whom exactly am I speaking?"

"Companion Lenaris, close childhood friend of Regent Ruarnon and advisor on the Tarlahn Royal Council."

Maharl nodded. "I am Prince Maharl, ruler of whatever is left of Galvatia. I sincerely anticipated southerners approaching us, seeing an advantage in working with us now Narz looks to the south, too late to be of much good to us. But people from the east, people without sorcerers at your command, seeking to free Zaldeaans and us with them? You are a dream. A dream we are most happy to welcome."

Lenaris smiled. Being occupied by a delusional sorcerer king who kept your kingdom desolate with a sorcerous sky enchantment must be terrifying, and that fear would grow, with his acceptance of the state of

Narz's mind. But Ruarnon had the alliance they sought. They would be keen to plan to free the Zaldeaans and Galvations both, as swiftly as possible, with the news Narz had captured Elite Guard scouts and may know of the Timabalen army's presence and of the impending sorcery war it signalled.

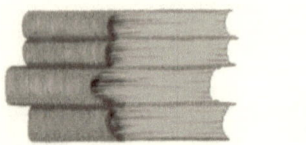

CHAPTER 10

ON THE RUN~ LINH

Linh tensed. Why was Michael riding alone when Lenaris and Ruarnon were still in the marketplace? The sheltered stone platform was fast approaching. She'd have to decide who to ride after. Thought of Michael heading off alone tightened her shoulders. She made a snap decision and steered left of the stone shelter, racing past its tables and stalls on Michael's tail.

Something shadowed the beats of her horses' hooves. Was that *more* hooves? Thudding behind her? She jerked in the saddle. A man rode close by. Into the marketplace, pursuing Ruarnon and Lenaris. Further back, more guards pursued Mawana up the hill from the battlefield.

Linh's heart hammered against her ribs. The man was getting between her and Ruarnon. And she couldn't be sure which way the guards behind her rode. She looked back, straining to see over her shoulder.

The guards pursuing Mawana had seen Michael. Several broke away, making a beeline for him. Mawana veered right on the hillside, leading the other guards around it, out of sight.

Linh's heart beat faster. Her horse was slower than Michael's. She was gaining on him, but the soldiers closing in on him were faster. They were going to outpace her and cut her off from Michael.

Linh turned her reins, her horse whinnying as she steered it to double back along the city walls, towards the marketplace. There was just one man up there. Could she get round him to Ruarnon?

Stone cracked. Linh reined in, her heart hammering against her ribs. Was the man the sorcerer? Had he just blasted a wall?

She turned west again. Neither Mawana nor the soldiers pursuing him rode near the burial mound hills. Mawana must have continued his ride around the hills. And the soldiers riding towards Michael were still pursuing him, instead of her.

She healed her horse among the burial mounds. Maybe she could meet up with Mawana. She scanned between the burial mounds on both sides. The man was riding through the western gate, into the city. There was no sign of Mawana or patrol soldiers. She gazed back, wondering if more soldiers had come up the hill. Michael was turning. Soldiers from the battlefield were still angling towards him. And in the distance, a whole patrol rode towards him. Was this an ambush?

Linh's horse rounded another burial mound hill.

"What was that?" someone shouted downhill behind her.

"Only one. Most entered the city. After them!"

Linh healed her horse down the southern side of the burial mound hill, searching frantically for soldiers. Several soldiers rode after a horse among brown, dead looking trees ahead to her right. Nothing moved on her left. She turned left, angling down the slope, hoping those riding for the gate wouldn't see her as they crossed the marketplace.

She reached the outside of the city walls unhindered and followed the wall across the back of the city.

"Another! Southwest corner!"

Linh glanced back. At least four soldiers were exiting the trees, riding across the plains at the base of the hill the city lay on, towards her.

She rounded the corner of the city walls and they disappeared from sight.

Something lay ahead, where the city walls ran along level ground. A bump on the flat soil. Another patrol. Stationed at the southern city gates. They hadn't seen her yet. More hills rose across plains further south. Linh steered her horse towards them, angling away from the city wall, but keeping it in sight so she didn't get lost.

She held her breath as she crossed bare, exposed plains, hoping the south gate guards didn't spot her. She repressed the urge to bite her lip as she jostled in the saddle, gripping the reins unnecessarily tight instead.

Larger rocky hills lined the horizon further south-east. A whole row, the perfect cover, if she could reach their far side. They even seemed to angle towards Ancient Valley, where General Imphin would have messengers stationed. That might be the safest way to regroup with the others.

She turned further from the tall, red stone city walls. Four men from the trees still followed her further north, but they didn't seem to be gaining ground.

She heaved a sigh as she passed the first hill. Then she tensed. Distant hooves thudded. A second group of guards chased Michael around the corner and east along the city walls. They were closer to him and gaining ground. She wanted to call out to him as he hugged the city walls, to warn him of the south gate guards ahead. But her pursuers rode parallel to his path. If she drew their attention to Michael, they could turn and cut him off. She growled. If these pricks wanted a chase, she'd give them a merry one.

She veered further southwest, zig zagging among and putting more small rocky hills between her and the four riders. Shouts rose from nearer the walls. She turned back. Soldiers at south gate were pointing to Michael. Two were mounting horses to cut him off. She turned over her other shoulder. Her pursuers had reached the first hill and were still hot on her tail. *Good.*

She continued swerving around ever larger hills, the city wall falling further away on her left, and fading into the darkening sky. The south gate guards were distracted by Michael. Only the four pursue her as she rode parallel to South Gate in the hills.

Her horse slowed gradually, as it dodged more hills. She angled it further east, to keep the southern wall in sight, when the gate guards became dots in the distance.

A dip in the land ahead took her by surprise. She slowed her horse. The riverbed. A long way to her left lay a bump over it, the bridge she had crossed when entering the city a few hours ago, kilometres away. The place where Ruarnon had told them to regroup in the riverbank north-west of the city if they got separated. She was a long way southeast from there, further away than when soldiers first pursued her.

"Shit!"

Linh selected an earthy patch of riverbank to steer her horse down, between the rocks, some of which may not be stable, and rode over the small trickle of water that used to be a river and up the far bank. Maybe she could lose the soldiers in the mountains, and double back to the river?

Galvatia City was retreating into the horizon behind her and it was getting harder and harder to see. The dim light was darkening, rapidly. But her pursuers continued their beeline, keeping her racing into the wilderness. Bastards! Who did whoever set the ambush think she and her friends were?

Taller rocky hills a short way ahead were vague dark blurs now. Soon it would be too dark to ride without risking injuring her horse's legs on rocks it couldn't see.

She squinted at larger rocky hills, for one that gave cover on multiple sides. It was a challenge in the half dark, but eventually she spotted darker darkness in a rock formation, a crack that looked large enough to climb into. Would the horse fit?

She dismounted and steered her horse towards the crack. The horse snorted, lowering its head, but somehow followed her into a space just large enough for it to lie down, surrounded by rock on all sides. She tied the reins to a rock jammed between a boulder and the ground, then flung her saddle blanket on earth rising above the horse and lay down.

There was no use blundering through the dark. Hopefully her pursuers thought the same or rode past without noticing her. Either way, someone was bound to search this area at dawn. Now was the time to sleep, while darkness cloaked her and hampered her pursuers.

Sleep didn't come easily. Linh kept imagining the thud of hooves and couldn't help shuffling to see if it was friend or foe. It was usually nothing. Once, it was distant riders carrying burning torches, *not* friends. She lay awake, dreading the torches coming close. Eventually she forced herself to lie still and drifted off.

The world returned slowly in the morning, daylight revealing that the rocks around her were just taller than the horse, concealing them both from patrols. She sighed. Where were her pursuers? And where was Michael? She grit her teeth. Where were phones and app messaging when you needed them?

She sat and took a deep breath, trying to encourage the tension in her shoulders to loosen. Returning to the city and staying here both seemed unsafe. The crack was too small to canter through on horseback and the city was probably crawling with soldiers. The riverbed may also be crawling with soldiers.

She couldn't search for the others without great risk of bumping into patrols. Which left giving them up for lost and riding back to camp where General Imphin's people managed scout reports. Could she make it all that way by herself?

A distant shout rang over the hills and Linh tensed. She was a sitting duck here. Best get moving while the light was still pale. Before the patrols woke to full alertness and hunted her relentlessly again.

She climbed the rocky ledge and peered over. Flat ground lay head, scattered with stones, and in the distance, abandoned farmhouses and occasional cattle skeletons. There was no sight or sound of anyone. Did that mean her friends had been captured? Or chased west of the city?

A guard stepped out from behind a farmhouse on the right. She stared. One by one, half a dozen guards shifted, across the barren farmland. There was no sign of the mounted riders who had scattered her friends. And these strangely still guards weren't marching like a patrol. One paced before a farmhouse. Another stood on a hilltop, surveying the barren farmlands. They seemed stationary and were cutting her off from General Imphin's camp.

Linh swore. Avoiding capture was all very well, but she couldn't sit here until her meagre food and water supplies ran out. And the guards looked set to remain in their places at least that long. The southeast, across open land, looked bad.

Opposite her stretched another row of hills, higher and steeper, forming a rock-strewn gorge, the row she'd seen last night. No guards patrolled this side of the hills. Had her pursuers ridden past already?

There were still hills and open spaces between her and that row. She'd need Troy's ability to sneak without being seen by guards on the plains. But turning west now meant being seeing by Galvatia City's gate guards, as did turning north. And Ruarnon had warned that travelling south could mean accidentally crossing the border with Azula. Southeast along the rocky valley was by far the best option.

After a quick breakfast of water and hard biscuit, Linh took a deep breath, secured her horse's saddle blanket, led the horse out of the cracked rock and mounted it. She turned the horse towards the hills between her hiding spot and the gorge. Mountains were visible on the horizon, where Imphin's base camp lay. Navigating should be easy enough.

She set the horse at a walk, keeping the hill she'd hid behind and another between her and the nearest guards. Her ears strained beyond the clop of her horse's hooves, across the eerie silence of lifeless ground. She slowed at a gap between the hills and waited until two guards stepped behind a distant hill. Then she tugged the horse's reins and led it swiftly across.

She soon reached the gorge and led the horse on foot. Rock rose on both sides, and the gorge was rock scattered, with dry red soil. Silence stretched beyond. Her horses' hooves sounded loud against the hard ground. When the horse trod on rock, an echo bounced off rocky hills and sheerer cliffs on her right, but over time, the absence of other sounds convinced her she was alone and helped her relax.

Linh rode on beside hills and three more gaps behind sentries' backs, to a section of gorge edged with cliffs, hills and then mountains on her right. A hiss rose among the hills. She reined in, holding her breath and straining her ears. A damarian screech split the silence, followed by more hissing. Her chest tightened and breathing became slightly difficult.

She scanned the reddish-brown rocks for a hint of grey but there was none. Her shoulders tightened anyway. The damarian city must be behind the cliffs on her right. That was why the Zaldeaans didn't patrol this gorge. It was too dangerous. And she was unarmed, while the farmland on her left was guarded and damars or guards could threaten her ahead, in the east. The only safe option was to turn back west.

She slumped and turned her horse around with a heavy heart. Where did she go? The west was also wilderness, but more open and easier to be spotted by a patrol. Could she follow these hills and then the stand of trees, then make a break across the western end of Galvatia for the river?

"In the gorge!" a voice cried.

Linh tensed. She was riding at a walk alongside a gap in the hills, through which a Zaldeaan sentry pointed. Two riders cresting a nearby hill turned their mounts towards her. Linh healed her horse to a gallop.

"He's heading west!" a man cried.

Linh smirked. Only a *boy* could avoid them overnight could he? She'd show them! But where could she hide?

Shouts rang out through a gap between hills on her right. Riders further west galloped towards the gorge. They were going to cut her off...

She bit her lip and turned her horse south between two hills, scanning the slopes for damars, but ascended unchallenged. Perhaps she could hide in Azula, though she'd *have* to avoid being seen.

The hill behind her was higher and screened her from approaching riders. She exhaled with relief.

Her horse stopped at the top of the hill. The downward slope before her was a sheer cliff, stretching twice as far down as she had ridden up. She gasped, as vertigo tugged at her.

The cliff ended at a high, brown stone wall. Guards lined battlements atop the wall. They peered inwards from regularly spaced guard towers, down at a city of stone cottages, punctuated by free standing guard towers. A prison city.

Linh gaped. An enormous field and orchard spread beyond buildings, bordered by oppressive stone walls. Countless people stood in lines between rows of green shoots in the field. More stood along aisles, passing along buckets and upending them. Grey clouds barred the sky. The prisoners were watering the field and orchard by hand. Men in armour strutted along laneways near them, Zaldeaan guards.

This was where the missing farmers, inhabitants of the burnt villages and city had gone. The buildings were small, timber and thatch, built on a grid of dirt roads devoid of palaces, temples or culture. It was a purpose-built prison city and its high walls and forced labour put Linh in the mind of Khmer Rouge or Nazi death camps and made bile rise in her throat.

"Back this way! On the hills before Black City!"

Linh tensed at the shout and wheeled her horse around. A young man rode to the foot of the hill her horse stood on. Another rider approached from her left. A third rode round a hill on her right. Her breaths came in ragged gasps. She was cornered.

"Don' worry 'bout them," said the man on her left, nodding. "They get fed well enough, and we 'aven't 'eard a whip crack since Gov Poran came."

Governor Poran?

"How is it you haven't been captured yet?" asked the man on the right. "Where you from?"

What had the world come to that for the first time in her life, Linh sincerely wished she was Troy? He would probably lie his way out. But lying was never a talent of hers…

"Australia," she replied, feeling too ignorant to pretend to be from elsewhere on this continent.

"What'd she say?" muttered a forth rider as he reined in beside the youngest.

"Astriya," said the rider on Linh's left. "Where's that?"

"It's in the south," Linh replied honestly.

The guards frowned. They might think she was from a southern kingdom they'd never heard of. Her heartbeat quickened. Maybe she *could* talk her way out.

"I've come to deliver a message to Companion Karmarn," she gambled, avoiding looking directly into anyone's eyes, in case they perceived the lie in hers.

"And what interest does Astriya have in his Lordship?" the man on her right asked.

"Companion Karmarn's king hired us to deliver a message," she improvised.

"Why didn't they sail to Commander Karmarn directly?" asked the soldier on her left.

"We got lost," she replied, which was certainly true.

"Sounds dubious to me," the man replied.

"If you're a messenger for a king," said the man on his right, "where's your escort? And why were you riding directly south, when Commander Karmarn lives several leagues southeast from here?"

Linh flushed. The youngest man eyed her critically, but kept his mouth shut.

"What do we do with 'er captain?" asked the man on the left.

"Bind her hands. We'll take her to the Forest Prison," the man on the right replied.

Prison? They were taking her to *prison*? Linh's heart pounded out of control.

"Not Fang Mountain, captain?" asked the fourth man.

"Fang Mountain is for important prisoners! Not just any rebel!" the captain objected. "Don't worry girl, Commander Coroth won't let anyone hassle you," the captain added.

Linh frowned. Why would someone 'hassle' her? Why would a Zaldeaan prison master take her side? Weren't Zaldeaans sexist? Or were these the type of sexist men who thought it their duty to protect 'defenceless' women? As her guards in prison, that might not be a bad thing…

The youngest guard dismounted, eyeing Linh critically. She glared at him, a habit from people who mocked her at school at home. His lips twitched, just like Michael's used to when he held back a smile. But all the youth said was, "Put your hands behind your back."

Linh fought her instincts to flee, or punch him in the nose, which would do a fat lot of good while three of his companions stood close at hand and complied. Something rough, but not too hard, cord perhaps, bound her wrists tightly.

"Take her reins and you and Dirg escort her to the Forest Prison," the captain ordered the young guard. "We'd better keep searching for strangers."

Strangers? Did the Zaldeaans not know who they were hunting?

The young guard took Linh's reins and Dirg, the fourth soldier, rode beside her. She bit her lip. Though if the guards at the prison were like this, being in prison might be alright. The problem would be contacting her friends, though if Ruarnon *did* manage to help free Galvations and the prison was full of Galvations… she might not be stuck for too long. *Curse Umarinaris and its ifs*!

Her captors led her horse between two sentries on a nearby hill and into barren farmland. The sentries nodded to her captors, their blue eyes scrutinising her, but they said nothing. Travelling north would be easy now she couldn't achieve anything by doing so.

As they rode, Zaldeaan newcomers handed their reins to sentries on nearby hills, who rode west, towards the east gate of Galvatia City. Were they working shifts? And this was the end of a shift?

The young soldier's gaze studied her. How much had he guessed, or could he guess?

"You are not from here, are you?" the young man asked.

"No," Linh replied.

When he said nothing more, she opened her mouth to question him, but he shook his head and angled it in Dirg's direction. Who was this boy and what could he possibly want to discuss with a Galvation rebel in secret?

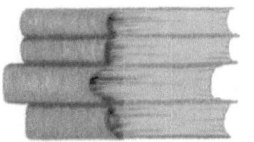

CHAPTER 11

THE FOREST PRISON - LINH

L inh blinked and gazed alertly through the darkness, feeling hard ground beneath her. She sat awkwardly, hampered by bound wrists, and peered through near total darkness in search of what had woken her. Surely there weren't wild animals on these drought-stricken plains? But no, the small fire framed Demune sitting upright on watch, facing her, while Dirg lay snoring softly on the far side of the fire.

"There are some things I did not want to say in front of Dirg," Demune said in a low voice. "The idea that we serve Narz against our will does not make sense to him. So when Narz's spies ask him questions, he doesn't understand that he should hold his tongue. But your black hair and dark eyes… don't North Landers, or East Islanders have that colouring?"

His gaze was intense. Was that hope in his voice?

"Why would you be glad to find a reclusive, sorcery-wielding North Lander here?" Linh asked. "Or a subject of Tarlah's allies and therefore your people's greatest enemies?"

The youth's face lit up and he smiled. "We thought it would be Governor Iagl who'd come for us. But if you are a North Lander or from the empire… has Regent Ruarnon come? To free their uncle and parents?"

Linh smiled. "Oh they're more forgiving, wildly ambitious and creative than that. They want to free your whole army. And probably bring about world peace, if they can nudge that into being."

Linh's cynicism surprised her. But Ruarnon's optimism exceeded hers. Things seemed so complicated, so messy and so many powers opposed them here. Yet still Ruarnon's plans refused to give ground.

The young man's eyes widened. His lips pressed together, surprise and worry mingling in his eyes.

"Are some of you resisting?" she asked, remembering how Monin had half expected Karmarn to escape and bring a good chunk of the army back on his own.

"Karmarn has already tried an escape plan, but Narz's spies got wind of it. Narz truly seems to believe the worst of my comrades will go straight to war with Tarlah if they return home. He thinks our forced service here is kinder. He might even be right. Karmarn would never go to war against his nephew, but the army would likely swear loyalty to Governor Derlan when we get home and there will be no peace under Derlan, whatever the arrangement Prime Ruler Ruarnon has."

Linh smiled. "That traitorous prick is dead. When he besieged Governor Syenne and she asked if he killed Kyomi, apparently his face gave away his guilt and her soldiers killed him on the spot.

"Governor Iagl still holds it against her, but Iomar was genuine in his support of Ruarnon's peace and Iagl seems to trust his brother's judgement and respects Ruarnon. He's been happy to let Ruarnon keep peace between him and Syenne."

Demune exhaled deeply. He slowly smiled. "Coroth said his cousin was clever. Good at reading people. I didn't think they'd get the chance for that to help, but with Derlan dead, I can see it working. But I'd still be nervous of what Governor Iagl is planning in Ruarnon's absence, if Ruarnon is here."

His worried gaze met hers.

Linh smiled again. "Governor Iagl is here too and seems enthusiastic in following Ruarnon's lead to free his people. They train together, get on well and I suspect Iagl hopes to get the chance to fight alongside Ruarnon."

"They're a warrior?" Demune asked.

"Lenaris is the natural fighter, but I suspect they have as much skill as she does. They just lack her aggression. They led the fight against damars in the Realm and came face to face with Governor Iagl's soldiers in Zaldeaa. They ordered their soldiers to stand down and that won Iagl's respect."

Demune nodded. "Governor Iagl being here also makes me nervous. Some of our people are accepting Narz's bribes to spy on us, thwarting future escape attempts. I can't see Iagl being merciful to them."

Linh's mouth dropped open. "You *want* people who are keeping you imprisoned for self-gain to be handled with *mercy*?"

Demune sighed and his shoulders sagged. "Coroth is sure there are sorcerers watching us. The spies are just giving the sorcerers advance warning. Coroth and I don't think we'd have much chance of escape even without traitors hampering us.

"Besides, we've pretty much been at war for nearly a year. Most of us want to get home and be with family and at peace. I don't blame them for trying to make our forced servitude more pleasant."

Linh shook her head. "I'd have to slap them all at least once before I was that forgiving."

Demune smiled slowly. "You sound a bit like how Coroth always described Lenaris."

Linh wrinkled her nose. "We're more like each other than we care to admit."

"Who are you?" he asked.

"I'm from a lot further away than the empire," she replied.

She explained how sailing with Timbalens answering Omah's call for aid and her homeward quest had brought her to Tarlah, and she and her friends had helped and befriended Ruarnon.

"Please tell only the people you trust most, who have guarded tongues this," said Demune. "Teliph, Coroth's girlfriend, said Narz is experimenting with the gateways. She said very few sorcerers can operate them, but he is one and she is likely another. She feared it might kill him and anyone he has messing around with them. But if she learns to operate them, perhaps she can help you get home?"

Linh's breath caught. Narz's sorcerers *were* the ones who could operate gateways. Red Cloak must be Narz's lead guinea pig. And Ruarnon being her friend, and Teliph Ruarnon's cousin's girlfriend, perhaps that tenuous connection could help them get home…

"What's your connection to Coroth?" Linh asked. "You sound like friends."

"I am Demune, Companion Nish's son, whose was regent while Companion Armar rode to Tarlah seeking aid against the damars. My father sailed west after me when the army was captured."

"What happened to Companion Nish? And Companion Karmarn?"

"My father resides with his Beneficence King Narz, as hostage. He told Karmarn he didn't care if he was killed as punishment for escape attempts, but Narz didn't even hurt him in retaliation to the only escape plot."

Linh's mouth fell open. Presumably Karmarn and Nish were friends and Nish was well known among the army. Wouldn't Narz at least torture, if not publicly execute Nish to deter future attempts?

"Commander Karmarn lives in the mountains south-east of here and guards the plains from rebels and oversees the hunt for strangers."

"Who else is in the Forest Prison?" Linh asked.

"Galvation soldiers captured in the war, and people who cause trouble in Black City."

Demune's manner and distant gaze suggested he accepted what was beyond his power to change there.

"Who's in charge of the Forest Prison?" Linh asked.

Demune smiled. "My friend Captain Coroth. Companion Karmarn's son."

Linh stared into the distance. Her jailor was Ruarnon's cousin... and her cellmates would be soldiers who opposed Narz. If only she had a way of telling Ruarnon...

But one man, a personal friend of Commander Karmarn as hostage didn't add up. "What else has Narz done to stop patrols from escaping?" Linh asked.

"Two thousand of our men are guards in the capital cities of Azula, Tiama and Arveta, which have many resident sorcerers, making escape impossible. Two thousand hostages against our good behaviour, taken after the failed escape attempt.

"Narz has bribed some of our men to spy on us, but Coroth keeps spies away from the ground floor of the Forest Prison, where prisoners are babbling, or ceasing to eat their food in one cell after another. Coroth thinks their madness is feigned to frighten away guards and conceal tunnel digging, but he has not investigated for fear of drawing the spies' attention."

Linh's mouth dropped open. "Coroth's turning a blind eye to escapees?"

"It is not our war. And Narz will not suspect Coroth because Coroth is in love with Lord Tarz's daughter, Teliph, and probably dependent on Narz's approval to sway Lord Tarz to let them marry."

Teliph... Lylah had mentioned that name. "Is Teliph a sorceress?"

"Yes, and that complicates things. Lord Tarz sees little point in teaching her magic because as a woman, a wife and mother is all she will ever be. But when Narz found out how powerful Teliph is, he began teaching her magic himself. She respects and admires him, and Coroth hesitates to tell her the truth of how we came to serve him because it will shatter her illusions about him."

Linh shook her head slowly. "I suppose he looks as wonderful to her as he did to Poran, Dargus and Darius. He helps people who need it, and they don't like to admit the extent to which he screws over people he doesn't consider to be his people. But why are you telling me?"

"I want you to tell the Zaldeaan King, so Ruarnon understands our situation. Even if they succeed in freeing any of us, Coroth will not want to leave Teliph."

Linh frowned. "You mean Ruarnon's cousin might not want to be rescued from slavery?"

"Like I said, its complicated for him. But if he can find the nerve to tell Teliph the truth about how we came to be here, if she can admit to herself that Narz isn't a flawless, wonderful person and can be as cruel as he can kind, I think there is a chance she may help us. I want you to tell Ruarnon that."

Linh shook her head. She had known Karmarn was head of the Zaldeaan patrols, but for her to be captured by a good friend of his son, and his son being the prison master had been wonderful strokes of luck. She was about to have the kind of adventure Troy probably always dreamed of having: getting arrested, taken to prison, and likely breaking out again. She fought back a laugh.

She hoped Fiona wouldn't be too worried and that Michael had escaped the patrol. Hopefully Fiona and Troy had the sense to follow Ruarnon and Lenaris, the more likely path to safety.

"In the morning, we must pretend not to have had this conversation," Demune's voice broke into her happy thoughts. "Narz's spies will question Dirg, and he does not realise that is what they are or that he should hold his tongue."

Linh nodded and they both lay back down.

Next morning, five mounted guards joined them on their ride north. The mood became more solemn. Demune didn't speak to Linh and she avoided eye contact with him, struggling to adjust to falling into the role of captive, when only last night she'd spoken openly to him, like a friend.

They rode passed the white-washed homes and skeleton-filled paddocks beneath cloud-barred skies. Every now and then Linh would scan the horizon, near hills, homes or anywhere her friends might be hiding, hoping to catch a glimpse. But there were too many sentries. Sentries standing in paddocks or on cart tracks, among cattle skeletons scattered through barren land that had once been fields, all dimly lit beneath an oppressively charcoal, cloudy sky.

As she rode on, she noticed how rarely anyone spoke. They merely nodded to sentries as they passed, and her captors gazed ahead now and then but tended to keep their heads down. Their speed was slow, as if the world wasn't turning, and there was no need to hurry, in complete opposition to the world Linh called home.

Finally, the riverbed neared and mercifully, the clouds thinned overhead and the dull grey light became gradually brighter. The horses forded the shallow trickle of water effortlessly, then followed a dirt trail through the tangled branches of healthy green forest. The light continued to grow brighter, wind rustled leaves around her, rain fell in the distance and pale sunlight shone beyond. It was almost enough to promise the world could get better, were this not the road to prison.

Sensing her destination was near at hand tightened Linh's shoulders. It made breathing a little more difficult. She fought the urge to craft shield magic, as her fear and nervousness spiked. It didn't help either when her guards' un-strapped bows from their saddles and nocked arrows.

Wild hissing sounded and a bowstring twanged. A savage damar fell dead on the path. Linh shook her head at this hideous extra layer of prison security. So Narz *was* using damars against people here. He had in battle too. Did his subjects and other kingdoms not know that?

They rode towards patches of stone wall between trees, which resolved into a three-storey castle with every window barred. Linh tensed when two guards reached for her but was surprised how gently they lifted her off the saddle blanket and lowered her to the ground. Maybe Zaldeaans in these parts *were* sexist in a gentlemanly way. She shivered and Demune shot her a worried look, but she shook her head.

She tried to put a bold face on things as six strangers and her only ally in these parts surrounded her and marched her towards the castle prison. A small group of guards marched down the castle steps to meet them and Linh's guards backed up. Demune hadn't spoken to her for hours, but she was reluctant to leave him. He gave her a subtle nod in farewell, as her captors retreated, mounted their horses' and rode away.

She stood with a heavy heart, surrounded by prison guards, who gently pushed her towards the doors atop the steps.

She took a deep breath, eyeing the dark interior beyond the double wooden doors held open by big beefy guards in leather armour. She bit her lip when their gaze pierced her and didn't stop as she stepped into a high-ceilinged anteroom. Her new guards steered her left, towards a small desk with a man behind it, like a check-in counter at a perverse version of a hotel.

"Name," the man said.

"Linh Mai," she replied.

The man recorded her name and said, "Take her to cell three-hundred and twenty-one."

Linh's guards marched her towards more double doors. Four heavily armoured guards stepped aside, revealing a dark corridor lit by burning torches. She blinked to adjust to dim lighting as they crossed the corridor and climbed a wooden spiral staircase. When they stepped off the stairs, the stench of broken toilets and unwashed bodies made her breathe through her mouth, and her guards wrinkle their noses.

Her guards marched her past another pair of guards and down a cold stone corridor lined with heavy wooden doors reinforced with iron strips, with wooden flaps in the bottom. Cells, she assumed. The corridor was lit by burning torches and dark as night. Would there be any daylight in her cell? Or would she be trapped in stink *and* darkness?

He shoulders remained tight, as if bracing against attack, but she suspected anything that assaulted her here was going to be more psychological in nature. She walked through three more sections of corridor divided by stone archways with burning torches on both sides. Three more grim dark realms of prison before, mercifully, a large day-lit room walled in with iron bars spread across the end of the corridor.

Inside the large cell, a man backed up against the wall and a youth stepped before a third figure. The guards unlocked a barred door, untied Linh's hands and pushed her inside. The door clanged shut behind her and the guards locked it and walked away.

So they were the kind to throw people in here to rot, not torture them. That was… good? What about her cellmates? She could smell them from a distance. Breathing carefully through her mouth, she faced them grimly. Daylight shone through two barred windows onto greasy brown hair and a man with a plaited beard. His skin might have been white, under the grime, but it was hard to tell.

"A soldier?" the man asked. "At ease. There's no fighting in here."

Linh fought back an ironic smile. She'd never smelt or seen anywhere that put her less 'at ease'.

The young man blinked, and a girl stepped out from behind him, which for some reason reassured Linh a little.

"You are not Galvation," said the man.

"No, but I assume you are," she replied.

He bowed his head, a Tarlahn gesture… or was it from whatever culture Tarlah and civilisations here were descended from?

"Then who are you? Who else would wander into these war-torn lands, if they had anywhere else to be? I thought none of our neighbours cared for us, not enough to risk peace with Narz."

"I can't speak for them," Linh replied. "But your whole country is mostly deserted. Anyone who wasn't captured might be in hiding in neighbouring kingdoms, for all I know."
"Captured?"

"There's a prison city, with prisoners growing crops and tending orchards under guard. I assume all the captured civilians are there."

"Civilians?"

"Non-soldiers. I got separated from my friends and was caught atop the cliff overlooking the prison city because I had nowhere else to run."

"But what are you doing here in Galvatia?"

"Narz didn't just invade you. He's attacked multiple lands in the east and he stole the soldiers occupying you from the east. I've come with an eastern regent. They want their army back."

"No one who cannot combat Narz's sorcerers has a chance of that now. Narz gains more sorcerer followers and popularity by the day. It is what keeps our captors loyal; they dare not antagonise him nor endanger their comrades on duty in cities Narz controls. I think some of them resent having to guard us because our position feels to them like a mockery of theirs. We are all prisoners in this castle, but most guards treat us decently for that.

"My name is Captain Shafar," he added. "This," he nodded to the young man and the girl, "Is Pazi and Sarma."

The young man nodded gravely, and Sarma nodded shyly.

"Our unit was heavily engaged when the retreat was called, so we fought on and were captured. We have spent half a year in here, mending clothes and doing odd jobs in exchange for food. I am not sure how many soldiers have been moved on to Black City and how many remain here, but I am one of few captains not sent to Fang Mountain Prison."

Six months… Demune better be right about what was happening in the basement.

"Unfortunately," Shafar added, "our level is difficult to break out of, but the rebels are tunnelling into ground floor cells, save those blocked by dungeons underneath."

Linh's face split in a fierce smile.

"We however, are trapped by corridors, guards and damars."

Linh's shoulders slumped.

"We believe the ultimate security measure is a sorcerer using magic to spy on corridors," Shafar added. "Interestingly, they don't seem able to hear us. It was amusing testing that."

Linh shivered. An actual sorcerer monitoring the prison she was locked in? If Ruarnon did want to free the Galvations here while freeing Zaldeaan guards, the Tarlahns *would* contend with sorcery…

"Someone's coming," Pazi warned.

Linh tensed. Guards coming to question her?

Robed figures strode down a distant corridor, carrying baskets. Linh frowned. No armed guards accompanied them.

"It's alright," Shafar whispered.

The figures marched down the middle corridors. The daylight of Linh's cell showed them to be women, their skin far cleaner and sweeter smelling than her cellmates, all wearing deep purple robes, with their hoods up. Like a religious order, or a cult. What on earth were they doing?

The leader was a tall and stately red head, who greeted Shafar with a smile. Pazi and Sarma moved towards the bars, approaching the other women, who beckoned and began speaking to them in low voices. The leader motioned Linh and Shafar closer.

"She's an outsider," Shafar whispered, nodding to Linh. "From the east."

The woman eyed Linh keenly. "So his quest for Guardians met someone, and battle? And your people are come for revenge?"

Something about this woman told Linh she would see through lies. And Shafar seemed to trust her. But was this a set up?

"How are you walking free?" Linh asked. "If you know and are on friendly terms with my cellmates?"

The woman smiled. "Not everyone was at home when the Zaldeaans and damars came to call. Some of us were rallying support in neighbouring lands, where we were wise enough to own property, wealth and to have established connections."

Linh frowned. "But Galvations hate magic. Why would you go mingling with people in countries where sorcerers live?"

"Not all of us are narrow minded dear," the woman replied. "Nor are all of us inflexible or unadaptable. Being both is very useful when your homeland is occupied and your people have no allies outside it, bar yourself and your associates."

Linh frowned. At the corner of her eye, she glimpsed a blonde woman slipping apples out of her pockets, and into Pazi's. Her frown deepened.

"The bounty of Luvaras," said the woman, following her gaze. "The temptation we offer to convert the foolish Galvations to worship Luvaras, true God of Sorcery, Narz's personal god. Or so we have convinced the guards, as a ruse to smuggle prisoners' food."

Linh gaped. A *fake cult* as a front to smuggle prisoners food?

"Are there *actual* Luvaras Priestesses?" she asked. "Could you get caught?"

"Real priestesses are far more secretive and while they travel widely, none of have ever come here. They are sorceresses and their interest is in training young sorceresses. Everyone knows there are no sorcerers in Galvatia because we hate magic and would throw them out, if such people existed."

"Then why would you be here?"

"Most people only know myth and rumour about actual Luvaras Priestesses, Luvaras priests and The Dedicated. Ignorance is widespread enough that we could distort the myths to mask our intentions.

"And it is common knowledge that Narz is offering Healers to win popularity, so if priestesses came here and healed prisoners of their wounds, perhaps that would be part of Narz's attempts to win over and benignly rule the entire continent?"

Linh smiled. There was something of Governor Syenne in this woman, though she had even greater talent for using her enemies' beliefs and ignorance as an elaborate weapon against them. Linh liked her.

"How did you know I was here?" she asked.

"We heard rumours of unidentified wanderers in Galvatia. And you are the first new prisoner to be brought here in weeks. It seemed likely you may be one of the wanderers, so we wished to make contact. Galvatia is not a friendly place to strangers of late. So who would come here and why?"

"I'm part of an expedition to ally with Galvatia, free the Zaldeaans, and in so doing, the Galvations," Linh told her, deciding she could say that much because it was crucial Ruarnon reach the people they needed, but not daring to mention the Timbalens until she had a lot more evidence she could trust this woman, because the stakes of sorcery war were too high.

"A delegation from the Zaldeaan Prime Ruler, Regent Ruarnon of Tarlah?"

Linh blinked.

The woman smiled, reading the question off her face. "No one on this continent wants to offend Luvaras Priestesses, let alone anger them. We are careful not to abuse that power, but it gets us into places and among people no one else who opposes Narz has a hope of accessing. Which, along with some talented servants, keeps us well informed.

"We would very much like to speak to your King," the woman added.

Linh wasn't sure how much of her racing heart was nerves and how much was excitement. This could still be an elaborate trap, but it could also make her escape that much easier.

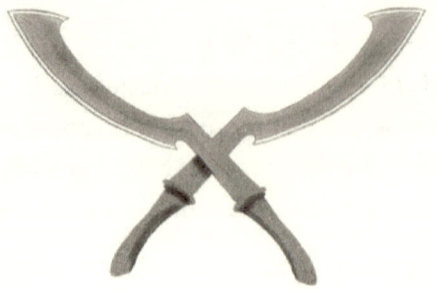

CHAPTER 12

LOST PERSON -RUARNON

Ruarnon blinked in surprise at the feel of a soft bed beneath them. It was quite comfortable and very strange. They hadn't had this for days. Not since… they left their cabin onboard the Iylena.

They sat up to survey their surroundings. They lay on a small bed against a wall, with a writing desk on their right and a wall with a door made from metal bars on the left, set in a stone wall. Their gold rings were still on their fingers and their pack lay in a corner.

Ruarnon's mouth split in a smile and they laughed softly. They had been right. All they needed to do to contact their uncle was get captured, though they hadn't seen being waylaid by a sorcerer coming. That was the most likely reason for their gentle and respectful treatment, and accommodation in what their Australian friends would probably joke was a 'luxury hotel'.

The risk was what hold did Narz have over Karmarn and how might it impact Ruarnon? As in the Urai capital city, among a culture they'd had barely a week to study, Ruarnon would have to watch everyone around them, and take their cues from the Zaldeaans as to how this would play out. Spies were a possible partial hold on Karmarn, as was magic.

Ruarnon smiled. Was that excitement they were feeling? Anyone in their situation should be afraid. But it seemed their uncle had their back and could at least ensure they were decently treated. And so long as they were in prison, the only person they had to be responsible for was themself.

It was more freeing than riding through the gates of Tarlah City as merely Heir, not Regent. It was going to Ruarnon's head like alcohol. But as their Australian friends defined such things, they had never had a true holiday in their entire life. For once, the only things they were likely expected to do were answer questions, eat, sleep –life's basics. To Ruarnon, that *was* a holiday. Though it may get a bit boring…

They strode to the door and peered through its barred window, down a long a stone corridor stretching left and right. A deserted corridor. Surely this was a castle? Was it Karmarn's residence?

Soft footsteps fell. A woman in a Tarlahn green silk dress just like Aunt Telena's walked towards them. Ruarnon stared and fell very still. The last time they had seen their Aunt Merlah was at the Festival of the Gods before the war, nearly two years ago.

Ruarnon hadn't known their uncle was Zaldeaan then, or that the family lived in the Zaldeaan Realm and their marriage had sealed King Kyomi and Ruarnon's father's peace treaty. Everything had changed since then, in Tarlah and Ruarnon's life.

How had the confidence in Aunt Merlah's blue eyes escaped their notice? The decisiveness?

Her porcelain face was care-lined, and her loose blonde hair was half streaked with silver, but optimism shone in her grey eyes, perhaps reawakened by their presence and what it signalled.

"Ambassador Drake," she said with a warm smile and a wink as she approached.

Ruarnon smiled back. How had she known Tor's adopted son was someone Ruarnon would trust with a task like establishing contact with her? The perfect fake identity?

"It is so good to see you again and that you made it safely through the war!"

Ruarnon smiled as she approached. "I was very glad to hear you made it safely too. I hear Coroth was heroic in that."

Some of the light in her eyes faded and she bowed her head solemnly. "He came through well enough to be appointed Captain of the Forest Prison here. Narz sees his quality."

Ruarnon frowned slightly. She *did* mean that literally, but by her wording and knowing look, she was warning Ruarnon that Narz had taken a special interest in Coroth. And in making him captain at the Forest Prison, Coroth was likely outside Karmarn's protection. A hostage?

"How is my brother's child?" she asked.

Ruarnon smiled. "They are quite well. They re-established relations with the Urai earlier this year, survived assassination attempts thanks to servants gifted by Governor Syenne and have decided they like sparring with Governor Iagl."

Merlah's mouth opened in surprise.

"I suppose that's what came of being raised by King Urmilian," they added. "He expected the world of them, and they somehow learnt, with the help of good friends, to deliver it."

Tears welled in Merlah's eyes. She shook her head. "That is more than my husband or I hoped for.

"I wondered, when King Narz sent us two sorcerers and told us we were to capture strangers in Galvatia, if it was someone from the east. I know of the expedition he sent against the Timbalen Empire. I feared for the worst.

"But I am afraid it will be some time before our work here is complete. His Worthiness will most likely say the same, though my husband shall wish to speak to you and confirm this."

Ruarnon frowned. Her eyes were full of meaning. They were 'Drake' because someone else was listening. It was also a subtle signal to Ruarnon to watch what they said. Incomplete work... was she implying they would be able to escape, but not yet?

"What is the nature of the soldiers' work here?" Ruarnon asked. "Kyura's death and Regent Nish's departure left Tarlahn impressions confused."

"Most of the soldiers are securing Galvatia under my husband's leadership, but two thousand serve in the capitals of His Worthiness' cities. King Narz is a visionary leader, like our own King Fra."

Ruarnon cast their mind back to Tor's history lessons. There were legends about King Fra, a Timbalen king… he had united the Timbalen Empire through conquest and was the emperor to whom Guardians sent their children to serve as Elite Guard. Was she saying King Narz was training sorcerers to occupy conquered territories?

Ruarnon kept their face impassive, smiling when appropriate. It was like the game Emperor Yarath had played of 'casual conversation' when they first met, but the addition of knowing they were being listened to and quite possibly watched by spies made it more interesting.

"Meanwhile, in his role at the Forest Prison, Coroth aspires to imitate the Urai," Merlah added proudly.

Ruarnon frowned. The Urai had come between two great powers when… they refused to aid Tarlah in its first war with the Zaldeaan Realm, costing an ambassador his life and many lives in retribution attacks. Did she fear her son was caught between the Timbalen-Azulan war?

"Farewell Ambassador," said Merlah.

Ruarnon said goodbye and sat back on their bed to think. Her second use of that title struck them. *Ambassador*. Karmarn wanted to play Ruarnon's visit as an incursion into occupied territory as a diplomatic visit, despite that the incursion's destination suggested the visit was intended to reach Narz's enemies, the Galvations? Aunt Merlah hadn't just come to visit and catch up with the family member she hardly knew, she'd come to prepare Ruarnon for their meeting with Karmarn.

Galvatia City was the first man-made thing of any size they had seen on this continent. They could claim they assumed the Zaldeaans would have occupied it and used it as a base for their military operations. That would have been the sensible thing for their uncle to do. Why hadn't he?

Ruarnon stood at the sound of heavy approaching footsteps and the sight of two bronze armoured guards approaching. They opened Ruarnon's cell door and escorted them down the corridor past airy frescoes of forest, flowers and a waterfall lit by skylights. Door frames were carved and painted to resemble trunks, and the grain of their wood rose up between it, suggesting the castle had belonged to an artistic Galvation noble.

Ruarnon's guards halted, and guards flanking the last door opened it. They revealed a round room with a central skylight. Forest frescoes blended with shelves made of branches around its walls, and a pool of water surrounded by plants filled the centre. Ruarnon's Uncle, Commander Karmarn sat behind a desk cut to blend with a vast tree trunk fresco behind it, his long brown and iron-grey hair tied back as he perused a scroll.

He motioned absently for Ruarnon to sit in the chair before the desk. Ruarnon composed themself, suspecting this visit would be more formal.

They sat and the show began.

Karmarn looked up, revealing a lined, perfectly controlled face, his dark brown eyes as passionate as ever. He looked Ruarnon right in the eyes and asked, "Who are you and what are you doing in His Worthiness' Realm?"

"I am Ambassador Drake, sent by Their Benevolence Ruarnon, Regent of Tarlah and King of the Zaldeaan Realm, to learn of the agreement by which the Zaldeaan Army serves His Worthiness," Ruarnon replied formally, deciding Karmarn was too important and busy to recognise a Tarlahn Companion's adopted son from the far side of the world.

"If that was your purpose in His Worthiness' Realm, why were you interested in Galvatia?"

"We understand the Zaldeaans are deployed in Galvatia. I assumed they would use its capital as the base of their operations and came seeking their advice on how best to establish contact with His Worthiness."

A flicker of Karman's eyes was the only sign of approval that showed through his mask.

"Does the name 'Galvatia' mean anything to you?"

"No."

"You are unfamiliar with the ancient tongue?"

"My regent has been too preoccupied in wars with the Zaldeaan Realm to bother about learning ancient dead languages," Ruarnon answered.

"It means 'City of the Guard,'" Karmarn replied, emphasising the name as if it was important.

"Guard against what?" Ruarnon asked, playing along.

"Guard against sorcery. His Worthiness is a sorcerer. Such a place is tainted, ill befitting any of his operations."

Ruarnon suppressed a frown. That wasn't a commander's strategic decision. It wasn't diplomacy or politics of any sort. That reason was almost sentimental, or ideological.

Light headedness almost disoriented Ruarnon. The Warrior's Creed sometimes had Zaldeaans make foolish, costly decisions in battle, because it wasn't strategy. Linh would say it was ideology. Adhering to ideology could be irrational sometimes. Narz's fears may have been validated as ideology, and it was the ideology his followers had bought into and that impressed his fears on Poran and Dargus. Was Narz irrational, or an ideolog? Both? Was there a difference?

Karman eyed Ruarnon pointedly.

"My apologies," they said. "We are regretfully unfamiliar with Azulan culture. That was another reason we wished to approach Narz via our acquaintances."

A spark of amusement in Karmarn's eyes, there a moment, gone the next, made Ruarnon fight back a smile. They'd struggled to think of an appropriate word there.

"Why does your king wish the Zaldeaan army to return?" Karmarn asked, hinting at why Ruarnon hadn't referred to the Zaldeaans as 'subjects', which they were, of Tarlah.

It couldn't hurt to tell the truth… "Their Benevolence understands they were wanted for a conquest over half a year ago, and there is a labour shortage in the Zaldeaan Realm."

"The army has successfully captured the capital and townships of Galvatia but are yet to defeat the resistance. It is unlikely His Worthiness shall consider their task complete any time soon."

Did that mean Narz might be prepared to hand the Zaldeaans back? If they defeated the rebels? That possibility hadn't occurred to any of Ruarnon's advisors, or to Ruarnon. But it would likely apply too late, *after* the Timbalen invasion.

"I shall convey that message to Their Benevolence, if I am permitted to return to my ship," Ruarnon gambled.

"That will be up to His Worthiness. I shall inform him of what you have said."

Ruarnon inclined their head and was escorted back to their cell. Only once the guards had left and they'd sat down did they exhale deeply. A staged conversation with a fake identity to their uncle while Narz's spies listened in felt like… like all the early Royal Council meetings Ruarnon led as regent. Like everything they had said in front of an audience of one or more strangers since they became regent. To be a leader was to be an actor.

But Uncle Karmarn was something else. His command of his face, expression, posture, tone –all of it was perfectly calculated for his role of busy, dedicated official for Narz. He must have been the perfect Tarlahn spy during the war…

But what would the conversations true audience make of it? What would Narz, who responded to anything he saw as a threat with damar invasions and war, make of diplomacy and an 'ambassador?

Several days later, Ruarnon was summoned again. They kept their breathing slow and steady as they marched into Commander Karmarn's office. Again, Karmarn was seated at his desk pouring over a scroll, convincingly indifferent.

"As I anticipated," Karmarn said when Ruarnon reached their desk, "His Worthiness does not expect the Zaldeaan army to complete their task soon. They are needed to defeat the resistance; at which time he shall consider their service complete and give them leave to depart. Until that time, if you wish to enquire on their progress, His Worthiness advises you to march to my residence bearing the flags of Tarlah, that you not be mistaken for rebels."

Ruarnon's mouth fell open slightly before they could catch it and smooth it over with a smile. Narz *had* responded to diplomacy? Karmarn knew him well. Ruarnon filed the thought aside, lest it distract them further.

"I am grateful to His Worthiness for his advice," said Ruarnon, struggling to play act as well as Karmarn this time.

"His Worthiness also bids you to inform your king. My men shall return your horse and grant you safe passage to your ship."

Ruarnon's body hummed with energy at the idea of being released so easily. They bowed their head, Tarlahn style, in thanks.

But how did they inquire inconspicuously about the fate of their friends, Mayrun and the guards?

"Sorry to trouble you further Sir, did His Worthiness know what happened to the rest of my party?"

"They may have gotten mixed up with Guardian spies recently apprehended on the border with Azula. If so, it will take a great deal of time to verify their identity, so you had best leave them behind and collect them when you return for the army."

Karmarn met Ruarnon's eyes then. That was a warning. But he may mean literally what he said: don't try to free your friends until you're ready to free the whole army.

Karmarn turned to his scroll and a guard unbound Ruarnon's hands and led them to the ground floor, where their horse and four mounted guards awaited them. They mounted the horse, and the guards led them over forested hills and across flat grassy plains beside burnt forest on their left, indicating they were south of the fleet.

Their guards stopped at a sandy coastline, and Ruarnon rummaged in their pack and withdrew the Urai horn Mocco had gifted them for their seventeenth birthday. If Mawana were anywhere within ear shot, he would recognise that horn and come looking for Ruarnon. Tor would recognise its call too.

Ruarnon withdrew the horn from their saddle bag and winded it in three long blasts, then waited some time before a rowboat appeared on the horizon.

"Why's your ship so far out?" one of the guards asked suspiciously.

"The winds died east of here and we had to row to shore," Ruarnon explained truthfully. "I assume the winds have yet to return."

"The new king, a Tarlahn king, wants to bring us home?" another asked, and Ruarnon noted the longing on his face.

"Yes."

"Why's he want us back?"

"They," Ruarnon corrected with a smile.

To their credit, these soldiers responded with polite confusion, not the rudeness Ruarnon had encountered on their first visit to the Zaldeaan palace.

"And as you are Zaldeaans, they probably think your place is at home," Ruarnon answered.

Raised eyebrows and stupefied looks conveyed the soldiers' doubt.

"Surely our place is where His Worthiness wants us to be?" the man who wanted to know why Ruarnon's ship was anchored beyond sight, Narz's spy Ruarnon assumed, asked.

"And how was Tarlah to know where that was?" Ruarnon replied incredulously. "Their Benevolence' opinion is that Zaldeaans belong in the Realm, and when your service to His Worthiness is complete, we will ship you home."

Out of the corner of their eye, incredulity, surprise and hope spread across three faces. Only the spy didn't seem keen, probably because on honest soldiers' pay was far less and perhaps because his comrades wouldn't be kind to him if they knew he had sold them out.

The boatload of soldiers the Iylena sent gaped at sight of Ruarnon standing, alone, with Zaldeaan soldiers. Ruarnon smiled and fought down a laugh at the absurdity that so much had gone wrong during the war with the Zaldeaans, so much had been out of their hands, and yet this time so much had gone right, despite much of it *still* being out of Ruarnon's hands. Umarinaris was a funny place. For perhaps the first time, they understood why Troy laughed so much.

"We have found the army and His Worthiness has told us when they will return. Our mission here is complete," they announced to the surprised Tarlahns rowing towards them.

"So soon?" asked a soldier who, from her hasty blinking, realised they were acting.

"Indeed, Commander Karmarn was able to make enquiries with His Worthiness on our behalf."

Ruarnon dismounted and allowed a guard to lead their horse into the deep hulled rowboat. "Ah, it shall be good to return to Tarlah," they said as they walked towards the boat. "The weather here is too gloomy. Thank you for your escort," they added to the Zaldeaan soldiers, three of whom bowed.

They didn't ride away until the Tarlahns rowed Ruarnon a long way from shore. Ruarnon suspected the spy was under orders to confirm they had left the continent. Ruarnon smiled and wondered if their ancestors had been a little too hasty in abandoning the gods. Because they now knew where Karmarn, Merlah and Coroth lived, and had established a means of legitimately contacting Karman *and* Narz in future. Esirah appeared to be shining on them and Mijora to watch over them as they traversed Her lands.

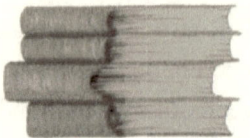

CHAPTER 13

REUNIONS~ FIONA

Fiona bit her lip, as she sketched with charcoal on spare parchment. Linh was the bravest and she and Michel were the cleverest of the four. They could cope out there, on their own, if they had to. But could Troy? How far would he get with no one to curb the impulsivity and restlessness he had been fighting to control? She was grateful to be safe and in the pleasant company of people who meant well, but she missed and worried about her friends.

"They've gone," said Rila. "We will leave as soon as you are ready."

Fiona smiled. A corset of tension slipped away and she breathed freely.

Shella smiled at her. "I suggest you get packed. Rila can lead you to the farmlands."

Fiona rolled her bedroll, returned her spare clothes to her pack and swung it onto her shoulders, then stood before her hosts of three very long days.

"Thank you," she said. "I appreciate you taking Troy and I in, your patience with him and you keeping me safe."

Shella smiled warmly. "You are welcome dear. Having a young person to stay broke the monotony for us."

"And thank you for giving me something to do," Fiona added, as she rolled up a half-finished sketch of her three friends.

Shella smiled again. Then Fiona turned to pat her horse goodbye and followed Rila up the secret passage. Her heart sped up in anticipation. Worry gnawed at her, about leaving the concealing walls of secrecy behind. But stepping outside was anti-climactic. The sky was almost as black as pitch, and the buildings were so dark they blended in, while the air was almost as still and stale as underground, and a heavy silence blanketed the night.

Rila carried a dark lantern, the grey light of which seemed bright against total blackness beyond the circle it cast. Fiona stubbed her toe on the step of a building she could barely see. It startled her, but it was good to walk in the open, once her eyes adjusted.

It didn't take long to reach an open square near the riverbank. Rila led her carefully down the side of the riverbed, then took hold of a heavy looking rock and lifted it, revealing a ladder at the top of a shaft.

"It's a bit of a climb with dark lanterns, but we can light torches at the bottom," she said. "It'll be at least a day's march on foot, so we'll sleep when you get tired tonight, and keep marching in the morning."

Fiona sighed about going back underground, but the sooner they hiked through the tunnels, the sooner she could get to the open farmlands, and to rebels who may have news of her friends. She climbed down a sturdy ladder into sewers that didn't smell as much as she feared, perhaps because the city had been all but deserted for months. Which was good because they walked for ages beside the sewers in a tunnel. They also slept in the tunnel, completing their hike in it the next day.

When she walked out into a dry riverbed under a cloudy sky, west of Galvatia City, Fiona inhaled fresh air with enthusiasm and smiled to see open spaces around her once more.

They walked under clouds that became gradually lighter. Thunder cracked nearby. Fiona's mouth dropped open. Large drops of rain fell meters away, while the air before her remained dry.

"Sometimes sections of magic fail around the edges," Rila explained. "But it looks like this one is mostly rain, not too much lightning. It'll be safe to walk under, but we will get wet."

Fiona grinned at something as natural as rain and walked forwards, laughing as heavy drops splattered into her clothes and soaked her to the skin. The rain was lighter ahead and a bright rainbow shone across the sky. Then, quite suddenly, they stepped out of a shower into sunshine.

"Time to leave the riverbed," said Rila.

Fiona overtook her, rock hopping agilely up the side until she stepped into a bright green field of plants heavy with grain. Grain fields stretched ahead of her, towards farmhouses. Wind rippled through the fields on her right, while on her left rose a rainbow before showers of rain. Further left, lightning flashed, thunder rumbled, and white and grey clouds were dispersed by the wind. Fiona smiled broadly at the enchantment crumbling at the edges.

"Has Narz tried to repair it?" she asked, as they paused on the edge of the field.

"No," Rila replied. "It was weak here in the beginning and has slowly but consistently broken up at the edges. King Narz seems content to let it wear out."

"Does that mean his power's focused elsewhere?"

"It is not focused here, allowing us to feed ourselves, and eventually we hope the whole thing will collapse, the drought will end and Galvatia will be restored."

"It's beautiful here," Fiona added.

Rila led her onto a narrow dirt track through the grain fields, towards the white-washed, thatch rooved farmhouses. Fiona enjoyed the cool wind on her skin as they walked through greenery, and the smell of soil and plants.

"It *can't* be…" she said, stopping in her tracks.

It was. Troy was running towards her with a big grin on his broad, honest face. He met her in the middle of the field opening his arms. She smiled as he picked her up, then swung her around. She leaned into his kiss, then pushed him firmly back a step.

Troy stared.

"I'm very glad to see you, but that was silly and you left me on my own and Linh would punch you in the arm, but hitting you doesn't feel right," she added, her affection and frustration that his behaviour had endangered him and left her on her own colliding.

"I'm sorry," he replied. "It was. And I really didn't mean to leave you."

He wrung his hands, guilt plain on his face.

"Of course you didn't. So next time *don't*."

She softened it with a kiss on the cheek. She meant that. It seemed he was at the point where he needed to be told. And he did listen. She *did not* want him running off alone, unprepared, again.

"It was reckless. I just…" He trailed off.

"You hate being trapped," she finished for him. "I don't know if you're a bird made to spend most of its life in the air, or a loose cannon, but you're certainly not built for staying put."

She smiled. Some of the guilt and pain left his face, smoothed away by a smile.

"It's probably a good thing you didn't have to spend three days underground," she added. "It wouldn't have done you any good, whereas I managed. Did anyone else make it?"

Troy's face fell and he took a deep breath. "Linh's not here," he replied.

Fiona sighed. "She'll do better on her own than either of us."

"I'm still worried about her," he said. "Prince Maharl hasn't heard anything about her from his rebels. We think she must have been captured. Ruarnon too."

Fiona bit her lip. It had been three whole days since the sorcerer scattered her friends. Anyone who hadn't turned up since, with so many soldiers searching for them… part of her wanted to fight the idea her best friend was a prisoner, but the rational part knew it was the most logical possibility.

"Mic's coming," said Troy. "Lenaris and Mawana made it too, but we think Ruarnon, Mayrun and the guards got captured."

Michael jogged towards them and surprised Fiona by reaching to hug her back as soon as she reached for him. He wasn't big on affection, but they did like each other.

"I hoped you'd find your way to safety," she said.

"I didn't," Michael said with a smile. "Troy did."

Fiona's mouth dropped open.

"He likes to pretend he's not responsible," Michael added quietly, but loud enough for Troy to hear. "But he can be."

"Don't worry," Michael added seriously to Troy, "we won't tell anyone."

Troy grinned and Fiona smiled proudly. Maybe she could forgive him for running off, if he'd rescued Michael from the wilderness.

"Fiona!" Mawana called.

He smiled and embraced her tightly, then Lenaris greeted her.

Fiona smiled at them all. After the chaos of the ambush, she hadn't expected so many of her friends to make it to safety. But it made the fact Linh hadn't harder.

Weariness made Fiona's feet drag as Troy led the way to Joharlen's farmhouse. Michael eyed her with regret and Troy gazed into the distance. They all felt Linh's absence, especially now the three of them were together.

"Apparently she was behind me, but we were being chased by guards and I didn't see her," said Michael, his gaze downcast.

"I should have stayed atop that hill," Troy said darkly. "And not followed Mawana."

"And I should have told you to come back, instead of riding with you," Fiona told him firmly. "Only Linh remembered herself and didn't let hope distract her."

"And she's the one paying for it," Troy added bitterly.

"Don't beat yourself up," said Michael. "I could just as easily say I should have noticed her and slowed so she could catch me up and you could have found us both, but I didn't."

"It was chaos by then," said Troy. "Which is my fault."

Troy winced. Mawana was poking him in the back. "If you keep blaming yourself my friend, I may have no choice but to keep doing that until you stop," he said in what almost passed as serious tones, until he grinned at Troy.

Fiona smiled when Troy returned that grin. Troy looked up to Mawana. Mawana not blaming him ought to help dig him out of the pit of guilt he seemed stuck in.

"And I have good news, that arrived just after you ran out to greet Fiona," Mawana told Troy. "Joharlen received a letter from Tor. Ruarnon's coming. They made it back to the fleet on their own. They're sailing north and should arrive at a Galvation harbour further west in four or five days."

Troy slowly shook his head. "They made it back *to the fleet?*"

"Do we trust the letter?" Michael asked.

"It has Ruarnon's official seal, which they left onboard the Iylena," said Lenaris. "Unless Narz has captured the fleet, it's from Ruarnon."

Everyone smiled. The Iylena's approach felt like home coming to Fiona. And when Ruarnon joined them, proper negotiations with the Galvations would begin and they could find out how to help Linh.

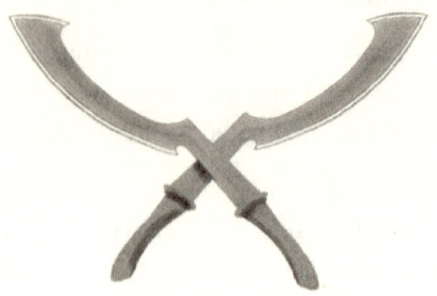

CHAPTER 14

PLANS AND MAGIC~RUARNON

Ruarnon supervised magic shield practice on the Saeron's decks. Their news the stormfront was real made the soldiers who believed it nervous, but ultimately more determined. Some didn't believe. Ruarnon was concerned about those soldiers.

While their ships waited for news from Lenaris or Mawana, Ruarnon encouraged soldiers in their training, until the winds picked up and thunder rumbled in the distance. Lightning flashed at the edge of the cloudbank. Thunder rumbled again. The nearest clouds deluged a heavy shower of rain, dimpling the sea and deafening everyone on deck.

"It's real!" a soldier shouted over the downpour. "The clouds are real!"

A section of cloud broke away and drifted sideways, trailing rain. Other clouds broke up from the stormfront, raining heavily. One blew over the fleet, soaking soldiers and sailors staring in awe. Even those who 'believed' Ruarnon were awed to see their belief proven.

Eventually the sky above cleared. Showers of rain became lighter and the cloudbank became clearly visible further away, now a lighter shade of grey.

"Yes," they announced, projecting their voice to carry across the Tarlahn and two Zaldeaan decks, "those clouds are real. King Narz has found a way to bind them, but his power is crumbling at the edges. The sky is returning to Erhmun, its rightful master and it makes way for Esira to shine through."

"What can we do against it Benevolence?" asked a nearby soldier, his eyes wide.

"We cannot oppose power like that, but we do not need to," said Ruarnon. "Cloudy skies are no obstacle to access prisons or armies. I have travelled safely under them. It is only here at their edge that violent storms are a danger. With more storms, you will row ashore under clear skies and move swiftly beneath the edge of the cloudbank on land. If that makes you nervous, I suggest you return to shield magic practice and hone your defences."

Ruarnon managed a smile. Some soldiers smiled in return, others nodded gravely or stared, while a few young people returned eagerly to shield magic practice. Tarlahn magic shields flashed over three ships, smaller than usual, some shrinking, fading or vanishing instantly. Ruarnon praised soldiers, encouraged those whose shields shifted erratically, then rowed to Governor Iagl's ship, where soldiers stared at the stormfront, or at small magical shields shifting erratically.

"We have never faced power like this," Iagl said quietly, as Ruarnon climbed from their boat suspended beside the main deck. "But I have an idea. Does your Benevolence fancy a duel?"

Governor Syenne had warned them that Iagl was skilled with a blade but so was Ruarnon. They nodded and Iagl had his soldiers make room. Ruarnon and Iagl drew their swords, bowing and circled each other. Iagl tested them with probing strikes, prompting parries and footwork. Ruarnon stayed on the defensive, watching Iagl carefully.

Iagl launched a series of attacks, each stroke flowing into the next. Ruarnon shifted their stance to meet the strokes. Iagl pushed hard, smiling as Ruarnon matched him. Ruarnon smiled back; here was an opponent against whom even Lenaris would struggle.

"What does one do when one is the best swordsmen in one's kingdom?" Iagl wondered aloud, pausing his assault. "Find a worthy opponent in another, it appears."

He launched another series of attacks and Ruarnon loosened up, fighting with an instinctive rhythm against familiar and unfamiliar attacks, until Iagl paused again. "But can my men do the same?"

"It appears my Tarlahn subjects can," Ruarnon replied, nodding to the shields forming on their Tarlahn ships. "Are the Zaldeaans their equals?"

Iagl smiled and they exchanged another flurry of blows, pivoting, blocking, parrying, probing and lunging.

"I am undoubtedly equal in skill," Iagl replied, meeting Ruarnon's eyes. "Perhaps my men shall prove the same."

They exchanged another round of blows and Iagl nicked Ruarnon's forearm. Ruarnon nicked his shoulder instinctively, making Iagl smile. Only when they paused did Ruarnon notice shields forming around them, large ones, which flickered or faltered at first, then began to stabilise. Uncle Omah's words came back to them; "If one of your subjects can see you, you are on stage."

Ruarnon smiled, realising Iagl was an effective leader as well as a skilled swordsman.

The rest of that day, and the next, storms broke out periodically, and Ruarnon continued to encourage, praise and push their soldiers in training, and train with Iagl. Their soldiers developed a grim determination about skirting Narz's powers, acknowledging that was all they needed to do, and trained hard to be equal to the task.

Ruarnon wondered how Commander Octharl was preserving morale, when his army intended to battle the power that bound leagues of clouds before them head on. Then the first letter from land arrived.

Tor,

We have succeeded in ways unexpected, involving regrettable separation. The freedom of others will be the first desire. It will require you to go to my husband's uncle's side via those who call our leader

Prime Ruler and involve aiding our friend's relative and their companions.

Lenaris, via Mic.

Ruarnon lay the letter on the table in their cabin for Companion Tor and General Takanis to read.

"Kahorn's side is west on our continent," Takanis added, "and as the North Landers call your Benevolence 'Prime Ruler,' I assume Lenaris wants us to sail north to western Galvatia if the letter is not a forgery. Can your Benevolence be certain?"

"It refers to 'Mic'," Tor replied, "the name by which only Troy calls Michael; a subtlety I would not expect an imposter to incorporate."

"Writing in riddles to preserve the secrecy of the message sounds like Lenaris," Ruarnon added. "I presume she suggests the western coast is a better base to launch my expeditions."

Ruarnon rowed to Octharl's ship to discuss it with the Timbalen Commander. Octharl stood tall on his foredeck, and was broad and square jawed, with piercing blue eyes and a perceptive, lined face.

Octharl froze in his seat when Ruarnon confirmed that Elite Guard scouts had been captured. He relaxed a little on hearing that Narz's only known response was to send out Zaldeaans to capture Ruarnon's party.

"I am not sure if he delays in attacking us because he is busy interrogating my scouts, or if he waits for us to make the first move," Octharl mused. "Whichever it is, things may move very quickly for my fleet from here.

"But I will send Elite Guard with you. Until we know where King Narz's forces are massed, it would ease my mind to position Elite Guard off the western coast too. I shall send General Imphin on my behalf, now his surveillance is complete, to represent me in Galvation negotiations. Depending on King Narz's movements and the outbreak of war, the Elite Guard may assist the prison breaks."

Octharl organised a Timbalen scout ship and Elite Guard packed and began boarding Ruarnon's ship. When the scout ship had set sail and the Elite Guard were ready, Ruarnon nodded to captain Dargeth.

The Iylena's sails were set, and she began to sail away from the fleet, north along the coast.

Cries rose up from the deck. Sailors and soldiers pointed back to the Timbalen fleet, which was becoming indistinct, without being far away enough to shrink from sight. It blended into sea and sky, disappearing altogether, drawing exclamations across the deck.

Ruarnon shook their head on witnessing the magic that concealed the fleet.

"What are we sailing into?" Tor asked them.

"A place unlike any most Tarlahns have been," Ruarnon replied.

But with the Timbalen fleet vanished, contact with Karmarn established and Ruarnon's ships setting out to meet the Galvation resistance, their expedition had truly begun. With Narz aware of Elite Guard scouts and knowing an invasion force must not be far behind them, Ruarnon fiercely hoped they could plan fast enough to attempt their rescue before the impending war broke out.

They sailed beyond Galvatia's burnt coasts, past green forests under bright blue skies, well wide of fishermen's boats, leisure craft and life as normal in an unknown northern kingdom, in a several-day trip to the western port city.

Ruarnon left General Takanis with the fleet and travelled with Tor and General Imphin in Prince Maharl's carriages through healthy farmland, to Joharlen's farmhouse. Mawana, Lenaris, Michael, Fiona and Troy met them in the carriage, and Lenaris updated Ruarnon on what they had learned since they were separated.

Two men greeted Ruarnon at the front door. The younger, whose ordinary features could belong to anyone, introduced himself as Lord Joharlen, and the older, his brother, as Prince Maharl.

Joharlen's eyes were dark and slightly bloodshot, while Prince Maharl stood tall and proud and greeted Ruarnon confidently, reminding them of Emperor Yarath. Ruarnon sincerely hoped Prince Maharl was in a better emotional state.

"Our spies report that Keepers of the Peace are pursuing a traitor sorcerer denouncing King Narz and spreading stories of the damarian invasion of the Zaldeaan Realm," Prince Maharl said, as they sat down to dinner, with Lenaris, Mawana, Troy, Fiona, Michael and Tor.

Troy and Fiona smiled, but only one sorcerer being mentioned made Ruarnon worry about the other.

"A captive I released in the east," Ruarnon replied. "That was my condition of his release."

Maharl's eyes flared with surprise and a hint of awe.

"Did your Benevolence bewitch him?" Joharlen asked.

"No. I made them see the brutal man King Narz becomes when he is frightened, a man I presume you know too well."

Joharlen bowed his head.

"You certainly convinced him," Maharl replied. "The Keepers are anxious about not having caught him yet and speculate that many sorcerers have been put off by his stories, whether or not they believe them. He has sown seeds of doubt in Tiama and is now in Arveta. My people say Zaldeaan guards on patrol gossip about it whenever they think their superior officer cannot hear them."

Ruarnon nodded. Betrayal by his own probably shocked Narz. Ruarnon just hoped it didn't unhinge him the way meeting Narz's sorcerers had unhinged Emperor Yarath.

"How did your kingdom face King Narz alone?" Tor asked Maharl.

Regret made Maharl's face sag slightly, then it was blinked away.

"With great difficulty. There has been little point asking the nearest southern kingdoms for aid. King Narz manoeuvres subtlety in the South Lands, infiltrating them with sorcerous law keepers, whose loyalty is to him alone. The southern kings fail to perceive this, noticing only a reduction in crime because Keepers are efficient, and mistaking the happier public mood for an increase in their own popularity. By the time King Narz moves into the open and the southern kings realise he rules them through his Keepers, I fear only the God Kings will rival him in power."

That was the kind of cunning the letters persuading Kyura to war had shown. Was this Lord Vye's influence?

"My friends tell me many of your soldiers are imprisoned in the Forest Prison, with my friend Linh," said Ruarnon, "while the captains and King Narz's opponents are in Fang Mountain, with my best friend's father. Meanwhile, my cousin runs the Forest Prison. I have personal interests in both prison breaks I presume you intend to carry out."

"Magic is our greatest barrier," Maharl replied. "Sorcerers guard both prisons. We have tunnelled most prisoners out of the Forest Prison ground floor, but the corridors are watched by sorcerers, and we cannot infiltrate the guards. We need people on the inside."

"I suspect the sorcerers who watch the prisoners are also watching my cousin," said Ruarnon. "His rank as captain masks the fact he is a hostage to ensure my uncle's co-operation in supervising the Zaldeaans patrolling your kingdom."

Maharl eyed them thoughtfully, while Joharlen frowned.

"Unfortunately," Ruarnon continued, "King Narz has two thousand Zaldeaans garrisoned in Azula, Tiama and Arveta. If the Zaldeaans patrolling Galvatia flee, they risk exposing their garrisoned comrades to torture or death."

Maharl's eyes grew dark. "Azula is crawling with sorcerers, many of whom support King Narz, and Tiama and Arveta are little better. Trying to free those soldiers would be folly. Unless you plan to invade Azula."

Ruarnon breathed carefully. The Timbalens weren't ready to reveal themselves to the Galvations yet, or their intention to invade Azula. "Then it appears our first task is to liberate the prisoners in the Forest Prison, and to capture my cousin and the Zaldeaan prison guards."

Maharl frowned.

"There is a way to combat sorcerers," Ruarnon added. "I suspect there will be many practical challenges, but the ability to wield magic should be of substantial aid, specifically use of sleep magic."

"How is it King Narz has angered magic-wielders in the east? I would have expected him to seek your allegiance."

Troy scoffed, then flushed when the prince eyed him critically. Ruarnon explained their parents' and Companion Pamoran's abductions, the damarian invasion and abduction of the Zaldeaan army.

"The Zaldeaans did not resist King Narz with magic?" Maharl asked.

"They do not know magic. However, my friends from the jungle do and we learnt it through them after King Narz's attacks."

"You are sorcerers?"

Maharl eyed Ruarnon worriedly, and Joharlen gripped his sword hilt.

"No," Ruarnon replied, meeting Maharl's eyes.

"Impossible," Joharlen protested. "Only sorcerers can wield magic! We have known this for centuries!"

"The Gods' Blessing in battle," said Maharl. "I wondered if the feats we sometimes perform in battle, which defy ordinary explanation, were magic. If in moments of desperation we tried to wield it, and some of us succeeded."

Joharlen eyed his brother in alarm. "You believe this?" he asked. "After all the centuries we have opposed sorcerers and the corrupting influence of their power, you believe we could *all* have that ability?"

"That is not how it works," said Mawana. "Sorcerers *are* different. Their ancestors have trained in wielding magic for centuries, strengthening their abilities. My people have long practiced shield magic, and we are stronger than Ruarnon, who is gifted, but has spent less time practicing."

"Show me," said Maharl.

"You want them to perform magic in here?" Joharlen asked, his posture rigid.

Maharl nodded. Ruarnon nodded to Mawana. Joharlen stared in horror at the white dome shield which appeared over the table. Ruarnon watched Maharl's gaze trace the dome intently.

Was it wise to teach them magic? How could they overcome centuries of fear, mistrust and hesitation in time for the prison breaks?

"Would you like to touch it?" Mawana offered.

Joharlen looked worried, but Maharl reached upwards, pressing his hand firmly against the dome. It didn't budge. He shivered and withdrew his hand.

"How do you do it?" Maharl asked, his intent gaze impossible to read.

"Concentration," Mawana replied. "We learnt shield spells in a peaceful place without distraction."

"You can *all* produce shields?" Prince Maharl asked, a strange light shining in his eyes.

"Yes," Ruarnon confirmed.

"Then why could you not shield yourself against the sorcerer when the patrol scattered you?"

"We did not wish to alert King Narz to the extent of our powers yet," Ruarnon replied.

Maharl nodded. He drew a deep breath, closed his eyes and raised his hand before him. Joharlen's mouth dropped open, as Maharl's palm turned white, pushing against something flat. He nodded and lowered his hand.

"You have used magic knowingly?" Ruarnon asked, registering the colour draining from Joharlen's face.

"Yes," Maharl replied, his gaze distant. "In earlier times everything happened so quickly. I could not be sure. But when I led the retreat beside the damars…"

"You shielded your soldiers," said Mawana.

"I must have. My best people tried to haul the wounded away, and their guards were being overwhelmed. But the front line of damars stood hissing until my men lifted the wounded, giving the guards time to secure their retreat. I started shaking, let go of something, and the damars surged forwards. I should have realised I was not powerful enough to be… but I was afraid…"

"You feared you were a sorcerer," said Mawana.

Joharlen took a deep breath, and said to his brother, "I do not blame you... But you should have told me. I knew you worried, and it troubled me."

"Why are you so scared of magic?" Michael asked.

"For all that legends of the Sorcery War dwell on the Gods," said Maharl, "on the corruptive influence of the evil Chaos, and the divine intervention of the Creator Gods in the form of the Guardians, the fact remains the massacres, enslavements and endless wasteful battles were carried out by ordinary people granted extraordinary power, corrupting them utterly. Many on this continent choose to forget that sorcerers are human. That King Narz and the God Kings of the Far South who treat their subjects like game pieces are still people, and the only thing that separates us is the ability to wield magic."

"You feared your ability to wield it?" Michael asked and Prince Maharl nodded.

"The atrocities of the Sorcery War were not only committed by sorcerer-kings like Narz," said Joharlen. "There are stories of slaves gaining sorcery powers and using lightning, which they considered a godly power, to murder their masters' families. Their vengeance for the brutal way sorcerers had treated them was legendary, until greater atrocities committed by kings caused memory of them to fade.

"And here we are, many of our people imprisoned, or enslaved by King Narz, and you offer us magic. What is the point of liberating our people if magic corrupts us and we become its prisoner instead?"

"I have no doubt that our fear of the corruptive power of magic is why so few of our people realise they can wield it," Maharl added.

"You fear the worst of your natures, and how the ability to wield magic will affect that part of you?" Ruarnon realised.

Maharl shuddered and Joharlen sighed. They saw magic as the enemy of peace. Given the damage it had done in the Sorcery War, and to their kingdom, Ruarnon could understand that.

"I think you fear too much," said Ruarnon. "I am Heir Ruarnon, Regent of Tarlah, King of the Zaldeaan Realm, Prime Ruler of the Northlands. I wield magic, and I have ruled my people's former enemies for over half a year. I sent my people to the Realm to ensure crops were planted and harvested. I negotiated with Zaldeaan Governors and left them in power, ending a succession war and bringing peace and stability. Power is not evil in itself; it is what you do with it that is good or evil."

"And how are we to know that we will overcome its corruption and wield it justly?" Joharlen asked, looking pale, almost ill.

"Prince Maharl, are you corrupted by commanding an army or controlling a treasury?" Ruarnon asked. "Is the power of a ruler so utterly different to the power of magic?"

"I have never seen it in that light," Maharl admitted. "Magic appears more terrible because of the destruction it has caused; but King Narz is not extremely dangerous because he is a sorcerer. He is extremely dangerous because he is an emperor."

"When we think of powerful people who wield magic, we think of King Narz, or his ally Lord Tarz," Joharlen added.

"Is there no one else?" Fiona asked.

Maharl looked dumbfounded.

"But we have always thought…" Joharlen objected.

"It is one of only two explanations…" Maharl replied.

There was a pause. Then Maharl said, "We have never viewed her as such, but there is one, a great queen, in the north. And she is of the kindest nature… Unwilling to fight, even to help us…" he trailed off, frowning.

"A sorceress queen who's a kind ruler?" said Troy. "There's your proof. If she can do it; so can you."

"We always assumed she had another power. Sometimes I suspected Queen Ziliene was a Guardian," said Maharl.

"But you suspected that because you couldn't believe a good person was also a sorcerer," Michael challenged.

Maharl eyed him sharply, then nodded. "I will need strict laws governing use of magic if we use it."

"If you do not; your people may be useless in our plans to free your subjects in the Forest Prison," said Ruarnon.

Prince Maharl's eyes lit up and he smiled gratefully. "Then it appears we have an alliance."

Ruarnon smiled. "We do."

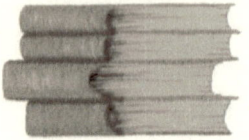

CHAPTER 15

TIME STOOD STILL -LINH

L inh sat with her back against a stone wall. Once upon a time a wooden floor to sit on and a stone wall as a backrest would have been uncomfortable. But she couldn't spend all day standing, walking, or lying on the rectangular pile of straw on her left that served as a 'bed' in this place.

A breeze wafted in through the barred window behind her and she breathed in deeply. It could be cool at night, there being neither glass nor window shutter. But was there anything better in a place lacking flushing toilets or showering facilities, than fresh air blowing in from mother nature? She couldn't go to nature, but it could come to her.

She smiled, as a butterfly flapped lazily through the bars and around the cell. Pazi and Sharma ceased practice fighting to watch it, ensuring they didn't harm this pleasant distraction from prison life. Even reflective Captain Shafar looked up from his thoughts, in his corner, watching the white winged insect flutter lop-sidedly about their cell.

All four of them watched as it paused for a second on a bright button on Sharma's shirt, then took flight when she laughed. It turned, but on finding no more appealing colours in the dull room, it fluttered back through the window.

Linh sighed. Visitors were such a rare novelty. The false Luveras Priestesses were a gift; the only different faces Linh got to see aside from her three companions and the two guards who delivered their meals. And the false priestesses brought news of the outside world, not that there was much to report. Minor raids. Rebels dodging patrols — again. Rumour the southern armies were stirring and that Narz would soon be at war with more enemies.

Anything new, anything that brought colour or variety to Linh's world was to be cherished. Because this was all there was now. This hard stone floor, with patches of straw to sleep on. The windows that brought blessed light and allowed her and her companions to still experience night and day. A stone corridor going down to guards who obeyed orders not to speak or communicate with them in anyway. A dull, quiet place, where life was plain, monotonous.

Linh turned to watch as Pazi and Sharma resumed their bare-handed practice fight. Captain Shafar looked down, deep in thought, and their cell returned to its normal state of near silence, but for the gentle patter of Pazi and Sharma's bare feet as they paced, leapt and all but danced around each other's attacks across the cell.

"Will you join us?" Pazi asked, noticing her studying them and perhaps spotting a change in her expression.

"I'm not very good without weapons," she replied, eyeing his wiry strength warily. Sharma was reasonably solid for her biological sex and both were relatively skilled with hands and feet.

"Have you something better to be do with your time?" Sharma asked playfully.

Linh smiled and stood. They began rotating as a three, each person watchful of the person left and right of them. Linh ducked Sharma's blow. Sharma leapt Pazi's kick. Linh leapt Pazi's kick and stumbled.

"Pot!" Captain Shafar cried.

Linh looked over her shoulder and swore, then ducked Sharma's blow and leapt under it, away from the curtain concealing a chamber pot no-one wanted anyone to knock, nor disturb the contents of. The intense smell ought to have warned her. Had she got used to it by now? Or had her sense of smell died from overexposure? Neither was a problem.

"Supper," Captain Shafar called, when Linh, Pazi and Sharma were all sweaty and breathless from their practice and all sporting at least three bruises. Linh had worried about both, but she knew Sharma trained because she refused to let the smell of sweat stop her from adding variety to her daily routine. Pazi said the same about bruises. And after five boring days with nothing to do but watch, Linh had given in today.

She suspected she would every day from now on. She had to do something to retain some level of fitness and strength. It might even let her work off steam and forget that she could no longer walk more than twelve steps in any direction without hitting a wall.

All four of them stepped against the back wall, as a pair of guards approached, one carrying a tray with four bowls of gruel in it. Linh's stomach rumbled. She didn't know why. The stuff had little flavour. She wasn't sure what it was. She suspected she didn't want to know. But her body still craved sustenance as much as it always had. And they were only served breakfast and supper, so she hadn't eaten for hours and was always hungry by this time, having still not quite got used to skipping lunch.

The first guard lowered the tray before the bars separating them from the freedom of the corridor, keeping an eye on all four inmates, while the second lifted the bowls through the bars, placing them on the floor one at a time. No one moved to attack either guard. They had no chance to escape, and attacking the people who fed them wasn't clever, but apparently some prisoners who hated being confined to a single room had done so, hence the routine of standing back when meals were delivered.

The guard keeping an eye on them inclined his head to Shafar, who returned the gesture. The guards never spoke, and the man who placed their meals in the cell always avoided looking at them, as if it made him uncomfortable. But there was something reassuring about one guard acknowledging the captain as a human, while all four stood, filthy and smelly, their cell stinking from chamber pots only emptied at dawn and dusk.

If one of their guards, a man who could leave this floor, this building, who was free to go outside, could nod to her cellmate like he was human, ignoring the stink of everyone's daily existence, then there was hope. There was hope he wasn't the only one like that. That Coroth did care. That the Zaldeaans weren't any keener on being their jailors than Linh and her cellmates were about being prisoners.

The second guard placed the fourth bowl on the ground, and both turned and retreated. She and her cell mates took a bowl each and sat in a circle on the floor, as they did for every meal.

"May this meal be our last here. May the govern$or trip and break his neck." Shafar intoned the ritual blessing over their meal, then they all began to eat.

Governor Mandarkin was universally hated in the prison. On her second day Shafar had spoken about it too soon and she was sure one of those guards overheard him as they retreated with the tray, because the man had smirked, before continuing on his way.

Linh copied the others, spooning the worryingly grey, soup-like substance into her mouth and swallowing, trying not to think what could turn safely edible food that colour. Hunger helped. As did her hope that her friends and Ruarnon had figured out where she was by now and were doing something about it. Because she was going to count every day she had to eat this muck, and if they left her to do it one more day than was necessary, they were going to hear about it!

The usual wonderings flit through her mind. Had they found the rebels yet? Had they persuaded Prince Maharl to work with the false Luveras Priestesses? Were they planning to break Galvations at ground level and above out of gloom and monotony yet?

There wasn't much point wondering. The false Luveras Priestess had reported only yesterday that nothing had changed. Surely Ruarnon could persuade Maharl to change? If they weren't locked up here too, or on Fang Mountain. Best not to think about that. But even then, Lenaris was stubborn enough to try something, and Mawana reckless enough to back her. Surely someone was trying to get her and her new companions the hell out of here. She sighed.

"Thinking unhelpful thoughts again?" Captain Shafar asked.

He had a talent for giving her and the others space when they needed it, despite that they shared the same room, and the only time they were out of each other's sight was when someone drew the curtain to use the chamber pot. But he also seemed to know when it was best to pry, and cut off someone else's thoughts before they made themself unhappy.

"Yes. I'm normally not the restless one. I'd use Troy's strategies to help me, but they usually involve horse riding, or swimming in enemy waters or doing something reckless in open spaces. None of it works in here. And it feels wrong not wielding magic. We trained every day on board the Iylena during the voyage. It became second nature to me. I had to fight my instincts to wield it so hard when the soldiers cornered me. And now I can't risk using it or sensing whatever enchantments the sorcerers here are casting... it feels like my sixth sense has died. Like I'm mourning it."

Pazi and Sharma listened keenly to her words. No-one they knew had ever talked about magic, until the skies became filled with dark clouds and the rain never fell. And until they came here, and guards always arrived in cells when people tried to break the locks, responding so quickly the Galvations realised a sorcerer was spying on them and could immediately send guards running.

They both seemed a few years older than Linh, but had a youthful eagerness to hear about magic. Linh suspected many Galvations could rapidly overcame whatever misgivings they had about magic, if someone offered to use it to get them out of this bloody place.

To her surprise, the captain replied, "That makes sense. Before the war, it was my job to train levied soldiers in spear and sword. And before that, I trained the regular army. Unable to lay hands on either weapon now, it almost feels like I have lost a limb."

Linh nodded. "I'm sorry, for everything you've lost."

"Let us not mourn too much. Some things are lost for now and may be mourned a little each day we are here. But they are not lost forever. We must learn to wait until we can have those things again. Learn to wait until our freedom returns."

Pazi and Sharma inclined their heads. Linh sighed and did the same.

Linh wasn't used to waiting. She was used to fighting. If people didn't listen when she spoke, she shouted at them. Her will to defy things had always served her well. But there was nothing she could actively do about her present situation. She couldn't shrink herself to fit between the bars or fly out the window. And the guards who delivered meals didn't carry keys to cells, so even if Pazi and Sharma trained her well enough to take both guards down with her bare hands, it wouldn't get her out of here.

She could rail against it. She could yell and scream and punch the air. All yelling would do was hurt Pazi, Sharma and the captain's ears, and perhaps worry the Galvations in the cells sealed by wooden doors and stone walls along this corridor, who would not be able to see what the shouting was about.

In prison, regulating your emotions wasn't just about your own wellbeing, it was about the wellbeing of everyone who could see and hear you. Captain Shafar had told her that on her first day, and she was beginning to understand how right he was.

That was why she looked for the positives in everything. It was a distraction from her anger. From her helplessness. Though sometimes it made her cry, because she had been inspired to adopt that strategy because she was sure it was what Fiona would do if she were here. Linh missed all of her friends, very much.

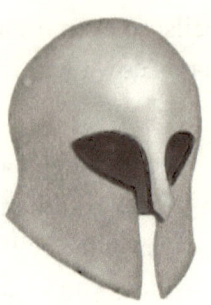

CHAPTER 16

PRISON AND FREEDOM-TROY

T roy resisted the urge to groan, or stand up and pace around Joharlen's kitchen, as Maharl spent eternity outlining intentions for the prison break to Ruarnon, their companions, Joharlen and General Imphin.

"If my soldiers only put guards to sleep from the tunnels and ground floor," said Ruarnon, "we risk guards on higher levels alerting Coroth before we reach them. We also risk magic-wielding soldiers outside being attacked by Zaldeaans and damars. If there is a sorcerer, we risk them informing King Narz of our attack. Have you a way to enter other levels of the prison?"

"Not that I trust," Maharl replied.

"What do you not trust?" Ruarnon asked.

"A group of women I believe are imposters, who have access to the entire prison. I believe they intend to dupe us into alliance, infiltrate our rebellion and sabotage us, as Companion Karmarn has attempted."

Troy's attention span failed. He exited the house via the front door and wandered along a dirt track through the nearest grain field to walk off restlessness, while his friends talked their way through a maze of obstacles. Why hadn't he thought of doing this sooner? Fiona could catch him up on the main points later and his restlessness would only distract Ruarnon or the others.

Two young men stood talking at a crossroad ahead, both wearing cloaks concealing objects that bulged suspiciously, one resembling a bow in shape. Why would farmers need bows? Umarinaris didn't seem to have rabbits or other introduced species of pest animal it was legal to cull. The young men talked in hushed voices, sounding lost.

They hushed as Troy approached. A woman approaching down an intersecting road paused, frowning at the two men and Troy.

"Ah, good afternoon," one of the young men said awkwardly to Troy.

"Hi," Troy replied, his casual greeting raising the other young man's eyebrows. "You look lost. I'd offer directions, but I only arrived recently."

The first young man's soldiers relaxed.

"Did you volunteer too?" he asked.

It was Troy's turn to frown. "For what?"

"But then… are you one of the visitors?" asked the second.

"You could call me that," Troy replied. "You don't mean volunteering in the tunnels? A sort of… liberation?" he asked, trying not to be too obvious, in case they were just clumsy farmers.

Both young men smiled.

The woman approached, then said in a hushed voice, "That was lucky. We don't normally discuss these things in the open. There's only one farmhouse in this area where innocent farmers won't be confused by such talk."

"I came from there," said Troy. "Everyone's planning."

The woman studied him. Damn. Even the rest of the resistance might not know about the large-scale prison break plan. These rebels might just be joining the basement break. Troy's impulsive tongue had struck again.

"I'm glad to hear it. Another week or so and we will have run out of locations we can access, and our operation will come to a standstill."

Troy's eyes lit up. He could spend the next week listening to planning, bored out of his mind and restless out of his body, or maybe he could help this lot...

"I don't suppose I could join you?" he asked. "Some of my friends might like to come to."

The woman considered him. "Can you fight damars? And do you have any weapons?"

Troy sighed. "We left our weapons on board the ship, but we've fought damars before."

The two young men stared. "We've only heard rumour of them in the west."

"What's it like there?" Troy asked, noting the cautious look the woman gave them.

The first young man smiled. "We are soldiers from the port city. We were garrisoned to counter naval attacks on Galvatia's west coast during the war, unaware that King Narz's army was approaching overland. For some reason, his clouds don't extend to the coast and while he captured two castles as his army advanced here, his soldiers neither reached nor disrupted our western coastline."

"Your people are *free* further west?" Troy asked, his grin spreading, as the woman smiled at his sincerity and both young men mirrored his smile.

"Narz seems less concerned about those of us too far away to act as bases for his enemies to invade him from," said the woman. "And we suspect his magic isn't powerful enough to threaten us any further west."

So anyone who escaped the war *did* have somewhere to live and grow their own food, even while the eastern side of Galvatia was drought stricken...

"When do you leave for the prison?" Troy asked. "I'm Troy, by the way."

"I am Captain Anar," said the woman. "We leave at dawn. It is a two-day ride. The digging will not be pleasant," she cautioned. "The prisoners are underfed, unwashed, and the tunnels are cramped, smelly and dark."

"I'll let my friends know," Troy replied. "But I'm up for it."

She bowed her head at his words, and the young men smiled their goodbyes. Troy walked back to Joharlen's farmhouse, where he waited impatiently for a pause in discussion to tell his friends.

"Anar was not exaggerating," Maharl cautioned, when Troy finished. "The prisoners in the ground floor will be raving to disguise sounds of digging, and to keep guards back so they do not discover empty cells or tunnels."

Troy swallowed nervously. "It achieves more than I will sitting here," he asserted.

"I'm not sure how I feel about working in cramped tunnels," said Fiona.

"Or feigned madness," Michael added.

"The main tunnels are larger, more like regular corridors," Joharlen reassured them.

"I don't like missing out on what's being said here," said Michael.

"Our planning will take some time," Ruarnon informed them. "We will do everything we can to conceal the Forest Prison break, but King Narz may learn of it swiftly, so we must plan and be prepared to carry out Fang Mountain Prison Break soon after. That will involve climbing a mountainside under the gaze of sorcerers, requiring General Imphin's expertise and will take a great deal of planning."

"Meaning our next likely chance to see Linh could be weeks away," Michael concluded. "And we just might be able to free her if we get lucky with where she's imprisoned. I'll go with you."

Fiona eyed Troy sternly. He lowered his gaze, unable to meet hers. She smiled and took his hand. She really did seem to forgive him for running off, she just seemed to be channelling some of Linh's force of will, which he probably needed to keep him in line. He smiled, feeling Linh was with them in spirit.

They departed on horseback early the next morning, carrying their packs, and wearing the swords Familon had given them on Myleth Island belted at their waists, Ruarnon having brought them ashore. Troy found the volunteers at the edge of the road, wearing quivers at their hips and bows strapped to their packs. The two young men nodded in greeting and Captain Anar addressed everyone.

"To our new volunteers," she said, "welcome. We are about to begin a two-day ride to the prison. We shall sleep in a cave off the riverbed, then leave our horses with my companion in a secret tunnel. Most of the ride will be down a riverbed beside land patrolled by Zaldeaans. If I hear a patrol, I shall raise my arm, signalling a halt. If I do that, stand against the riverbank and wait in silence. When I angle my arm forwards, you may continue walking."

Troy didn't mind the start of the ride, in sunlight, under blue skies, but soon they moved beneath static dark clouds, down a riverbed beside barren plains. The ruined land made him resentful, as did the fact there was nothing he could do to change it. He tried to ignore it, staring into the distance without seeing as they rode through a post-apocalyptic deadscape.

The next day, when the greenery of the damar-infested forest came into view, it occurred to Troy that this was his chance to strike back. He couldn't do anything about the drought, but he could free the farmers levied as soldiers in the prison ahead. Maybe they could take their farming further west.

Captain Anar halted the volunteers at the tunnel mouth, and they dismounted, handing their reins to a single rebel, who bound the reins together.

"The damars will be sleeping while we move through the forest," Captain Anar addressed the volunteers on foot, "but their sense of hearing is excellent, so we must move quietly. Their sense of smell may also wake them. I want all bows strung now and every archer to walk with bow and arrow in hand. If you think you see a damar, wait until it hisses or screeches, otherwise you'll waste arrows. Aim for their heads and necks, as only lethal wounds will stop them. Any questions?"

"We've only got swords," said Michael. "How do you want us to proceed?"

"Keep to the middle," the captain replied. "Leave the damars to us if you can, otherwise, stab at their throats. Slashing is too dangerous in dark and confined spaces."

Fiona grimaced and Troy's stomach twisted, but they knew how brutal savage damars were.

Captain Anar led the volunteers up the tree lined riverbank at nightfall. They moved down an animal trail under a quarter moon. Troy tread carefully, struggling to dodge bushes and branches he could sense rather than see, and trying not to snap sticks on the dark ground. But the prospect of waking savage damars didn't wipe the excited smile off his face. He was taking part in an *actual* rebellion.

Fiona smiled at him, probably reading his mind.

Michael halted. Troy almost walked into him. Fierce hissing rose from the left. Bowstrings twanged, as a damar rustled through the undergrowth. A second short figure moved in shadows on the left, followed by a third, fourth and fifth. More bows twanged. Troy tensed and drew his sword, but silence followed the last twang.

He listened intently as he followed Michael round shadowy branches again, until Captain Anar signalled a halt before an earthen mound. She reached for the mound and knocked against wood. Knocks sounded inside, and she knocked a second pattern, then the mound swung inwards and admitted her.

Troy ducked through the concealed doorway after Michael, into a low earthen tunnel. Torchlight flickered against the ceiling, revealing sawn off tree roots, while more roots grew down tunnel walls. He followed the others further in, where the walls widened, and the ceiling retreated until he could stand upright. Scaffolding spanned the roof periodically, like an old-fashioned mine.

Muffled voices travelled towards him. He frowned and Fiona whispered, "The ground floor prisoners are feigning madness to conceal prisoners are missing, remember?"

Something in Troy tightened at the reminder. He wrinkled his nose as the scent of unwashed bodies and a rarely cleaned toilet drifted towards his nostrils.

"Breath through your mouths," Michael advised, as the stench built in intensity.

They reached a fork, and the captain led them right, past small, narrow tunnels. Cries of people raving travelled down the tunnels and the stench almost made Troy gag. He hated to think what the toilet situation was. Clearly human rights and sanitation weren't respected in the cells above.

"Do you think Linh's doing ok up there?" he asked.

"She's probably scalding the guards ears off for the poor sanitary conditions," Michael replied with the hint of a smile.

"I hope her temper doesn't get her in trouble," said Fiona.

Troy squeezed her hand. He suspected Linh's tendency to resist anything she didn't like extended even to poor living conditions.

"I hope she's in the level above," said Fiona.

Troy did too. It would be fantastic to get her back, without waiting for Ruarnon and the others to finish planning and without the sorcerers who watched over the prison corridors delaying her. It was a long shot, but Troy couldn't fight his hope.

"There shall be a great light!" a voice overhead declared. "A star shall shine yonder and the hero will come forth! With Guardians at his right hand, he shall lead us to freedom and drain all sorcerers of their powers! And the stars shall rain from the heavens to rejoice with us!"

Troy smiled, reminded of Life of Brian, his father's favourite film.

"Why Queen Marius! I thought you was dead forty years gone! What a fool I've been! Prince Rugan isn't dead either? Splendid, I'd love to see him!"

Troy's face fell. How long could you fake hallucinations before your mind started to manufacture them? He shivered.

The smell of unwashed bodies hit his nostrils harder then before. A pair of filthy men crouched on the left side of the tunnel, grinning. Fiona smiled at them, seeing straight through the grimy faces and tangled hair to happy men underneath. Maybe it was worth listening to feigned madness, to witness happiness like that when people were freed.

Captain Anar stopped before the end of the main tunnel.

"You will be relieving the diggers either side of us," she told the volunteers. "The ropes in each tunnel will help you measure the approximate length to dig. There is a wooden triangle to lean on to measure the angle of your digging.

"The tunnels are too narrow for torches, and you may need to crawl back down to catch your breath and push out loose soil. End of shift tunnel diggers!"

Grubby people crawled out of narrow tunnels on all fours, the largest commando crawling. How narrow were those tunnels?

"I'll go at the top," Troy offered, hoping it wasn't too tight and not wanting to trigger Fiona's discomfort of enclosed spaces.

"I'll go next," Michael volunteered.

Fiona smiled her gratitude. It struck Troy that she needn't have come. She could have stayed above ground, in the open air, admiring the clear sky above the farmlands that still made Troy smile because of its novelty. But these people needed help. So here she was, discomfort or not. That was Fiona.

"I suggest you unbuckle those swords," said Captain Anar. "They'll only get in your way."

Grubby rebels passed pickaxes or shovels to volunteers while Troy, Fiona and Michael unbuckled their swords. Troy took a pickaxe, while Michael took a shovel. Then Troy crawled into a tunnel on his left.

It was a claustrophobic's nightmare. The curving structure soon blocked torchlight from the main tunnel. He groped blindly in the dark, until his pick struck the end of the tunnel. He reached for the wooden triangle, rested his left arm on it and wielded the pick by feel, periodically pushing loose soil to Fiona or grabbing the rope to check the tunnel's length.

The air became stuffy, Troy's muscles cramped and within minutes he crawled out for fresh air and stretched. Eventually, he managed to block out confused shouting from above, and got into a rhythm with his digging.

Over the next four days, Troy worked determinedly, helping to free thirty-five smiling, grimy faces from most basement cells not blocked by the dungeons. The stench of unwashed bodies and unemptied chamber pots still made him nauseous at times, but the smiles on faces as people crawled towards freedom made it worthwhile.

With each day that passed, each shift that ended, he scanned every grimy face as everyone marched to the bedrolls they slept in, in the main tunnel. Every night he hoped to see Linh, but every night Fiona's sigh marked her absence. The tunnels gradually extended towards what Captain Anar said was the end of the basement corridor above. Each cell dug into left fewer for Linh to be in. Until the fifth day, when there was only two cells left.

Long shot or not, Troy was pacing the corridors trying to burn off his restlessness before everyone else rose for breakfast that morning. His heart rate was up, he couldn't help hoping, and his whole body buzzed with nerves that the last two tunnels could lead to Linh, and they may not.

He reined in his mood when Captain Anar rose, and she didn't seem to notice his clenched fists when she said, "You three may take one of the last tunnels."

Fiona smiled at the chance to free the last prisoners, until Ruarnon and the others put their main prison break into action. Escapees climbed up tunnels nearby, to shout their ravings up through cracks in the cell floors and hopefully disguise any sounds the last two dig teams made breaking into the last two cells.

Troy moved determinedly, his arms tense as he dug with the pick. His chest buzzed. Hope of seeing Linh and dread of leaving her in miserable living conditions for an unknown number of days more warred inside him. He didn't realise his digging angled more sharply upwards than the triangular tool, until his pick ground against stone sooner than expected. He frowned.

Adrenaline began to hum in his veins. He took as deep a breath of the stuffy, smelly air as he dared, then levered the stone up with the pick and sat it on the floor above. Dim torchlight shone down through the gap. Troy cleared more dirt, then levered a second stone. He caught a third stone with his left hand and pushed both up onto the floor, then a fourth. Time to free some more people. Hopefully Linh!

He raised his arms and stood waist deep in the stone floor, checking if the prisoners needed help moving, as some were poorly fed and too weak to climb unassisted. A stone wall rose opposite him. The prisoners must be behind him.

He pushed off the floor, lifted his legs out and stood in the prison cell. The first wall met a second, which ran along empty floor to a third wall with a door in it. He frowned, as Fiona's head and shoulders appeared, and he wondered how the cell could be empty.

They'd heard prisoners raving from the tunnels moments ago. But now it was silent. There were no prisoners in sight and none speaking to him. Something was wrong.

His breath caught, as he turned past Fiona. There was no forth wall. The floor stretched on to an archway with torch brackets on both sides, more corridor, another archway with torches, a third corridor and a distant guard standing with his back to them.

Troy gestured Fiona frantically down. But she sat on the prison floor frozen, her eyes widening as she stared down the corridor.

"They've stopped," said a distant guard.

"Maybe they've lost their voices," the other replied.

"You don't think… they've gone and… killed 'emselves do you? Captain Coroth won't like that."

"I suppose we better check, not that I fancy goin' closer."

Silence fell.

"Get back in, I'll seal it," Troy whispered frantically.

Fiona took a deep breath and lifted her legs out of the tunnel, then stuffed the first two stones back into the floor. Troy's heart hammered against his chest, as she shoved the third and fourth stones into the gap, sealing them on the wrong side.

Fiona looked up, her face white with fear. She motioned him determinedly to the nearest wall, pressing herself against the wall opposite.

She didn't think they had time to climb back without being seen. Getting caught in the tunnel would lead the Zaldeaans to the freed Galvation prisoners… but how did Fiona and Troy hide.

Troy leapt to the wall, as both guards walked towards them. He pressed his back against stone and blinked sweat out of his eyes. Torches cast a band of shadow where archway met wall in narrow corners ahead. Fiona was creeping into the shadows opposite. Troy crept into the shadow on his side. He tried to press his stocky frame further into a corner, and to not breathe so loudly, as footsteps drew nearer.

"Nothin' to see with all them doors shut," a guard said from the other side of the arch.

"We could peer through the flaps what let's food in."

"An' get kicked in the face!"

"But we gotta see if they's alive."

"Alive! We're alive alright you son of a whore! Rotting down here every day! A plague on both your houses! Lots of plagues; rats and locusts and everything that oozes and pusses and eats your crops, and your innards!"

Troy jumped at the voice from behind the door he'd tunnelled to the wrong side of.

"Happy now?" asked the second guard.

Troy exhaled deeply as their footsteps retreated. That had been far too close.

A new voice made him freeze. "What are you two doing away from your post?"

"The prisoners stopped raving. We thought they might be dead."

"Did you check?"

"One of 'em started yelling again."

"Only one? Do you know how much corpses stink? You get back down there and check *every* cell!"

There was a loud smack and a yelp, followed by two sets of hasty footsteps. *Every* cell...

Troy turned to Fiona. She was deathly pale and reaching for the torch burning in the wall bracket near her. It was desperate, but their swords were in the tunnels and fire might distract and threaten the guards long enough for them to make a run for it.

The guards' footsteps approached. Troy tensed, as they stepped past him.

"You've been at the inn again haven't you?" a woman's voice yelled from the last cell. "Cavorting with drunks and whores! I'll tan your hide, you useless lump!"

Why so hostile? Had she realised Troy's mistake? Was she trying to put the guards off ? She certainly put Troy off.

Both men froze at her words.

"Shall we just wait 'ere a bit longer and tell 'im we searched 'em all?" the first guard asked.

Sweat trickled down Troy's back, as he waited for them to leave. His fingers itched for the torch burning on his left. Enemies were close and he wanted a weapon.

"I'm going fire walking! There'll be flames of every colour and they change colours when you walk through. It's ever so much fun! Are you coming?" a young woman's voice called.

Both guards trembled. They met each other's gazes and spun on their heels. One cried out, staring at Troy. The other pointed at him in shock. Fire moved behind them. Troy seized a burning torch, as a guard tried to duck Fiona's torch. Fiona's guard overbalanced, hit his head against the wall and was knocked out. He slumped to the floor.

Troy waved a torch at the remaining guard, who stared as if he'd seen a ghost. Troy kicked him in the shins, hard. The man went down, cracking his head on the stone floor.

Both guards lay silent. Troy sucked in air.

"Well Poso? Filain? You incompetent fools; did you check the cells or not!?" the nasty voice demanded.

There was a pause, in which Troy held his breath.

"Answer me, you toe rags! How dare you ignore a superior officer? I'll have you flogged!"

The man's voice was coming nearer. Fiona motioned Troy to the arch. He backed up, as she crept to the opposite side. Footsteps approached. Then they halted.

Troy took a deep breath and peered around his arch. The man stood two corridors before him, frowning at Fiona's hand returning a torch to its bracket.

One shout and he would have every guard in this place on them.

Instinct kicked in. Troy charged at full sprint. The guard opened his mouth, frowning in confusion. His eyes jerked to the burning torch in Troy's approaching hand and his flushed cheeks drained of colour. He reached for his sword and fumbled to extract it from its sheath.

Troy took the torch with his left hand and punched the man in the nose with his right, jarring his wrist. The guard went down heavily, and Troy stood panting and nursing his sore wrist. The collapsed man didn't move.

"Bleardmoor, what are you fussing about?" called another voice.

Troy's heart sank. They weren't escaping through the tunnel. This guard would check their corridor too. He could wait here to be caught or make an unlikely bid for freedom...

Troy ran, fuelled by adrenaline. A slight echo scuffled behind him. Fiona ran too, her mouth a grim line, her eyes wide. She really was channelling Linh tonight.

They reached the end of the corridor without meeting guards, taking the final steps slowly. Troy peered around a corner, along a corridor lit by periodic torches, at four hulking guards standing either side of open double doors. Two dozed where they stood.

Something tingled. Fiona was wielding sleep magic. Troy stared. They could put the guards to sleep, walk through the front door and release the magic. No one would know who they were, or that they hadn't escaped from the cells.

Troy slowed his breathing and focused on sleep, making the third guard's eyes droop and the fourth blink heavily. He held tight to the magic, focusing on chests rising and falling slowly, until both men relaxed into the wall. Then he stepped around the corner, gripping the magic tightly in his mind.

A man in bronze armour stared at him from inside the doorway. Troy froze. The man's eyes drooped, and he didn't speak. Fiona had him. But Troy's guards were stirring. He tried to grip the magic particles scattering against his will, but his heart hammered against his chest. He was too stressed to project sleep.

"Upstairs!" Fiona whispered, moving past.

Troy hurried after her, onto the wooden spiral staircase on his right.

"Huh?" said a guard behind him.

"Escaped prisoner!" a second shouted.

Pressure hit Troy's sleep magic. He released it, knowing the door guards were awake.

Heavy footsteps approached the stairs behind him.

Troy puffed his way up to a landing. Fiona kicked a guard's feet out from under him and his head hitting the ground silenced him. Troy stared, then shouldered the second guard into the wall. He punched the man's jaw and swore at the pain flaring in his wrist. The man's head cracked against the wall and he slumped.

Doors barred the entrance to a corridor. Guards shouted on the other side.

"This way!" Fiona hissed, clambering up the next flight of stairs.

Troy took a deep breath, braced himself and stayed put. Maybe she could hide somewhere. If he could buy her time. He didn't want her captured because he'd screwed up. *Again.*

One of the doors before him swung open. He kicked it shut. A man cried out. He shoved the second door into a second guard. A burly man pushed between them, drawing his sword. Troy lunged with his left hand and the man backed away from his burning torch. Troy kicked the guard's legs out from under him and he toppled, taking the second guard down.

The first guard stumbled through the door, and Troy drove the base of the torch into his temple, toppling him, then hurried up the stairs. When he reached the top, an empty corridor spread before him.

"Fiona?" he whispered.

There was no answer. Footsteps on the stairs below drew rapidly nearer. A breeze blew against him from his right. The corridor in that direction ended at a balcony. A balcony meant outside…

Two guards jerked out of their doze, as Troy's footsteps thudded towards them. Another pair stood on the left, barring stone steps leading down. Hope flared within Troy.

The second set turned alert gazes towards him and his adrenaline surged. He rode it, charging the first pair of guards with flaming torch raised. Their eyes widened with fear and one fumbled to draw his sword.

Troy swung the torch, and both jumped aside. He kept running. The other two had drawn their swords.

He swung his torch at them. A blade cut its burning end off. Troy threw the wooden end in the second guard's face, and seized the first's sword arm, twisting it, as he kicked the second guard. The first guard jerked free and Troy overbalanced, stumbling.

A blow caught him on the jaw and he fell. The top stair met him swiftly. The side of his head collided painfully with the ground and everything went black.

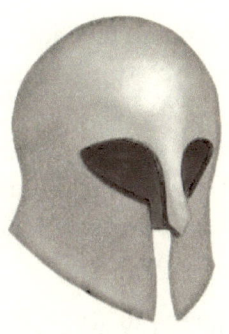

CHAPTER 17

PRISON-TROY

Troy blinked to clear blurred vision, ignored his pounding headache and wondered why he was wet. He sat in a chair. Trying to move his hand to wipe the water away revealed that both hands were bound, and his right wrist was sore. He looked up into the eyes of two strangely overlapping, young blonde-haired men, with stern authority on their faces.

"Where are we?" he asked, as his head throbbed, and the torchlight glared into his eyes.

The young men frowned and asked, "You do not know?" with one voice.

Troy frowned. His head spun and his stomach roiled.

"Are you ill?" the young man asked, his double frown deepening.

"Seem to be," Troy replied.

A vague image of a tunnel came to mind and something about Linh. "Do you know where Linh is?"

"You came looking for a friend?" the young man asked, his features wide and incredulous.

"I think so."

That didn't sound quite right, but Troy's throbbing head deterred further thought.

"Who are you working with? How did you get in here?"

Who was this man? Best not to mention tunnels. They were incriminating.

"Who are you?"

The young man looked puzzled and blurred, but there was almost only one of him now. He looked thirty odd, but his youthful authority reminded Troy of Ruarnon.

"Do you know Ruarnon?" Troy asked.

The man's eyes widened. "You are Tarlahn. What are you doing here? Ambassador Drake returned to Tarlah."

Who?

"Nicked off without the rest of us did he?" Troy asked, feeling like he had been left behind in… King Narz's continent in the West. It was coming back.

"So you broke into a prison? Looking for this Linh. Our new prisoner, Linh Mai."

Troy smiled. "That's her."

The young man's eyes narrowed. The ambush came back to Troy, and something about chasing Michael through wilderness.

"This is the boy?" a cold voice asked.

The young man sat up straighter.

"His fall appears to have addled his mind Governor," the young man replied. "He claims to be a Tarlahn guard abandoned by Ambassador Drake, seeking a captured friend."

"How did you get in?" the Governor demanded; his eyes boring into Troy.

"By magic," Troy replied, seizing the best lie he could think of.

"Preposterous," the man snapped. "The rebels fear magic!"

"What rebels?" Troy asked.

A third, burly man stepped into view and backhanded him. Troy's head snapped aside, and pain stung its way across the right side of his face. He flinched, as the man backhanded the other cheek. But the stinging pain cleared his head, jolting his memory.

He needed a good lie to protect rebel tunnels under the prison. Adrenaline exploded inside him and his heartrate sped up to counter the threat.

"Do not lie to me," the Governor said coldly.

Troy took a nervous breath, looked his inquisitor in the eyes and said, "It was a test. They wanted to see if they could get me inside. They wanted to know if King Narz's sorcerers could stop them. The God Kings," he breathed, looking at the floor.

He cried out as a second stinging blow struck the right side of his face.

"Get me a whip!" the Governor ordered.

"They have gateways," Troy whispered, clinging to his story and trying to ignore his own trembling. "Magic gateways. They made an archway appear on the rocky plains and I stepped through, and I was here, downstairs. They said the Faeron helped them."

There was a sharp intake of breath. Whoever this prick was, he knew about the Faeron. Maybe he wasn't angry because he thought Troy was lying. Maybe he was scared.

Troy winced, as rough fingers gripped his stinging face and held it close to eyes that burned with a hate so strong it made him shiver.

"What did this gateway look like?" the man whispered.

Troy ignored the taste of bile his throat and recalled real Faeron gateways.

"The archway was made of stone, with a golden swirl of writing I couldn't read around it. When I looked through it the writing glowed. I couldn't see the rocky plains anymore. The plains were either side of the archway and the sky was above it, but through the archway was a dark, torch lit corridor."

"And these men who made the gateway, where are they?"

"They stayed on the rocky plains and told me they'd kill me if I didn't keep walking down the corridor. I fought off three guards and then there were too many, so I tried to run."

"And they didn't bother testing if they could get you out again?"

"Why would they care about me?" Troy asked. "I'm Tarlahn, a left behind guard of Ambassador Drake."

"How do you know about the God Kings?"

"One of their attendants made me lie down bowing before them," Troy invented. "And then told me I wasn't allowed to speak to His Divinity."

The man's eyes were still boring into Troy's. He was shivering uncontrollably now.

"And this friend of yours?" the man asked.

"I hoped to find her before I got caught, but I couldn't see through the doors. In my country prison cells have bars you can see through."

"Why was a God King using sorcery to get a man into this prison?"

"He said this was the bastard sorcerer's prison. That's all I know."

"Illegitimate use of sorcery. They plan to assault His Worthiness because he offends their sensibilities?"

"They seem the sort of people who step on anyone they don't like," Troy invented, inspired by the burly man standing beside the governor.

Troy gasped, as his aching face was released. It stung more sharply than the dull ache of his head.

He spent several moments sitting in fear. The prick seemed to believe him, but what would they do with him?

"I have much to think about," the Governor announced. "And you are far too soft Coroth," he added contemptuously. "Alert me immediately if anything else happens."

"Yes Governor," Coroth replied.

The Governor left the room, taking the burly man who functioned as his fists with him.

Troy's eyes widened. What about Fiona? Didn't they know about her?

Coroth studied him, but his next words were addressed to a soldier who entered the room with a whip.

"Get rid of that and get Tars up here to bandage his head properly," Coroth ordered.

The soldier left, and Troy tried to think through the pain. He was alone with Coroth, Ruarnon's cousin. How did he say what Ruarnon would want him to know? There had to be something meaningless to the Azulans that Coroth would associate with Ruarnon.

"It's nearly the Festival of the Gods," he said. "The King will make sure everyone attends this year, even the Urai."

Coroth stared in amazement and Troy was glad Linh and Fiona paid so much attention to Tarlahn culture and that he recalled some of what interested them.

Put it together, he willed. Ruarnon's coming for you and they've got shield magic.

"I think you need to rest that battered head of yours."

Coroth didn't understand... or were spies listening? With a stroke of inspiration, Troy raised both forearms in a Tarlahn salute. Coroth's jaw dropped, then he returned the gesture, meeting Troy's eyes with a mix of hope and worry.

Footsteps approached and Coroth's arms dropped. Troy lowered his arms, just before a gruff looking soldier entered with a bucket of water and a roll of clean bandages.

A wet cloth soothed Troy's face, but stung part of it, and he stared at how much blood was wiped from the side of his head. The man bandaged his head, his hands were unbound and Coroth ordered, "Take him to cell three hundred and twenty-one."

Tars nudged Troy forwards, and two guards outside flanked him, while Tars led him. Troy heaved a sigh. He'd spent four days freeing people from prison, and his reward was getting his head bashed in, his face slapped off and locked in a cell. He cracked a smile, even though it stung. The world was a funny place sometimes.

He was led back down a flight of steps, wondering with every step what had happened to Fiona. No one mentioned her, and the nasty bloke had behaved as if Troy was the only person he had to question.

He blinked. The guards were leading him down a corridor on the top floor of cells, through archways lit by torches like the ones he'd fled earlier. They marched him to the end, where one face widened in surprise.

"Linh Mai," he said and his face split in a grin, cut short when his cheeks stung.

"Troy!" Linh cried.

"Is that perfume you're wearing?" Troy asked. "I can smell it from here, latest from Paris is it?"

Linh laughed, a deep throaty laugh he'd rarely heard. It made him smile until tears came to his eyes.

Her face fell, and she gasped when Troy neared her cell. His cheeks felt puffy and the bandage round his head was probably bloody.

The guards unlocked the cell and pushed him in wordlessly, locking the door behind him and left without a word. Linh eyed his face worriedly.

"Wanted to know how I got in," he replied solemnly. "I had to tell them about the Faeron gateways."

Linh chortled.

"You know, the ones the God Kings are experimenting with to infiltrate places King Narz has sorcerers guarding?" Troy added.

Linh laughed again. "I believe mine and Michael's brains are rubbing off on you," she said, making him smile. "Did they believe you?"

"That nasty prick of a governor bought it hook, line and sinker."

"And the others?" Linh asked, her posture tense.

Troy took a deep breath. "All safe, except Fiona. We were digging prisoners out of the ground floor, and we accidently dug up the corridor."

Linh's eyes widened.

"And I promised her I wouldn't do anything silly again," Troy realised. "Shit. She's going to be mad."

Linh frowned. "Fiona, mad?"

Troy smiled. "She's been a bit firmer with me since I went on an ill-advised expedition while we were hiding in Galvatia City."

He didn't add 'and it was for my own good and thanks to both of you,' but the way she frowned at him with the hint of a smile made him wonder if she guessed.

"Fiona got ahead of me on the stairs. I don't know what happened to her. Coroth and the prick of a governor didn't mention her."

"I think we're going to get along with you too," a youth in the cell behind them said approvingly. "We got caught after the battle, but none of us has been Questioned."

"I don't recommend it," Troy replied, his pained smile mixing genuine humour and nerves. He could still see the hate and fear in the Governor's eyes, feel the burly man's hand striking his face and hear the Governor shouting for a whip. He'd never been so close to serious trouble…

It was time to be more careful. He couldn't stand being as organised as Linh, but this was where the line of easy-going and ADHD restlessness and impulsivity crossed into a world of pain, and he didn't fancy that. It was time to give his luck a well-earnt rest, wake up his common sense and somehow force his impulsivity out of the driver's seat. He had no idea how to do the latter, but the idea of actively pursuing common sense made the rebel in him laugh.

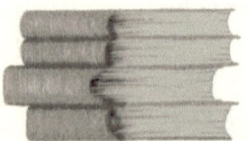

CHAPTER 18

LUVARAS PRIESTESSES - FIONA

Fiona raced up the stairs, her heart pounding faster than her feet. She'd never been anywhere near this level of trouble before. Never tasted such adrenaline. It was kind of… fun? She smiled.

Troy took things to extremes. He wasn't a subtle guy and this was outside everyone's comfort zone, but the adrenaline hit of racing up those stairs with guards not far behind… she kind of understood why Troy had taken off through the gardens.

It should have been her removing the last stone. She'd known there was a risk he'd get overexcited, carried away and miscalculate, *again*. But there was something infectious about his excitement, his smiles. She'd wanted to let him have that moment. And now it had produced her own adrenaline pumping, flying by the seat of her pants experience. It was quite a ride, but she fancied getting off, before the runaway carriage crashed.

She reached the top of the stairs and paused to take in her surroundings. A stone corridor wound away on her left, a second on her right. A cool breeze drifted from the right corridor, carrying a snatch of conversation. Figuring it led to a guard tower, Fiona hurried down the left corridor. Pale light appeared ahead. She tried to stop, but momentum carried her around the corner. A tall young man, in a light silk shirt and dark pants, with a sword at his hip and an oil lamp in hand, closed a door on the right. He turned, revealing an intelligent gaze.

Fiona dropped her head automatically, not just out of shyness, but because she feared he would see straight through her. If she avoided that, she might be able to pull a Troy with the gate guards. She dropped a curtsy and bowed her head.

"I didn't mean to startle you," the young man said quietly, turning to the handle and opening the door as if he was expecting her. "You must be from Black City," he said kindly. "I did not mean to be here this late, so you are not interrupting. In you go."

Why did he want her to go through the door? Black City was a slave labour city… did he think she was a cleaner? And he was leaving. Fiona bowed her head Tarlahn style and entered the room, her heart drumming against her chest.

"Best if you keep this shut," the young man added. "Some of the guards are not very polite when I am not around."

He closed the door, and she scanned the room. There was a wooden shelf on the left, a desk before her and a small table on her right, an office. He *did* think she was a cleaner, which made more sense than an escaped prisoner roaming an upstairs corridor. She smiled. So this was how riding adrenaline, improvising and pure luck felt? It *was* fun to be Troy!

She tensed as footsteps thudded, but they didn't near the office. Had Troy turned towards the guard tower? She reached for the handle, but more footsteps pounded up the stairs.

"What is going on?" the young man's voice demanded, full of authority.

"Escaped prisoner Captain. From the ground floor. He came upstairs."

Fiona's mouth dropped open. 'Prisoner' not prisoners? Hadn't the guards seen her?

"Search the outside stairs!" the young man ordered.

The castle had *external* stairs?

Many footsteps moved down the corridor, likely between Fiona and Troy. She bit her lip. She'd never manage to get round all those people to join him.

Several men cried out. Faint sounds became returning footsteps.

"Take him to the spare office," the young man's voice ordered.

Fiona's heart sank. A few footsteps moved past the office door and another door creaked beyond.

"How in Creation did a boy get loose and climb three flights of stairs before you caught him?" the young man asked, the anger in his tone making Fiona cringe. "Governor Mandarkin will be furious. You will spend a week in the basement cells, to remind you that if you do not desire Galvation status, you must do your job properly!"

He must be Captain Coroth, Ruarnon's cousin, the prison overseer. And the governor would be King Narz's Galvatia overseer, which meant Troy's unintended visit had got the Zaldeaans into serious trouble.

Silence followed Captain Coroth's outburst. Fiona held her breath, waiting for a soldier to admit that a girl had been seen on the stairs. None of them did. The silence stretched, and she wondered if they hadn't seen her properly, or perhaps lacked the guts to admit a second escapee had got past.

"Obin; lock them in the first basement cell on the left," Coroth ordered.

Footsteps clunked on the wooden stairs. Fiona tensed as the sound moved towards the door she stood behind. But they continued softly past, and another door creaked open and closed. Was Coroth questioning Troy in a spare office?

Fiona took a deep, long breath. If she put Coroth, his guards and guards on the outside stairs to sleep with Troy's help, could they walk out? And creep back through a damar-filled forest to the farmlands? If she didn't try, if she maintained the act of a servant and tried to walk out alone, unarmed… was that *more* dangerous?

She sighed. She might be able to sneak through the forest without damars hearing, but Troy's distractibility made him clumsy. Damars *would* hear him sooner or later. Without weapons, they'd have to outrun the creatures. Could they do that?

Her heart hammered against her chests as she opened the office door and stepped into the corridor. On her right, a pair of large guards stood either side of a second door.

"Come child. Guards make poor company," said an imperious female voice.

Fiona jumped. A woman in hooded purple robes stood at the top of the stairs. She smiled knowingly and turned, descending the stairs almost as silently as she must have climbed them. Fiona had a hunch that antagonising this confident stranger by questioning her wishes was a bad idea. She took a nervous breath and followed the woman onto the stairs.

The woman paused a few steps down and whispered, "Did you come from the ground floor tunnels? Was there an accident?"

How did she know? And if she saw it as an accident…

"Yes," Fiona whispered, assuming the woman was linked to the resistance. But why hadn't Prince Maharl mentioned her?

"Put this on, follow my lead and do not speak when guards can overhear us," the woman instructed, handing Fiona a purple, hooded robe.

Fiona pulled the robe over her head and lowered the hood, then followed the woman downstairs, where guards on the landing eyed them nervously, one biting his lip, the other bowing his head. The woman ignored them. Who was she that they feared her?

On the ground floor, the woman strode towards double doors barred by four new burly guards, who swallowed awkwardly, one shoving the man next to him aside, another opening the door. The woman strode imperiously through and led Fiona across an open room, lit by moonlight shining through its barred front windows. A man at a desk on the right bowed as they passed, while guards barring the front door stood like statues.

The woman turned, leading Fiona down a corridor on the left and up a spiral stone staircase. They stepped off the stairs onto a landing of polished wooden floorboards. Along the corridor ahead, elegant metal brackets held oil lamps on walls painted with spiralling blue frescoes, an artistic depiction of wind.

Lamplight flickered beneath a door ahead. The woman Fiona was following opened it, revealing a dining table at which another woman in purple robes sat. The second woman eyed Fiona with interest, her wizened eyes kind, like a clandestine, cheery cult member. Who on Umarinaris were these women?

The door shut behind them, the first woman motioned Fiona to a chair and took her own seat at the head of the table. Fiona sat, and the second woman lowered her hood. She had grey hair, a kind, lined tawny face, given this seemed to be a secret order inside a prison, surrounded by damars.

The first woman also removed her hood, revealing red ringlets, and pale, freckled skin with green eyes, high cheek bones and a narrow, commanding face.

"She was hiding in the Captain's office, posing as a servant," the woman told her older companion. "Unfortunately, the boy was caught before I reached him."

"And that cousin of yours does not consider the resistance appropriate employment for women," said the elder woman, producing an amused smile from the red head.

Why hadn't Prince Maharl mentioned his cousin was *inside* the prison?

"What is wrong child?" the red head asked. "You must know who we are, even if my cousin was too prejudiced and afraid to accept our assistance."

"He mentioned 'imposters' who had access to this prison, but that was all," Fiona replied.

The red head rolled her eyes. "Then he is unchanged, despite his desire to free prisoners through tunnels beneath the ground floor. He is a fool if he thinks we have not noticed. How did you manage to infiltrate the prison?"

"By accident," Fiona replied, deciding the truth wouldn't give away anything they didn't already know. "We got careless because we were digging the tunnel to the last cell, misjudged the angle and dug up into the corridor. Will my boyfriend be ok?"

The red head sighed. "Is he clever, or a good liar?"

"Both," Fiona replied.

"Then Governor Mandarkin won't have reason to seriously hurt him before he gets whatever 'truths' your boyfriend tells him. No-one but Coroth may notice your disappearance, but making your boyfriend disappear after he was captured is more than we can achieve tonight."

Fiona bit her lip. She hated thinking of Troy in pain, but deep down she knew it would cause him more pain if it was her, or Linh or Michael in his place. She shivered and hoped the woman was right.

"Where did you come from? King Narz despises Galvations and we have become outcasts because the southern kings wish to avoid provoking him."

"The east, from the continent King Narz abducted the Zaldeaan army from."

"And Prince Maharl was delighted to offer you an alliance," the red head speculated, her gaze distant. "We were not so fortunate. I am Prince Maharl's older cousin, Lady Amina, former resident of the castle Companion Karmarn has made his residence. Laria," she motioned to the white-haired lady who resembled a kindly and stern grandmother, "formerly lived in the castle now converted to the prison on Fang Mountain."

"How are you still free?" Fiona asked.

"Laria's and our other companions' husbands were captured and imprisoned on Fang Mountain early in the war and our households were sent to Black City, but we were absent when war broke out, having purchased estates in Arveta, where we mingled with the nobility, posing as Tiamens.

"We learnt what we could from the inside and sowed seeds of doubt and fear of King Narz from within. Princess Amia knew of our plans, but she and her guards were slain as they fought off Zaldeaans approaching straggling families evacuating Galvatia City, so there are few left to verify our identities.

"After the war broke out, we remained in the south to learn about Luvaras Priestesses. They are commonly known as sorceresses in purple robes, and, like Luvaras Priests and The Dedicated, they have temples all over the continent, from which they convert people to worship Luvaras, the god of sorcery."

Fiona's mouth opened and Amina paused. Fiona didn't like to interrupt, but now Amina had given her the chance, she asked, "Who are The Dedicated?"

Laria smiled. "After the Sorcery War, sorcerers who did not flee this continent had no one to teach them how to control their powers. They were a danger to themselves. Over time, Luvaras Priests began training men. But sorcery power had been used to exploit and abuse many women during the war, and many women who did not feel comfortable learning magic from Luvaras Priests began learning it from Luvaras Priestesses.

"Over time, the way both orders taught magic became gendered. But there are more genders than male and female. And this influences not merely how those people style their hair, make up (if they were it) and clothes. It influences their behaviour too, as they often do not conform to or else are selective in conforming to expectations of men or women. This made the way they viewed, learnt and wielded magic more flexible, so they founded their own order. In time, it also embraced sorcerers who do not perceive Umarinaris the way many people do. People quick to make connections, or highly logical, with clear visions of right and wrong and uncensored speech, people with too much energy, even people with illnesses or injuries that prevent their bodies from operating the way most human bodies do."

Fiona beamed. A secret order of queer, neurodiverse and disabled sorcerers? Troy was going to have a field day when she told him about this.

"I know someone who'd like to join that order," she said in explanation to Laria's raised brow at her smile. "How did posing as Priestesses help you?"

"It was the perfect way for us to travel from our estates in Arveta to Galvatia, to enter this prison and Black City to 'convert' Galvations. We could show them the 'bounty of Luvaras', giving prisoners food from our estates, while the guards dare not watch closely. With our guise prepared, we sailed back to Galvatia and contacted Joharlen to offer our aide, but we came too late.

"Companion Karmarn had sent enchanted imposters posing as myself and my wife, and they led a raid on a convoy in which tens of rebels were captured. After that, Prince Maharl dared not believe I was who I claimed to be and declared that if I was, I would have returned sooner.

"He felt we had abandoned him. And he mistrusted the magical healings Laria's servants performed in this prison. Prince Maharl feared we were a genius plot of Companion Karmarn's, offering crucial allies to free prisoners, which would culminate in the capture of rebels."

Fiona's eyes slowly widened. It sounded like these false priestesses had been more open minded and smarter about Narz's rise to power and the threat of war. Like Maharl thought them too good to be true, compared to his humble resistance.

"If you don't mind me asking, you already guessed why I was here when you saw me in the corridor, so what do you want from me now?"

"We can escort you safely back to my cousin. I would ask you to reason with him on our behalf. We have access to the upper levels of the prison. We may even approach the rooms the sorcerers work in. He needs us to free the rest of our people from here, and Black City. We can help him liberate them all and move them out of Narz's control, if only the fool will listen to us."

Amina sat straight in her chair and her tone was calm. But Fiona detected the frustration in her voice.

"Has he truly rejected your help, just because it seems too good to be true?" she asked.

People always said that about scams at home: if it seems too good to be true or a random stranger contacts you with a prize for a competition you didn't enter —it was a scam. But this world didn't seem to have any equivalent to scams that were rife with digital technology back home. How had the fact Karmarn had deceived Maharl once made him too paranoid to recognise his own cousin?

Amina sighed. "Men here are foolish. They wear the crowns, carry the swords and believe they are the brains of civilisation. It is usually women working behind the scenes who are the brains, as is our case. But Maharl has shown little interest in women and Joharlen's relationships have all been with men. Both are acquainted with the traditional, official role of women as wife, mother housekeeper etc and neither knows our true roles as spy, strategist and advisor. Most successful Galvation men lean heavily on their wives —and take most of the credit. But my cousins are yet to understand that, so my friends and I remain in the category of things they fear and do not understand, alongside Narz."

Fiona's mouth dropped open. It sounded like the vague impression she had of the 19th and early 20th century west on Earth. But hearing about it as a present-day reality was something else. How did you reason with someone who was too prejudiced to recognize how clever you were?

Fiona shook her head. "It's a shame my friend Linh was captured by patrols. She's strong willed enough to make him see reason."

That was the problem. Linh wasn't here. Michael would help, if Fiona explained to him, but he'd be all cold logic, when it was Maharl's feelings that held him back. Fiona suspected it was Linh's force of will, her confidence combined with her passion that might be needed to push Maharl to overcome his life-long fears and trust these women. Could Fiona do that?

"My friends are staying at Joharlen's house," she said. "If you take me back, I can speak on your behalf. My friends will want your help in the prison break, and Prince Maharl may have to accept you, because his plans won't succeed without my friends."

"Then our meeting tonight is most fortunate," said Amina.

"It may be wise to tell her the rest," Laria said to Amina.

The two women exchanged stern, thoughtful looks until Fiona chewed her lip. Then Amina nodded and Laria explained, "Should the situation with the Far South grow any more volatile, we are considering conducting our own prison break without Maharl. It would be foolish for us not to work together, and his rebels could hamper our efforts if we do not. But we are wary of leaving our people languishing here, vulnerable for much longer."

Fiona shivered. "What's happening in the Far South?"

"The Princes of Bovey and Adriga recently swore allegiance to King Narz," Laria replied. "Like Narz, they pay Healers out of their private purses and the Healers provide services free of charge. It earns the goodwill of their subjects, which the usurper Bovey needs. They also employ Keepers of the Peace, whose reputation for justice and willingness to arrest nobility as well as commoners, and their skill in protecting nobility from assassins and theft, have also made them popular, generating more goodwill for Bovey.

"Adriga, meanwhile was concerned the popularity of Healers and Keepers would result in commoners abandoning their labour to flock to the health and safety King Narz's kingdoms offer. He employs Healers and Keepers to stabilise and pacify his population, and to place a solid ally, Narz, at his back.

"But we suspect the other southern princes' squabbles have ceased. Sceptical and untrusting princes are stalling negotiations with King Narz, because they see Healers and Keepers as a ploy to install sorcerers in their princedoms, through whom King Narz intends to rule by force. They believe the princes of Adriga and Bovey are self-serving fools, and we suspect these southern princes have formed an alliance against King Narz.

"They know Narz's sorcerers are few, inexperienced, undertrained and they may believe now is the best time to crush him.

"We have heard rumours of southern armies mobilising. We want our people out of the prisons and Black City before war overtakes these lands."

Fiona slumped and her gaze fell to the table. "The southern princes aren't the only ones," she said softly, explaining Narz's invasion of supposed Guardians in the Timbalen Empire, and the retaliatory invasion it had provoked.

"Mother preserve us," Laria whispered.

"They intend to initiate sorcery war?" Amina asked, her face paling.

"As they see it, they intend to finish one," Fiona replied. "Narz seems paranoid and bent on destroying them, so they've come to destroy him first."

"Two sorcerer armies controlled by frightened rulers..." Laria whispered. "Azula would be destroyed. Thousands would die."

"I thought Keepers weren't trained in combat?" Fiona asked.

Amina took a deep breath. "One of Laria's sorcerer-servants swore allegiance to Narz to spy for us. He suspects Lord Vye is recruiting and training a sorcerer army. If word reaches Narz that his 'Guardians' have come, he will fear them targeting his Keepers and Healers, and openly recruit sorcerers to counter them."

Fiona sighed. If lots of people appreciated the work Healers and Keepers did, people with magic craft may queue up to protect them. The Timbalens could face off against an army of well-meaning Poran's.

Tears sprang to Fiona's eyes. "We can't let that happen."

"Telling Prince Maharl his new allies will only make things worse will not go well with him," Amina cautioned. "Tell these Elite Guard not to attack."

But Fiona didn't know any... except the three Elite Guard she'd fought beside in the sewers of Timbala City. All three were here. They would understand. But would Commander Octharl?

Laria was eyeing Amina with an eyebrow slightly raised. There was *more*?

Amina sighed, then added, "For centuries, the God Kings of the Far South have claimed that sorcery power is evidence of their divinity, and that non-royal sorcerers are royal bastards, whom they have recruited, or else murdered. But the presence of Healers and Keepers in Bovey and Adriga will soon be known to God Kings. And when they hear of sorcerers peddling their skills to non-magic wielders, whom they view as sorcerers' subjects and servants by rights, they will be insulted. If they are farsighted, they will realise King Narz's Healers and Keepers undermine their claims to divinity, and the basis of their rule. If Narz's power and sorcerers continue to spread closer to the Divine Realms, I foresee war with the God Kings."

Fiona's heart skipped a beat. What would happen if this continent disintegrated into a four-way war, between three sorcerer armies?

"I'll do whatever I can to get you an audience with the Prince and Timbalen leaders," she promised.

"We will depart for the farmlands at first light," said Amina.

With a mass of new information and worries whizzing through her mind, Fiona struggled to sleep in the quarters the fake priestesses had claimed in the prison castle. Laria woke her at dawn, and she dressed hastily in purple robes, then followed the false priestesses and their servants to the stairs, trying to hold her chin high like them. The two false priestesses descended proudly, and guards hurried to open external doors and stepped back for them, determinedly averting their gazes.

The outside guards straightened as they walked past. Hissing rose. Beyond the stone steps, two horse drawn carriages waited, with guards seated atop them. At the treeline beyond, several damars rushed the horses. The guards atop the carriages loosed arrows and damars fell. The false priestesses ignored them and Fiona followed the women into their carriage, taking a cushioned wooden seat beside Amina, opposite Laria and two servant women.

The carriage window shutters were closed, letting in only cracks of daylight, but it looked safer than the mad dash Fiona had planned, if she succeeded in freeing Troy.

Amina handed out oatcakes for breakfast and the energy they provided allowed Fiona to question something else the false priestesses had said. "Laria, how did you end up employing sorcerers? I thought Galvations fear sorcery?"

"They worked on my estate near Fang Mountain," Laria replied. "They tried to hide their powers, but while my husband busied himself governing, I discovered what they were. They are well-meaning, shy and fearful of judgement, but having known them and their parents most of their lives, I trusted them and found better ways for them to serve us.

"My mother was a sorceress. She dismissed beliefs about sorcerers being Chaos spawn as 'talk of fools' and declared that if Mijora allowed us to come into being and then rejected us, then she is not worth serving. I deeply regret that Prince Maharl has not been so open-minded. Much of the hardships he has faced could have been prevented had he accepted the aid of sorcerers."

"He's learning," said Fiona. "He's accepting magical aid now."

Laria's eyebrows rose and Fiona explained that she and her friends were planning to use magic to aid the prison break.

"You do not fear magic?" the maid sitting on Laria's right asked.

"Magic itself?" Fiona asked. "Yes. Using it makes me nervous. But I fear meeting people who wield it powerfully against me a lot more."

"With Mistresses' permission," said the maid, "I would use magic to show you Keepers and Healers I have met, to draw your own conclusions."

"That is wise," Laria replied. "The Elite Guard *must* distinguish between Healers, Keepers and combat sorcerers, if they invade. Killing Healers would be a travesty, and Keepers roused in righteous anger may be more dangerous than sorcerers trained in combat."

Fiona shivered at the latter thought. Poran and Dargus had merely released damars against Zaldeaans in righteous anger. But on the field of battle against invading sorcerers, what would magic crafting people desperate to protect their own be capable of?

The servant focused on window shutters, and images began to appear; a paved stone laneway between city buildings at twilight, and a lone man with a pale, frightened face walking swiftly down it. Two figures blocked the lane. Two more stepped in behind.

"Where's the money?" asked a figure ahead.

"I... I don't... we only just opened the shop after the fire. We haven't had time..."

"Time's up," said the other figure, advancing in a menacing strut.

He fell on his face, as did his companion. Men behind fell too, and two men in red cloaks approached. The man fell onto his knees.

"Thank you!" he said.

"You will have to repay the debt," said the first red cloaked figure. "But the courts will allow you time to earn the money. And these men will be charged with intended assault."

"Street guards patrol Arveta at night," said the maid. "Some criminals do not yet realise even the darkest laneways are now patrolled."

The laneway blurred and vanished.

"Keepers are more fearless and effective than anything in Galvatia," said Amina. "They investigate crime thoroughly and are not convinced of the guilt of any party without substantial evidence. They have proven people innocent who, in Galvatia, would wrongly be found guilty. People of every class are now required to judge each crime, so that class-based arrogance, ignorance or prejudice does not dictate verdicts. King Narz has stripped nobility of their legal benefits, making all equal before the law."

Fiona shivered. That didn't sound anything like a megalomaniac unleashing damars the world over. It sounded like a revolutionary. And if that memory of the maid's was anything to go on, his legal revolution *was* making city streets safer.

Amina nodded to the maid, and Linh turned to the window shutters again, as more colours swirled and formed into a row of grand-looking apartments, with a domed temple in their midst. The viewpoint was from the street, looking towards the temple steps, down which a young man came bounding, and up which a group of people rushed to meet him.

"Oh Tamar! We feared we were too late! The Healers said you were at death's door!" a woman exclaimed.

The young man laughed. "Took me five days to recover from healing!"

The family embraced him and turned down the road, the children eagerly asking questions.

"Do they look funny? Do they use weird instruments to do magic? Do you think I could be a Healer?"

The double doors of the temple opened, and a dozen people in green cloaks strode down the green tiled steps, into a carriage, its doors painted with a tree.

"There is plague on Bovey's borders," Laria explained, as the colours blurred and vanished. "All Healers who can be spared are being sent to halt it."

Plague, among a population without modern medicine or vaccines, where plague probably ripped through populations, like smallpox when it first landed on Australia's shores. But Narz's healers were trying to halt it in its tracks… Just how much was Narz trying to change the world?

"Did King Narz build that temple?" Fiona asked.

"He has built Healing Temples throughout Azula, Arveta and Tiama. He built the first temples in Bovey and Adriga too, to serve as examples," Laria replied. "Narz uses taxes to keep them supplied, and Healers and Keepers are paid by the crown."

"Do *you* think Keepers and Healers are part of a plot to expand Narz's empire, seeing as they're all sorcerers loyal to Narz?" Fiona asked.

"I doubt it," Laria replied. "A man who desires power does not use taxes to pay for the upkeep of Healing Temples; he uses them to pay his army."

"There is also sinister evidence that Narz intends Healers and Keepers as ends in themselves," Amina added. "Did it not seem strange to you that not a single one is corruptible?"

Fiona shivered.

"Any whiff of corruption from a Keeper and that Keeper is removed. The same occurs with Healers who accept pay from people they heal."

"Flawed Keepers and Healers are not the only ones who go missing," Laria added. "There are rumours of sorcerers who use their powers to oppress others. We suspect that Luvaras Priests, Priestesses and certainly The Dedicated killed some, but we doubt it is coincidence that across all three kingdoms Narz has direct control over; they have been weeded out. They die in 'accidents', are poisoned by 'rivals' or taken 'hostage for ransom' and never seen again. Those in kingdoms Narz has recently come to control are investigated by Keepers and found guilty of breaking laws written to target them."

Fiona shivered more violently. Was Narz be trying to build a Utopia?

"The only exception is Lord Tarz," said Amina, "who rules a small kingdom between Azula and Galvatia. He is a self-serving tyrant, who taxes his people ruthlessly. We believe Narz tolerates him because he is the bastard son of a God King, who came north seeking a throne his illegitimacy denied him. His family would be deeply offended if he were murdered, so killing Tarz may risk open war with a God King. If he is wise, Narz will fear the God Kings using their bastard children to undermine his Keepers and Healers and assassinate him."

Fiona shook her head. She had heard of people who opposed the government's ideals disappearing before. Stalin's Russia came to mind. But this time Narz wasn't attacking potential opposition; he was weeding out imperfection within his own ranks and on guard for subterfuge. He wasn't just a dictator; he was an *idealist* dictator.

"What happens to people who disappear?" she asked.

"That," said Laria, "Is the strangest thing of all. We are quite certain that all sorcerers who abuse their powers are killed. But some corrupt former Keepers and Healers have been identified working as labourers, under guard, on Narz's private estates. Of those who oppose Narz, a few are unaccounted for, but most are in Fang Mountain Prison."

"One thing we have learnt," Amina said softly, "is that Narz is not so evil, and we are not as good as we once thought. Common people's rights are better defended, and they are happier and healthier under Narz than they were in Galvatia before the war.

"I think he truly believes that anyone who opposes him, his Keepers, Healers, or sorcerers, is a threat to peace. Opposition could prevent healing and engage Keepers in violent conflict, but the only spells he has taught Keepers to apprehend criminals are shield and sleep spells."

He *was* pursuing utopia, and prepared to enslave anyone he believed threatened it, because he felt it was justified …and necessary.

"I want our people freed," said Amina, "but if the Elite Guard defeat Narz; his alliance of five kingdoms will fail, three kingdoms will face a succession crisis because he has no family, and I worry what will happen to Healers and Keepers."

"Keepers, Healers and Elite Guard have a lot in common," Fiona replied. "I've met some Elite Guard who will listen to me. I'll try and track them down."

Her own words replayed in her head and she wondered how on earth she would do that. But the Elite Guard captain she remembered had been nervous of her friends' enchanted swords. Nervous of innocent sorcerers being murdered, the way those weapons had used during the Sorcery War.

Captain Rilmar and her companions would see the good in Healers and Keepers. Fiona could reason with them. Maybe Captain Rilmar could speak to whoever was in charge of the Elite Guard and sway them. Though what would happen if the Elite Guard Commander Octharl and the emperor's orders were at odds, she had no idea.

Fiona spent half the rest of the carriage journey wringing her hands and wracking her brains about what to say to Prince Maharl. Laria and Amina had advice, but she hoped to get to speak to Ruarnon first. With Ruarnon knowing what she knew, it would be easier for them to convince Maharl to trust Amina together.

Too soon, the carriage was rolling towards fields, then stopping down a cart track from a farmhouse. Amina, Laria and the maid wished Fiona luck. She took a deep breath, then climbed out and walked towards the farmhouse, her heart drum rolling against her chest. She could almost hear Troy telling her she was more than ok, and Linh telling her to put her chin up. She smiled and fought the desire to keep her head down or bite her lip.

If she wanted Maharl to take her seriously, she'd need to look him in the eye. She didn't like doing that. It felt like demanding people's attention, imposing on them. There were so many people to listen to at her house, so many siblings. And they all had important things of their own to say. She didn't like to take too much of her parents' attention. And her friends wanted to listen when she spoke. She wasn't used to insisting anyone do anything, except Troy, very recently.

By the time she reached the front door she could feel the heat radiating from her flushed cheeks and neck. She tried to ignore them and steeled herself as she knocked on the door.

It opened and she bit her lip, as Joharlen's face peered out.

"Are you well?" he asked her.

"Yes, I just…" why did it have to be Joharlen? True, it was his house, but couldn't it have been someone else answering the door? And now he was eyeing her expectantly.

"I need to tell Prince Maharl something important. And I know he won't want to hear it."

Honestly always seemed the best policy to Fiona.

Joharlen's gaze narrowed as he studied her closely. "Have you learnt of a new threat?"

"I know why his prison plans might fail and how they can succeed."

That had been Amina's advice. Focus on what mattered to Maharl. Then make what mattered to Fiona matter to him too.

"Who have you been speaking to?"

Was that just curiosity or was that quirk of his brows a sign of worry? Was she going to have to explain everything on the front doorstep?

"Is that Fiona?"

That was Michael's voice.

"Is it?" Joharlen called over his shoulder.

Fiona's mouth dropped open. "I've been gone for one night and you think I'm an imposter?"

"That's her voice," Michael called.

"But is it *her*?" Joharlen asked, looking Fiona right in the eye.

Fiona gaped. How could he think… what would Linh do? Fiona took a deep breath and forced her chin up to gaze upwardly into Joharlen's pale eyes. Then she formed a misty white shield between them.

Joharlen jumped. Michael stepped next to him in the doorway, staring.

Fiona bit her lip and Michael smiled.

"That's Fiona," Michael smiled. "Though you're acting more like Linh."

"She's got… a way of making herself heard," Fiona replied.

Michael smiled. Then he frowned. "You've got news?"

"I do not know if we can trust her source," Joharlen cautioned, as he gestured them both into the kitchen and closed the front door.

Fiona started at Ruarnon sitting at the table. They smiled at her and she smiled back. Tor, Mawana, Lenaris and Prince Maharl also sat with them around the table.

"Who is your source?" Prince Maharl asked, his gaze narrowed in suspicion.

Fiona looked away from the intensity of those hyper focused blue eyes, but made herself look back in the general direction of his face. Being the peacekeeper she was among her siblings would get her nowhere here. She had to be more like Linh and stand her ground.

Stick to the facts Amina had advised. Well here went nothing.

"The same false Luvaras Priestesses who've been smuggling food into the prison since they returned to Galvatia," she answered.

Maharl's gaze hardened.

"They guessed I was an escapee from the basement. They already know about that prison break and they want to help with the one you're planning. That's why they delivered me here."

Maharl waved his hand. "A small, false gesture of good faith to gain our trust. We have seen imposters before."

Fiona's heart hammered against her chest. Heat radiated from her neck and cheeks. His words battered at her hopes. His determination to mistrust was relentless. But Linh wouldn't give in that easily and neither could Fiona.

"If you won't include them in your plans, they'll carry out their own. They don't want to wait until after the southern princes invade Azula. They worry the food supply will be cut off, and Narz will pull the Zaldeaan guards to fight, and prisoners could starve. They aren't going to let that happen."

Maharl frowned.

"That's an odd threat," said Joharlen. "It does not sound like the sort of thing Karmarn would have an imposter say."

Fiona summoned all her courage and inhaled deeply. Amina was sure these words would convince him Fiona's source was truly his cousin, but Fiona worried they would anger Maharl, to the point he might kick her out.

She couldn't quite look him in the eyes, so she settled for gazing at the top of his head. "Amina says that if you won't except her aid and your bumbled prison break plan sabotages hers, she will contest your right to the throne."

Joharlen gasped.

Colour drained from Maharl's face.

"Surely she would never?" Joharlen asked.

Maharl fidgeted with his wine glass. "She might."

Fiona gaped. "You *knew* she could *truly* be your cousin? All this time? And she could have helped you for *months*, and you wouldn't let her?"

Maharl's wine glass ground against the table as it turned in his hands. "Where was she when the advance of Narz's army was concealed by lookouts at her own and her closest friends' castle? Where was she when we were attacked? Why was it only after we fell to our knees that she at last offered her hand in aid?"

That wasn't fear in his eyes. Anger burned there. But his tone was somehow hollow; regret.

Fiona exhaled and shook her head. "Maybe Amina was right. Men here are foolish."

Mawana's chortle became a cough at Tor's stern look. Maharl frowned at Ruarnon, but they shrugged.

"I have always found the idea that your behaviour is determined by the manner in which you contribute to making babies somewhat ridiculous," said Ruarnon. "So when entire civilisations invent elaborate rules about how one gender is supposed to behave..."

"You take them for fools," Maharl finished and Ruarnon nodded.

Joharlen gaped at them.

Michael shook his head. "Troy will be so disappointed he wasn't present to witness *you* being rude to our allies."

Ruarnon smiled. "This all comes partly down to Galvation gender roles, doesn't it?" they asked Prince Maharl.

The prince turned away. "It is for men to rule. I would have welcomed her as my right hand. But she was off Chaos' knows where..."

"And you didn't trust her because she wasn't acting on *your* orders?" Lenaris asked. "I see the problem."

"Princess Amia knew," said Fiona.

Joharlen's face fell. Tears started in Maharl's eyes. "Another woman who didn't do what I told her. And..."

So she wasn't defending refugees at the gates on his orders. He blamed her death on disobedience?

Fiona but her lip, then forced herself to voice her realisation. "Another woman who dared act in ways you didn't. She saved a lot of refugees from slavery in Black City by helping them escape Galvatia. And with Amina's help, you *might* be able to liberate Black City itself."

Maharl's mouth tightened, and anger flashed in his eyes. He breathed heavily and Fiona flinched, but he wasn't looking at her. "Just tell me my cousin didn't encourage my sister to do that? Tell me Amina wasn't a contributing factor in Amia's death?"

He met her gaze then, his own eyes earnest, not angry.

Fiona's mouth fell open. "She was already… She fell before Amina knew the city was under attack."

Maharl sighed.

"If she was capable of fighting, I assume she was more than capable of making her own decisions," said Lenaris.

"She was only twenty-two," Joharlen said softly.

"*I* am twenty-two," Lenaris replied firmly and Maharl stared at her.

Fiona smiled. She often forgot Lenaris was that young herself. As an arm's instructor and eldest sibling in her household, Lenaris often seemed the going-on-forty, mother of how-ever-many younger people were in the room.

Maharl sighed. "Please tell my cousin I would like to see her," he said quietly, tears in his eyes, his gaze softened.

Fiona smiled sympathetically, at the grief she suspected he hadn't expressed for his sister, and lost time and lost aid from the cousin who lived. Then she fetched Amina. The door opened as they approached it, and they entered the kitchen, where everyone sat at the table.

"Has the presence of capable young women among your new allies showed you our merit, or have you by some miracle managed to set aside your prejudice against magic and those who wield it?" Amina asked Maharl, looking him squarely in the eyes.

"How could you live in *his* domain?" Maharl asked, as though he considered her owning an estate in Arveta an act of betrayal.

"How do you hope to learn anything about Narz by hiding in farmhouses and underground tunnels?" she retorted. "Did you not learn anything of intrigue in the palace? I am surprised Aunt Shella did not have more to say about you cutting me off."

Fiona's eyes widened. *Aunt* Shella? Her kindly guardian of three days was Galvation royalty?

Prince Maharl's eyes gave him away.

"You did not tell her?" Amina asked incredulously. "Curse those Zaldeaans for killing Amia!"

"I have forgotten what confidence looks like Amina," Maharl said softly. "It has been too long since I saw you in happy times, strutting the palace with the authority of a man, for me to recognise you as yourself. I thought I saw the arrogance of a sorcerer, of someone in league with people who have the upper hand."

"I can remind you of confidence extensively," Amina replied. "When I tell you how you need to revise your prison break plans, making appropriate use of myself, and my false priestesses."

There was a pause, then Maharl turned to Joharlen saying, "And she wonders why I do not have a burning desire for marriage."

Maharl's lips quirked in a near-smile, but Joharlen looked tense.

"Joharlen," said Amina, "did you really think Companion Karmarn or King Narz would invest sorcerers in altering our appearances for months on end, until you finally accepted us as allies, so we could betray you, or does it make more sense for us to have been who we claim this whole time?"

"Fear and suspicion have been conducive to our survival," Joharlen replied with dignity. "Extended use of reason has been something of a luxury we could not afford."

"Yet now it appears that reasoned inclusion of us in your plans is crucial to their success," Amina retorted.

"I begin to understand why I could never like you Amina," Maharl said quietly. "You make everyone else look incompetent."

"Only when people lack the humility to utilise my differing strengths to complement their weaknesses," Amina replied. "That is why my false priestesses have been so successful. We have happily delegated responsibilities we cannot fulfil ourselves to sorcerer-servants which we cannot complete ourselves, such as spying on Narz's underlings, curing prisoners abused by their guards, and gathering intelligence. Because of our tolerance, acceptance and respect for others' abilities, regardless of their gender or social status, our success has been great.

"That was always your flaw Maharl. You do not have to *be* and *do* everything. You are not a failure if you delegate tasks others can complete to a higher standard; you are then a wise and efficient leader."

"You should have been Prince," he replied quietly. "I was happy as commander of the army, but I do not have your head for politics."

"Perhaps you should change the law," she said gently.

"I will," he replied. "Will you remain to advise us?"

"Of course," she replied, her expression warming.

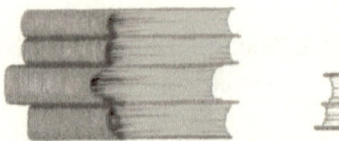

CHAPTER 19

STEALTH- FIONA

Fiona watched with a smile, as Amina took over discussion around Joharlen's table, once General Imphin and Governor Iagl had joined them. Maharl didn't object, and he and Joharlen listened keenly. General Imphin seemed intrigued by her leadership, but Governor Iagl didn't quite look at her, possibly because she was the embodiment of everything his late, treacherous father had raised him to believe women could not be and he didn't quite believe her abilities yet.

"The sorcerers can see anything that happens inside the prison," Amina reported, "viewing one corridor after another, but they cannot hear us. While my false priestesses and I walk around pretending to convert prisoners, we can inform prisoners of your plans. But the sorcerers can notify the Galvation Governor Mandarkin of disturbances magically and immediately. You must overcome them first."

When Ruarnon looked contemplative and Maharl's expression darkened, Fiona wondered how Maharl and Ruarnon had anticipated succeeding at that without Amina.

"My rebels are not ready for such a test," said Maharl.

"That will be my task," said Mawana.

"Zaldeaans fear sorcerers," Amina added, "and they make Coroth nervous, so footsteps approaching the room they work in may rouse their suspicion, as they are not used to visitors. If you overcome them too slowly, they will notify the Governor. He will send the Zaldeaan army and sorcerer trackers, who may identify and track escaped prisoners as they march to safety."

"We can overcome the sorcerers without approaching them," Mawana said. "If you take me to the prison corridor beneath the sorcerers, I can wait until they make the slightest sound and use that to direct my sleep magic at them. Others can pretend to convert prisoners until the sorcerers are asleep, then put the guards to sleep."

"You can put people beyond your sight to sleep?" Ruarnon asked.

"I have formed shields to block snakes as soon as I hear leaves rustle at home," Mawana replied. "Using sound to target sleep magic will be easy for me, but I suggest everyone who accompanies me practices putting people in the kitchen to sleep from the basement."

"You intend to put the prison guards to sleep as well?" Governor Iagl asked and Ruarnon nodded. "Then I suggest you station me near the exit, where I can challenge my countrymen should anything go wrong. They will fear magic, but their forced service under a sorcerer-king may have increased their tolerance to it sufficiently to cause trouble."

"We need to attempt the prison break at Fang Mountain soon after," Ruarnon reminded him. "I ask you to fulfil the same role there."

"Fang Mountain is guarded by sorcerers," Maharl warned. "They are spread across the outer battlements and monitor the mountainside."

"They are also atop the three main towers *inside* the battlements," Amina added.

"Then Elite Guard are needed at Fang Mountain," said General Imphin. "I shall report to Commander Octharl, confirm his timings and seek his permission."

"If Zaldeaan guards at Fang Mountain work under supervision of sorcerers," said Iagl, "Any open conflict between magic-crafters will send them running for cover."

"How can we help?" Michael asked. "At either prison break?"

"You can join soldiers under Companion Tor's command at the Forest Prison front entrance," Ruarnon replied.

"I've already posed as a sorceress," Fiona reminded them. "I walked out of the prison through the front door in priestess' robes."

"You also dug up the ground floor corridor," Maharl objected.

"I climbed through it after Troy," Fiona added, "concealed the tunnel by putting the stones back in place, then bluffed my way out of Captain Coroth's presence."

"How is my cousin?" Ruarnon asked.

Fiona smiled. "I should have guessed who he was. He has the same quiet confidence and authority of someone twice his age as you."

"How do the Zaldeaans think Troy got in?" Maharl asked.

"Sorcery," Amina replied. "A prisoner overheard the sergeant telling the day guards to be vigilant against people appearing out of magical Faeron gateways inside the corridors, after Troy was caught."

Michael laughed and Fiona smiled proudly. "He lied to them," she explained. "Faeron gateways are magical stone archways that let you travel instantly over long distances, and the prison corridors are subdivided by stone archways."

"The Zaldeaans believe such gateways exist?" Joharlen asked.

"Laria knows of them," Amina replied. "Her servants saw a Luvaras Priestess examining one in Tiama and she believes they are operated by sorcery."

Fiona's breath caught. Did that mean *real* Luvaras Priestesses might be able to send her and her friends home?

"How did *you* learn of such things?" Maharl asked Fiona suspiciously.

"Ultimately, we came to Tarlah by Faeron gateway," Michael replied, making Maharl frown and Joharlen shift uncomfortably in his chair.

"I should like to join Fiona and the false priestesses," said Lenaris. "Mawana needs to watch over the sorcerers, whereas I could accompany the female soldiers Ruarnon will send downstairs as they overcome guards and revise our plans if we encounter unforeseen difficulties."

Ruarnon approved, then they, Maharl, Joharlen, Iagl and Amina left to discuss specifics, while Fiona went to the basement with Mawana, Lenaris and fourteen women Tarlahn soldiers to practice shaping sleep magic in the room above. Michael and Tarlahn soldiers sat at the kitchen table making random noises for the others to target magic at.

They practiced for several days, and everyone's hearing became more sensitive, but only Mawana could hear soft sounds, so they agreed that he and Lenaris would target the sorcerers. The finer details were agreed upon and a date was set and swiftly arrived.

Fiona tried to remember to breathe normally. Twanging bowstrings atop nearby carriages silenced damarian hissing in the dark of the trees, while torchlit Zaldeaan guards opened the Forest Prison's double doors. Amina led the purple-robed procession up the front steps, her false priestesses at the sides, Fiona in the middle with Mawana, who wore his hood pulled low and Laria, with Lenaris and female Tarlahn soldiers behind them.

Fiona followed the purple robed crowd across the atrium and up the spiral stairs. Guards stood stiffly to attention but avoided the false priestess' gazes ,as they passed. Fiona's heart sped up as they entered the top cell corridor and the women split into adjoining corridors. Tarlahns behind Fiona mimed speaking through the cracks of iron braced wooden doors, but Laria led Mawana further down. Fiona and Lenaris trailed behind, Lenaris walking with an upright, commanding posture and proud expression that made Fiona wish she had half the other woman's confidence.

Fiona couldn't help gazing up at the whitewashed stone roof dividing her from sorcerers who saw everything. She stepped softly, straining her ears, but heard only her own breathing. As the silence stretched, her balance of hope and nervousness shifted towards nerves. What if the sorcerers sat still for hours, giving Mawana no clue as to their location? If his sleep magic missed so close to sorcerers, he'd alert them to his presence and the fact he was targeting them.

Lenaris nodded to a cell on Fiona's right. Fiona drew a deep breath and walked towards the iron-braced wooden door, hearing shuffling, as prisoners shifted to listen. She mouthed 'virtues' of Luvaras and 'benefits' of worshipping him until she ran out of ideas. The prisoners wouldn't know when to mime replies because they couldn't see her. If the sorcerers watched closely enough, they would get suspicious.

Fiona listened tensely for sound overhead, and resisted the urge to look at Mawana or up. She heard nothing, and Mawana didn't stomp, the signal he had crafted his sleep spell. She sighed and mouthed to the next cell that Luvaras was the mightiest God, offering his worshippers magical protection and healing, and wondered what real Luvaras Priests, Priestesses and The Dedicated actually thought of Narz.

A soft thud overhead made her freeze. That tingle wasn't nerves, it was magic. Mawana stomped and Fiona turned. Mawana and Lenaris were staring at the ceiling on their right. Footsteps shuffled softly overhead, and she instinctively seized magic above her. She imagined eyes closing, slowed her breathing and relaxed her body, then tried to project the sensations upwards.

Something pressed against her magic. She gripped it tightly. There was a soft thump, as the person she had put to sleep hit the ground. Pressure pushed against her, and she held firm, breathing slowly and projecting relaxation until the pressure subsided.

"Got him?" Lenaris whispered and Fiona nodded.

"Good work," Mawana whispered.

"Come with us and hold that magic tight," Lenaris added.

Lenaris and Mawana led Fiona out of the corridor, treading lightly as cats, and the purple robed, soldier false priestesses followed with Laria.

Fiona kept her breathing slow and tried to relax her muscles. She lifted her purple robes, as they climbed the stairs, focusing on her projection of sleep.

Mawana and Lenaris took the left turn at the top and Fiona tensed in anticipation. They rounded a bend in the corridor. Coroth lay fast asleep ahead, his body orientated towards the room which must contain the sorcerers.

Fiona stopped beside Coroth, projecting deep breathing onto him, while Mawana, Lenaris, Laria and the soldiers approached a door on their right. Laria kept her chin up, a proud priestess about her business, her familiar face hopefully distracting the sorcerers from multiple unfamiliar faces.

Fiona held her breath as Mawana reached for the door handle. The door swung inwards, revealing a man slumped in a wicker chair, sleeping with his mouth open. A younger man lay on a bed on his right, sleeping with an apple with a bite out of it on his chest. Opposite him, a third sorcerer stirred on a bed. Fiona sensed magic tingling and he relaxed.

She exhaled deeply, as Mawana smiled and Lenaris turned back. Magic tingled at Fiona's feet. She had almost let go of Coroth. He relaxed into the floor as Lenaris's sleep magic enveloped his body. Fiona sighed.

Mawana and Lenaris stepped into the sorcerer's room and closed the door. Clubs cracked against two heads, then a third, then there was silence. Coroth stirred and Fiona projected sleep at him, and nodded to the soldiers, who gagged and bound him.

"This is much easier with you and your friends' abilities," Laria commented.

"And with your identity as disguises," Fiona added.

Laria inclined her head.

Coroth stirred again as linen was shoved into his mouth and bound round his hands. More more magic tingled, the soldiers supporting Lenaris and Fiona as their work nudged Coroth awake. The pressure of keeping him asleep built. Then the knot at his hands was finished and the soldiers nodded. Fiona let the magic go slowly.

Coroth's eyes opened. He blinked in recognition.

"I'm Troy's friend," she said. "I came back to finish some unfinished business of your cousin's."

Coroth stared and Fiona smiled.

"The sorcerers are unconscious, and we are taking over the prison," Lenaris told Coroth softly, as she stepped out of the sorcerer's room.

"Your cousin wants you to know that you and your guards are about to be abducted by Tarlahns, with the aid of Galvation rebels. We will leave evidence of fighting that never occurred and burned bodies wearing Zaldeaan armour in the forest."

Coroth blinked mutely.

Lenaris motioned two soldiers to lead Coroth to Mawana. The remaining purple robed soldiers moved to restrain guards on the external stairs, clearing the way for Laria's servants, and for prisoners to escape. Laria moved to direct her servants.

Fiona and Lenaris turned back down the spiral wooden stairs.

"It's always nice to speak to Coroth and his friends," Lenaris said loudly, the cue signalling to Tarlahn soldiers on the top cell level that Coroth and the sorcerers were asleep.

"If only his guards could join him in intellect," Fiona added, signalling the soldiers to begin putting guards to sleep.

Magic tingled, but when they stepped into the corridor, two guards shifted nervously. A pair of purple robed Tarlahns approached, wielding ineffective sleep magic.

Lenaris's magic tingled towards the guard on the right and the other magic stilled. Fiona turned to the man on the left, as his eyes widened in surprise. She pushed sleep on him firmly, and he slumped to the ground beside his companion.

Fiona held the magic tightly, as the soldiers' shoved linen scraps in the men's mouths, tied gags around them and bound their hands. Then she let go and her pressure headache eased as both men's eyes jerked open, and they stared at false Luvaras Priestess leaning over them.

"We are fake priestesses, soldiers of your new king," Lenaris whispered. "And your service to King Narz is ended."

The men stared, and one flinched when Lenaris unbuckled his belt, removing a ring of keys and handing them to Fiona. Fiona smiled as Lenaris beckoned to the four Tarlahn soldiers and led them downstairs, where they would pretend to convert prisoners until they had enough soldiers to restrain all the mezzanine guards.

Fiona waited until four more purple-robed false priestesses walked swiftly to the stairs, nodding their success to her, then she smiled and strode to the nearest corridor with the keys in hand. She stepped up to the first door on her right and said quietly, "It's time."

She tested keys until she found the right one to unlock the door, then pulled the door open, breathing through her mouth against a powerful stench. Her eyes watered, as grotty faces inside creased into smiles. She smiled back, as people filed out silently, grinning from ear to ear.

Amina reached her as she unlocked the next cell. "Would you like me to take over?" she offered quietly. "One of my servants noticed a strange name; 'Linh Mai' in the entry book and believes the cell number corresponds to the end of this corridor."

Fiona smiled broadly and handed over the keys, then walked swiftly to the end of the corridor. Quiet footsteps shuffled and she sensed tens of people behind solid timber doors on either side holding their breaths in anticipation.

The cell at the end was separated from the corridor by iron bars, with two barred windows in its back wall and a small crowd of people inside. Its timber floor looked polished, perhaps a former dance floor.

She scanned faces as she came closer. Among dirty haired blondes, Troy's brown curls were immediately recognisable. She beamed at him.

"Fiona!" two voices cried.

Fiona's broad smile remained in place as she strode forwards, directed at Linh's dirty-faced smile. She winced at the faded bruising on Troy's cheeks and a bandage around his head.

"Are you alright?"

"This knocked some sense into me."

He smiled sincerely and she smiled and shook her head.

"But getting away with lying to the Governor of Galvatia about the God Kings getting me here through a Faeron gateway was kind of awesome," he added.

Fiona smiled. "Convincing Coroth I was a servant from Black City was kind of the same, as was walking out the front door."

He gaped, then grinned.

Linh shook her head. "Have you corrupted Fiona Troy? I didn't think anyone could do that."

Linh shook her head and crossed her arms, but she was smiling.

"What happened Linh?" Fiona asked apprehensively.

Linh explained about trying to follow Michael, trying to lose soldiers and ultimately being caught before Black City.

Amina approached and unlocked the cell door.

Troy ran forwards to hold Fiona, kissing her tenderly.

Fiona looked up to see Linh shaking her head, arms crossed. Fiona laughed and raised an arm, welcoming Linh into a three-person hug. She was surprised how long the scent of their unwashed bodies took to bother her and they both noticed her nose wrinkle as they stepped apart.

"I know," said Troy. "I'd kill for a shower, and for everyone else to have one, no offence people," he added, eyeing his cellmates and escapees moving silently the corridor, many of whom smiled.

Amina continued unlocking cell doors, and Fiona smiled at a line of escapees doing a silent jig down the corridor and up the stairs. They would descend the external staircase, guarded from damars by rebel archers, into a protective rebel corridor through the forest. The escape had begun.

"You were good company," a young man said to Linh and Troy. "Your people have a wonderful sense of humour."

"And good spirits," said a young woman.

"You lot do alright," said Troy.

"I do not know if we will meet again," said an older man. "We will join our Princes, and probably be in battle before the month is out. And no doubt you shall re-join your friends and attempt to recover the Zaldeaans. We may walk different paths from here, but you were good companions in hard times, and we wish you all the best, whatever the future may bring."

"Thanks for everything you taught me," Linh said to all three of her cellmates.

She smiled and shook hands with them, as did Troy. Then their cellmates danced into the corridor, quietly joining dozens of excited prisoners approaching the spiral stairs to freedom.

Fiona, Troy and Linh followed them down the corridor at a walk.

"Where will they go?" Linh asked.

"There's a kingdom north of here," Fiona replied. "Maharl was tight-lipped, but apparently its Queen, Ziliene, has abilities that made Prince Maharl think she's a Guardian. The rebels held Karmarn's soldiers back with ambushes and nasty skirmishes during the war, so they've never pushed far north."

"But won't Narz invade the northern kingdom now?" Linh asked.

"Prince Maharl said Queen Ziliene has been neutral in the war with Galvatia so far. She didn't fight Narz to protect Galvatia when it fell. The princes don't think Narz will risk his truce with her when he's at or about to be at war with so many others.

"Besides, some of Ruarnon's soldiers will stay behind to capture Zaldeaans who approach the prison after tonight. And one of Laria's sorceresses can wield communication magic, so she'll receive and reply to magical communication from Narz, while the others keep his sorcerers' prisoner.

"The prison breaks will be covered up as long as possible, and the rebels have set traps and ambushes throughout the forest to delay the Zaldeaans, when Karmarn realises what's happened. But the Middle South are mobilising against Narz, and everyone expects war soon."

"Where are the others?" Troy asked.

"Mawana is guarding the sorcerers, and Michael's outside with Tor and Tarlahn Elites, who will put the guards on the ground floor to sleep. Ruarnon is in the farmlands."

Fiona looked around. The former cell doors were open. Some rooms were large, furnished with cushions, chairs, shelves of scrolls or sleeping pallets. It was filthy and smelly and would need an awful lot of cleaning, but this was a home now, a prison no longer.

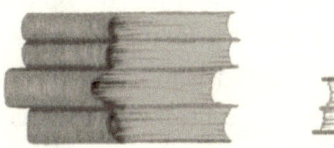

CHAPTER 20

FREEDOM-LINH

Linh hesitated. Twelve steps. That was the furthest she had been able to walk from the back wall to the bars. Thirty seconds. That was the longest the cell door tended to open for, as the chamber pot was passed out. But the door had been open for much longer than that. And her cell mates had already left.

Troy was beaming as he stepped into the corridor with Fiona.

Linh took a deep breath and stepped through the bars. Her foot touched stone. Guards didn't shout. Or didn't come running. No one stopped her. She took a second step. And a third.

A smile spread across her face, as she followed her friends down the corridor, past doors she had barely been able to see from her cell, all opening into rooms now emptied. Moonlight shone through them. They too had windows, granting merciful air and light to her fellow prisoners, for a much longer stay than she had endured. All of them already moved down the hallway ahead of her. Others must be on the stairs by now. It was *over*.

Tension across her shoulders began to dissipate. She took a larger step, then another. Then she ran forwards, enjoying sheer freedom of movement, neither walls nor guards stopping her.

"Linh's enjoying running," Troy said in a hushed voice to Fiona. "Should we be concerned?"

Linh laughed. PE had never been her favourite subject at home. But she would happily run for eight hundred meters now, as fast as she could, just because she *could*.

Escapees returned her smile, waving and gesturing in silent celebration as they filed out the corridor on her left, walking towards the stairs, and freedom. A second file of grinning escapees moved on her right, silently parting in theatrical twirls to let Fiona, Troy and herself through. She returned their smiles, following Fiona down the spiral wooden stairs, past a file of escapees coming up from the mezzanine.

"Let's head to the ground floor," Fiona suggested. "When Lenaris and the Tarlahns are ready, you can borrow priestess robes and Lenaris will lead us through the atrium. Then Governor Iagl will enter the front doors, explain our plan to Captain Coroth, and ask him to evacuate the Zaldeaans in the dorms opposite the false priestess' wing."

They descended below the mezzanine on deserted stairs, and Linh and Troy waited for Fiona to check the coast was clear.

"It's ok," she called.

Linh's steps sounded too loud as she descended into a quiet, dim stone corridor. She searched nervously for exits, used to watching out for guards and being ready to hush rebellious conversations, should one enter her corridor.

Guards lay at the end of four adjoining corridors, bound and gagged, and four burly figures were bound by Tarlahns at the double doors leading to the atrium. Linh sighed and her shoulders relaxed a little.

Escapees appeared on her right, led by a Tarlahn soldier in priestess purple, grinning and waving as they climbed the stairs. Another file emerged from the corridor on the left, led by another Tarlahn.

"Whose there?" a man's voice asked.

Linh tensed and scanned the room for the threat.

"That came from downstairs," Troy said quietly.

Two Tarlahn soldiers leading escapees descended to investigate and Troy, Linh and Fiona followed carefully. The spiral stairs ended in a short corridor, with two doors on each side, lit by a single torch. A Tarlahn unlocked the first door on the right, as a man's voice said, "Why are there so many people?"

The soldiers tensed and Linh frowned as the door swung inwards. The prisoners seemed large in the shadows. Because they wore boiled leather. She tensed.

"YOU!" yelled an angry man.

Troy started.

"It's *your* fault we're down here!"

"Zaldeaans, imprisoned in punishment for failing to catch an escaped prisoner," said Fiona.

All eyes turned to Fiona. She was wearing Priestess purple, which they seemed to think put her in charge. Fiona, the boss, of someone? Could she do that?

"Haven't you learnt your lesson yet?" Fiona asked, and Linh smiled.

That caused a ripple of nerves among the guards, but Troy and Linh were clearly escaped prisoners.

"TREACHERY!" the man shouted. "TREACHERY IN THE BASEMENT!"

"What are you doing you fool?" another guard asked anxiously.

"If these women are here with him; they ain't priestesses! They're fakes!" the man yelled. "This is a-"

His words cut off, his eyelids drooped, and he slumped to the floor, deeply asleep. Linh turned. Lenaris gazed intently behind her, flanked by Tarlahns in priestess robes.

Of course. Linh *could* openly craft magic now! They all could!

She reached out and formed a shield. For the first time, colours sparkled among the mist, perhaps because she wanted to see the thing she hadn't been able to touch for weeks.

The other guards stared in horror. But when her magic didn't attack them, two knelt, while the rest shivered in the shadows.

"We are sorry Your Worships," said the man who had questioned his companion, from his knees. "He did not know what he was saying. He was a fool."

But the Zaldeaan beside him frowned at Linh. "*They* aren't priestesses," he said. "They thought we were prisoners and they wanted to free us."

"But they can work magic!" the second man on his knees protested, his features wide with fear.

The suspicious man stepped towards Linh. She focused, hardening her shield, the colour of which vanished. The man smiled, assuming it was gone. He walked into her shield and strained against it, causing pressure to build in Linh's head. The pressure eased, as the man stepped back, frowning in confusion. He reached tentatively forwards, until his palm turned white against Linh's invisible shield.

"Whoever we are, *we* can work magic," said Linh. "Can you?"

The guards stared at the hand pushing solid air, wide-eyed. The pressure vanished as the suspicious guard stepped back in alarm.

"All of you on your knees," Lenaris ordered.

The suspicious guard and his fearful companions knelt.

"Line up facing the wall opposite your cell in single file," Lenaris ordered.

The man who apologised chewed on his lip as he shuffled forwards on his knees. The others eyed the ground as they crawled into the corridor and lined up along the wall.

Lenaris nodded to the Tarlahns, saying, "Gags first."

The women removed strips of linen and ropes from their purple robes and gagged guards, who outnumbered them two to one.

"Help!" a woman cried.

"That's us," said Troy.

He jogged back upstairs, and Linh and Fiona followed him. Four Tarlahns in priestess purple stood with their backs pressed against the double doors to the atrium, standing awkwardly over four bound Zaldeaans at their feet.

"Many footsteps are approaching," said a woman.

Linh tensed, suspecting Zaldeaans from the dorms were entering the atrium. Troy rushed forwards, bracing himself against the double doors, which moved steadily inwards. They weren't going to hold.

"Let them go," Linh said quietly. "Jump sideways and Fi and I can block the air before the doors with shield magic."

Linh crafted her shield behind the slowly opening atrium doors, joining it carefully to Fiona's. She sensed more shields forming on both sides and waited till they solidified.

"Now!" she yelled.

The four women and Troy leapt sideways. The doors creaked open, pushing the four bounds guards across the floor behind her shield. Two Zaldeaans rushed through and tripped over their comrades.

"There's people on the ground," yelled a third man, as the two stood and moved aside. "Move carefully."

Three guards leapt the bound men. Linh tensed at pressure, as one bounced off her shield. The others halted, then stared.

"Priestesses!" a voice behind the door shouted. "The treachery is Luvaras Priestesses!"

Guards dragged their bound comrades back through the doors, which opened fully. Linh forced an icy smile onto her face, and directed it at tens of tousle-haired, pale-faced Zaldeaans. They recoiled. But they controlled the atrium.

"Stand down," advised a familiar, young male voice. "The captain will not want us provoking their Worships. Retreat to the stairs and let them pass."

"Do as he says," a gruff voice ordered.

The Zaldeaans before Linh backed up. The men crowding the atrium flowed backwards in a human stream to the dormitory corridor, most carrying swords and shields.

Butterflies stirred in Linh's stomach. The priestess guise kept them safe but relying on fear to keep that many armed soldiers under control unsettled her stomach.

Lenaris reappeared, calling four soldiers, Linh, Fiona and Troy to her. "The rest of you have prisoners to convert," Lenaris added, to Tarlahns emerging from the stairs.

Linh let her shield go and the others faded. Lenaris led the people she named into the atrium, her posture tall and proud. The Zaldeaans melted back, exposing Demune.

"Rebels! Rebels have-"

"Form a shield wall!" the gruff voice ordered.

Men carrying bronze shields pushed to the front of the Zaldeaan crowd, forming a bronze shield wall across the atrium. Others moved behind it with swords drawn, angled towards the atrium front doors. Linh's hand itched to grip her absent sword. No-one's shield magic could hold off that shield wall if it turned on them…

Demune backed up, turning a worried glance to Linh. The external doors stood open and there was no one outside, meaning Tor had probably ordered rebels and Tarlahns to move back.

Zaldeaans forming the bronze shield wall stood tensely, Zaldeaan eyes scanning the doorway, but the gruff-voiced man did not give the order to charge.

"We'll outnumber them sergeant!" a soldier asserted.

"They've had all night to set an ambush while we slept," the sergeant retorted. "I'll not send you blundering into it. If their Worships stand aside, my squad is to secure the external stairs. You ten," he added with a gesture, "Find the Captain and search the cells. The rest of you; remain here and keep the atrium secure."

Linh tensed at footsteps on the stairs behind her. Prisoners were still evacuating, weakened from lack of food and proper sleep. They were unarmed and not in a good state to fight.

The bronze shield wall turned towards her, and Troy clenched his fists. Lenaris didn't move. She stood tall, barring the doors to the stairway and the soldiers followed her lead.

"Summon the other priestesses," she said quietly over her shoulder and one set of footsteps retreated.

"They're working together!" a man yelled.

"We've been deceived!" yelled another. "They're not real priestesses; they're rebels!"

"Take them," the gruff voice ordered.

The bronze shield wall parted, and grim-faced veterans advanced towards Lenaris, Linh, Troy, Fiona and the four soldiers, with swords drawn. The Tarlahn women looked to Lenaris, who stood her ground and did not draw the weapons Linh ver much hoped were concealed inside her robes.

Linh's shoulders grew tight until they ached. She took a nervous breath, then focused on hardening magic before them, concentrating on its colour, forming a shimmering, misty shield wall. The others extended it sideways.

The Zaldeaans gaped.

"You *dare* question me?" Lenaris asked. "You dare threaten a Priestess of Luvaras?"

The veterans halted.

"Sorcery!" a man shouted.

"They'll kill us all!" another screamed.

"Then we let their Worships' pass," Demune replied loudly, with impressive calm, given that he didn't know Tarlahns could wield magic.

"Real priestesses would not ally with rebels," said the sergeant, as he emerged from the shield wall, which parted before him. "Rebels hate sorcery and the Priestesses are sorceresses. These people are imposters. Perhaps the rebels learnt magic to combat King Narz. I've always wanted to know if swords can cut through magic shields. Let's find out. Shield wall; advance."

The shield wall wavered, then shuffled forwards. Linh swallowed nervously. Sweat trickled down her face, and pressure built in her head, as she maintained her largest shield yet.

"Stand down!" a calm voice ordered from the front entrance.

Linh peered at helmeted heads, but couldn't make out the speaker. She suspected the man had a narrow, commanding face, blue eyes and wore a gold coronet with a blue sapphire in its centre.

"Impossible," said the sergeant.

"Improbable yes," Governor Iagl's voice replied. "But not impossible."

Iagl had a temper and diplomacy was not his strong point. How did Ruarnon expect him to get the Zaldeaans to stand down?

"Illusion," the sergeant objected. "Another attempt to deceive us!"

Iagl smiled. "I challenge you to a duel sergeant. I will prove upon your blade that I am who appear to be."

The sergeant swallowed nervously and drew his sword. Iagl smiled as he stepped forward through the guards and said, "I think I shall evade wounding you. I like you sergeant."

He advanced with a flurry of brutal attacks, each strike flowing forcefully into the next, battering the sergeant's sword and forcing him back with every blow.

Iagl side-stepped several desperate thrusts with ease and advanced again, disarming the sergeant.

"NO!" a voice cried.

Two men leapt forwards and the unarmed sergeant retreated. Iagl smiled.

"Is he sure about this?" Troy whispered.

"Ruarnon says he's a superb swordsman," Linh replied.

Both Zaldeaans charged like bulls. Iagl danced out of their way, pivoting back and forth, defending against two sets of sword strokes simultaneously. He disarmed one opponent with a flick of his sword, elbowed the man in the head, and raised his sword towards the second man. The second backed away.

"That is Governor Iagl," said a voice behind Linh.

Tarlahn soldiers approached, with a young man in a silk tunic, whose hands were bound behind his back, Coroth, Linh assumed.

"Orders, Captain," said the sergeant, not taking his eyes off Iagl.

"I have command of the prison Governor Iagl," said Coroth. "Please explain how you came to co-operate with Tarlahns, and how this is to proceed without two thousand of our brothers in Azula being slaughtered because of our mutiny."

"He doesn't trust what we told him," Linh whispered.

Governor Iagl smiled. "You have your father's tenacity Coroth," he replied. "Your cousin occupied us with an army that was methodical and highly efficient against damars. An army any Zaldeaan would be proud to lead, and a commander we are proud to follow.

"As for this castle; my soldiers carry specially mixed red paint, which will be artfully strewn throughout the prison as evidence of how your men fought bravely against the rebels. Galvation skeletons from the battlefield, dressed in Zaldeaan attire, shall be piled and burned outside, freeing their spirits from their bodies and providing smoke to deliver them to the heavens in accordance with Galvation beliefs.

"The evidence of your having fought desperately and been slaughtered to a man by vengeful rebels shall be obvious to any who investigate, assuming anyone overcomes rebel ambushes in the forest to reach this castle."

"When sorcerers here do not respond to King Narz's sorcerers in Azula seeking confirmation all is at should be…" Coroth said quietly.

"We have sorcerer contacts taking care of that," said Lenaris. "There was an important woman in the resistance open-minded enough to keep sorcerer servants."

"Where do we hide?" Coroth asked. "King Narz can search this kingdom from where he stands if he becomes suspicious."

"The rebels know a place he cannot *See*," Iagl replied.

Coroth took a deep breath, then said to his men, "To attention."

The bronze shield wall lowered, Zaldeaan swords were sheathed, and the men straightened and faced Coroth.

"What are Their Benevolence's orders?" Coroth asked Iagl.

"Lower the shields," Lenaris commanded, and Linh sagged with relief as their magical shields winked out. Her vision was blurring. As she tried to blink it clear, footsteps thudded and Tor's voice cautioned, "Careful!"

The crowd of Zaldeaans backed up slightly, as a thin figure hurried past. Linh smiled at Michael. Michael ran forwards and Troy grinned and lifted him clean off his feet as he hugged him.

Michael laughed. Linh's browse rose as Troy pecked him on the cheek. Then Michael approached Linh. She smiled and hugged him. Troy had been good company in prison, good for her spirits and better company than she could have imagined, but it would be nice to have Michael to talk to again.

The Zaldeaans were retreating into their dorm corridor. Tarlahns in priestess purple led bound Zaldeaan guards to Coroth and Iagl, and Zaldeaan soldiers moved to unbind them. The former prison guards eyed the Tarlahns uncertainly, as Coroth explained their situation, then retreated into the dorm corridor, from which a column of Zaldeaans carrying small packs began to emerge, led by a grizzled sergeant with hope shining in his eyes.

Iagl led the column outside, to a human corridor of Zaldeaans in bronze armour, with bows raised and arrows nocked at the top of the steps, descending below Linh's sight. Only then did she notice the steady twang of bowstrings and damarian hisses and shrieks from the hillside.

"And I think *I'm* reckless," said Troy, shaking his head.

Linh followed his gaze. Mawana approached with a large smile on his face, and an unconscious sorcerer slung over one shoulder, escorted by young women who must be Laria's sorcerer-servants, who carried a second sorcerer between them. Linh grimaced as Mawana lowered his sorcerer to the ground.

"Linh and Troy!" Mawana cried as he straightened with arms wide. Linh smiled and hugged him, struggling to breathe until Mawana let go to hug Troy.

More Tarlahns followed, carrying a third sorcerer and probably casting sleep magic to help secure all three unconscious sorcerers.

"Linh, try not to wander off this time," Mawana added.

Linh smiled.

Troy turned to Mawana ambivalently. If Linh shouldn't wander off... Mawana grinned, then laughed until Linh worried his sides would split.

"Never change my friend, but try to stay safe eh?" Mawana said to Troy with a grin.

Troy grinned back at him, his shoulders relaxing.

Mawana's expression became more serious. "We will take the sorcerers to carts along the escapee column. Will you join us?"

"I'd like to wait for the original false priestesses," Fiona replied, and Linh, Troy and Michael waited with her.

Mawana hefted the sorcerer over his shoulder, and Tarlahns bearing the other two sorcerers and more guards followed, as they exited through the front entrance. A brief stream of escapees and more Tarlahns followed, led by Lenaris. The last people to leave the stairs were five smiling false priestesses, one of whom Linh recognised.

"The last files of prisoners from the mezzanine are on the stairs and the top floor is empty," Amina told Fiona and Linh. "This is the Forest Prison no longer."

"All that remains is to soil my floors with fake bloodstains," a blonde false priestess grimaced. "I have half a mind to ask Ruarnon to send those Zaldeaans to clean up after themselves before I set this place up as home again."

"What will you do now?" Linh asked Amina.

"We will return to our estates in Arveta. I wish to speak to our people there about rumours of sorcerers becoming restless as war approaches. We suspect that at least one, if not more secret sorcerer organisations are stirring, and we wish to investigate them and inform my cousins of the danger they may pose to our people and our new allies."

"So this is goodbye?" Linh asked.

"For now," Amina replied.

"Good luck," said Fiona.

"And you," said Amina. "All of us opposing King Narz tread volatile ground now, but the continent itself will become volatile when war breaks out. Take care, and use the spark that let you deceive Coroth into thinking you were a cleaner to overcome whatever challenges await you."

Fiona thanked her and everyone said their goodbyes. Linh and Troy expressed their gratitude for the role the false priestesses had played in freeing them and Linh thanked them for their company while she was locked up.

Then the false priestesses strode towards the front entrance and Linh and her friends followed them. In the doorway, she gazed beyond the column of evacuating Zaldeaans, downhill into a moonlit forest. She inhaled the scent of plants, as a gentle breeze blew against her skin. The air smelled fresh and clean. Freedom tasted good.

CHAPTER 21

FANG MOUNTAIN - LENARIS

The next night, Lenaris couldn't help staring at Mawana and the Elite Guard as they rode through the grassy plains by the pale light of a quarter, and a dim half-moon. Their Elite Guard escort's enchantment should make them appear as indistinct shadows to sentries watching from the prison atop Fang Mountain ahead, but the Elite Guard and Mawana rode too close to Lenaris for the spell to be visible to her. From where she sat, all three of them were perfectly visible for a wide radius, across grass that barely came halfway up their horse's legs. It made her feel exposed.

She rode upright and alert, on the lookout for any sign or sound of a startled wild animal. In the darkness of the forested hillside ahead, that may be their only warning of enemies or allies approaching under the branches. Enough danger lay ahead for Lenaris to probe the air with magic, alert for the slightest tingle.

She lifted her gaze above the dark mass of treetops ahead, which obscured the castle at its top, at a starry sky overhead.

A mountain top wasn't the worst place to be imprisoned. If he was lucky, her father would have a view of goings on in the land bellow.

Though witnessing his guards depart as search parties towards Galvatia wouldn't be reassuring.

Pamoran wasn't made to sit indoors. He spent his spare time sparring in the training courtyard and would sometimes take Lenaris, her younger sisters and mother on trips to the beach or rides through the forest at Week's End. He may not have fared much better in a cell than Troy.

She ought to see him soon, if all went well getting around his sorcerer guards. What had her father made of sorcerers? He'd have had little choice in denying their existence for as long as her grandfather had. Pamoran may have seen them craft magic; if he'd witnessed infiltration or escape attempts.

Lenaris shivered. His stay in prison had been longer and likely far darker than Linh's. In their march north from the Forest Prison, Linh had surprised everyone by riding ahead, or dismounting to walk or jog, when they knew she wasn't fond of exercise. Mawana had jogged with her, but that was his nature. Lenaris suspected Linh's new interest in 'exercise' was love of freedom, and that was how several weeks in prison had impacted her. What would her father be like after many months?

Wind blew waves of long grass before them, drawing Lenaris's attention. Somewhere beyond it, more Elite Guards and groups of rebels were moving. They would approach separately, so if prison guards concentrated their efforts on the first group they spotted, it would divert attention from others. Lenaris sincerely hoped her group wasn't the first the prison guards noticed.

"My magic will see us through this, do not worry," Mawana assured her with a smaller, more nervous smile than usual.

Their Elite Guard smiled but said nothing. *Their* magic would be the biggest help, but they weren't the bragging sort. They were one of many Elite Guard helping to protect rebels tonight. A hero possibly, but also a front-line soldier in an exceptionally dangerous magic battle, should things go wrong. Lenaris sincerely hoped it didn't come to that.

The three of them dismounted at the edge of the plains and followed the Elite Guard to a fallen tree, where Lenaris slowly made out dark forms. Suddenly, tens of horses tied to picket lines stood before them, guarded by rebels. Lenaris sighed at the effectiveness of the shadow enchantment, as a rebel approached to take her own, Mawana and the Elite Guard's horses.

All three dismounted, handing over their reins and Lenaris studied the dark terrain ahead. Her eyes adjusted slowly to dim light beneath the trees. She could see well enough not to walk into trunks or branches, but they'd have to move carefully to avoid rustling twigs or leaves on the dark mass that was the ground.

Mawana led them forwards, in single file along a small gap in the undergrowth that must be a track winding around trees ahead. They passed through quiet forest in which moonlight creeping around twisted branches cast strange shadows on forest floor, between a road zig zagging up the mountain. Then the Elite Guard led them along the roadside, toward two towers rising above the trees, and a high wall with gates in it barring the road.

They crouched behind bushes. Guards stood in pairs along battlements before and above them, spreading out from the gate towers, silhouetted against the half-moon. The guards gazed indifferently at their surroundings or talked amongst themselves. They seemed oblivious to Elite Guard in prison towers crafting sleep spells on sorcerers or rebels positioning to craft sleep magic on them.

Lenaris sighed. Now, they would wait for the signal the sorcerers had been overpowered and the guards could be safely put to sleep.

Above her, Zaldeaan guards paced. Two played a board game and another pair smoked pipes on the battlements. The faint tap of wooden counters across the game board drifted down, as did murmured curses of the guard who was losing and footsteps of guards pacing, through dark air heavy with anticipation.

Finally, something happened. White light flashed in the tower on their left. It rocked slightly and rocks shot out from its wall.

"What in the name of Chaos?" exclaimed a guard, as the board game paused, the pipes were dropped in surprise and every guard stared at the tower.

Mawana shot Lenaris an anxious look. If sorcerers had detected Elite Guard, there was nothing they could do to help.

White light lit up the sky, and Zaldeaan guards muttered prayers. Several ran for the gatetowers. A bird cawed on Lenaris's right and left. Guards along the battlements toppled in deep sleep and alarm bells tolled in the towers.

"GET DOWN!" The Elite Guard bellowed.

Lenaris dived, instinctively reaching for the blanket of magic Mawana cast over them. They hit the ground between trees. Light flashed behind them. Something rumbled. Clods of earth battered the shield she supported above. Then all was silent.

Lenaris sat up swiftly beside Mawana, maintaining her hold on her shield. Before the gates lay a crater. Clods of earth had flown in all directions, spattering into dust. But no one seemed injured.

Light flashed along the wall, then again on Lenaris's right. Trees on her right burned. Her escort Elite Guard crouched beneath a branch on the left, beside undamaged wall.

A lone set of footsteps strode through the night. A pale cloaked Elite Guard ran onto the road before the gate. The man dived and white light flashed. Both gates were blasted off their hinges and debris obscured Lenaris's vision. She tensed against pressure and gripped her shield tightly, as clods of earth rained against it.

The pressure eased. Lenaris blinked away lights dancing before her eyes and tried to ignore the ringing in her ears.

Three shadows disappeared between the gates, more Elite Guard, who had just tricked sorcerer-guards into destroying the gates to let them in. She shook her head.

Her Elite Guard mouthed to her, "Sorcerers on the battlements."

Light flashed overhead, making hair on the back of Lenaris's neck stand up and setting several trees ablaze. Fires sparked, then blazed across the treetops and Lenaris sensed a shield broadening under falling, flaming debris.

Were the sorcerers attacking the trees? Was hunching under burning branches any safer than charging inside?

Thought of what awaited inside reminded her of the Zaldeaans inside those walls. They'd be as terrified as Galvation prisoners in their cells.

General Takanis led rebels at the far gate, but was one level-headed woman enough to manage frightened, armed Zaldeaans? How would they react when the rebels entered the prison yard?

Lenaris stood. "I am going in."

The Elite Guard bowed their head and stood. Mawana grimaced at the force of fire lashing his shield overhead.

"Let's try to avoid their magic?" he asked, with a hasty smile.

She bowed her head, then ducked after the Elite Guard towards the crater before the gate towers. Other footsteps pounded on the road behind. Rebels, ready to confront guards and free prisoners. Light flashed and the ground rocked beneath them. The plan needed to change.

"Halt!" Lenaris ordered, in a tone that prompted even the rebel leader to stop and study her.

"I am Lenaris, Advisor and Companion of Regent Ruarnon. If you charge in there now, prisoners could be taken hostage by panicked guards. And if we evacuate the prison while sorcerers fight, rubble and debris could kill and maim. Stay outside, until the flashes of light and rumbling stop."

"And should Zaldeaan guards attempt to flee?" the leader asked.

Lenaris recalled the willingness to fight magic the Zaldeaans had demonstrated in the atrium of the Forest Prison. They may be terrified tonight, but they were experienced and deadly soldiers. Facing armed rebels would remind them of that.

"This is not their war. Move aside and let them pass. Ruarnon and I will take responsibility for rounding them up when our prison break is complete."

It was unlikely the Zaldeaans would run back to Narz when they realised they were free. Locating them could be as difficult as locating Galvation rebels had been, but that was tomorrow's problem.

"When the magic calms, we enter, leaving them room to escape, and only engage if they attack us?" the Galvation leader clarified.

Lenaris inclined her head, and the woman returned the gesture.

Lenaris strode forwards, her Elite Guard on her left, Mawana on her right.

Mawana gasped.

Shadows moved from the trees on her right, and flames flared along the battlements before them. Lenaris stopped in her tracks. The Elite Guards' orders were to take as many sorcerers alive as possible…

A man screamed and the flames vanished. A shadow moved through the smoke, then two figures enclosed in shields flew off smoking battlements and drifted into the trees.

Were the sorcerer-guards here like those who invaded the Timbalen Empire, ready to fight to the last man? Or were they more like Poran and Dargus, guarding their people from what they perceived as legitimate threats? Her safety and how to handle them varied wildly depending on which it was.

White light flashed overhead. The ground rumbled and wobbled beneath their feet and the shield the Elite Guard cast flashed, as small bits of dirt sprayed off it. Lenaris flinched at pressure against the small section of shield she maintained. Then the tugging resistance ceased, and the dust cleared.

Two Elite Guard inclined their heads as they overtook Lenaris. A third sat in the crater she was skirting just before the gateway, holding his foot. Then he too rose and ran, as if there was no pain, or injury. The Elite Guard seemed very capable, but the sorcerers were using a level of force likely to kill prisoners incidentally. Could they be reasoned with?

She moved along the inside wall to get her bearings. Three separate towers rose before her. Zaldeaan guards huddled along the wall. A small spray of stone fell between two towers.

Footsteps thudded along the walls, and panicked moans and a voice shushing them from a nearby tower suggested Zaldeaan guards were hiding in the guard towers.

Light flashed overhead. More stone showered the courtyard.

"We run for freedom!" one Zaldeaan was yelling. "Before the sorcerers kill us all. And if anyone tries to stop us, we cut them all down!"

Mawana peered at her with widened eyes. The dizziness and tingling when they entered Ancient Valley truly had been a language enchantment. And it was still working on them now.

Zaldeaans roared and raised their swords and spears in agreement. Then they charged around the left tower, towards the exit behind Lenaris. She strode into their path. They halted before her.

"Shield wall!" the man yelled.

"Prime Ruler Ruarnon means their Zaldeaan subjects no harm," she said loudly and clearly.

Zaldeaans gaped at her.

"Our allies mean to free their people, but they will let you pass. As shall I."

She moved aside, leaving her short sword in its sheath and clearing their path, Mawana and the Elite Guard moving with her.

"The… the Tarlahns have come?" asked a lone voice.

"Ruarnon has come to recover their parents, their uncle, your commander, and as many of you as they can. This is not your war. You do not belong here."

"What if the sorcerers kill us as we flee?" asked another.

"Our allies, the Elite Guard have a lot in common with your neighbours, the North Landers. Their orders are to protect you, as well as the prisoners, if they can. All of you evacuating at once will make that easier for them. It is less space to shield."

"And the faster we go the harder it is to hit us. Full speed boys!" the leader yelled.

Zaldeaans roared, brandishing weapons. Some eyed Lenaris fearfully, as if she too were a sorcerer.

"Is the world ruled by midluns and women now?" one muttered as he passed, and Lenaris couldn't help smiling.

The crowd moved through the gates. Lenaris peered back anxiously. The rebels had moved into the trees. The Zaldeaans eyed them, raising shields. But they kept running. They cheered when the rebels didn't attack. Louder when they began to pass the rebels, no one stopped them, and they realised they were free.

"Where did…"

A small group of guards gaped at Lenaris from the foot of the right tower. More footsteps thudded behind them.

"Your companions are leaving," she said. "That way," and she pointed.

They stared.

"Does Syenne have a daughter?" one asked.

Lenaris smiled. A strong woman who appeared to speak Migryan, obviously she must be Syenne's daughter.

The Zaldeaans ran after their countrymen. Others followed, solo, in pairs or trios from around the courtyard, many hastily climbing down ladders from guard towers after their countrymen.

Light flashed above the towers. Elite Guard were still fighting sorcerers.

"That prisoner is staring at you," Mawana said softly.

Lenaris looked up. In a cell window near the top of the third tower, a man with a long beard, long hair and a thin face had his gaze locked on her. Light flashed again, briefly illuminating his proud face and the way he stared at her, like she was a star that had stepped down from the heavens.

"Father," she breathed.
The next flash of light came from the window a single floor above Pamoran's cell.

Then Lenaris was running. Her feet made short work of the ground between her and the tower. Torches burned at regular intervals inside the staircase. Shocked Zaldeaan guards gaped as she ran towards them on the tower stairs.

"Out of my way!" she commanded. "Join your companions on the road!"

They froze, staring. Some reached for weapons, but didn't draw them.

Doors on all four sides opened at the first level, and again at the second. Lenaris clutched at the wall as the tower shook. Elite Guard were fighting sorcerers up there. She wasn't sure what she could do to stop them. But she sure as Chaos wasn't letting her father get killed in the crossfire.

She climbed and climbed. A cold wind blew against her face. The staircase led right up to the roof and the top half of her torso was in the open air.

She froze. A wide-eyed woman stood before her; Elite Guard Captain Rilmar.

Captain Rilmar swallowed, peering around Lenaris. A darkly dressed man stood behind her, staring at her. Lenaris had stepped right between them. And from the tingling traces of magic in the air, she didn't stand a chance against either.

"The Middle South are marching on Azula," Lenaris told them both. "A God King is stirring. War is coming. But no one need die here tonight."

"You can barely wield magic," said the man. "Yet you dare confront us?"

"I have fought sorcerers before," Lenaris told him calmly, as she stepped up to stand level with him. "And damars and Zaldeaans. I know your power. I will fight if I have to. But if you are like Dargus, Poran or Darius, I would rather not."

The man frowned. "What do you know of Darius?"

"We captured him," said Captain Rilmar, "Alive, in the sewers of my home city in the Timbalen Empire."

The man gaped. "He *led* that expedition. Why didn't you kill him?"

"Their Emperor wanted to," said Lenaris. "But my regent stopped him."

"Why didn't your people kill him when they had the chance?" the man pressed. "Who are your people?"

"Elite Guard, of the Timbalen Empire," said Captain Rilmar.

"Why are the Guardians attacking a prison?" another man asked from the rooftop opposite. He tensed, as a male Elite Guard climbed up before him. The Elite Guard's gaze flicked to Captain Rilmar and he didn't attack.

The second sorcerer continued, not taking his eyes off the new Elite Guard, "I thought it was *your* style to break into people's homes and murder them in their beds?"

"Is that not why *you* invaded *us*?" the male Elite Guard asked. "You tried to wipe us out because of mere rumour and suspicion! You did not bother to establish our supposed guilt before you attacked our capital city!"

"Attack the Guardian homeland?" the second sorcerer objected.

"How else do you think we learnt of your existence? Why else would we sail halfway across the world to defend our people?" the male Elite Guard replied.

"Defend them from what?" asked the second sorcerer.

"From your paranoid king!"

"Paranoid?" asked the second sorcerer. "Guardians are tyrants! They tried to mass murder sorcerers down to babies during the war! If you exist in great numbers once more, it is no wonder he invaded you!"

"Are *you* not tyrants?" Captain Rilmar asked. "When you lock up people who have harmed no-one?"

Mawana tugged at Lenaris's leg from the stair well. She shook her head. If the sorcerers started fighting again, her father's life was in danger. Mawana sighed and nodded.

"The Galvation prisoners would see you kill us!" the second sorcerer yelled at Captain Rilmar. "They would see healing cease and innocents go to prison because of the incompetence of non-magical law enforcement. They would see plagues in the south wipe out entire cities, because they would rather the world die of plague than anyone wield magic!"

"You claim to imprison Galvations to allow your comrades to heal?" a second familiar Elite Guard woman asked, climbing onto the rooftop beside the male Elite Guard.

The second sorcerer shifted to keep both enemies firmly in his sights.

"Some prisoners here are well-connected, wealthy and would happily use assassins to weed sorcerers out of their cities," said the first sorcerer. "The Keepers suspect one has already done so, but they could not prove it; hence he is still alive."

"They chose not to execute him because of lack of proof of his crimes?" asked the woman Elite Guard.

"Of course," the first sorcerer replied. "No one can be found guilty unless evidence proves their guilt beyond reasonable doubt."

"But if this man is alive," said the woman, "then that is proof of King Narz's reforms, and that they apply even to his enemies."

"Why do you care?" asked the first sorcerer. "Why the interest in justice?"

"Justice is at the core of our creed," said Captain Rilmar. "It binds us to use our magic only for what is just, not merely what can, under limited, prejudiced circumstances be justified, like the slaying of all sorcerers during war.

"As Elite Guard, it is our duty to guard our people against all harm, including injury and illness. Some of us work as healers, disguising our use of magic with herbal remedies, so as not to alarm people."

"How have you pretended to be anything other than powerful sorcerers?" the first sorcerer asked incredulously.

"Our descent has always been claimed as mixed human and Guardian," Captain Rilmar replied. "Any use of magic makes people nervous, but why should the descendants of the Guardians not possess strange powers?"

"*Are* you descendants of Guardians?" the first sorcerer asked.

Lenaris help her breath.

"Our descent is truly unknown," Captain Rilmar replied. "Among our ranks, it does not matter. Anyone possessing 'strange abilities' in our homeland is considered of 'Guardian descent', trained in their powers and offered a place among our number, where our creed governs use of their powers.

"Personally, I believe that whoever we once were, our numbers have included hundreds of sorcerers over the centuries and continue to do so. There are some who flatly refuse this, and war between our people and yours will strengthen their position, allowing us to define ourselves as other and better than you, even to hate you. But I do not believe we are so different."

"How can anything you say be true, when you come to free people who oppose magic?" the first sorcerer asked.

"Galvation captains who fought in the war have not directly harmed anyone. I see their freedom as harmless."

"It is not!" protested the second sorcerer.

"Then persuade them to make it so. Release them. Let them see magic wielded for healing and just purposes. Let them see for themselves the benefits you claim to desire for this continent."

"So they can persuade hundreds to die of plague rather than let us heal them?" the second sorcerer demanded.

"I have healed people with magic without their knowing, so their ignorance and prejudice and unfounded fears did not kill them. There are ways to ensure all you wish for comes to pass. Your challenge is finding ways that least harm all effected."

"That is devious," said the first sorcerer.

There was a pause, then he added, "There are too few voices among King Narz's commanders. Your views deserve consideration."

"She lies!" said the second sorcerer. "She tries to deceive us into surrender!"

"Even if that is her intention; her logic stands," the first sorcerer replied. "You would argue the imprisonment of Galvatia is unjust? How do we know you have not come destroy sorcerers?"

"Would we announce our opposition so spectacularly as we have tonight, were that the case?" Captain Rilmar asked.

There was a pause.

"Do you have the authority to make peace?" the first sorcerer asked.

"On this night and at this location; yes. But further negotiations with representatives of sorcerers under King Narz would be necessary to prevent the outbreak of war."

"Not negotiations with King Narz himself?" the first sorcerer asked.

"If our commander, appointed by the emperor himself, ordered us to war against our better judgement; we would refuse him. Can you say the same?"

"If you can prove we resemble one another," said the first sorcerer, "and the prudence of, and opportunity to masquerade as Guardians has allowed you to succeed in what we struggle to accomplish; it may be possible to persuade King Narz war is unnecessary."

"How might that be achieved?" Captain Rilmar asked.

"I would meet more Elite Guard. I would see in your behaviour the proof of your words. And if you convince me, perhaps some of you would accept my invitation to live among us and judge us for yourselves. I am Jaygoff. My brother is Captain of the Keepers, and he will value my word. He may be able to arrange an audience for you with King Narz."

"You would put your life in their hands?" the second sorcerer asked angrily.

"Killing them is difficult, overcoming them costly," Jaygoff replied. "There were only ten sorcerers here tonight, and by my count, fifteen Elite Guard. Can you imagine the destruction if an Elite Guard army went to war against *all* His Worthiness' sorcerers?"

"I don't trust them," the second sorcerer objected.

"I am not saying I do," said Jaygoff. "But this must be tried."

There was a pause, in which Lenaris wished the pale light of the moons let her see the sorcerers faces clearly. Then the two Elite Guard were holding the collapsing second sorcerer upright.

"What have you done?" Captain Rilmar asked.

"Put him to sleep," Jaygoff replied. "His fear would reignite a costly, unnecessary battle. If I place him and my unconscious comrades in a carriage, will it be permitted to return to Tiama?"

"You have my word," said Captain Rilmar. "I will see it safely beyond our allies."

Jaygoff turned to Lenaris. "You intended to get us talking? You endangered yourself by intervening for that purpose?"

Lenaris smiled. "Zaldeaans prefer to solve things with swords, but Tarlahns like myself are fonder of words. I was in the sewers beneath Timbala City with Captain Rilmar. Not everyone survived that confrontation. I know the power of sorcerers, and you were fighting above my father's cell."

Captain Rilmar blinked.

"My father is Companion Pamoran. He was Regent of Tarlah during the siege."

Captain Rilmar nodded in recognition, but Jaygoff frowned. "There are no easterners here."

"We came to free the prisoners," said Captain Rilmar. "Will you oppose us?"

"Where will they go?" Jaygoff asked carefully.

"North," said Lenaris. "We understand there is a neutral kingdom there."

Jaygoff's face brightened. "Queen Ziliene wished no part in any war. If she will take the prisoners… but what made her change her mind?"

"The coming war," said Captain Rilmar. "Her message to the Galvations was that all refugees are welcome in the Forest Realm."

Jaygoff considered it. "If she will take them in, we shall let them go."

"What will Narz think of this?" Captain Rilmar asked.

Jaygoff sighed. "Rebels relocating to the North is the same as staying here: they no longer threaten his Worthiness work. It is better. They shall be happier in the north. And not guarding them frees us to defend our people. We will free the prisoners, on condition your people let us march freely with you, to the border of the northern kingdom, to witness their departure."

Captain Rilmar inclined her head.

"Can I see my father now?" Lenaris asked.

Jaygoff frowned. Then he handed Lenaris a ring of keys. "I will follow at a distance. They may not leave their cells if dreaded sorcerers are in the corridor."

Lenaris thanked him.

"Galvations!" Captain Rilmar yelled down into the courtyard below the tower. "Stand by to support the prisoners' exit. We are opening the cells!"

Several stories bellow, the rebel leader Lenaris had spoken to led the rebels into the courtyard. There was no sign of Zaldeaans on the ground below. If the sorcerers kept their word, the evacuation could begin.

Lenaris almost knocked Mawana and the Elite Guard down the stairs as she rushed to the landing and unlocked the first door. Confused faces stared when she pushed it open.

"This is a prison break!" she said loudly enough for everyone on that level to hear. "The Galvation Resistance awaits below to escort you to the North."

Prisoners stared as she opened the next door and the next. When all four doors were open, she rushed down to the next level, leaving Mawana to persuade the bemused prisoners it was safe to come out. The next cell revealed a few confused couple. The next two men. But the third…

Pamoran turned from his window in surprise, then his smile lit up his whole face. Even by the faint light of torches on the landing, she could tell his face was more lined, his hair streaked with grey. He'd lost too much weight, but he still stood tall and proud.

"How in Chaos name are you here?"

Her Elite Guard smiled and reached for the keys, to continue unlocking cells while Lenaris answered, "If you thought you were bold as regent of Tarlah, you won't believe what Ruarnon's like. They've met four friends from a far distant country, who have empowered their more radical thinking. They united the Realm during civil war —behind their leadership. Even Governor Iagl respects them. And Governor Syenne took them under her wing.

"Father, I've sailed the eastern seas with Ruarnon. I've been to the Timbalen Empire, Cauldron Island, even the Island of the Guardians. And it was all so Ruarnon could train soldiers and prepare them for this. For rescuing you, and their parents, and if they can manage it, even the Zaldeaans."

Pamoran slowly smiled. "I leave Tarlah at the height of siege, and that youth brings peace then travels the world? How is my father coping with all this? I assume Monin advises Ruarnon?"

Lenaris smiled. "He said something about needing King Urmilian back because advising Ruarnon's changes of the world were too much for his twilight years."

"You both matured enough for that old bastard to speak honestly to you?"

Lenaris laughed. She may have called her grandfather that too, but never to her father. "Yes."

Pamoran smiled and stepped to hug her. She ignored the smell of his unwashed body and held him close, trying not to tense at how much thinner his once powerful frame was in her arms.

"So Monin's plot to have you marry Ruarnon and influence our young regent backfired spectacularly?" Pamoran said as they stepped apart. "I suppose you had a hand in that?"

Lenaris laughed. "I did. But just because I am more vocal doesn't mean Ruarnon's will is not incomparable to mine. They would never shout anyone down, but they have the patience to move mountains. They want to help stop the war between the Timbalens and Narz."

Pamoran gaped. "Narz invaded the Elite Guard? Mijora protect us!"

Lenaris grimaced. "Umarinaris is given to fears and Chaos himself since you were in touch with it. But it hasn't all been bad news. The Urai were so impressed with how Ruarnon established peace in the Zaldeaan Realm that we have re-established relations with the Urai. Which is how I met my husband. Mawana!"

Mawana entered the room with a shy smile. It still amazed her, seeing a man that tall and broad hunch his shoulders, appearing unthreatening and modest, despite his size.

Pamoran took in Mawana's height, breadth and smile in a sweep.

"A warrior, clearly. Are you sure his mind is as sharp as his blade?"

"I try not to show it Sir," Mawana replied. "I don't share my cousin's ambition to be an apprentice Elder. Catching and studying animals for the Institute of Learning is more my style."

"Full of physical challenges, the great outdoors and a good way to mask your intellect?" Pamoran asked.

Mawana's smile broadened.

"Yet you came here?" Pamoran added.

"I wasn't going to part with my wife for an unknown period of months. Besides, Ruarnon isn't the only friend we are supporting here."

Pamoran turned expectantly, and Lenaris turned from his gaze. "Arlian and Ethlin fell in the siege," she told the wall. "But I have been training four new students. Troy is as reckless and funny as Arlian. Michael's mind is as sharp as Ruarnon's. Fiona is more like Telena. And though she'd hate to hear me say it, as we can clash, Linh is a girl after my own spirit."

"And Ruarnon manages to travel with you *and* this Linh?" Pamoran asked, shaking his head. "They have grown!"

Lenaris glared at her father, then at Mawana for laughing, which didn't stop him.

"How would you like some fresh air?" Mawana asked, offering Pamoran his arm, as they turned to the stairs and Pamoran moved frailly after them.

"I should like that very much," Pamoran replied.

Lenaris took her father's other arm, and they began descending the stairway, as other escapees cheered above them and many escapees footsteps joined them on the stairs, all flowing down toward the open air, the forest and freedom.

CHAPTER 22

ON THE MARCH -RUARNON

W here will your people go, if we succeed?" Ruarnon asked Prince Maharl at Joharlen's kitchen table, the day before the Forest Prison break. Tor, Joharlen and General Imphin sat with them, but the room felt quiet and empty.

"If we succeed, our land no longer has the resources to feed so many," the prince replied. "I wrote to Queen Ziliene. Taking in our refugees could be seen as a betrayal of her peace agreement with Narz. But she agreed to that. On condition that anyone who wishes to settle in her lands swears they are done with war. Even aiding our rebellion."

"You agreed to that?" Ruarnon asked.

"All that would remain then is to free Black City," said Joharlen. "All who wished to help could rally in the west, where we can feed volunteers."

"Narz's sky enchantment is failing," Maharl added. "If he lacks the resources to restore it, our land will become more fertile, and we can return. Especially if the Zaldeaans are gone. We may regain our kingdom without war, while Narz fights the South. But for now, I would see our people safely sheltered in the west. With Queen Ziliene."

Ruarnon inclined their head.

"The Queen had a message for you," Prince Maharl added, eyeing Ruarnon intently.

Ruarnon frowned. "You told her about me?"

"No. But she seems to know who you are, that you seek your parents, and she wishes to meet you before you attempt to do so."

"Did she say why?" Ruarnon asked.

"Only that there are things you should know first that she will not commit to writing."

Secrets she did not want to risk being exposed, like Lylah's sisters...

Ruarnon had a legitimate means of communicating with Narz and they could ask to have their parents returned... but Narz could have just told 'Tarlahn Ambassador Drake' he was done with the Tarlahn king and queen and let them accompany 'Drake' back to Tarlah. Yet Narz hadn't mentioned Ruarnon's parents. And Darius said Narz was reluctant to talk about them.

Time was running short, and Ruarnon could scarce justify a side trip, but with Narz's fearful powers, and his courteous response to diplomacy, it appeared he could be reasonable when approached the right way, and exceptionally dangerous when not. But how did Ruarnon convince Narz they were not an enemy, and persuade him to respond to their request to free Ruarnon's parents?

Queen Ziliene had negotiated peace with Narz. Visiting her was a likely opportunity to learn things that may be necessary to succeed in freeing their parents.

Tor inclined his head.

"Please tell her I accept and look forward to meeting her," Ruarnon told to Maharl.

"There was more to her invitation," Maharl added.

Tor frowned.

"She is aware that you sail with the Timbalens but do not intend to go to war. That your forces are to remain neutral. She has invited you to anchor your fleet in her harbour."

Ruarnon frowned at an offer that was a provocative move for a supposedly neutral territory.

"What do you think her intentions are?" Tor asked Maharl.

Maharl sighed. "She offers shelter to anyone who wishes no part in sorcery war. Queen Ziliene is as much protector and guardian of her people as she is ruler. She has taken in runaways from the south, even escapees from the God Kings. There are rumours sorcerers have found refuge in her Queendom. That is why I wondered if she were a Guardian. She acts like one, in the way she protects, teaches and nurtures any who entrust her with their care."

He slumped. "Narz approached us by stealth. But she knew he was coming. She warned us. That is how we had time to evacuate Galvatia City. She is already harbouring Galvation refugees. She took everyone from our city who made it to her borders, and sent wagons to pick up stragglers, just before Narz's army arrived."

Ruarnon's mouth opened in wonder. The connection to Lylah's desire to protect the Urai by teaching them magic was obvious, but what stood out more was that Queen Ziliene had *already* taken in refugees from Narz's enemies, months ago. And he was still at peace with her. That must be why she was willing to take in refugees from the prisons. But more, it suggested she knew something about Narz, at least how to deal with him in her favour. Ruarnon was determined to speak with her.

"Once my Elite Guard reach Fang Mountain Prison," said General Imphin, "Narz will know we have arrived in force. From the moment that prison break begins, so does our countdown to war."

Ruarnon inclined their head. "It would be best to relocate my fleet now, before the Elite Guard move openly."

"It is a risk to trust a strange harbour to receive our ships," said Tor. "But remaining with the Timbalens puts us at risk of immanent attack. And if our ships are sighted in Galvation waters, we may be presumed guilty by association. Relocating our fleet would send a clear message to Narz that we have no intention of using it against him."

"Save the small forces of Zaldeaans and Tarlahans involved in the prison breaks," Ruarnon said slowly. "We will move the fleet. And greet General Takanis on our arrival in the North."

Orders were given. Then General Imphin left to check up on Elite Guard preparing for the Fang Mountain Prison Break, and Ruarnon helped Prince Maharl, the cook, Tor and Joharlen pack food supplies into a wagon, ready for their journey to hopefully meet Forest Prison Escapees and lead them to Queen Ziliene's Forest Realm. The princes' personal luggage was loaded and the cook climbed in, while Prince Maharl and Joharlen stood before Ruarnon and Tor.

"I am sorry we could not include Black City in our plans," Ruarnon said.

Prince Maharl inclined his head.

"Thanks to Amina, we know a number of our soldiers have been moved there," said Joharlen. "And that Damaria is beside Black City."

"Neither of us has the forces to neutralise Damaria," Prince Maharl added.

"It feels unfinished," said Ruarnon.

"My hope is that when my people move north and respect Queen Ziliene's peace with him, and when war with the Middle South begins, Narz may recall every soldier he has guarding Black City, to pit them against the Middle South. If we should be so lucky, both my people and your Zaldeaans working there may be freed without us lifting a finger. If not, I think it likely Narz will empty Damaria to fight the Middle South. If he does, we can attempt a Black City Plan."

Ruarnon inclined their head, then shook hands with both men. Tor did the same.

"We wish you well with your parents," said Joharlen.

"And I wish you well with your people," said Ruarnon.

"Thank you, for the magic and hope you have given us," said Prince Maharl.

"Thank you for your hospitality," Tor added.

They bowed their heads to each other, then both princes boarded the wagon, and the cook inclined her head, before flicking the reins. The wagon trundled away.

Ruarnon spent that night at the farmhouse and the next day smiling at a distant dark line that was surely a column of Forest Prison escapees marching north around the damar infested forest.

Ruarnon sat the next night on Joharlen's porch, beside Companion Tor and Captain Arleath, their bodyguards waiting around them. Their shoulder's tightened when flashes lit up the sky above Fang Mountain.

"Now Narz knows the Elite Guard are here," they said quietly.

Tor inclined his head. "There were too many sorcerers at Fang Mountain. It was always possible one would tell him before they were overpowered."

"It feels…" said Ruarnon, "like Timbala City. Watching other people act, and someone else react, and Chaos having his way."

"This is far from over," said Tor. "Lylah said you too were crucial to better futures."

"You trust her?" Ruarnon asked.

"I trust you will do anything you can to make a difference. And trying to recover your parents may present that opportunity."

Ruarnon nodded. Perhaps diplomacy could find a way…

They were grateful when the hour to mount their horse came. They set out under starlight with Tor and their bodyguards, the latter carrying three dark lanterns, against which the grain fields they rode through shone grey.

Ruarnon hoped their uncle found the prayer book they had had a scout drop in a courtyard of Karmarn's castle. Its quality could only belong to Karmarn, and Governor Iagl was confident it would be 'returned' to him. Under *Prayers to the Mother*, the Zaldeaan protectress, Karmarn would find Ruarnon's orders to renege, should war with the Middle South break out. Orders to be passed on to Companion Nish, and captains held hostage in Tiama, Arveta and Azula's capital cities. Their orders were to mutiny. Lives would be lost overpowering the few sorcerers guarding them, but fewer than if they fought.

Ruarnon sighed. No Zaldeaans leaders in Narz's other kingdoms had dared attempt a mutiny. But now all two thousand captive men could be punished for Zaldeaan failure to secure Narz's prisons against enemies. And the Zaldeaan king (though whether they accepted Ruarnon as such was another matter) was ordering them to mutiny. Ruarnon sincerely hoped it was possible for Companion's Nish and Karmarn to obey those orders.

The mountain range in the distant south-east concealed two pieces of unfinished business, Black City and Karmarn's castle. But Ruarnon turned northeast, entering the riverbed their friends had used as an escape highway. Unknown to their friends, the other branch rounded the Damarian Forest, and ran under a magic barrier that kept damars out, then flowed into the Forest Realm.

Ruarnon's guards dark lanterns shone on the footprints of Forest Prison escapees who had marched down the riverbed to safety earlier that day. Ruarnon crossed their tracks and reined in atop the far bank. The distant grey patches of tiny dark lanterns showed Fang Mountain's escapees marching towards them, perhaps a league away.

When the head of the column neared the river, Mawana's height and size stood out from a small group at the front. The group almost reached the river before Ruarnon made out Lenaris's smiling face. The face beside her smiled too. Even in the dark lanterns, it was older, beardier and thinner, less full of life and restless energy than Ruarnon recalled.

When the three crossed the river, they paused to greet Ruarnon. Captain Rilmar inclined her head as she rode on past, leading the escapees in the riverbed onwards.

"Lenaris has been telling me of your Benevolences' adventures," Companion Pamoran greeted Ruarnon. "Urmilian himself will struggle to believe what you have achieved."

Were those tears in his eyes? Tutor Pamoran's? Regent Pamoran's?

Pamoran smiled. "I would offer my advice in days to come, but I fear you have outgrown it."

Ruarnon smiled. "Your father does not agree. I have had to wrestle him into place with words many times."

Pamoran laughed. "Quiet, unassuming Heir Ruarnon putting my brick of an old man in place. There is a sight I regret not seeing."

His expression became more serious. "I tried to free your parents. The Azulans believed I was wielding magic to help them. At first, I thought it absurd. But when I tried wielding magic, I caught the attention of a sorcerer on Fang Mountain. And now Lenaris tells me you can *all* craft magic?"

"If my former tutor is willing to learn, I would happily teach him," Ruarnon replied and Pamoran laughed. "Though I may not have time in coming days."

"No," said Pamoran. "But I look forward to it."

The sparkle in his eyes suggested he was serious. Teaching him magic would likely be as dangerous as learning to spar with him. Pamoran smiled fiercely, as if reading Ruarnon's mind and Ruarnon smiled back.

Pamoran turned to Tor. "Hello old friend. I see you've been letting the youth's ideas run away with them. Or have you been encouraging their pursuit of Chaos and dreams worthy of the Creator's themselves?"

Tor smiled, clapping him on the arm. "Someone had to do it. As you were not available to prod them into wild things…"

Both men grinned at each other.

"There is one more thing you need to know Ruarnon," Pamoran said, steering his horse beside theirs, as the group rode into the riverbed alongside escapees marching on foot. "When I was accused of using magic to free your parents, Narz's response was strange. He didn't look at anyone. And he said, 'The parents must be kept safe.' Not the 'King and Queen.' 'The parents'.

"I suspect he feared my ability to craft magic could put me in conflict with the sorcerer guarding us, and that that would endanger your parents. But why did it matter to him that you are their child and they are parents? Or whether they are kept safe?"

Pamoran took a deep breath. "I wonder if his emphasis on 'parents' implies he has some use for you, and that their safety is important to his plans for you. It may be that I have been alone too long, with too many hours to think, but I wonder."

Ruarnon gazed into the dark of night. "What use could *I* be to Narz?"

"I do not know," said Pamoran. "But Lenaris has told me of Lylah's ability. And she said you were crucial to better futures here. What if Narz has similar powers?"

Ruarnon sighed. *Seeing* Elite Guard training could had been what made Narz believe the Elite Guard were mobilising against him. But as was always the case with Narz; Ruarnon couldn't see how it made sense. Not yet.

They rode on.

Gradually, the sky turned grey, and stars faded, as the river curved, leading them north-east. On Ruarnon's left, barren rocky wasteland obscured pale sky with jagged, dark rock formations, while on the right, trees of the damar-infested forest provided shade from the first rays of sunlight.

Ruarnon's guards, Lenaris and Mawana strung their bows and nocked arrows, their eyes keenly studying trees right of the riverbed. Bowstrings twanged as damars hissed, screeched and fell dead. Ruarnon and their friends rode in the riverbed a league beyond where the last damar fell, then up into the forest, where they slept.

The next day they rode until their shadows grew long and the light turned golden. Then Captain Arleath pointed at figures reclining beside the road ahead, watched over by Tarlahn soldiers, their horses grazing nearby. Michael roused his friends and Ruarnon smiled, dismounted and greeted them. Linh looked paler than they remembered and thinner, but she still hugged Ruarnon and her smile hadn't changed.

As Lenaris introduced her father to their friends, Ruarnon noticed someone else beside the trees. Coroth looked taller, older and wiser than at the festival of the Gods, two years ago. The laughter in Coroth's eyes had dimmed. His expression was more reserved, a slight smile. His round cheeks and the burden of leadership in his eyes and the frown of his brow mirrored Omah. But his blue-eyed, blond-haired colouring resembled Ruarnon's father. The combination caught Ruarnon's breath.

Coroth smiled, then his expression sobered. "My mother deeply regrets her ignorance your parents were captive in Falls City during the siege. We would have tried to recover them had we known."

"From what I heard, you hand your hands full defending Aunt Merlah against warmongers," Ruarnon replied, and Coroth bowed his head.

They recognised the lilt of their cousin's Zaldeaan accent now, but Coroth's air of authority was wholly foreign.

"I saw your parents," Ruarnon added and Coroth gaped. "I was captured by a sorcerer," they added when Coroth's eyebrows raised. "I woke up in their castle. Your mother greeted me, giving me a false identity. Your father is an outstanding actor."

Coroth sighed. "Narz watches them more closely. He trusts them less than me. He knows I'm in love with his protégé, Teliph. I was a hostage, and I think he anticipated them coming for me and trying to help our people escape again.

"Narz can seem relentless, but I think it's because he anticipates tenacity from his opposition. Perhaps the same tenacity that let him become king in a kingdom where everyone fears sorcerers.

"It's strange, he kept me and my father captive, and he doesn't trust my father. But he seems to respect us. I only met him twice. First when we arrived. After a month sailing with people who could set the sky on fire. Our worst fears of the North Landers, our captors who could burn our fleet to the ground. 'Do not worry,' he told me. 'You, your friend and some of your soldiers are not old enough by my judgement. You will not fight against the Galvations. You may wait in safety, then patrol Galvatia once it is conquered.'"

Coroth shivered.

"That sounds like a psychopath, pretending to care about you," said Michael, and Ruarnon started, realising their friends had finished speaking to Pamoran.

Coroth shook his head. "No. The look in his eyes. He has strong views about young men fighting. He was angry at my father for allowing it. Said we should have a chance to live, before granting us a chance to die. The look on his face when he spoke …it made me wonder who he lost.

"We didn't fight. He wouldn't let anyone under twenty take the field, even though in the Realm a burly fifteen-year-old would be given arms. We stayed at his castle during the war. He even told us how far we were from the fighting, as if to reassure us. That's when I met Teliph. Narz was anxious at first. He referred to us as his 'guests', children of the army occupying Galvatia.

"Teliph was conflicted about the war. She didn't argue with him, but to me she questioned the need to occupy Galvatia. She worried about Narz, that he was becoming crueller to protect his Healers and Keepers, his dream of using sorcerers to create a better world. I feared she was right. And when the Galvations were defeated and rounded up, and prisons chosen, I asked the honour of running the Forest Prison.

"Narz was … *proud* of me. He knew I feared him. He knew I felt sorry for the Galvations. He seemed proud that I took a stand for what I believe in."

Ruarnon stared in wonder. How could Narz be so fearful and untrusting of adults, yet show care towards young people and make them feel …*welcome*?

"It's the same pride he has of Teliph," Coroth continued earnestly. "She does question him sometimes, and though he may rail against her arguments, he never tells her to shut up, like her father, Tarz. He lets her speak, even when he doesn't want to hear it.

"I don't think he trusts adults. He seems wary of them. But half his Healing Temples were founded in areas with high infant mortality rates. I don't understand it. And when my friend Demune," he nodded to a young man waiting nearby, "asked if he could work in the forest prison, Narz let him, knowing we were friends. He *smiled* when *we* smiled about it.

"I sent Demune on patrols when Narz learnt you and your friends were here. I wanted to ensure you were treated well if a patrol caught you."

"That plan worked," Linh said with a smile.

"If you are seeking your parents," Coroth said urgently, "I know this may sound strange, but from all your friends say you achieved in my homeland and the east... Narz may think the world of you, as a bold young person with big dreams. As a leader. He may respect you. Your best bargaining chip to free your parents may be asking him in person."

Ruarnon sighed. Of all the ways they could attempt to recover their parents, why must the best insight they had into Narz's character suggest the most effective one was walking into a sea monster's mouth and seeing what happened?

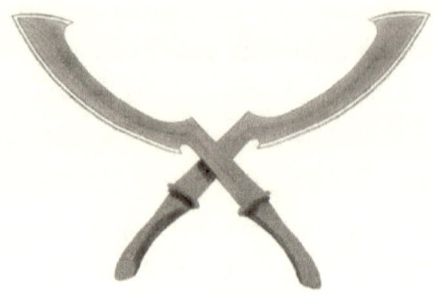

CHAPTER 23

A YOUNG MAN'S WAR -RUARNON

Later that day they rode until the trees thinned and Ruarnon made out bright green, crop covered hills ahead. The forest curved to the edge of sight left and right, embracing a vast land of fields.

"Is that a cornfield?" Troy asked.

"The Great Forest conceals this kingdom on all sides," Ruarnon replied. "Prince Maharl says it has done so since refugees fled here during the Sorcery War. Everyone who lives here takes a vow to do no violence and tell no-one outside this land of its existence. That is why Prince Maharl was so vague about it, until Queen Ziliene invited me."

"So that's why they're happy to take in refugees, but not fight?" Troy asked. "They're all pacifists?"

"Perhaps not all of them," said Ruarnon. "Prince Maharl says that over the past year the strongest, most adventurous and bravest people of Queen Ziliene's court have vanished. He suspects they have combated Narz in some way and failed. I do not think he had the nerve to ask Queen Ziliene how."

They followed the column of Fang Mountain escapees along a dirt track. Cornfield covered hills gave way to orchards. Wattle and daub cottages with thatched roofs rose among plantations. A village of log houses lay beyond, with Forest Prison escapees lining its main, road as far as Ruarnon could see. Villagers and farmers handed out cloaks, sandals or bread, and two villagers raised buckets of well water for thirsty escapees. Their four Australian friends stared.

"If this was our country," Fiona said to Ruarnon, "these people wouldn't be allowed to just rock up and wander about, or regarded with such compassion. The Galvations are lucky to have neighbours like this."

They rode through more villages scattered between animal paddocks, fields, orchards, meadows and streams. Deeper in the Forest Realm uncertainty, even fear was writ on local faces as escapees marched down their roads. Did they fear the presence of so many outsiders threatened the secrecy of their land? Or the Forest Realm's neutrality in wars further south? But the locals didn't hinder anyone.

"Are these people safe?" Troy asked after a while. "From Narz?"

"Prince Maharl and General Imphin suspect Narz wants the northern wasteland searched," Tor replied, "but they doubt the patrols will venture this far. They expect Narz to see the fighting on Fang Mountain as Guardian aggression and anticipate him rallying his armies to defend against them."

"Why hasn't Narz attacked the Timbalens yet?" Michael asked.

"We think he wants to give Lord Vye more time to train his sorcerer army in combat," said Tor. "He will be nervous about pitting inexperienced sorcerers against highly trained Elite Guard."

"And we suspect Octharl awaits Narz's forces assembling to determine his invasion route," Ruarnon added.

"So once Narz's armies mobilise, it'll be the eve of war?" Michael asked.

Ruarnon nodded.

It was strange, riding purposefully and overtaking uncertain Galvation refugees wandering to unknown destinations at a hesitant pace. Ruarnon shivered. The evacuees of Tarlah City might have walked a similar path into the Urai jungle, had the Timbalens been too late or not come at all, and Tarlah City fallen to the Zaldeaan army.

As they rode past refugees, Ruarnon saw who their people had been, and who many people on this continent would become, if the war between the Timbalens and Narz was not stopped.

They shivered. The Middle South and Narz's kingdoms could be reduced to this even if the Timbalens *did* go home. Especially if they went to war against each other *and* a God King and his sorcerers joined the war. This line of displaced people without homes, or work, could multiply in weeks to come. And there may be nothing Ruarnon could do about it.

Lost in thought, they didn't notice Coroth ride alongside them until he spoke. "I am sorry about Uncle Omah. He was my favourite Tarlahn relative."

Ruarnon met blue eyes like their father's, darkened around the edges by a strain of leadership like Omah's. They bowed their head.

"You must have known all along," they said, "that your parents' marriage was a diplomatic one and there was risk your people would go to war against the other half of your family."

Coroth's gaze fell. "I always knew something was amiss. There were people who resented my mother even in my earliest memories. When I asked, father said he would tell me when I was older. I was seven when they told me how their marriage began."

Coroth smiled and Ruarnon wondered what could be happy about the situation.

"My mother threatened to kill him when they first met. Father says that for all she presents as a respectable, indoors Zaldeaan woman, she's always been a skilled fighter. I helped defend her during the war, but she killed more assassins than I did. It was an odd notion for someone raised in the Realm, the idea that your mother could kill with a sword, when Zaldeaan culture says mothers are loving and nurturing people who need men to protect them. Yet my mother trained me to fight. Father was too busy, and he said she was more skilled."

Ruarnon smiled. "It's a shame she had to live in the Realm. I suspect she would get along well with General Takanis. And Lenaris would like her."

"She *is* friends with General Takanis. They learnt to fight together when they were young. They've been in correspondence ever since she moved to the Realm."

Coroth took a deep breath. "Uncle Omah asked me to speak to Kyura during your diplomatic visit. He asked me to help him see reason. But Kyura would not see me. As things got worse, the whispers of war, the attempts on Governor Iomar and Governor Kia's lives, my parents started to keep me out of his sight. Father said when he looked at me, he saw Tarlah. He saw the people whose lives war would destroy, even worse so than his own people's.

"I saw the same guilt in Narz's eyes, the second time I met him. When he was not keeping us young Zaldeaans safe from war and there was no pretence of my status as guest. When it was clear I was a captive.

"He does whatever he believes is necessary to protect his people, but I suspect it pains him, as it pained Kyura. Narz is stronger and I do not think he would ever take his own life. But I fear what he might do, if pushed as Timbalen invasion and the Middle South marching against him would push him. And mother preserve us if the God kings march on him. They will have none of the Elite Guard's restraint."

Ruarnon sighed, their concerns weighing upon their shoulders like sandbags.

"If your parents are still in his castle," Coroth added, looking Ruarnon directly in the eyes, "your plans may need to allow for his guilt. If you need to communicate with him again, you must be very careful."

Ruarnon frowned.

Coroth sighed. "I think my parents kept me away from Kyura in his final days because they feared his guilt on seeing me, a half-Tarlahn, half-Zaldeaan, person he had failed to protect from war, would destroy him. As sight of the destruction and deaths on our shores *did* destroy him. But you may not be able to avoid that confrontation with Narz. If not, you must be prepared to manage him carefully."

Ruarnon's insides tumbled. *Manage* Narz?

Then they remembered the sobs, the angry voices, the rage in Iagl's eyes and the terrible sadness in Syenne's, as they stood around Kyura's sarcophagus. They remembered how they had started a conversation among people in a state of strong, heated and volatile emotions, arguing with each other, and had ultimately led every party present to sign a peace agreement with Tarlah, which also secured peace between Iagl and Syenne.

Coroth wasn't asking anything of Ruarnon they hadn't already achieved. The difference was this time it was an entire continent, at least two sorcerer armies and armies of non-magic wielders at stake, not merely the Zaldeaan Realm. Dare they speak to a man of irrational fears about what scared him most?

Ruarnon had had little sway over Emperor Yarath or Commander Octharl, but from what Lenaris had overheard First Captain Rilmar say at Fang Mountain Prison, Rilmar may be able to swear the Elite Guard to peace. Could Ruarnon do the same with Narz?

Coroth's surprises weren't finished. His posture remained still in his saddle, and his uncertain gaze fell upon the road, as he licked his lips. "I may be able to help your parents," he offered. "If I tell Teliph that Narz holds my aunt and uncle captive… She can contact me by magic. She is a sorceress, and Narz's favourite pupil. I've yet to find the courage to ask how much she knows of his darker side, and she is yet to ask how exactly my people came to be here. She knows something is wrong, but he is the father she never had. If he loves anything, it will be her. If I ask her to speak on my behalf, he will listen."

"What is the status of your relationship with Teliph?" Ruarnon asked.

Coroth took a deep breath and said, "If Narz approves and persuades her father, she will be my wife. She is his only family. But she is troubled, perhaps because the worst in him is rising and she knows it. It may be dangerous to ask her for favours if the request conflicts with his cruel intentions and the benign ruler she believes him to be. From what she has said, Narz is complicated, and any dealings that prompt inner conflict for him are fraught. I hope your parents do not fall into that category."

"You would ask me to advocate for peace with him, but you think it too dangerous for you to do so?" Ruarnon asked.

"You're not here as a captive, or hostage, but of your own freewill. Narz's abduction of father's army secured peace for your people. He may believe he has helped you, whereas he knows he has wronged me, my family and my people. He will associate me with his guilt, which is why I would ask Teliph to speak for your family. But you and he may speak as free people, as equals, ruler to ruler."

Ruler to ruler… Ruarnon knew exactly how lonely it was to rule. Of the burden, stress and anxiety of carrying your people's wellbeing on your shoulders in hard times. And that was apparently exactly what Narz believed he was doing. How wonderful would it have been to speak freely, with no burden of leadership, knowing the other person understood exactly where they stood, during the siege of Tarlah? The occupation of the Zaldeaan Realm?

Ruarnon had never had that opportunity for support. But they had seen the difference it made with Maharl and Joharlen. How challenging the insular thinking of a fellow ruler under pressure could help them see the truth and find hope, and make and carry out plans that improved their peoples' future. They could attempt the same with Narz.

Ruarnon shivered, as they climbed hills barred by high stone walls. The road passed between gate towers with open, iron reinforced gates roofed by a stone arch. A second pair of gates stood further back; their towers joined by a stone ramp. Both gates could be shut to trap an enemy between, while archers loosed arrows. Queen Ziliene may be a pacifist, but the city she ruled had been built by people familiar with war, who knew how to defend themselves.

Two guards in bronze plate armour stood on each ramp, holding elaborately engraved, ceremonial battle-axes. Ruarnon's guide raised a hand, and the guards returned the gesture, their eyes flicking between Ruarnon's bodyguards and examining their friends, as they entered the courtyard between the gates.

Familiar sounds drifted towards Ruarnon, the hum of conversation, jingling money pouches, clacking of hooves on stone, the burble of children's laughter and clink of tools in workshops. The smell of freshly baked bread and sizzling meat wafted with the jumble of sounds carried on the breeze.

The second set of gates opened onto a crowded street in which children chased dogs, people carried bread baskets or pulled handcarts, a poor family rode in a wagon, a wealthy family travelled in a painted carriage, and a stream of people headed down a side street where distant cries of wares for sale and haggling rose. Above it all rose tall, narrow stone buildings with slender, gracefully framed balconies, outlined by the pinks, purples and blues of sunset.

A powerful longing for home rose within Ruarnon, as they rode into an oasis of ordinary life, unaffected by the sea of war threatening to flood the continent. They had struggled to understand Queen Ziliene watching Narz's sorcery batter Galvatia, his soldiers round up farmers and villages and imprison them in Black City, or the Galvation army lose the war. Now Ruarnon understood. She was protecting the safest realm on the continent, perhaps its greatest refuge since the Sorcery War.

They spent the evening in Queen Ziliene's palace, at a balcony dinner with their companions, in the peace and normality of the Queen's capital. Anxiety about the Timbalens or Narz antagonising each other into war's outbreak gnawed at them, but the scents of rich food and laughter and chatter from distant buildings on the wind wrapped them in the comfortable bundle of normality. They decided to soak it in and pretend for one day that all was well in the world.

The next morning, Ruarnon admired the rising sun reflecting off towers and spires linked by graceful bridges and domes of gold or glass. It seemed familiar… like the architecture of the City of Peaks on The Island of the Guardians, or the paintings of cities in caves painted by the faeron on Cauldron Island. Like a mythical city of a time now forgotten, the time before the First Sorcery war.

"Benevolence, it is time," said Tor.

Ruarnon strode out of their quarters. Tor would meet Queen Ziliene as their advisor. Lenaris and Linh waited as their companions, and Coroth waited too, Queen Ziliene having requested his presence, but also that they keep their party small. Ruarnon wasn't sure why.

Fiona waved them off, Michael nodded and Mawana and Troy wished them well. Then a servant led Ruarnon, their three companions and Coroth down a pale stone corridor, then past painted panels of children dancing through forest trees and under timber archways carved and painted to imitate flowering vines. The designs exuded beauty, mirroring the oasis of peace the Forest Realm was.

They descended a staircase carved with rippling railing and steps, then turned into a corridor ending in a grand arch with a green curtain beneath, flanked by guards in full bronze armour.

Ruarnon kept their breathing steady, noting tension in Tor's posture. Tor likely suspected the Queen was a sorceress. If her lands were like the North Lands, they may resemble what Narz aspired to, making a partnership between them natural, yet she appeared to distance herself. Ruarnon wasn't sure what to make of her.

The servant announced, "Ruarnon, Regent of Tarlah, King of the Zaldeaan Realm, Prime Ruler of the North Lands, and their advisors request an audience with Her Grace."

"They may enter," said the guard on the right, pulling the curtain aside, and Ruarnon led their companions into the hall beyond. To their left, glass windows overlooked a garden of flowers, with a path running to a stone chair atop a hill. Before them lay a dining table with green cushioned seats, covered with a green tablecloth and silver candleholders.

At the table's far end sat a tall woman. Long dark hair flowed over her shoulders. Her fine boned face was beige and faintly lined, but her black eyes resembled deep pools of knowledge from someone infinitely older. She wore a pale green gown and a gold circlet with an emerald in the middle, presenting as a ruler, unlike the Sisters, yet she radiated the same sense of power.

"Welcome, be seated," she said, in gentle tones, with unquestionable authority.

She gestured to rows of seats either side of the table. Tor and Lenaris sat either side of Ruarnon, Linh on the right edge, sitting straighter and more confidently than she had when translating for them on Cauldron Island, a lifetime ago.

"I am Ziliene, Queen of the Forest Lands," the Queen continued. "There is much I wish to discuss, but first, I wish to know of the manner in which Ambassador Drake left the house of Karmarn."

Ruarnon smiled. "My apologies. That name is fake. Companion Karmarn is my uncle by marriage, half-brother of the late Zaldeaan King Kyomi and my subject. He treated my arrival as a diplomatic query about when the Zaldeaan army would return to its homeland and Narz responded to it as such."

"What binds Commander Karmarn to King Narz?" Queen Ziliene asked, not missing a beat.

"Two thousand men, serving in Narz's kingdoms as hostages."

"You are certain that is their status?"

"He was determined to divide us when he heard of our numbers," Coroth replied, "When we first arrived and he wanted his Keepers to 'monitor' us."

"You do not think he was concerned that you serve his people as guards, rather than domineer them as soldiers?"

Coroth blinked in surprise and Ruarnon frowned. Surely she wasn't duped by the sorcerer's image of Narz as an idealistic hero? How could anyone sharing borders with Galvatia believe that?

"You are wary of me." Queen Ziliene eyed Ruarnon sharply, with eyes Ruarnon suspected were more common in the East Islands. Her servants had the same long black hair, flowing robes and dark eyes. Did the East Islander's also descend from people here in the west?

Ruarnon pushed the thought aside. "You look as though you could reach out with one hand and pluck Narz from power. You have aided Galvations, but still Narz sits on his throne, destroying their land with his sky enchantment perpetuating drought, maintaining a prison city full of Galvation slaves, and you make no move against him. Why?"

"My power will not stop him by force. And my influence is as likely to harm the state of his mind as to positively influence his actions. Narz debates whether he can risk sending his forces against Elite Guard, unaware at times they sit on his doorstep, but frightened of their presence at others. He knows the God Kings view Healers and Keepers of the Peace as frauds, or royal bastards, traitors and deserters, and that either way they will plot to destroy his people.

"Ideology would have forced Narz to war with the God kings eventually but having failed to destroy the people he believes are Guardians, provoking their wrath, knowing the Middle South is stalling negotiations and rallying against him, Narz sees enemies on all sides. He is paralysed by his fears."

Ruarnon gasped. Narz paralysed? After all his lashing out in the east?

"But the army of at least one God King is mobilising," Queen Ziliene continued, "and armies of the Middle South will reach Azula's southern border in two weeks. Once Narz learns of their approach, his sorcerer army will be unleashed, and anyone that comes between his sorcerers and the Divine Army will perish. Lylah has *Seen* it."

Ruarnon shivered. How on Umarinaris did this woman know what Lylah had seen?

"That gives us two weeks," Linh interrupted. "We must be able to do *something*."

"That is why I requested Ruarnon's presence, and invited Selenia, Captain Rilmar and the sorcerer Jaygoff, brother of the Captain of the Keepers."

Selenia entered the room, followed by a middle-aged woman with a calm face that gave away nothing, and a blonde man who appeared curious, yet reserved. Ruarnon struggled to return Selenia's smile. How did Flariah's task for her family, against Narz, tie her to this?

All three sat on the Queen's left, at her gesture. Selenia smiled at Ruarnon across the table, but their gaze was drawn to Jaygoff, who tingled with magic. Ruarnon had sat down to talk to Narz's sorcerers before, but not free ones, who could still craft magic. The notion made them tense, and Captain Rilmar sitting calmly beside Jaygoff, without a flicker of her own magic, puzzled them.

"The diplomacy begun between Captain Rilmar and Jaygoff on Fang Mountain may have been beautiful over time," Queen Ziliene continued, "and I hope it still shall be. But to prevent a sorcery war as devastating as the last, we are almost out of time.

"Captain Rilmar has convinced me the Elite Guard wish to avoid Sorcery War. If they can convince Narz of this and form an alliance against the God Kings, the worst of the coming war may be averted."

"But Narz thinks they're Guardians and is paranoid about Guardians!" Linh objected. "You'd have to cure his paranoia to make him believe the Elite Guard aren't enemies!"

"Not quite," Queen Ziliene replied. "We would need to counter his greatest fears. To prove them false. There is a way. Lylah is certain you and your three friends are bound to it and Ruarnon's assistance will be crucial."

Lenaris frowned. "How can you prove the Elite Guard are not Guardians?"

"We cannot. But we can prove their intent is not what Narz fears, by a means Narz is unable to deny."

"How can you be so sure?" Lenaris asked.

"Because I know and understand what caused the state of his mind and thus how to counter it. You Linh, have knowledge of trauma, of the effects of war on your mother. Do you not see where Narz's fears stem from?"

Linh's expressions flashed through surprise to conviction, to uncertainty. "But the war most likely to scar him like that…how can *he* have experienced the Sorcery War? Wasn't it *centuries* ago?"

"My mother told me the Sorcery War began when her mother was a child, with a city holding out against a long siege, its inhabitants fearful of slaughter by their enemies. When the city fell, the conquering army burst into flames. Survivors fled in terror and word of a new weapon spread.

"Kings desired it to protect their borders, reclaim conquered cities and settle old scores. They sought sorcery, and several kings waged war with it at once. Others feared it, fell to it, then learnt it and revolted with it. War and civil war tore the kingdoms of the known world apart. Thousands died, tens of thousands were enslaved, and the fighting raged until all knowledge of how it began was distorted and forgotten, and sorcerers were feared and hated the world over.

"Then the Guardians' appeared, and sorcerers died steadily, until they learnt to fear Guardians and rallied against them, but those in the north were too slow. The most powerful and well-known northern sorcerers fell in battle or were slain in hiding. Their slaves, servants and subjects escaped, their families went into hiding, the God Kings retreated to the Far South and the Sorcery War was ended.

"But during the war, not all sorcerers used their powers aggressively. Some used them only in self-defence. Narz's father was one.

Narz saw his father murdered by an enchanted sword which pierced his magical shield. Narz used his powers to fight off the attackers, and fled with his mother, younger brother and sister. They fell in with other sorcerer families, retreating to an abandoned castle which they made their home.

"Word of a city inhabited by sorcerers spread, and some sorcerers believed they could enslave them. War came to the castle, but Narz and his sorcerer-comrades used their powers to fight. They defeated their attackers and realised their power. They became an army under Narz's leadership, and freed two kingdoms from the rule of tyrannical sorcerers, restoring relatives of rightful kings to their thrones and returning a little order to a world that had descended into chaos.

"Then the Guardians came. They feared Narz's army had arisen to re-conquer kingdoms for sorcerers and attacked it. Narz was severely wounded and left for dead. When he awoke, he healed himself and fled in search of his family, with the few of his comrades he could heal. But his family had sorcery powers too, and fear of sorcery was at its height. His little brother, little sister and mother died as their powers were extracted by Guardians in the next town. His companions were slain trying to protect their families from the same fate."

Ruarnon stared into the distance. It would be like, after Ruarnon's allies had lifted the siege of Tarlah and people had come home to celebrate, everyone they loved had been slaughtered. How could anyone *live* with that?

"Narz fears the Elite Guard are merciless sorcerer-murderers because he encountered Guardians who were exactly that during the Sorcery War. Memory of those murders haunt his dreams to this day; seven centuries later. The only reason Narz survived, was because shock and horror paralysed him, suppressing his ability to wield magic and preventing Guardians from detecting him."

Ruarnon caught Lenaris's critical gaze at the words 'seven centuries later.'

"When he recovered from his initial shock," the Queen continued, "grief struck Narz and turned to rage. He joined a last alliance of sorcerers against Guardians, slaying as many as he could to avenge the family and community they had taken from him. Until he met a Guardian carrying an enchanted sword, like the one that killed his father. The pain and memories it stirred were too great, and he fled, after severely wounding that Guardian.

"The Guardian gave the weapon to a passing merchant, describing Narz to him, and making the man solemnly promise to deliver the weapon to anyone who could kill Narz. Unintentionally, he cast an enchantment as the agreement was made, so only the merchant and anyone he freely gave the weapon to could wield it.

"From that day, Narz roamed the countryside alone, swinging between grief and rage, attacked by and fighting Guardians, who hunted him, until rumour reached him of a weapon of great power in Tira. He decided it would be safer to seize the weapon than to flee, lest one of the Guardians chasing him recover it. But when he reached Tira, the city guard recognised him and attempted to apprehend him. He knocked them down and turned their spears to dust. A warning bell tolled and Tirans in the street fled to their homes in panic. Guards rushed from the gate towers, but all but one froze where they stood.

"Knowing that Guardians would arrive any moment, Narz seized the remaining guard and demanded to know where the man who alerted them to his presence lived. The guard looked instinctively in that direction. A dozen houses burst into flame. The trembling guard said the merchant was on the move and had the weapon with him.

"The Guardians would soon arrive, and Narz was unlikely to find the merchant first. Hating the Guardians, fearing them, wanting no one to help them find the weapon that could kill him, Narz lashed out, touching more magic than he had ever shaped before, and froze the city in time.

"Fleeing Tirans hung suspended over the streets, flickering flames were smothered by a statue of flame-like crystal, wagons and horses halted abruptly, screams and shouts cut off. Narz fixed more magic in place than left him energy to stand. It should have killed him. The spell should have broken instantly. But it did not. He had found a way to hold it in place without actively maintaining it."

An entire city frozen in time. It was worse than the enchanted sky over Galvatia, drawing on the same sorcerous skill...

"When Guardians arrived, Narz lay unconscious with a heartbeat so faint they left him for dead a second time. He awoke a day later and was taken in by a passing merchant. In his weakness, his rage gave way to terrible grief, and the merchant's wife took pity on him, finding him work on a farm.

"Years passed. He worked mechanically. Depression masked his powers and visiting Guardians searching for sorcerers could not detect him. He heard rumours the sorcerer army he had led was trying to re-conquer the continent, and whispers of sorcerers who were captured and then released, by Guardians who did not believe they were dangerous.

"Gradually, Narz accepted that the Guardians who had attacked and killed his army had done so out of a misguided desire to protect the people his army had freed. He acknowledged that the Guardians who had killed his mother and siblings were extremists, not representative of most Guardians, and that his vengeance against all Guardians may have killed innocent people, who were trying to protect non-magic wielders.

"Remorse overpowered him, and despair plagued him like an illness. His master kept him on, having lost family during the war, and suspecting that grief, as opposed to guilt, was to blame for his lethargy.

"More years passed. Narz noticed that not everyone lived in peace under the rule of the new kings. Some lived in fear, untrained sorcerers, struggling to control and hide their powers. Narz left the farm, seeking and teaching young sorcerers. He learnt to use his own powers extensively in healing, when close friends of his students fell ill.

"By then, he ought to have been near the end of his life, but he felt strong and looked young. He reflected on a time when he desired above all else to protect his family. and realised he had enchanted them with unnaturally long life. Magic had killed his parents and siblings, but aging may not kill him. He had a purpose, and all the decades a man could want to convince people that sorcery could make a better world.

"Six hundred years passed. The spell that holds Tira frozen in time survives, and he uses the same magic to hold the clouds in place over Galvatia."

Setting aside Narz's impossibly long life… the story made perfect sense of the extreme fears that drove Narz. Of his desperate desire to protect those he cared about. Ruarnon could see how his past positioned him to overreact to perceived threats.

The Elite Guard and Narz together were a perfect storm. But what jarred Ruarnon most was that in the end, Narz understood the Guardians were not out to slaughter sorcerers. He knew *all* Guardians they *weren't* the enemy. Yet, when he became king of Azula and expanded his rule to Tiama and Arveta, *Saw* Elite Guard training in the empire and mistook them for Guardians; he forgot.

It was like Narz's mind had gone back to the murders he witnessed, to the fear, grief, pain and the anger that drove him to lash out against all 'Guardians'. As if he could not distinguish between the Guardians who murdered his friends and family in the distant past, and the Elite Guard of the present. Would destroying a weapon that could kill him be enough for First Captain Rilmar to convince Narz of anything?

"What happened to the weapon Narz was so worried about?" Lenaris asked. "The one he froze Tira to counter?"

"When the merchant heard the alarm bells, he and his wife took up the weapon to confront Narz, as their house and those around it caught fire. Moments later, Narz's spell hit the city and they were frozen in the street. The city, and all who lived there are frozen in time, atop the Forbidden Mountains, south-west of Fang Mountain.

"Under the merchant's instructions, his maid fled with his infant daughter. The spell hit the child, but not the maid. The maid went east on a refugee ship, hoping to break the enchantment. When she arrived in what is now the Timbalen Empire, she searched for Guardians rumoured to be nearby. They could not break the enchantment, but they sent the child to Cauldron Island, where she remained in safety for centuries. But Narz's magic is weakening, and the spell freezing her in time broke sixteen years ago."

"I suppose the maid is long dead…" said Selenia. "I wish I could thank her. Can the enchantment on Tira be broken?"

"In moments of remorse, Narz *has* tried to break it. But his guilt is so strong, and the balance of power required to unbind people without harming them so fragile, that he gave up for fear of killing them. But the enchantment is bound to Narz's lifeforce, perhaps connected to the enchantment that keeps him alive. If he dies, it will break instantaneously, the safest way to free the inhabitants of Tira."

"Are you saying we cannot free Selenia's parents without killing Narz?" Ruarnon asked.

"I am saying that is the safest way. But if Narz survives the coming war, I shall attempt to break the enchantment myself. As for the weapon, the enchantment binding it to Selenia's father also binds it to his bloodline. Anyone of his blood may give it safely to another to carry. I would have Selenia give it to Captain Rilmar and Jaygoff, and them bring it before Narz.

"That weapon represents everything he most fears and hates about Guardians. By destroying it in front of him, Captain Rilmar will prove that whoever her people are, they are different from the Guardians who wielded that blade to murder his father, and others who wielded weapons like it to murder sorcerers during the war."

"Is he not likely to assume Captain Rilmar has come to kill him with it?" Tor objected. "Would it not seem more likely to him that Jaygoff was betraying him and helping Captain Rilmar kill him?"

Queen Ziliene sighed. "That is where we need Coroth and Teliph's help. Were Narz to lose his grip on his emotions and rational thought entirely, I believe Teliph is the one person he would not only listen to, but actually hear. Were she to accompany Captain Rilmar and Jaygoff and reassure him, I believe he would hesitate to strike long enough for you to begin destroying the weapon."

"Will Teliph help?" Ruarnon asked Coroth.

"I believe she would. Her father made her life a misery and magic is the main factor in his arrogant belief that he is worth infinitely more than the servants he treats so cruelly. Teliph has seen people suffer at the hands of a tyrant. The last thing she will want is for Narz to become like her father."

"But would she object to the weapon being brought before him, for fear it would destabilise him?" Ruarnon asked.

Coroth sighed. "I regret having not spoken honestly and openly enough to her to answer that. But he knows I was the kindest gaoler this continent has had. Governor Mandarkin told me to my face he thinks I'm too soft, yet Narz rejected Mandarkin's calls to remove me.

"I think part of him doesn't want to hurt even people he views as enemies. And this plan will make that part of him doubt. It may persuade him peace is possible, lives can be spared and then perhaps he can push aside what else he feels, to put someone decent in charge of negotiating peace, like he put me in the Forest Prison, or Governor Poran in charge of Black City."

Ruarnon gaped. That was not a compromise they had thought Poran capable of, once Ruarnon convinced Poran what had really happened with the damars Narz sent to the Zaldeaan Realm. But when they set their surprise aside, the Galvations were as vulnerable to Narz now as the Zaldeaans had been to damarian attacks. Poran must want to protect vulnerable people now, as he failed to in the past. And Coroth's intentions would have been the same. Surely Narz knew that? Yet he'd appointed both to rule over his captive enemies…

"You're right," said Linh. "The Zaldeaans who captured me said they hadn't heard a whip crack since Governor Poran took charge in Black City. Narz can lash out terribly; we know that from the Timbalen

Empire. But if he can still show restraint to Galvatia by appointing good people to rule Galvations, I think part of him will be interested to know an enormous war he thinks is inevitable is in fact avoidable."

Ruarnon shook their head. Narz was beginning to sound like Kyura *and* Governor Derlan rolled into one person, the best of the former competing with the worst of the later. Lylah said there was a great struggle, and Narz, Red Cloak, Teliph and Lord Vye stood at the heart of it. Red Cloak may be well intentioned, Teliph must be, while Vye's intentions were likely awful. Perhaps the struggle was Narz's heart and mind, and the impact each sorcerer had on his policies. But if so, what on Umarinaris could Ruarnon or their Australian friends do to help the best in Narz win?

"You would have me destroy this weapon as a gesture of faith," said Captain Rilmar, "That our intentions are what we profess, we honour our code and are prepared to cease war on Narz, if he ceases war on us?"

Queen Ziliene inclined her head.

"And you would have me destroy the object of his nightmares to gain his trust. But if Narz fears memories the weapon holds, how do we ensure he allows it to enter his castle? Or that he allows me, his mortal enemy, to approach him?"

Beside her, Jaygoff shook his head. "You would have me help deliver a weapon that could kill His Worthiness? You would have me believe he is seven hundred years old and his mind is irrevocably wounded by the Sorcery War?"

"How much have you seen of him?" Coroth asked.

"Behind closed doors?" Ruarnon added, "when he presents more a man, less the image of ruler he projects to his subjects."

"You think he is an imposter?" Jaygoff asked.

"I *know* how much a ruler's moods, attitudes and beliefs can inspire and motivate their people. I know how important it is to project calm and confidence when you fear defeat, and I can imagine the panic that may ensue, should the people see how frightened their ruler truly is. I questioned Commander Darius in the Timbalen Realm myself."

Jaygoff's eyes widened.

"He said Narz created the damars to combat something no man should face. He was convinced by Narz's fears, as was Poran and Dargus, whom I questioned at Cauldron Island."

Jaygoff gaped. "They were some of the earliest sorcerers to serve him. Part of his inner circle, to which I am not privy. But if any of your claims about him ring true, my brother, Keeper Captain Melroth will know of them."

"You wish him to confirm what I tell you before you agree to help us?" Queen Ziliene asked.

Jaygoff nodded.

The queen nodded to two people Ruarnon had assumed were her guards, standing at the far end of the table. An oval appeared over the table, facing Jaygoff. Shape and colour swirled within it. Muffled voices drifted out. Then a man with Jaygoff's brown hair and similarly clever, yet more open and honest face appeared, gaping.

"Brother? How… where are you?" Melroth asked, turning sideways and perhaps seeing the queen on the edge of his vision.

"I am with Queen Ziliene, who is making extraordinary claims about His Worthiness. That he acts now out of fear of the Guardians, from the Sorcery War itself, which he supposedly survived."

Melroth looked solemn at the first, though his mouth opened at the latter claim. "What do they want from you? Is that a Timbalen beside you?"

"This is First Captain Rilmar of the Elite Guard. She commands the Timbalen magic wielders and she is interested in peace with his Worthiness."

"Then why doesn't she offer it to his Worthiness? Why are both of you plotting with Queen Zieliene?"

"You know of his fears," said Queen Ziliene. "I see it in your eyes. Were an Elite Guard to knock on his door offering peace, would he answer the door?"

Melroth's gaze fell. "At this time, I fear he would not. His Worthiness list of friends and trusted parties is few. You seek my brother's help to get her an audience?"

Queen Ziliene explained her plan to have Captain Rilmar destroy a weapon to prove to Narz that he could trust the Elite Guard, her honesty sending shivers down Ruarnon's spine. It was risky enough asking Jaygoff's help, with whom Captain Rilmar was only recently acquainted.

But Teliph was also in the castle and Coroth would speak to her. She may also speak to Melroth. There was a chance they could work together, though the connections in this alliance were tenuous.

"We will meet you at the castle," Melroth decided. "I shall escort you both to His Worthiness. But be warned, the castle and throne room especially are well defended. Should you attempt treachery, you and anyone you bring with you is unlikely to survive."

Captain Rilmar inclined her head. "I accept your terms."

How was she so calm? So accepting? All Elite Guard seemed to have their emotions well-tempered, but she was extraordinary.

"Then I too shall help," said Jaygoff. "If Melroth can get us an audience with Narz, I can use my ability with magic to show Captain Rilmar's destruction of the weapon to sorcerers nearby, so they receive the message that act symbolises, independently of his Worthiness' reaction."

"I will do the same for the Elite Guard," Captain Rilmar added. Then she turned to the oval pane from which Melroth looked on. "If you can command the Keepers not to attack us, I can do the same with the Elite Guard. If we can convince each other of our good intent, our restraint and refusal to fight may convince Narz, if destruction of the weapon alone does not overcome his fears and doubts."

"But how will you calm him if sight of the weapon stirs his fears and prompts him to lash out with sorcery?" Tor asked.

Queen Ziliene sighed. "You may stir grief about his father's murder by producing the weapon, or anger at the deaths of his friends by similar blades. I anticipate a strong emotional response."

"Lady Teliph should be privy to this plan," said Melroth. "She received her magical education from Narz, and is his intended heir. Her views of war are coloured by Coroth's stories of atrocities committed during the Tarlahn-Timbalen-Zaldeaan Wars. She is deeply ambivalent about war and may be open-minded to trusting Elite Guard and reassuring Narz when Captain Rilmar presents the weapon. But she is not with me and it will be very dangerous for you to contact her by magic."

Queen Ziliene inclined her head ever so slightly.

"I will speak to her, in person," said Coroth. "She does not know Narz survived the Sorcery War, but she knows something terrible haunts him. She will be determined to prevent past mistakes from recurring, if there is anything she can do about it."

"It is my intention to ask for her help," said Queen Ziliene. "I will not keep you," she added to Melroth, who was gazing uneasily to his right, distracted by something Ruarnon could not see. "Thank you for your assistance."

He acknowledged her formally, Jaygoff said goodbye, then the pane of magic vanished. Lenaris and Tor were still staring at it. Linh was smiling, as if talking to someone far away in real time, able to see and hear them was not a great novelty defying everything scholars new about the nature of the world...

"I would ask more of others here," said Queen Ziliene. "Selenia; I ask that you go to Tira to recover the weapon from your father's hand. To do so, you will need keys to break the enchantment which renders the gates immobile. One key was sent to the Timbalen Empire long ago. When Ruarnon's ship sailed past, I recalled the bird guarding that key, knowing it would make its way here, and I see that it now hangs around Linh's neck."

Linh looked down at the leather necklace from which the bronze-iron sheened key hung with surprise.

"So Red Cloak didn't send it," she said, frowning. "All he did was bring us here and open the door to Myleth Island?"

"Where will I find the second key?" Selenia asked.

"Lord Tarz guards it," Ziliene replied. "The weapon can kill Lord Tarz as easily as Narz, and Narz trusts Tarz's self-preservation to keep the key well protected. The key is located in a cavity inside Tarz's chest. To retrieve it, he must die."

"That may happen anyway," said Jaygoff. "My brother and his Keepers are eager to uncover the truth about Lord Tarz and lock him in the deepest darkest dungeon. They suspect he is the bastard son of a God King, that he came north to claim a kingdom his illegitimate birth denied him at home, and that he plans treachery against his Worthiness."

"They are watching him with spy magic?" Ziliene asked.

"At all times."

So that was what distracted Melroth...

"What does Lord Tarz know of the Elite Guard?"

"There are rumours of an eastern empire with sorcerers called 'Elite Guard' in its midst," Jaygoff replied, "who are seeking to expand their sea trade in the western seas. Only Narz's Defenders know the Elite Guard as 'Guardians.'"

"His 'Defenders'?"

"Those of us recruited to guard Fang Mountain Prison, King Narz's castle and his kingdoms."

"A sorcerer army?"

"You could call us that."

"And do you think the prospect of an alliance with sorcerers' independent of Narz would appeal to Lord Tarz?"

"Melroth would think so. Lord Tarz may incriminate himself to Keeper spies, were a band of Elite Guard to knock on his door."

"And the Keepers would arrest him?"

"Melroth would set out with the best of his Keepers and Lord Tarz would underestimate them, because he does not know Narz trained them personally. When he realises he cannot escape, he may make it necessary for them to kill him, because capture would be too grievous an injury for his pride."

"After which, the Elite Guard will return to retrieve the key," Ziliene finished.

Two things struck Ruarnon. One was that Jaygoff was too honest and open minded, given how little he must trust them so early on, and was probably a spy for Melroth and Narz, which would convey the groups good intentions, and later prove them people of their word. The other was that Ziliene's plans to incriminate Lord Tarz were all well and good, but they put whoever went after the key in terrible danger.

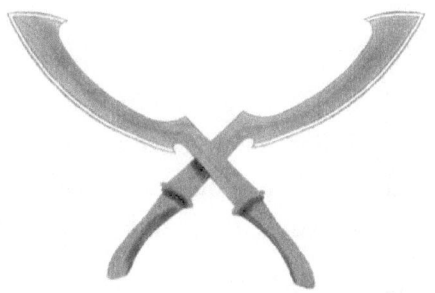

CHAPTER 24

THE QUEST -RUARNON

W hat's between Lord Tarz's house and the weapon?"
Linh asked Queen Ziliene and Ruarnon listened
carefully.

"Tira lies in the Forbidden Mountains, north-west of Fang
Mountain. The enchantment that froze it generated rumours of ghosts in
mountain villages, and they are long since abandoned. Magic-affected
animals roam the mountains now. They are unnaturally fast and will
attack humans. Recently, Narz and Lord Tarz crafted additional
enchantments to guard the weapon against the God Kings. Teliph alone
has the knowledge and skill to overcome these, and I shall seek her aid,
with your help Jaygoff and Coroth."

Jaygoff and Coroth inclined their heads.

Linh shivered. "We're going to get Teliph's father killed, then ask
for her help?"

"Lord Tarz had little interest in a daughter," said Coroth, his gaze
on the table. "He murdered Teliph's mother in a jealous rage when
Teliph was little and left servants to raise her, until Narz discovered
Teliph's power and neglect, and educated her. Lord Tarz is her father in

name only. She will not miss him and will probably be relieved he can no longer abuse his subjects."

Ruarnon shivered. With her father a tyrant and Narz taking time to notice and educate her himself, who had raised Teliph to be the decent person Coroth was in love with?

"How will Teliph know we aren't retrieving the weapon to kill her teacher and king?" Linh asked.

"If Teliph decides she does not trust you," said Jaygoff, "she will have plenty of opportunity to stop you from reaching Narz's throne room when you enter his castle, as will my brother and I."

"He is right," said Ziliene. "Trust must work both ways, if we are to succeed."

"I trust you, and she will try to trust you because of that," Coroth replied, eyeing the table as if the conversation made him uncomfortable, but from the tactical way they were discussing the woman he loved, Ruarnon didn't blame him.

"Teliph may have reason to trust Ruarnon," said Ziliene. "Part of Narz was always rational enough to know the God Kings may succeed in assassinating him, and that war increases the chances Teliph will succeed him soon. I suspect he retained your parents after questioning them so you could become regent, an experience positioning you excellently to advise Teliph. She may know that he intends you as her advisor."

For a moment, the idea shocked Ruarnon. But it was the same cold pragmatism and foresight with which Narz had abducted the Zaldeaan army, and pit it against the Galvations, in a misguided attempt to protect Azula and end war with Tarlah.

"Before the gates of Tira, there is a final enchantment Teliph will not be able to undo," Ziliene warned. "It will come from the dragons guarding the gate, Narz's ultimate defence against God King minions. They will twist your thoughts and feelings any way they can to dissuade you from entering the city. Have a care that your thoughts and feelings are your own and do not distract you from your purpose when you reach them."

"They'll trick us into leaving?" Lenaris asked.

"Most definitely. I suggest you confront your fears and doubts before you approach those dragons. Anything you leave unresolved may be used to distract you."

"How do you really know so much about Narz?" Tor asked Ziliene.

Ziliene sighed. "He is my nephew. It took years to find him on that farm and convince him to teach healing. I supported him in winning the throne of Azula, and his plans to bring sorcerers into the open. I knew something was wrong when Keeper's disappeared. I tried to talk to him when he stopped the clouds over Galvatia, realising fear could drive him to cruelty. But he would risk nothing now his most careful plans were being put into action. He began raving when I reasoned with him and became terribly upset. His rational thinking was beginning to crack under the strain of achieving his dream, and my presence added to his distress. I had to step back and hope that my teachings would guide him where my presence could not."

"You did nothing!" Linh cried.

"He is *broken* child. Any attempt to persuade him not to lash out reminds him of innocent blood he has already spilt and increases his guilt, which he cannot deal with, and which accelerates his descent into irrational thoughts and delusions. There are rare times in life child, when to do something can only make things worse, because there is no positive thing to be done."

"I assume you have the power to restrain him, yet you choose not to?" Tor asked.

"There were times during the Sorcery War when he came close to being killed or stripped of his powers by Guardians. He is scarred by it. Any attempt to control him takes his mind back to the War. He will believe anyone trying to control him is a Guardian and try his best to kill them. Only when I was dead, and he no longer felt threatened, would he return to his senses and realise what he had done."

"Is it his enchantment that kept you alive all these years?" Lenaris asked.

Ziliene nodded.

"But if he dies…" said Ruarnon.

"I will die also, knowing I have done all I can, hopeful of what will be achieved after I am gone."

Ruarnon stared. She spoke calmly, at peace with the knowledge, an ideal Tarlahn ruler in the flesh.

"Does that not mean he'll fight more fiercely, because he knows that if anyone manages to kill him, you will die too?" Lenaris said softly.

Ziliene's eyes glazed with tears, and she stood and turned away. "He wants me to see the days of peace; of sorcerers and non-magic wielders living openly together. He knows he shall not see it, but he should like his old auntie, who lived through the Sorcery War, to see it.

"He is not evil. He is *broken*. And I believe the only gesture powerful enough to overcome his deluded fears about Elite Guard, and to avoid Sorcery War with them, is to destroy the weapon in his presence. Will you help retrieve it?"

Linh smiled slowly. "An insane quest to win over Narz himself? Troy wouldn't be caught dead doing anything else. Fiona won't turn down a chance to reduce human suffering. And Michael and I won't say no to the chance to end a war."

Lenaris sighed. "Mawana would say the four of you are courting danger and hope instead of inaction and uncertainty. He will respect your decision and join you. As will I."

"Why did you not plan this sooner?" Tor asked Ziliene. "Why did you let Narz invade the Timbalen Empire?"

Pain flaired in Ziliene's eyes.

"I was distracted by a powerful enchantment, which I feared concealed that Narz had adopted the Sorcery War practice of breeding monster armies. I was so busy trying to learn who was breeding what and to deter him, that I did not realise he was planning an invasion until after his fleet departed in secret.

"I confronted him then. He created crystal walls to block every palace entrance and walled off his mind from magical communication for weeks. It was impossible to speak to him until his defences were weakened by the knowledge his invasion had failed. He sent Teliph to stay with me then, to protect her from how distraught he was."

He had walled off every entrance to his house and his mind itself to block out his aunt? Perhaps she was wise to keep her distance and avoid destabilising him further...

"When you learnt they existed, what did you do about the damars?" Ruarnon asked.

"It was too late. If his attack on the Timbalens provoked them and they attacked him in turn, he would need the damars to defend his kingdoms. Even if they didn't retaliate, have you ever wondered why, if the God Kings are so powerful, they do not rule this entire continent? The Middle South, Narz's kingdoms, Galvatia and my kingdom are small, primitive backwaters to the sophisticated, richer domains of the God Kings. They have not conquered us because it is hardly worth the effort.

"But Narz's Healers and Keepers serving non-magic wielders will spur them to invade. And when they do, I have no objection to Narz unleashing every damar against the Divine Armies, such is their terror, and complete disregard for anyone who does not do as they desire. My own sorcerers may need to break their vows of peace if that army leaves the Far South."

"They sound like they have changed little since the Sorcery War," said Captain Rilmar. "If they attack; my kin may wish to fight them."

"How is anyone to enter Narz's castle if war breaks out first?" Tor asked.

"Fiona learnt from the false Luvaras Priestesses," said Linh, "that Narz sent Healers to cure plague in the Middle South, despite the Middle South rallying armies against him. And his legal reforms and Keepers are plans for a more just society. Fiona thinks he's trying to promote life and peace and has only initiated wars and oppressed the Galvations and Zaldeaans because his delusions make him think his people are threatened. I agree with her that Narz is fragile and oversensitive, but won't he listen to people who share his concerns?"

Ruarnon sighed. "Who better to lead that delegation then an Heir aspiring to peace, who, with Narz's brutal assistance in the form of damarian invasion, has already fostered a successful peace between two age-old enemies? And who better to escort me to Narz's castle than Teliph's beloved, my cousin, Captain Coroth?"

The only question was how Narz would receive them, especially if war broke out before the weapon was recovered.

"Narz witnessed the Zaldeaan Governors signing your constitution," said Ziliene. "He respects you as a peacemaker and is likely to recognise your mutual interest in peace and justice, and to listen to you. You are uniquely positioned to make yourself heard, despite the ravages of his mind."

Ruarnon remembered the fear and dread they had felt many months ago while warlords manipulated Kyura to a war that shattered both their worlds, a war that brought the Realm to its knees and ended Kyura's life. So far, Ruarnon had only been able to fight battles underway, or pick up the pieces when the fighting was done. They were unable to dissuade the Timbalens from sailing to war, but the chance to prevent carnage was not yet lost.

"There is no question of me acting as Peace Ambassador," they said. "I can ask Narz to return my parents, negotiate the return of the Zaldeaans, and try to negotiate peace between Narz and the Galvations and Narz and the Timbalens in person."

"The most honourable thing, though it places you in the greatest of danger," Tor asserted.

"You shall stand right beside me," said Ruarnon.

Tor gave a small smile. "Monin would suffer heart failure at this decision, but the opportunity to prevent Sorcery War gives your Benevolence a duty to this entire continent, and I am sure your Benevolence' parents will respect that. I will of course accompany you."

"May I consult my other friends?" Ruarnon asked the Queen.

At Ziliene's nod, a servant fetched Mawana, Troy, Michael and Fiona, whom the queen eyed with interest, as they entered the room and Ruarnon explained the plan. They gave their friends a moment, then eyed them for a response.

"I've wondered what I'd say to Narz," Michael replied.

"So have I," said Fiona.

"Some risks are worth taking," Linh asserted.

"We're going to have a lot of trouble explaining to your parents why the girl who comes home from Noriyong Island is so different," Troy said seriously.

"That might be the least of our problems in that department," said Michael.

"One of which being answering the question, what do we want to achieve here?" Fiona pointed out. "I think this might cover it."

All four smiled. There was a nervous edge to it, but determination firmed their expressions.

"My parents are going to kill me, if I survive," Mawana said with a shake of his head.

"You could always blame the corrupting influence of our friends," Lenaris offered, eyeing Troy.

Troy tried to glare but was too busy laughing.

Mawana smiled. "I don't think they'd buy it. If I blamed my wife, however…"

Lenaris gave him a steely look and Ruarnon smothered a laugh.

"I have a great deal of advice for you on how to avoid triggering Narz's guilt and fears, and how to engage the rational part of his mind in your negotiations," said Ziliene. "After which, I suggest you depart with all speed to Lord Tarz's Castle and the Forbidden Mountains."

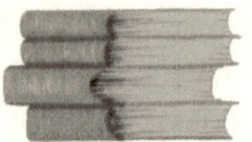

CHAPTER 25

PURPOSE ~LINH

L inh tried not to think too much, as she descended the stairs with her friends and Selenia. Her pack slowed her down, the enchanted sword General Takanis had delivered hung at her right hip, and a quiver of arrows at her left. It felt strange to be armed again. It also quickened her heartrate and heightened her sense of impending threat.

The idea of meeting Lord Tarz made her uncomfortable, confronting magic-affected animals in the Forbidden Mountains made her tense, but meeting Narz frightened her most of all. Ziliene had given advice, everyone had planned and Jaygoff and Teliph may be positive influences, but the bottom line was that when Captain Rilmar presented the sword that killed Narz's father; his reactions would determine everything. And he could do *anything*.

Confronting danger in circumstances they had no control over truly frightened Linh. That was how her mother became an only child in the Vietnam War and what she disliked most about conflict. Yet, everything they achieved here had ultimately been in reaction to Narz's actions. And now anyone's best hope of influencing his actions was to confront him.

A servant led them out of the palace, between green lawns, around bubbling fountains and bright flowerbeds, to a path where Queen Ziliene, Captain Rilmar and a person in a riding cloak with a quiver at their hip, whom Ziliene introduced as their guide stood waiting. The queen's eyes flashed to every enchanted sword buckled at Linh's and her companions waists.

"Those should serve you well against magic-tainted animals of the Forbidden Mountains," Ziliene advised. "But you had best discard them or have Captain Rilmar destroy them when you leave the mountains. Sight of them would utterly undermine your visit to Narz."

That suited Linh. She had cut through sorcerer's magic shields and killed them before, and she wanted never to have to do that again. But feeling her sword resist as she jabbed it forwards, the fear in the eyes of the man she had wounded but not killed, wasn't her only stark memory. She also remembered the raw power of Darius' magic. His lightning hadn't tingled, it had crackled, and all the magic in the air had pulsed with it.

Sorcerers like him were deadly. The only thing worse than giving up her weapons and never having to carve men as if they were meat again, was what sorcerers in that palace could do to her and her friends if they had no enchanted blades to protect themselves.

Ziliene's words cut into her thoughts. "Lylah took great risk in contacting me, and I in listening to her, but she is convinced that in every future; your presence on this quest, and in Narz's castle is crucial. Her final advice is be true to yourselves, and do as you have done, until all is resolved. May Esira shine upon you."

"And upon you," Ruarnon replied, and they bowed to each other in a gesture of respect.

Linh started, as Lenaris hugged Pamoran goodbye and Ruarnon bid him farewell.

"He is not well enough to accompany us," Tor whispered on her right. "He needs to restore his strength."

Close to, Pamoran almost looked thinner than Ruarnon, whose build was on the slight side. Pamoran looked ill.

The guards approached everyone else with horses, each of which had a bow bound to its saddle. Linh mounted with the others and rode onto a path leading to a gate in the outer walls. Their guide led them towards where the palace's inhabitants lined the path, scattering white lilies, roses and daisies before them.

"We also have this tradition," said Captain Rilmar. "White represents purity and the casting of flowers is to remind soldiers of their humanity, that war does not take it from them. I suspect it originated in the Sorcery War."

"They think we're involved in Narz's wars?" Troy asked.

"They see it," Tor replied. "And they mean well. They also fear war."

As they rode into the city streets, more people approached the road. Linh's path was a column of people silently laying flowers, some smiling hesitantly, while others hunched, uncertain or afraid. Their numbers gradually impressed upon Linh how many people the outcome of their quest would affect, and the world weighed on her shoulders, until the city walls approached. Then all too soon, the sights, sounds and smells of normal life were behind her, and they were exiting the gates of the safest city on the continent.

Ruarnon bid their cousin goodbye at the gates. Coroth and his Zaldeaan guards rode south, having 'escaped' Galvation rebels to return to Narz's loyal service and be in place to 'escort' everyone through Narz's castle, while Ruarnon turned west to Lord Tarz's castle and the Forbidden Mountains.

Linh had a moment of nervous apprehension. Then a sheep baa-ed from a paddock on her left. The sun shone between fluffy clouds overhead, and a shepherd boy's pipe notes reached her ears. Life went on in the Forest Realm, and in the fields, farms, villages and orchards of Western Galvatia ahead. Linh tried to imitate Fiona and enjoy their pleasant surroundings while they lasted.

Troy broke the companionable silence as they left their second village. "She didn't say anything about Red Cloak bringing us here? Didn't confirm our theory on him organising an evacuation plan for Narz by faeron gateway?"

"I'd forgotten," Fiona replied before Linh could admit she hadn't thought to ask. "Keepers wear *red* cloaks."

"We were brought here by Narz's *police*?" Troy asked.

Michael frowned. "Maybe we weren't just guinea pigs and it wasn't just about the escape route. Narz wanted Ruarnon's parents and Pamoran for information. What could he have learnt from us?"

Linh shivered. "His reforms. Laws, police and courts work differently in this world, but Narz's reformed legal system as Fiona described it is familiar to *us*. Keepers of the Peace rely on evidence to be convinced of guilt, and identify more falsely accused, innocent people than Galvations. We call that assumption of innocence and proof beyond reasonable doubt."

Michael stared into the distance.

"They've got juries of every social class. *Representative* juries. And nobles don't get special treatment anymore, equality before the law. And they have public healthcare that's free or subsidized by the government. Sound like Medicare?"

"His reforms are like home?" Troy asked.

"They all have roots in liberal democracy, which informs *our* government and is entirely out of place in this world."

"Where did you learn all that about home?" Troy asked.

Linh gasped. "From a book my grandmother gave me for my sixteenth birthday. I was reading it on the excursion bus and thinking about it on Noriyong Island."

"It was like Red Cloak could speak into Sryah's mind," said Michael, "when he communicated with her by magic on the Island of the Guardians. What if they could *See* each other's thoughts? When he didn't block her, like Narz can block Ziliene? If all that was going through your head when Red Cloak opened the gateway, what if he *Saw* your thoughts and reported them to Narz?

"And Narz had him stow us safely on Myleth Island, while Red Cloak picked Linh's brain for knowledge and designed a new legal and healthcare system?" Troy asked.

The world lurched beneath Linh. The idea was staggering. Some of Michael's associates, whom she now suspected weren't close friends of his, had teased her about reading so many non-fiction books, saying it was pointless when search engines told you anything and everything. But if she and Michael were right; her knowledge may have helped inform a revolution spreading across an empire.

"I guess we *were* just along for the ride," Troy said softly. "Accompanying the brains."

Linh was struck by his humble smile.

"That's why we had to work so hard to create a role for ourselves," Michael added. "Everything we've achieved here, persuading Ruarnon to unite the Realm, Linh saving everyone's necks in Imperial City, Fiona persuading Maharl to accept the false priestess' aid, and using magic to stop Zaldeaans from attacking Tarlahns; that was to *our* credit."

"So we *did* stand a chance all along?" said Troy. "But why did Narz let us wander into so much danger, if Red Cloak brought us to Myleth Island because it was safe?"

"When Red Cloak *saw* Elite Guard training and mistook them for a Guardian army," Michael replied, "Narz might have realised his Keeper had opened a Faeron gateway *inside* the Timbalen Empire and if he opened it to contact us, the Guardians could detect it and trace the Keeper here. That might be why we never heard from him in the empire, or near Lylah."

"It finally makes sense," said Troy. "We *were* abducted by a madman, who wanted Linh's knowledge to revolutionise his empire, and dumped us in a backwater where he could have his minion magically pick her brains and was scared to contact us because he thought we were in the homeland of his mortal enemies."

There was awe in his gaze, but a smile playing around his mouth. Linh shook her head. A stint in the Forest Prison hadn't taken the mad adventurer out of him.

"If Linh's been an inspiration to him, and he brought us here, how's he going to react when *we* meet him?" Fiona asked.

"Keepers and Healers sound like his masterpieces," Linh replied. "He might wonder what the person who inspired how they operate thinks of them."

"And why we've sided against him in *every* conflict," Troy added cynically, identifying a possible trigger. Any relaxed muscles in Linh's body tensed.

"We're about to navigate the edge of a cliff on a unicycle," Troy added half-seriously, unable to stop himself from grinning at the thought.

Linh managed to smile at the absurdity of the image, and reality itself.

"Then the person Lylah predicted needs you is Narz," said Ruarnon. "Your influence stems from the fact you helped inspire and are sympathetic to his reforms. With our influence combined, beyond Teliph, he is most likely to listen and respond well to us. That is why all better futures Lylah foresaw involved all five of us sailing west."

Linh blinked. For all the frightening things Queen Ziliene said could happen, all the extreme danger beyond their control in their quest, there was reason to hope, and the only way to avoid being overwhelmed by fear and doubt was to focus on that hope. Linh set her mind to it.

Two days later, Linh gazed across Galvation farmer's fields and grassy plains at the Forbidden Mountains. Jagged peaks barred the horizon. The safety of the farmlands would soon be behind them. She wasn't looking forward to the wild.

A Tarlahn scout approached and Ruarnon beckoned her to report.

"We captured three patrols approaching Fang Mountain a few nights' past. A fourth patrol was captured near the Forest Prison. Patrols in the abandoned farmlands and plains were recalled yesterday. We suspect they have retreated to King Narz's castle. Black City remains heavily guarded."

Linh frowned. That sounded like the Zaldeaans had abandoned Galvatia…

"Companion Karmarn knows Elite Guard were present at Fang Mountain," said Tor. "He may assume both prisons have fallen and withdrawn patrols to prevent their capture. Once his soldiers have assembled; Narz may order them to war."

"In which case my uncle has orders to revolt," said Ruarnon. "I worry that Narz will recall them to Azula to defend it. Is there any sign of Narz rallying his armies?"

"Not yet Benevolence," the scout replied. "Our allies expect them to mobilise soon. We believe King Narz knows the Middle South is mobilising its armies to march on him."

Linh tensed. Narz seemed in no hurry to act against the 'Guardians', whose scouts he'd captured weeks ago. She wondered how he'd respond to the prison breaks, but the approach of the Middle South would surely force his hand.

"Inform my captains that our soldiers in northern Galvatia are to fall back to the Forest Realm," Ruarnon ordered.

Ruarnon dismissed the scout. Linh and the others followed the guide down dirt tracks between grassy paddocks in which sheep grazed, towards the edge of the grassy plain.

"This is grazing land owned by Governor Arnack and Lady Laria," said their guide. "We tore the fences down and used them to trap patrols some time ago. The land is now open to the forest in which Lord Tarz's castle lies. There is only one road, leading up through the Forbidden Mountains to Tira, so you must beware creatures coming down from the mountains. I will lead you to it. If you follow it beyond Tira, it will lead you east out of the mountains, to the plains before the Trine."

Linh gazed across the grassy plains at tall, dense, ancient forest blanketing the foothills and Forbidden Mountains beyond. It was dark beneath that dense canopy; full of shadows for enchanted creatures to hide in. She almost wished it was full of damars giving warning of their approach with hissing and screeching.

The sea of grass gradually slipped behind them, until the guide led them in pairs down a dirt trail beneath leafy trees. Linh scanned shadows for threats, and her ears strained for sounds beyond the faint clop of hooves on soil. Occasional gusts of wind rustled leaves overhead, but silence beyond suggested animals and birds had fled.

"This is where I leave you," said the guide and everyone reined in. "May Esira shine upon your quest."

Ruarnon thanked them, and they rode back through the trees.

"If this is as far as they dare ride, it is where I should wait," said Selenia. "Jaygoff is the first sorcerer I have met and Captain Rilmar the first Elite Guard. I have not had time to become accustomed to them or to pose convincingly as Elite Guard. I fear I would give you away."

"Meaning you are not as reckless and accustomed to improvisation as we," Mawana replied. "Fair enough."

"I would feel better about sparing guards to remain with her if your Benevolence stayed as well," said Captain Arleath.

Ruarnon's regret showed in their lowered gaze, but they nodded and steered their horse alongside Selenia, as did Tor, while Captain Arleath motioned four guards to accompany them.

"Good luck," said Ruarnon.

"This is small," said Lenaris. "Mawana's devious enough to achieve it without you."

Ruarnon's lips twitched, and their eyes shone in reply. Mawana grinned too, as Linh and the others dismounted, unbinding bows from their saddles and set off on foot.

"If we had any sense, we'd be staying with them," said Troy.

"No one can accuse you of having sense," Linh replied automatically.

Troy smiled and replied, "I think that's what used to annoy you. You saw how much fun I was having ignoring sense, and you were jealous."

Linh tried to glare, but ruined the effect by smirking.

"I would rather you went with them," said Tor.

"I'd rather be close enough to help when this goes pear-shaped," Michael replied.

Tor sighed. "I will not argue with you after Imperial City. But I sincerely hope this goes differently."

"So do we," Linh assured him, and he bowed his head.

Silence fell and Mawana led them into the trees. The atmosphere sharpened as Linh, her friends and guards scanned their surroundings with a hand on sword hilts, Lenaris and six guards holding bows, everyone treading lightly.

Large, vague shapes appeared above the trees. Linh froze, as the shapes darkened and resolved into tower tops.

Mawana motioned them forwards. Linh's muscles tightened, as she crept after her friends. There were monsters here somewhere. But as she crept under trees, moving towards darkness which resolved into moss-covered stone walls, there was no sign of danger. Knowing Tarz had used the shadow spell to hide his entire castle, that only made her tenser.

Captain Rilmar motioned right. Linh hardly dared breathe, as she stepped under a row of arrow slits, to the castle walls. Something moved. A large something flashed high above ground and disappeared behind the wall on her right.

"What the hell was that?" Troy asked.

Linh's heart beat faster. Something large moved into view again, a blurring, shifting pillar of black shadow. It resolved into a large, blue scaled serpent.

Linh's shoulders tightened. It didn't appear to have seen them.

"I'd rather sorcerers," Troy breathed.

"Monsters cannot set you on fire," Mawana countered.

Linh shivered as a second head slid into view. The first head and its elongated, gigantic torso slithered back.

"Their scales are imbued with magic," Captain Rilmar warned quietly. "They will be impervious to ordinary weapons."

"What about magic?" Mawana suggested.

"Fire magic to the mouth should kill them," Captain Rilmar replied. "But you need to distract one while I slay the other; they are too fast to target both at once."

"I can shoot magic shields at the right while you slay the left," Mawana replied. "My shields are strongest."

"And the rest of us?" Tor asked.

"Distract them with arrows," Mawana replied. "Aim for their heads and hope to hit eyes and mouths."

"Do not approach closer than the edge of arrow range," Captain Rilmar added.

Mawana nodded to their guards, who fanned out beside the wall with arrows nocked, and crept towards the serpents. Mawana walked with Captain Rilmar, while Linh's friends fanned out to form a second line behind the guards.

Linh drew and nocked an arrow, pointing it skywards as she advanced. Her heart pounded fiercely. The second serpent head moved into view, as the first moved towards the wall.

"Loose!" Mawana cried.

Linh loosed, barely remembering to aim. A dozen arrows arched before her and glimmering shields shot. Fire blossomed in her peripheral vision. Her arrow went wide, but Mawana's shield struck the serpent's mouth. Arrows bounced off it. It hissed, gushing blue blood and streaked towards Mawana.

Mawana dived. The serpent's head streaked past. Lenaris's shield shot forwards. Tor's did too. The shields collided. Tor pushed Linh and Fiona down. Bright light flashed. Linh hurled into Troy. Blue gore spattered from her right as she hit the ground. Guards were blasted off their feet and a headless serpent fell beside Tor.

Linh sat clumsily, dazed. She blinked. Shields were flashing in and out of existence on her left. The second serpent dodged Captain Rilmar's shields with astounding agility. Every shield shot wide.

The serpent lunged with fangs bared and the Captain vanished, reappearing to attack it from behind. Captain Rilmar and her shields winked in and out of existence, while Linh gaped at her.

The serpent wove round shields, diving to attack. Mawana's shield hurtled towards the serpent. It ducked and dove towards him. He drew his enchanted sword and slashed. Blue blood sprayed. Mawana cried out, as scaled muscle knocked him to the ground.

Troy's enchanted sword flew forwards. It embedded itself in the serpent's side. The serpent lunged for Troy.

Linh drew her sword and stabbed the air over Troy's head. Blue blurred, her blade met resistance and she stabbed with all her might. The serpent wrenched her off her feet, as Fiona stabbed into scales beside her. The serpent shuddered and Linh let go of her hilt, dropping to the ground as the serpent collapsed.

Linh knelt, staring at a blue scaled, fang-bared head and elongated body beside her, thrashing on the ground. It fell limp.

Her heart was racing, but she hardly dared to breathe.

It was so *fast*. There was only a fraction of a second between it noticing and moving to kill you.

Troy kicked its head, moving it slightly. "It's definitely dead," he said. "I should be too. I saw its fangs plunging towards me and Linh stabbing it. You two saved my life."

He was too shocked to smile.

Linh smiled at him. Part of her may have been tempted to leave him lost in the wilderness when they first arrived on Umarinaris, but anything that threatened him was in mortal danger of her now.

"Thank you," Tor said as he approached. "We should have planned better use of the swords."

"Troy is as reckless as Mawana," said Lenaris. "You do not need to state wild intentions to either; they can read your mind."

Lenaris turned to smile at Mawana, who sat upright, blinking, probably concussed from the small explosion when Lenaris and Tor's shields collided. His smile suggested his hearing was fine.

"You are hurt?" Lenaris asked Mawana.

"Some cracked ribs, I think," Mawana replied with a grimace. "Had it struck me front-on, it may have shattered my ribcage."

Michael shook his head as he and Captain Rilmar approached, while Tor supported Mawana to stand, and Troy steadied him.

"You alright mate?" Troy asked.

"Dazed," Mawana replied. "My balance is addled and vision blurred. But the colliding shields saved my life. Those creatures were a death trap."

Linh looked around, wondering if that was all. The guards had formed a loose protective circle around them, facing outwards with arrows nocked, but beyond them, everything seemed still.

"Apparently the man hates visitors," said Troy. "Let's go knock on his front door."

Captain Rilmar led them up a path and across the lawn, to bronze plated double doors. The doors swung inwards as they approached. No one was visible in the candle-lit, high-ceilinged corridor beyond. The only faces were life-size frescos of proud looking men and women in fine clothes lining both walls.

Captain Rilmar entered the corridor. Mawana walked beside her. Linh took a deep breath and followed. She tread softly, scanning the corridor, but there was still no sign of anyone. Just the portraits lining the walls, those at the far end larger and bordered with gold.

The last portrait was larger-than-life, of a tall dark-haired man whose face was alive with power. Linh didn't like the smile hinted at by the curl of his lips. Below it hung a small fresco of a girl with Lord Tarz's blue eyes and long dark hair, beautiful, but sad.

Mawana froze. The man from the portrait was entering the corridor, his long, dark blue silk cloak swishing behind him, clasped with silver over a black silk tunic and pants. His face was framed by a thick silver circlet and his blue eyes glittered. He smiled slightly, as he stopped ten paces away.

"Do you like my family portraits?" he asked lightly. "Visitors do not often see them, but you have proven yourselves. I am Lord Tarz, ruler of a small independent kingdom bordering Galvatia and Azula, and I am pleased to meet you."

He spoke smoothly, but the half-smile remained, and Linh wasn't sure how to read the look in his eyes. Was he amused, angry or afraid?

"We had not expected such a welcome," Captain Rilmar replied in a neutral tone.

"I assume you are aware of my allegiance to his Worthiness, King Narz?" Tarz asked conversationally.

The captain nodded.

"It is courteous to offer him allegiance."

Courteous? Given that Tarz was a sorcerer living at the edge of Narz's empire, necessary was more like it...

"We are aware of that," Captain Rilmar replied.

Tarz bowed his head slightly. "Courtesy is always important, as I have told my daughter, who is under Narz's personal instruction."

Linh sighed. Tarz knew he was being watched and was trying to sound loyal, while informing his guests he was at Narz's mercy.

"We understand that King Narz has great respect for sorcerers," Captain Rilmar said conversationally.

Tarz's eyes flickered across everyone, and Linh thought he looked nervous.

"Surely you have heard of His Worthiness sorcerer-healers, trained and stationed across his Empire, and of the sorcerers who pursue his justice by enforcing his many legal reforms?"

"But what of those who do not wish to be recruited?" Captain Rilmar asked.

"They receive magical education," he replied. "For now."

What did that mean?

Soft footsteps made everyone turn, as a young man, the image of a youthful Tarz, emerged from the far end of the corridor. Linh glimpsed anger flaring in Tarz's eyes before it was smoothed over, and he said, "My Lords, my Ladies, this is my only son, Tazron."

Tazron smirked. He had his father's good looks, but his sly smile suggested he lacked his father's sharp intelligence.

"I am pleased to meet you, as pleased at my father," said the young man.

Tarz's expression became openly cross. "If you cannot show due respect to our guests, you may leave."

"But I will show them respect father. I know that woman is a sorcerer. I know why-"

"I am not convinced you are ready to meet guests from other lands."

"I'm not a fool! You want an alliance..."

Panic flashed on Tarz's face, and Tazron frowned, then strained to open his mouth.

Tarz strode forward with his hands in an open gesture, inviting his 'guests' to the sitting room on his right, but Tazron burst out angrily, "Why don't you trust me father?!"

He seemed upset as well as angry, and was red in the face, tears in his eyes.

"I'll make a better king than Narz! You'll see I'm worthy of his throne when you get it for me!"

Horror flashed in Tarz's eyes. Magic tingled, as a misty shield appeared around Tazron. Tarz's eyes widened in alarm.

Something pinned Linh's arms to her sides, wind rushed past, and everything became a blur. She was flying backwards down the corridor and confused sounds around her suggested she wasn't alone.

She landed on the path outside, staggering between Fiona and Troy, as her feet hit the ground. As if someone just picked them up and carried them like stuffed toys...

Linh turned to the corridor in confusion. Figures garbed in red appeared inside it. Blinding white light flashed, and the ceiling began to cave in. The hallway filled with rubble and dust clouded her vision. Light flashed and the wall on the right began to burn.

"They were inside the whole time," Captain Rilmar said faintly. "I thought the walls were enchanted, but I was sensing the illusion magic concealing them..."

Tazron stumbled forwards over dusty debris, the misty shield still around him, wide-eyed and horror-struck. He stopped behind their guards, as though wanting protection. The earth shook, and a large section of side wall blasted out of the castle, knocking down trees in the forest.

"I didn't mean to," said Tazron.

Linh turned. Tears splashed down Tazron's face. "I didn't know they were watching. He didn't tell me. I wanted to meet the visitors. We never get visitors and I'm never allowed to see them. It's not fair."

Light flashed through upper story windows. Stone exploded from the roof. Someone screamed. The scream cut off, silence fell, and the castle was still. The shield around Tazron vanished and he hunched on the ground, sobbing.

Linh stared. Tarz was dead. They'd just got the father of this intellectually disabled young man killed. Fiona knelt beside Tazron, speaking softly.

"Tarz never intended him to succeed," Michael said quietly to Linh and Troy. "His portrait wasn't on the wall, and it sounds like he was shut away and he and his disability hidden from the world."

"Tazron?! TAZRON!" a woman's voice shouted.

"Nurse!" Tazron cried, standing.

A flustered, solidly built matron ran around the corner, covered in dust and swept Tazron into her arms. "You shouldn't have slipped away like that!" she scolded as she held him. "You gave me such a scare!"

The fear in the woman's eyes eclipsed that in her tone. She eyed Linh, her friends, and their guards nervously, while Tazron clung to her.

"Lady Teliph will be glad to see you, Lord Tazron," a man's voice said from the castle.

Four young men in red cloaks emerged from the dusty debris-strewn corridor. The speaker wore a gold circlet with a small ruby at its centre, Keeper Captain Melroth, looking far more confident and surer of himself in this setting.

"We shall escort you to her, with the rest of your household," Captain Melroth added, as half a dozen people in pale linens cautiously emerged from the corner of the castle the nurse had come from.

Tazron turned to face the Keepers. "Teli wants to see me?"

"Yes," Captain Melroth replied kindly.

"But daddy said she was busy. He said she didn't have time."

"She is busy, but for you, she will make time."

Tazron smiled.

"But who are your friends?" Captain Melroth asked, his eyes flashing to Captain Rilmar, then the guards who formed a protective circle around Linh and her friends.

"That woman is a sorcerer," Tazron replied, pointing at Captain Rilmar. "And that girl was being nice to me," he added, pointing to Fiona, "but I don't know who they are."

"I am Captain Rilmar, of the Elite Guard of the Timbalen Empire."

She didn't mention having met him previously by magic. Nor did he. Linh wondered if two red cloaked men and the red cloaked woman behind Melroth knew anything about that meeting.

"So Teliph was correct, the Elite soldiers of Coroth's enemies' allies are indeed sorcerers," said Captain Melroth. "What brings you here?"

"I suggest we speak in private," Captain Rilmar replied, nodding to Tazron.

Captain Melroth turned to one of his men and said, "Please escort Lord Tazron and his servants to our horses. I will see you soon Tazron, and take you to Teliph. But I am afraid you will not see your father again."

"He's dead, isn't he?" Tazron asked roughly, trying to blink away tears. "Why is Teliph with Narz when daddy wanted Narz's throne? I thought Narz was bad, but Teliph is good!"

"It was your father who was bad," Captain Melroth replied carefully.

"Is that why he made you cry?" Tazron asked his nurse, who shivered. "Don't worry nurse, and everyone," he said, turning back to the servants, "I won't be mean to you. And Captain Melroth is a friend of Teliph's. We can trust him."

Nurse's eyes brimmed with tears and pride as she beckoned the servants to follow, and Tazron led them after the Keeper, across the lawn and into the trees.

"What do you know of Coroth's arrival in Azula?" Tor asked Captain Melroth.

"I know the army he travelled with would have attempted the fourth Zaldeaan conquest of Tarlah, had King Narz not sent threat of damars to lure them to sea, and capture them," Melroth replied sternly. "I know their work securing Azula's border with Galvatia and preventing Galvations from spreading lies and fear makes it easier for Healers and my comrades and I to do our work. It also prevents the Galvations from jeopardising King Narz's negotiations with the Middle South, though those have soured for other reasons."

So as much as Daxius.

"I am Lenaris," said Lenaris, "friend to their Benevolence Ruarnon, King of the Zaldeaan Realm, Regent of Tarlah. Their Benevolence sent King Narz a letter about Lord Vye's use of damars in the fall of the Zaldeaan Realm. Did he receive it?"

"I believe he did. I was ordered not to investigate Lord Vye some time ago. His Beneficence said he is a traitor worthy of death, but his execution shall wait until his work is complete. We suspected his kinship to the God Kings before then, but how do you know of Lord Vye's misconduct?"

"The slaughter in the Zaldeaan Realm was obvious to all," Lenaris replied. "Our only doubt was whether it occurred at King Narz's orders, or Lord Vye's."

"Slaughter? Coroth never spoke of such things… Though he has always feared his Beneficence. I was troubled by the extent of his fear, which does not tally with the Emperor I know."

"It matches the one you fear," said Captain Rilmar.

Melroth shivered. Then he looked Captain Rilmar in the eye and asked, "What brings Timbalens to Azula?"

"King Narz's invasion of us," Captain Rilmar replied.

"*Invasion*? Daxius spoke of a raid. He had a band of sorcerers with him, two or three at the most. How can he have led an invasion?"

"The same way a handful of sorcerers were ultimately responsible for slaughter in the Zaldeaan Realm," Lenaris replied. "Do you know of the city that lies between the border of Galvatia and Azula?"

"There is a prison there. And an area where all travel is forbidden, because a remnant of the Sorcery War makes it too dangerous."

"What do you think that remnant is?" Tor asked.

"I thought it was an enchantment. But it makes Commander Karmarn too uneasy to be stationary. It is a mobile threat. Are you telling me creatures from the Sorcery War survived?" Melroth's eyes widened.

"It cannot be. King Narz cannot trust Lord Vye to… Lord Vye *bred* them. King Narz bound them himself. But who could he pit creatures like that against?"

He was catching on fast. How much of this had he suspected?

Melroth's eyes closed. "The Guardians."

There was a long pause, in which the two remaining Keepers shivered.

Melroth's eyes opened again. "He discovered an Elite Guard army and mistook it for Guardians, didn't he?"

"How did you guess?" Captain Rilmar asked.

"His Worthiness always had a terrible fear. I thought it was of the God Kings turning northward for the first time in centuries to confront us. But his fear intensified before Daxius led his band east, and increased when they did not return. I suspected there was another threat in the east, and Daxius had gone to assess it and been overpowered."

He swallowed awkwardly, his face paling, then met Captain Rilmar's gaze again. "You are here for a counter-invasion?"

"Commander Octharl, of the Timbalen regular army, is here for that purpose. But as First Elite Guard Captain, I am here to assess whether war with King Narz is necessary for the protection of our Empire. Queen Ziliene, among others, has convinced me that diplomacy must be tried with King Narz. But there is something I must obtain to enable that diplomacy, to convince King Narz we are not what he fears. The weapon we wish to destroy before him."

"You have come to ensure your safety, but not for revenge?"

"It is the blessing and curse of my family that our memories span well beyond our lifetimes," Captain Rilmar replied. "I recall memories of my ancestors, how they felt and what they were thinking at certain times, all the way back to the Sorcery War. I know of the course the war took, the flight to the east, the settling of the eastern seas, the Wars of Unity that created the Timbalen Empire. I know its lessons as if I lived them myself.

"I see the God Chaos as a metaphor for what humanity becomes when it allows its negative emotions, and all thoughts that feed or justify them during circumstances of danger and suffering, to run wild. I do not care to repeat the mistakes of our ancestors. And where my Emperor is concerned, I am not bound to do so. Were my emperor to initiate Sorcery War here, I have the right to refuse to lead the Elite Guard into battle. But I cannot make that choice while a frightened sorcerer-king breeds creature armies and rallies a sorcerer-army, either of which seem as likely to be aimed against *us* as at the God Kings."

"I will ask His Worthiness to begin co-regency with Teliph," said Melroth. "I think we both foresaw its need. I had so much work to do paving the way for the Keepers… I focused too much on my responsibilities, not asking enough questions about Galvatia, or when Daxius told me of his mission. As for His Worthiness, I fear he has a curse much like yours, but it is of no comfort to him. It is the force that drives him without mercy, perhaps with too little thought, and too much fear.

"I must return to him. But when you arrive, I will ensure the castle is open to you, now more so that I understand what is at stake.

"Be wary of Lord Vye. He has his own intentions, and if he feels you will upset them, I fear he will try to kill you."

He paused, his face pale, his posture bowed beneath a weight Linh hadn't recognised moments earlier.

"One of my ancestors once felt as burdened as you do now," Captain Rilmar replied. "She was a soldier in the Sorcery War, who fled east. She founded a small village and worked hard to farm in a new climate and ensure peace, despite that some of her people could work magic and everyone feared magic. Her humble village grew into Timbala City, capital of the Timbalen Empire. War can burn worlds to ashes, but new worlds grow from them. Your nightmare is real, but so are your dreams. And it is not over yet."

Captain Melroth inclined his head, Captain Rilmar returned the gesture, then the Keepers departed after their Captain, Tazron and the servants.

"We fought alongside the Elite Guard Leader in the sewers?" Troy asked Captain Rilmar quietly.

"I crafted the shield that protected us all," she replied. "My companions only shielded some space being assaulted. And no, it was no coincidence that I escorted four youths bearing weapons of the Sorcery War. I wanted to learn how you obtained them and your intent. Nor is it coincidence that I commanded the Elite Guard at Fang Mountain, our first contact with King Narz's sorcerers on this continent."

"If Coroth told Teliph about the Elite Guard," said Linh, "Does that mean she and Captain Melroth knew that's what you are all along, but they didn't tell Narz?"

"I think Captain Melroth assumed the Guardians King Narz feared were someone else," Captain Rilmar replied. "But I will not ask him, nor Teliph to explain it to Narz. If they convince him, he may become consumed with guilt for wrongfully invading us, and Queen Ziliene warned how guilt deepens the cracks in his mind. It may be best if he still believes I represent the Guardians, but we have not the resources to subdue him, and we come to offer him a formal peace. My genuine approval of his Keepers and Healers may help alleviate his fears."

"And if he does not trust your offer of peace?" Tor asked.

"I am prepared to trust the Keepers with my security while I remain in King Narz's castle, not killing him, until he accepts that we have no intention of doing so."

"It would be kind of hard to argue with that," said Troy.

Captain Rilmar smiled at him. Captain Arleath emerged from the trees with four guards and was immediately overtaken by Ruarnon and Selenia, who were both smiling with relief.

Lenaris returned with a bronze-iron sheened key in one hand, and a grim expression on her face. "There was naught of Lord Tarz but ashes," she reported. "The key was concealed within the pile, and I assume the Keepers knew nothing of it."

Linh shivered, as Lenaris handed the key to Ruarnon.

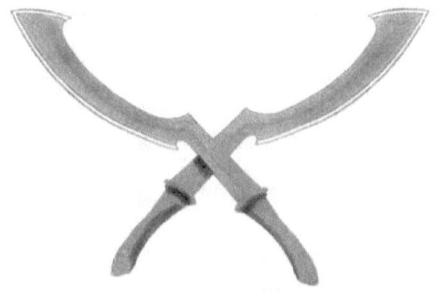

CHAPTER 26

LORD VYE-RUARNON

Ruarnon gazed across the steep mountainside ahead, as the sun set over a peaked horizon. The forest around them was dense, a quiet wilderness. It made the world in which Narz, the Middle South, Timbalens and God Kings stood on the brink of war seem remote.

Beyond the forest, an ancient, giant stone bridge arched from the road before them, its scale far beyond the highest and widest buildings Ruarnon had seen. It spanned across a valley, ending halfway up the next mountain. A forest grew beneath the bridge, but the bridge easily cleared the highest, most ancient treetops.

"I wonder how much was lost during the Sorcery War," said Tor. "I doubt any architect in the Eastern Ocean could accomplish that today."

"It is as ancient as Imperial City," said Captain Rilmar. "I suspect sorcery built that. Perhaps even the faeron."

"Unless," said Linh, "this is the peak of human engineering on Umarinaris, before the Sorcery War. If it was half as bad as Queen Ziliene and all the myths say, maybe humans *were* capable of feats like this, and they had more advanced technology, and it was all destroyed and forgotten in the chaos of the war."

Ruarnon sighed. How could anyone forget they were once capable of the engineering marvel rising ahead? A structural feat spanning an impossible distance? Timbalen knowledge of sea faring seemed unmatched by anyone elsewhere in the world, but had all aspects of engineering, of human knowledge, once been as great as this? What happened to the society with the money, skill and knowledge to organise and fund this project?

Tor was right, how much *had* been lost in the Sorcery War? Ruarnon shivered. Perhaps as much as could be lost, if the Elite Guard and or the God Kings Divine Armies fought Narz's sorcerers.

The sun began its descent, setting the sky ablaze with oranges and yellows as they crossed the weathered stone of the bridge, solid and sturdy under their horses' hooves, despite its impossible length and height. The sky flamed bright yellow, orange, pink, purple and blue as they rounded another large hill, and Ruarnon admired it until they set up their tents before a third bridge, while the sky filled with stars. Ruarnon tried to focus on the beauty of their surroundings, on the peace of these deserted heights, instead of war's rapid advance.

The next morning, Ruarnon rode between Selenia and Tor as they approached a bridge linking foothills to the Forbidden Mountains. Selenia's posture was relaxed. Merely having to hand the weapon to Captain Rilmar for its destruction seemed to comfort her.

"Companion Tor showed me Queen Ziliene's map this morning," she said. "He estimates we are two days from Tira."

She shivered, probably with excitement.

"Benevolence," a guard called from the bridge.

"What do you see?" Ruarnon asked, signalling everyone behind them to halt.

"A soldier," she reported. "There are more behind him, moving around the mountain."

Their scouts had seen no-one last night.

"A powerful sorcerer is among them," Captain Rilmar warned.

Should they retreat? But that meant going back to Tarz's castle, and nothing would stop the sorcerer pursuing them.

"He has shielded the road behind us," Captain Rilmar added.

Ruarnon shivered.

"Guards, ram the magic shield with your round shields!" Tor ordered.

Captain Arleath inclined his head and Ruarnon's bodyguards dismounted, raised their round shields and charged back down the road. They crashed into air and halted, leaning against their shields. Ruarnon gaped.

One man pushing against Mocco's shield had made Mocco collapse in Blue Bay. But this shield was withstanding seven men and three women heaving against it with all their might. For a moment. And another.

"Use your swords!" Captain Arleath commanded.

Ten swords were drawn, raised over round shields and stabbed. They halted abruptly, in mid-air.

"Hack it," Ruarnon ordered hoarsely. "Make them work to sustain it."

The soldiers withdrew their blades and stabbed. Sparks glinted as they hit resistance.

"We do not have time to break it," Mawana asserted.

"Then we will meet them," Ruarnon's voice answered, as their mind grappled with the idea that doing so was inevitable.

"Send me Benevolence," said Tor. "There is no need to expose everyone."

"I am afraid there is," Captain Rilmar warned as she reined in beside them. "That sorcerer is powerful enough to attack here and whoever meets him on the bridge simultaneously. I can only shield us effectively if we remain together."

Ruarnon exhaled deeply, as their heart raced out of control, and they fought down panic.

"Guards, return to your positions," they ordered, not looking at the retreat route the mightiest magical shield they had ever seen barred.

"May I lead?" Tor asked and Ruarnon nodded.

"I shall accompany you and shield everyone from in front," said Captain Rilmar. "We must not give away our power until the sorcerer attacks, so be ready to craft shields. I will attack if needed."

Guards inclined their heads at a gesture from Captain Arleath, then Tor and Captain Rilmar led everyone onto the bridge, while Lenaris rode beside Ruarnon, Selenia keeping to their left.

The burly, spear-wielding soldiers advancing at the far end of the bridge were led by a heavily armoured rider, who sat with an upright posture on a warhorse with bronze ring mail protecting its neck and chest. Ruarnon sensed magic, but the man wasn't wielding it. This had to be Lord Vye.

The man had light blonde hair and pale features. The sharp angles of his face were calm, a calm Ruarnon suspected came from being in complete command.

The sorcerer halted his guards ten feet away, and Ruarnon reined in as the man's grey eyes surveyed their companions coldly.

"But a single sorcerer to protect you from Lord Vye," he said disdainfully. "I expected an Elite Guard army. But I will not waste my time."

He turned to Selenia. Adrenaline sparked and Ruarnon instinctively formed a shield. It merged with Selenia's.

Bright light blinded them. Magic vibrated through the air. Sparks flew and rained before Captain Rilmar, who sat expertly as her horse reared and screamed. Tor's horse shied away and Ruarnon gripped with their knees as their horse shifted.

Light kept flashing, sparks rained, then stopped. Ruarnon blinked away spots of light dancing before their eyes. Captain Rilmar slumped in her saddle. Her horse settled on all fours and bolted around the guards, back along the bridge.

Ruarnon gasped. They couldn't resist this man without her.

Lord Vye smiled. "Hybrids. Not so disappointing. But insubstantial."

Something flashed in Vye's eyes. Magic crackled through the air; a beam of light pulsing towards Selenia. The impact hitting Ruarnon's shield was like physical force. Ruarnon groaned, their entire body straining as though pushing against a stone wall.

Ruarnon was vaguely aware of other magic tingling, as they shuddered with effort. Mawana's stronger shield pushed down, letting Ruarnon and Selenia shrink theirs, reducing the strain enough to make Ruarnon aware they were shaking.

Mawana growled, and Ruarnon sensed something moving towards Lord Vye. The shield halted, flashed and streaked backwards. It crashed into shield before Mawana. Mawana groaned, slumping and both shields vanished.

Light was still targeting Selenia. Ruarnon pushed against it, raising both their shaking arms. Selenia stood gasping beside them, sweat pouring down her face.

"A hybrid who can use two spells at once," Lord Vye said thoughtfully. "Perhaps I should take you alive."

Mawana shuddered, also straining against the light streaking at Selenia.

Fire flashed overhead. Thunder cracked and Ruarnon was thrown off their horse. Bright light flashed, blinding them. It vanished and they released their shield, euphoric with relief. They hit the ground gently and sat dazed.

Lights danced before them, while hooves struck the ground.

Ruarnon took a deep breath, sensing a powerful shield before Companion's Tor and Lenaris, who crouched on their left. Selenia sat beside Ruarnon, but Troy and Linh lay behind her, unconscious. Beside them, Fiona lay awake and Michael sat up.

Ruarnon's guards staggered upright. Their horses had bolted. Mawana was down behind Tor. Who maintained the shield Ruarnon sensed overhead?

Dust cleared, revealing chunks of grey stone scattered over the bridge, and a hole blasted into the space Tor's horse had stood on.

Soft footsteps prompted Rurnon to turn. A young woman walked around their friends, her pale face and bright blue eyes determined, her long dark hair in a braid. Her leather boots stepped carefully over chunks of broken stone, and she placed herself before Tor. Lord Vye's guards eyed her nervously, some backing up.

Vye frowned. "What in Creation are you doing Teliph? They mean to kill your precious teacher. *I* am protecting him."

"We are not strong enough to fight the Elite Guard, and the Middle South, and you know it," said Teliph. "The sorceress you just attacked means to destroy the weapon as an act of good faith."

"You are so easily taken in."

"And that is why I do not trust you?" she challenged.

"You realise their exposure of your father's treachery got Tarz killed?"

"I am sure Tarz's subjects can hardly contain their joy," Teliph replied coldly.

"Must two family members die but a day apart?" Vye asked with mock sadness.

"If you are so confident, why are we still talking?" Teliph demanded.

Vye's soldiers backed up. Their terrified eyes darted from Teliph to Vye. Vye drew his sword. His soldiers gave up pretence and turned and ran for their lives.

Ruarnon shivered. "Back up!" they ordered, staggering to their feet, their muscles aching, as Vye hefted his sword. The blade warped, the cross-piece sagging onto Vye's hand.

Tor turned Ruarnon around, supporting them with one arm. Lenaris half-lifted Mawana, while guards moved in either side. Ruarnon staggered forwards with Tor's help and gazed over their shoulder. Vye had drawn a dagger. Icicles crystalized in the air around him. They tilted back, point first, on the same angle as the dagger. Vye threw the danger. The icicles shot forwards.

"DOWN!" Ruarnon yelled, crafting a shield reflexively as they hunched, pulling Tor down with them. Tor's shield merged with theirs, joining Selenia's.

"CRAFT THEM ABOVE!" Lenaris yelled.

Ruarnon looked up, shaking with strain. Icicles above them fell. They gripped Selenia's hand and shuddered at the force of icicles hurtling into their shield, letting the deadly rain push the shield against their skin. The pressure and headache were too much... they released the gap over their head and sensed Tor's shield filling it.

The icicles stopped. Tor lifted Ruarnon to their feet. Their limbs hung heavily and their thoughts fuzzed. But Ruarnon could sense movement. Icicles burst into powder against an invisible wall over their head, and a second wall before Teliph.

They turned back, blinking to keep their vision clear. Lenaris's arm was bloody, but Mawana was fine. Michael and Fiona crouched, their helmets dented, puddles of melting icicles surrounding them. But Troy and Linh lay unconscious. Both their legs were bleeding from puncture wounds bellow their boiled leather kilts and their bronze breast plates were dented. Vye had tried to kill them all.

"RUN!" Tor bellowed.

Tor threw his other arm around Selenia and half dragged her and Ruarnon forwards. Ruarnon leant heavily on him while Fiona struggled to drag Linh and Michael heaved Troy by his feet, guards rushing to help him. Lenaris led the way, half-carrying Mawana, who was conscious, but sagging heavily against his wife.

Ruarnon staggered in a test of endurance, trying to keep their eyes open, and keep up with Tor and Selenia, as the bridge rocked under them. Captain Arleath paced them on their left. Magic tingled behind them. Their guards were shielding everyone.

Blasts, booms and a wild crackling rose like thunder. Stone cracked loudly and shards of stone rained around them. The ground shook again. Ruarnon flinched, as something cold struck them, but it was only water. Lenaris led them behind boulders lining the road.

Tor lowered Ruarnon to the ground. They sat leaning against a tree, blinking to clear their vision. Their heavy limbs sunk into the ground. Michael and a guard lay Troy before them, and Captain Arleath slumped beside Selenia, pale, his face drenched with sweat.

Ruarnon closed their eyes, trying to rest their aching body. Light flashed and they peered over the boulder. A firestorm raged over the bridge, waves of fire clashing and criss-crossing. Heat blackened pale grey stone. A stray lightning bolt shot from the flames and crashed into the cliff.

"They could kill us all," Linh gasped where she lay, beside Troy.

"That's what I like about you Linh, always focusing on the positives," Troy mumbled, lying beside her with his eyes shut, managing a grin.

Someone roared with fury, water rushed like a waterfall, and Ruarnon turned back. Cascades of bubbling water crashed down onto the bridge, into the fire. Jets of steam shot up and the flames vanished. Water drained away through holes blasted into the bridge, leaving steaming, blackened stone in its wake.

Teliph stood calmly in the centre of the bridge. Vye sat atop his horse, which was unnaturally still, enchanted, presumably.

"You have grown," Vye growled.

"I am *not* a child," Teliph replied. "I will not let you stop them."

Sparks flew around Teliph, presumably deflected by an invisible shield. Stone cracked around her. Vye and his horse lifted and floated backwards. He reached forwards but continued to move back. His eyes widened in horror, as Teliph advanced. She set him down on the far side of the bridge, then jumped back as stone cracked. Stones before her fell away. Vye kicked his horse and fled around the mountain.

Ruarnon exhaled deeply and turned to their friends. Tor tended Linh and Troy's bleeding legs. Linh blinked dazedly, Fiona sitting worriedly beside her, while Lenaris tended Mawana and the guards inspected each other for injuries.

A horse nickered as a guard led Captain Rilmar's horse into view. The First Captain sat in her saddle, unconscious.

More footsteps padded on pavement. Teliph walked around the boulder.

"I should have realised I would need to shield you immediately," she said, surveying them and shaking her head.

She knelt between Troy and Linh, focusing on their legs, then moved on to Captain Rilmar. Tor wiped Troy and Linh's legs with bandages, revealing slightly pink, raw skin. Ruarnon shook their head and Troy cocked an eyebrow, while Linh shivered. They would never get used to magical healing.

"This woman needs rest," said Teliph, studying Captain Rilmar. "I suspect Lord Vye stopped her heart. It beats normally now, but there may be damage."

"You four," she gestured to Captain Arleath, Ruarnon, Selenia and Mawana, "Need to eat, drink and rest. They are the only cures for magical overexertion."

Tor removed a drinking pouch from Captain Rilmar's saddle bag and passed it to Ruarnon, Selenia, then Mawana and Captain Arleath, while Lenaris found them biscuits. The water cleared Ruarnon's head and vision, and the biscuit helped. Now they were only slumped with exhaustion, instead of half-fainting.

Teliph watched them. "There is a rift between Queen Ziliene and King Narz that I do not understand, but Coroth says I should trust you. Yet I fear this weapon has a hold over King Narz that will worsen the state of his mind."

"You realise his mind is affected?" Ruarnon asked, surprised to hear someone so close to Narz admit it.

"Captain Melroth has not seen King Narz in his ravings," she replied calmly, but her eyes were haunted.

"Are you aware that he invaded the Timbalen Empire, and tried to annihilate the Elite Guard because he is convinced they are Guardians?" Ruarnon asked slowly.

"How?" Teliph asked. "There may be a sorcerer army now, but there was not when Daxius departed. He did not have enough men…"

Her gaze became distant. "Some threats no man can face. He needed Vye for God King dark magic. But if he thought he'd found a Guardian army…" she shivered. "That is why Coroth is so afraid of him, he sent that army to coerce the Zaldeaans here. And you think he will breed another, and strike again, until the Guardians are defeated?"

"Emperor Yarath is convinced of that," Ruarnon replied. "He believes a mad man thinks his Elite Guard are Guardians and wants to annihilate them. He wants to annihilate King Narz and his sorcerer army for the empire's own safety. But Captain Rilmar is the Elite Guard leader, and she wants to persuade King Narz to see reason."

Teliph shivered. "So that is what he fears. He has been fretting for weeks."

"He's not going to attack first, is he?" Troy asked.

"They are ready to invade?" Teliph asked, her face draining of colour.

"They await the outcome of Captain Rilmar's visit to King Narz," Ruarnon replied.

"Then he must confront his fears," said Teliph. "Before it is too late. If you can break the enchantments on the blade," she said to Captain Rilmar, "he will believe you are a Guardian, and it will force him to consider that your people mean him no harm. But you will have to handle him carefully, he is not rational when it comes to Guardians.

"But the timing… The Middle South march to war against us, the God Kings are stirring, and King Narz knows it. And in Daxius' absence, his illness has gotten worse. He will not share his burdens with Captain Melroth, because he wants Melroth focused on establishing the Keepers, and he is the same with Eligar, the First Healer.

"He summoned Governor Poran to consult him, but Poran is changed, and could not look Narz in the eye. He struggled to advise him and Narz dismissed him and was upset. Look at everyone sitting around you. He does not have the luxury of such support."

"He will soon," Michael replied quietly. "We'll be there. And Captain Melroth knows everything now and he'll want to help. He wants you to step up as co-regent."

"It is time. Is this what it was like?" she asked Ruarnon. "Knowing the wishes of rulers who came before you, and having to deny them, because circumstance forced your hand?"

Ruarnon nodded sympathetically. "That is how much of my reign has been. The old notions of Tarlahn kingship were incompatible with the challenges I faced. And you are right about how many people stand around me. Trust Captain Melroth. Trust Coroth. I once knew a king who tried to solve all his kingdom's problems on his own, and he killed himself."

Teliph sighed. "King Kyura. Coroth was vague about his death, but I knew that Lord Vye's fleet and its behaviour were at the bottom of it."

"Teliph, all of King Narz's enemies believe Lord Vye is related to the God Kings and see the danger he represents," Ruarnon cautioned. "Tell me you have someone watching him?"

Teliph smiled grimly. "The best. He has attempted several crimes here in recent years, but each time, when a Luvaras Priestess happened across him, he changed his mind. The Priestesses give even God Kings pause."

Ruarnon's mouth fell open. "How do you know Luvaras Priestesses?"

"They taught me to control my powers and gave me my initial education in magic when I was very young. Mother arranged it."

"Would the Priestesses be prepared to help, if the God Kings march north?"

"I suspect they would. They bow to no ruler and Luvaras Priests and the Dedicated are the same, but they dislike God Kings. I wonder if King Narz *has* approached the Luvaras Priests. God Kings make him less nervous than Guardians and an alliance may explain that."

"The Dedicated?" Ruarnon asked.

Teliph smiled. "An order founded by midlun sorcerers, who found Priest and Priestess training too gendered. It is now favoured by sorcerers who differ from the other orders in their physical and sensory capacities, and how their minds operate. It is rumoured they have infiltrated and freed captive sorcerers from the God Kings.

"Narz would not trust The Dedicated, but I hope the Priestesses can persuade them to help us against the God Kings, should it come to that."

"Why did Lord Vye try to stop us from reaching Tira?" Michael asked.

"Because he is not ready to commit high treason," Teliph replied, "so he feigns loyalty a little longer. I suspect he relished the chance to test his powers against mine, given that I stand between him and the throne.

"He will say nothing about today, because Narz will not believe I fought him, but he seems to think the Elite Guard want the weapon to assassinate Narz, and he does not want that to happen yet. He will try to stop Captain Rilmar from reaching the throne room.

"And you should know, Captain Melroth investigated Lord Vye before King Narz ordered him not to. He uncovered a trail of people who died in fatal accidents from the border of the Divine Realms to Azula, all of whom probably or definitely knew Lord Vye. He killed everyone with any capacity to reveal his exact relationship to the God Kings. Do not underestimate his ruthlessness."

"You forget that I occupied the Zaldeaan Realm after Vye visited it without Luvaras Priestesses watching him," Ruarnon replied. "He has no more conscience than a damar and is far deadlier."

Teliph shivered at the comparison.

"Captain Melroth said he would make sure we had access to the castle," Lenaris added. "There might be risk of Keepers clashing with whoever or whatever Lord Vye puts in our path."

"I will speak to Captain Melroth," said Teliph. "It is best if the Keepers stay out of this, other than letting you pass. Will you all accompany Captain Rilmar?"

Ruarnon nodded.

Teliph took a deep breath. "I will see you at the castle. For now, I have more of my father's nastiest work to dismantle."

She whistled and hooves clopped. She mounted her horse and rode away, determination plain on her face. Ruarnon gazed after her, unable to understand how Narz's youngest follower was the most open-minded, resilient and strongest of them all.

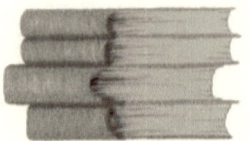

CHAPTER 27

THE FORBIDDEN MOUNTAINS -LINH

L inh appreciated rest, but she didn't appreciate the view, as they began riding the next day. The ancient stone bridge Teliph and Vye had fought on was charred, cracked and holey in places. Not to mention so high it easily cleared the treetops. Heights weren't her friend at the best of times, and this time the integrity of the structure was in serious doubt.

One of Ruarnon's scouts was scampering across the damaged stones, inspecting and testing its strength after the pounding it had taken yesterday. But the weight difference between a horse and a person was considerable. And they had quite a few horses to get across.

"I'll cross if you do," Troy said quietly and the warmth in his eyes made her smile. Neither of them would enjoy this, despite watching Ruarnon's scout step onto the road on the far side, having not caused chunks of bridge to collapse beneath her. The bridge withstood the weight of Captain Arleath's horse, as he led it clear of cracks and holes too.

"I've never appreciated how brave those guards are," Troy added, as guards followed Captain Arleath, leading their horses in single file. "You'd have to be brave to keep blundering into danger on someone else's orders."

"I suspect its braver to know you can walk away, but choosing not to, out of willpower alone," said Fiona.

Was Troy blushing?

"And out of an underdeveloped sense of self-preservation and refusal to listen to reason," Troy added. "It's important to remember those."

Linh shook her head. He was grinning, but partly serious and he was *right*. Facing serpents that could sink their fangs into you at lightning speed, let alone riding across bridges half-destroyed by sorcery wasn't something reasonable people did.

"You won us all over," she accused.

Troy grinned. "I'm glad of the company."

She suspected he meant that, as he led his horse behind hers and Fiona's onto an ancient stone surface that no longer seemed safe. She took a deep breath and followed Fiona's footsteps, determinedly not looking at holes. But as Linh neared the charred middle of the bridge, her gaze was drawn to dark green and rocky slopes of other Forbidden Mountains ahead, and to grassy plains flowing into farmlands in the distance on her right. It was beautiful and vast.

She blinked, stepping instinctively away from a large hole near the end, her horse skirting it gracefully behind her, then relaxed as she stepped onto solid earthen road winding along the mountainside, bordered by dense forest.

Her friends had mounted their horses and Linh, Fiona and Troy did the same. Guards fanned their horses out, riding with bows in hand, as everyone rode among branches tangling together above a forest floor teaming with prickle bushes.

Linh frowned.

"This place has been tampered with," Mawana said ahead. "It grows densely, making it difficult to stray from the road."

"Steering travellers into enchantments Teliph has been breaking, I suspect," Ruarnon added. "Vegetation and enchantments will not worry us but be on your guard against animals. They may have damar-like instincts to attack on sight."

Linh shivered and squinted through dim light filtering through the dense canopy overhead. Beyond their horses' hooves was silence. No ordinary wildlife appeared to live here, and the extraordinary kind seemed to be keeping to themselves, which suited Linh perfectly.

Tor flung up his hand halfway round a bend. Linh tensed. A prolonged hiss sounded.

"Shields!" Ruarnon called.

Linh crafted hers reflexively, then extended it to protect her horse's forelegs and flanks and her own legs. It was an awkward shape to maintain.

Grass and leaves rustled nearby.

"Serpent!" Mawana shouted.

A vague shadow flared into a giant head lunging for a guard, fangs bared. Linh's shield rippled, as fangs plunged into the guard's horse. The horse screamed. The guard fell off its back. The serpent flung the horse into a tree, where it lay motionless.

Linh instinctively thickened her shield.

A glowing white shield streaked towards the serpent. The serpent screeched, as its eye burned away. A second shield struck its' mouth. Its head blackened, smoked, and toppled, knocking down a tree. Serpent and tree snared in tangled branches and were suspended partway to the ground.

Only then did Linh realise she was panting heavily and sweating all over. The guard sat in bracken, staring at his dead horse. Ruarnon's biggest guard rode up and the fallen guard mounted behind him.

"I'm not sure I could shoot a shield that fast again," Fiona said breathlessly, and Linh stared at her best friend, who once wouldn't have hurt a fly.

"I will take the next one," Lenaris said grimly.

"I want our vanguards, Michael, Linh and Troy ready to release shields immediately after her," Ruarnon added, sounding strained. "We had best hit them half a dozen times before we pause to assess whether more shields are needed to kill them. The rest of us must avoid crafting magic and rest, if we can."

There was as uncomfortable silence, in which Linh's tension was eased by Troy's left hand taking her right and squeezing it.

"Breathe Linh," he said. "My shield failed instantly when I saw that thing. I'm relying on you on Fi to keep me alive."

She smiled at his nerves and squeezed his hand at the genuine fear in his eyes. Her shield magic was only better because she was more stubborn.

"Don't worry, I'll protect you both," Fiona quietly assured them, her blue eyes somehow dancing with nerves yet brimming with quiet confidence.

Troy leaned across the air between their horses to kiss her.

Captain Arleath joined two vanguards and led Linh, Fiona and Troy forwards, their friends following them through the dim forest.

Linh's heart had only just slowed when feet pitter pattered. Vanguards nocked arrows. Something fury raced round the corner on six legs. Linh stared as it snarled. Something overshadowed it, blurring from shadow to serpent head as it lunged. It sank its fangs into the fury creature, which howled.

Linh's shield formed before her, rippling like a pond showered with stones. The serpent opened its jaws wide, dislocating them, and swallowed the pony-sized fury creature whole. A bright flash incinerated the hairy creature and smoke gushed from the serpent's mouth. Its eyes glazed with death. Its head crashed to the ground, smashing branches off trees, and flattening a prickle bush.

Troy trembled beside her, gasping for air.

"That was you?" she asked.

"That was not a shield," said Mawana.

"I, kind of wanted to blast it out of existence before it got any closer," said Troy. "When you really want to hit out at something with magic, I guess you can."

"The Sisters said magic takes its properties from our desires when we shape it," Lenaris added. "I suspect we killed the first serpent with shields because that is how we envisioned them, but they can strike with the heat of lightning if that is our aim."

"That's how I killed that sorcerer in the sewers of Imperial City," Linh thought aloud. "I was angry and scared about what he'd done to Michael, and what he might do the rest of us that… I incinerated him…"

Her reins shook in her hands.

"That is why my shield merely threw Jandar across the deck of his ship in Blue Bay," Mawana added. "The properties our shields strike with are shaped by our feelings and desires as much as conscious thoughts; if they are strong enough. That is why Desriah insisted on our focus and hesitated to teach so many people, because once you master one form of magic, you can craft any, intentionally and unintentionally."

Linh shivered. She was grateful no one had altered their magic unintentionally when they were learning. Then, it might have put her off. Now, it may be their best weapon against sorcery-enhanced serpents.

Ruarnon sighed. "We swore to Flariah not to shoot shields or use magic offensively. And had you not, some of you may have died in Imperial City, or at Tarz's castle. We cannot keep either oath in these mountains. But I ask everyone to try to keep their magic in the form of a shield."

Troy shook his head. "I'm not suicidal Ruarnon. I'd feel safer using magic to fly than hurling lightning bolts."

Linh grinned, while Michael added, "I suspect magical flight is possible," with a wicked gleam in his eyes.

Linh shivered and Troy shuddered, smoothing the cynicism from Tor's face.

The mood swiftly returned to alertness, as they rode on under the shadows of twisted trees. Linh was grateful to reach the edge of that mountain without incident, though she wasn't keen on the enormous stone bridge at its end, arching up towards an even higher mountain with vultures and an eagle or two circling it. The eagles continued to fly away, but the vultures descended. She tried not to consider what had attracted their attention and was surprised to find herself halfway across the bridge.

Troy shook his head on her right, carefully gazing at the road ahead. That made her smile and the rest of the crossing easier.

Her good spirits faded, as they rode beneath the dense canopy of ancient forest, and the thing which had attracted the vultures came into sight. Vultures had begun eating its torso, but four reptilian limbs suggested it was a dragon, lying on its back.

"Where did that come from?" Troy asked. "And what killed it?"

Mawana dismounted and walked towards the carcass. Vultures scrabbled to its far side. Mawana pulled a long-hafted lance from the dragon's neck.

"Joharlen mentioned some of the Queen's bravest people going missing," Ruarnon replied. "Tarz's death may free these creatures to roam into western Galvatia. I wonder if the Queen sent magic-wielding hunters to slay them as a precaution."

Linh shook her head. Culling creatures that lived in these mountains sounded like a good idea, but she wondered what kind of people it wasn't suicide for.

They continued their ride. She tensed at a loud sound, which gradually became a roar. Trees thinned ahead, revealing a river flowing between two peaks on the left, cascading into a waterfall, their road becoming another bridge before it. Spray flicked her face as they rode closer, and the dull roar drowned out anything waiting for them on the far side.

Ruarnon halted everyone before the bridge, and Teliph turned to them, her face pale and tired.

"This is the last mountain," she said loudly. "Tira lies ahead.

"I received word the Southern Armies have set sail. King Narz is rallying his army and intends to march east, to meet them on the Azulan coast. If you follow the Mountain Flow east of here, then turn south along the Green Trine, making the best time you can, you may reach Narz's castle and have time to reason with him before the fighting begins. If you arrive after that, he will be preoccupied with the war, and likely in the wrong state of mind to hear you."

"Thank you for the warning, and advice," said Ruarnon.

"Teliph," said Tor, "May I ask what we have done to earn your loyalty?"

Teliph's stern expression softened. "I fear losing my father and king. The king is in peril, and my father does not wish to burden me with the entire truth of what he does to protect his people. He will speak more freely to you of war and peace. And in helping free the king from one of his greatest dilemmas, you will help save the man I call father."

Linh's features slackened in surprise. How could things be so complicated that Narz's adopted daughter thought strangers may be more able to reach him than she?

Ruarnon bowed their head. "Please inform Coroth we hope to meet him on the banks of the Green Trine, near Black City."

"On the second morning from now," Tor added, as he folded Queen Ziliene's map and returned it to his saddle bags.

"I shall. But when I saw Tira City, I was drawn to the enchantment. I did not realise how close I was to the walls until I saw two dragons standing guard at the gates. They stared at and tracked me, but made no move to attack or leave their posts. They seemed intelligent and may not attack until you approach."

"Their scales are protected by shield magic?" Ruarnon asked.

"More strongly than Tarz's serpents. Magic will only distract, not harm them, as will any weapons other than the enchanted swords at your hips. King Narz has made it so the only way to pass is to slay them, but I suspect they will remain at the gates if you retreat, so you may be able to regroup and reconsider if your first plan of attack fails."

"You already think like a ruler," Ruarnon observed.

"Uncle Daxius taught me. He gave me historical problems from king's reigns and helped me puzzle out possible actions the ruler could take. It made me realise I should become governor of Galvatia. King Narz approves, but I suspect he is ashamed of his treatment of the Galvations, and it would become clearer to me in that position, so he hesitates. Fear is driving him to compromise his beliefs. I hope you succeed in helping him overcome his fears."

"My hope is the same as yours," said Captain Rilmar. "We Elite Guard have been more privileged in our history and circumstances than King Narz, and his sorcerer-followers. I am mindful of the disadvantages you face, so I do not hold what King Narz did out of fear against him. But he *must* see reason. I will do what I can."

"Thank you. I shall do my best to be present when you arrive, but my brother's nurse is ill, and he foolishly insisted on waiting on Tarz's southern border till she gets better. I am going to order him and our household to ride immediately for Azula's capital, and I mean to escort them to the Luvaras Temple myself, so Lord Vye does not seek to use him against me. May fortune go with you."

"And remain with you," Ruarnon replied with a smile, which she returned faintly.

Teliph rode around them, and the sound of her horse's hooves retreated across the bridge, the roar of the waterfall swiftly drowning them out.

Linh braced herself, as the last protective buffer between her companions and the dragons rode away.

When they reached the rode on the far side and it curved, dimming the roar of the falls, Ruarnon turned their horse to address everyone. "Guards, I would have you split into two groups and distract each dragon with arrows, testing their speed and reactions, then distract them while the rest of us attack with our enchanted swords. Will you attack with magic?" they asked Captain Rilmar.

"I will try to shield the minds of anyone who approaches from their influence, though that requires complex craft, and I may not prevail."

Ruarnon inclined their head.

"I suggest we approach in small groups," they said to their friends, "with people we feel most comfortable with. We may need to monitor, remind and reassure each other against however the dragons try to distract us."

"Don't worry Mic, we'll make sure you don't get distracted pondering the universe," said Troy.

Linh smiled at how the comment lit Michael's face up. Then she shivered.

"You're sure you want to come?" Troy asked Fiona seriously.

"Yes," Fiona replied, smiling sincerely.

Troy turned to Linh. "I'll try not to fall behind this time," he said seriously, referring to being unable to keep up with her in the illusions they confronted to retrieve their enchanted weapons on the Island of the Guardians.

"We'll try not to get ahead," Linh assured, and he nodded.

Linh braced herself, then followed the others past trees, towards what she took for a rocky cliff. But the round boulders were faced, stacked to form a tall, long wall with a bluish tinge. The wall extended into trees on their left, then turned at a corner and stretched into the distance ahead.

Linh's spine tingled as they rode towards the walls of Tira. The road curved towards the walls, until the trees were on the downwards slope on her right, then it straightened across the mountain top, ending before a pair of tall arched gates blanketed with a substance like icy glass. Sunlight fell on it, but it showed no sign of melting.

"The enchantment that preserves the city," Fiona breathed.

"But where are..." Linh paused, as a large dark shape wheeled around the far corner of the city walls and landed at the end of the road. Another dark shape sat, its wings folded up like a gargoyles behind it, its legs arranged like those of a giant cat sitting primly before the gates. Both dragons turned.

Linh shivered, not taking her eyes off them as a gentle breeze blew towards her, bearing a metallic scent. The vanguards horses danced sideways, towards the trees and other horses neighed.

"Halt your horses," Tor instructed. "We will lead them into the trees."

Linh shivered at the horses being spooked by the dragons' scent. She dismounted, and led her horse after Fiona's, exhaling deeply to slow her rapid heartbeat. The guards' threaded ropes through reins and bound the horses to tree trunks, then stepped away with bows in hand.

"I will lead," said Ruarnon. "Guards, I want you to probe their willingness to move from their posts with arrows. Mawana and Lenaris, can you shoot shields for the same purpose, and check their speed?

"Those of us with enchanted swords must be light on our feet, ready to change direction, to run or attack, at a split second's notice. When we attack, I want the guards, Australians and Companion Tor to keep your distance and shield us with magic shields.

"If it gets too dangerous and I do not call a retreat, Companion Tor is to call it. If that fails, Lenaris or Michael are to call a retreat. If all of us are bewitched, I leave First Captain Rilmar in charge. Please form groups of four and decide which order within your groups you will shoot shields to distract a dragon if needed."

"You're first Linh," Troy said. "You're damned quick in a tight spot."

Linh smiled. Her survival instincts ought to serve them well.

"I'll go next, seeing as my shields are strongest," said Fiona.

"I'd like to go third," said Michael, "To give me more time to figure out what the dragons are up to and how best to counter them."

"If we all fail, it's up to you to do something wild," Linh added to Troy, wondering if the part of him that loved risk taking was about to step into its element.

He blinked, then nodded slowly, taking her seriously.

"Above all," Ruarnon said loudly, "remember the Timbalen fleet are ready to resume the Second Sorcery war. Remember Yarath's fear of Narz and Narz's fear of Guardians. Remember what we know of Keepers and Healers, the good they do, and the travesty it will be if they are ordered to fight Elite Guard. Remember our desire for peace, to help each other remain focused and protect each other."

Ruarnon linked hands with Selenia and Tor, and within moments everyone had formed a circle, holding hands. Linh took a deep breath as she held Troy and Fiona's hands and smiled when Troy gripped her right hand tightly. Ruarnon raised both their hands, Selenia's and Tor's in a double salute, which was mirrored around the circle.

Linh buzzed with nervous anticipation. Nervous, hopeful smiles were exchanged, hands were squeezed and then it was time.

Everyone let go, two groups of guards moved either side and Ruarnon, Selenia and Tor and positioned themselves to approach the right dragon. Linh led Troy, Fiona and Michael to the left, behind Mawana and Lenaris. Captain Rilmar stepped between both groups, stern and calm as ever.

For a moment, Linh was intensely aware of silent evergreens rising around her, of bracken brushing her ankles and the bright blue sky dotted with thick tufts of white cloud overhead and silence on all sides. Then Ruarnon raised and lowered their arm, and Linh gripped her sword hilt as she and her friends advanced on foot.

They walked to the edge of the trees. Mawana, Lenaris and half the guards advanced ahead of the others, through bracken covered grass, towards two huge dragons sitting on their hind quarters before the gates, long thin tails flicking through the air behind them. The long snouted, dark blue faces turned towards the couple, their giant yellow eyes considering.

Guards on the right advanced with bows poised and arrows nocked. Captain Arleath opened his mouth to give the order to fire. Flames glowed and gushed towards the guards. A shield wall flashed before them and was bathed in magical flames.

"RETREAT!" Ruarnon bellowed.

The guards on the right turned and ran.

"The dragons are enchanting the second group of guards," said Captain Rilmar. "I cannot sense how to counter them. My shields about their minds are ineffective and grasping the enchantment is like holding the wind."

The guards on the left were charging the other dragon, losing arrows from their bows at random and yelling incoherently.

"Abandon charge!" Captain Arleath yelled, as he retreated on the right.

The left guards ignored him, losing arrows that rained harmlessly on the ground.

"RETREAT!" Ruarnon ordered.

"This might help," said Captain Rilmar.

As the guards moved within forty paces of the dragon, a magical shield wall formed before them. Magic stirred on its near side, forming steps up the wall, which the guards climbed. Linh gaped.

The guards reached its top and moved steadily down the other side, their forms vague behind the shield. The shield wall vanished, but the stairs remained, until the guards hit the ground.

The guards charged the dragon. The dragon raised its left paw and a single swipe sent them flying. They tumbled to the ground, then limped away.

"They formed stairs over your shield wall?" Ruarnon asked.

"Yes," Captain Rilmar replied. "They are intelligent and capable of countering whatever I do with magic."

Lenaris was backing up. But Mawana strode forwards, his head turning slowly, as if every feature of the dragons mesmerised him.

"Mawana, get back here!" Lenaris called.

"I cannot reach him," said Captain Rilmar. "The magic in the air around him is fixed by great power."

Lenaris rushed towards Mawana, seized his arm and tugged him backwards. Mawana stumbled. Then he cried out in surprise and let Lenaris lead him back at a run.

"Proximity is the problem," Mawana called as he returned. "I was drawn to them, and all but forgot how dangerous they are. The closer you move towards them, the stronger their enchantment becomes."

"It did not tamper with our thoughts," said Captain Arleath. "It let us come close enough to scare us away with fire."

"I think that thing built up Mawana's curiosity to distract him from killing it," said Michael. "It distorted the guards' eagerness to do their duty until they were so focused on attacking that they didn't give a thought to how. Then it multiplied their fear and shock when they failed, to send them fleeing. They can't plant random thoughts or instincts into our heads. They can only use what we already have against us."

"Genius," said Tor. "If this is King Narz's idea, then he is a brilliant tactician."

"We need to identify which of our emotions they are most likely to heighten to manipulate us, and consider how to counter them," said Ruarnon.

Linh sat in the long grass before the gates and considered.

"The dragon on the left didn't try to kill the guards," she told her three friends, trying to understand why her fear was decreasing. "It pushed them away. And the other dragon drove guards away with fire, which Captain Rilmar can protect us against. I don't think the dragons will try to kill us. It seems their main goal is to stop us from reaching the gates."

Michael blinked. "That's what I was going to say. We need to be ready to dodge flames and stay focused."

Linh shivered. That statement was such a far cry from her fears when they had first blundered onto Umarinaris. But you didn't throw away the chance to dissuade a man suffering from paranoid delusions from a war that could annihilate two chunks of humanity; you seized it.

"I want you and the guards to watch us with First Captain Rilmar," Ruarnon told Captain Arleath. "Lenaris was able to bring Mawana back, and I suspect the dragons will let you drag us back. They seem to reserve enchantment for those seeking to attack or enter the city."

"Benevolence," said Tor.

"You can come with me," said Ruarnon. "But I do not want you stepping within the dragon's reach. Three of my guards have fractured ribs from the blow of a dragon's talon. I do not want you getting yourself killed by a creature you cannot attack trying to protect me."

"And Pamoran wondered how our young peace-loving heir was leading our people through war without him," said Tor, shaking his head.

Ruarnon smiled and Tor bowed his head. Then there was nothing to distract Linh. Was the ground rising up, or were her nerves sinking to meet it? She and her friends were about to fight their own minds, and the most powerful creatures, crafting the most complex magic she'd ever encountered.

But Troy was right. Being unreasonable, and it seemed, having Ruarnon's wild optimism, was key. Linh just hoped every uncertain day she and her friends had spent here, all several hundred of them and every risk they had taken were sufficient training for this moment.

One by one, her friends stood. Mawana's group stood in the middle, Linh's faced the dragon on the left, while Ruarnon's faced the dragon on the right. There was a moment to squeeze Fiona, Michael and Troy's hands, to smile when Fiona kissed Troy and Troy grinned after kissing her back, and then everyone was positioning themselves like sprinters beginning a race, and Linh's heart raced ahead of her.

"May fortune go with you," Ruarnon said quietly. "Now!"

Linh rushed forwards, her gaze fixed on the dragon on the left. Her vision wavered. She ignored it and ran on. It wavered again and she slowed, feeling dizzy.

"Please come home Linh."

Linh stopped. When had she last heard her mother's voice? A year and a half? Longer? She blinked, trying to breathe and look at the dragon, but everything was going dark.

"I'm phoning the police. We've searched the entire island! They're nowhere to be found!" a worried man's voice asserted.

"Mr Gentile?" Linh asked, frowning.

"Police," said Mr Gentile's voice. "Yes. Four teenagers have gone missing from an island excursion on Noriyong Island. We fear they have been abducted."

How long have we been away? Linh had pushed that question aside so many times. When had she stopped asking? Could they get back, if

Narz had brought them, and he lost his mind at sight of the weapon that killed his father?

"I'm sorry if I'm hard on you. I just want you to do well at school. To have a good life."

Her mother was always asking about her grades. Taking her to the local library to get extra background reading. She'd probably have a tutor for every subject if her family could afford it. Her mother wanted her to have the youth war had deprived her of, and the career that post-traumatic stress had prevented her from having. Linh knew that. But she shouldn't get distracted. There was something important she was supposed to be doing. The dragons!

Linh strode forwards determinedly, blinking, trying to clear her vision, because everything was dark and hazy. Where were the others?

She turned. Grassy clearing lay left and right. Two dragons sat at the end of it before a tall, blue stone wall, but everything looked vague, and she could hear nothing, not even her own footsteps.

She kept turning. Another blue stone wall lay ahead, split by another pair of gates, guarded by another pair of cat-like, dark blue dragons.

Linh exhaled nervously and turned further. A third stone wall, a third pair of gates and dragons, and further right lay a fourth. She stared. Blue stone walls lay in her peripheral vision and on every side.

"You clever bastards," she said, turning again, looking for a weakness in the illusion, a ripple, a fault.

Her vision on all sides became dark and blurry, like a reflection in a rippling pond. Which way was forwards? She might walk into a tree if she was going backwards, or a friend if she went sideways. Or a dragon, unknowingly.

Her enchanted sword hung at her right hip, but if she tried to cut through illusion, she risked hurting a friend she couldn't see. Her quiver was at her left hip. If she threw an arrow fletching first, it shouldn't hurt anyone. She drew an arrow and threw it forwards. It vanished a few meters away. She turned, throwing a second arrow at the second blue stone wall. That too vanished behind illusion. As did her third arrow and her fourth.

"Fine then!"

She still had a dozen arrows. If she stuck them end to end, like a blind man's pointer, it would be better than nothing. She squatted, emptying her quiver and tried to jam the point of one arrow into the fletching of another. She cut herself several times, and accidentally split two shafts down the middle, before she succeeded in joining three arrows end to end. Then she held her rudimentary pointer fletching first and strode forwards.

Troy's hands balled into fists. He ran as fast as he could, his face set.

"Troy? Where are you?"

He shivered, slowing. That was impossible...

"The excursion returned without you. Your teachers couldn't find you anywhere. But I can see you. You're running across a field with Fiona and Linh. Where are you?"

"Mum?" he asked softly, vaguely aware of the world around him dimming, sounds quieting, and of slowing. If she could see the field...

"Come back to us Troy! I know I can be hard on you, and that you don't relish being a babysitter for Tom and Sarah, but I'm getting a promotion soon. I'll be able to afford childcare. And your father has switched jobs so he can be closer to us, he will help look after Tom and Sarah too and you will see him more often."

Troy's eyes filled with tears. His father had taken that job after his parents got divorced. He'd said he needed time to rethink his life and then Troy hadn't seen him for four months.

"We miss you. I'm not mad at you for running away. I just want you home safe."

She sounded calmer, not as strict, not the way she normally reacted when she was angry. But how long had he been gone? What had that done to her? She thought he'd run away from home… how could she think he would abandon Tom and Sarah?

Yes, it was tiring and looking after them could be annoying, but he had time to blow off steam and have fun acting out at school. He would never run away. But if she thought so… what if Tom and Sarah did too? He joked and played with them, but you didn't tell your kid siblings you loved them… they might not realise… he had to go home. He *had* to tell them!

"Troy! Where are you?"

Troy stopped. Good question. It was so dark. Where was he? And who was that? It sounded like… Fiona and she was in trouble.

Troy wasn't sure what he was doing, but he clung to something, or strained against something. Then Fiona stood in a grassy field before him, with tears on her face, looking around.

"Fi. We've got to go home. My family thinks I've run away. I'm scared my younger siblings don't realise I love them! They think I've abandoned them!"

Fiona took a deep breath. "We can do this. We can."

A tear trickled down her face.

"Do what?" he asked. "Why are you so upset?"

"I could see everyone. My teachers, telling me Linh's smarter than me. You, saying she's braver. My parents, telling me which of my siblings they like better than me and why. All our friends saying they like everyone else better, because I'm not as smart, and I'm not as fun and I'm not as strong."

More tears ran down her face. "But they're wrong. They're wrong, and we can do this. But I need your help. They're over there."

"What's over there? What's going on?" he asked, stressed and confused.

"We're trying to stop something. It's important, and we have special swords, and it's not far away. We need to keep moving forwards."

Troy followed her gaze. Two dark blue dragons sat like cats, spiky tales swishing behind them, before the walls of a great city, which had a strange blue tinge. Great danger lay that way. Lives suspended, and the end of the world, or its rebirth. He couldn't remember enough to make sense of it.

He turned back. A familiar rocky island lay behind him, surrounded by sea on three sides and the channel between it and Myleth Island on the other. A stone gateway arched from its centre, open to a castle, and opposite the castle was a mountain top, and from there a voice called, "Troy, Fiona, Linh, where are you? Mrs Mason's doing her nut!"

Noriyong Island, the same day they left. He could get back, before his mother thought he'd run away, before Tom and Sarah thought he'd abandoned them… but something wasn't right. That was Michael's voice, but how could Michael be on Noriyong Island, when he was here? Where was here? Why was it so blurred?

"How do you know what's going on?" he asked Fiona.

"I remembered you telling me I was more than ok on the Island of the Guardians. I knew the you I saw telling me I was less fun wasn't real, and that none of it was, and that whatever is real is confusing us and trying to stop us. It's over there and we *have* to fight it!"

Fiona, advocating fighting? Something shifted in Troy. He didn't know what was going on, but he remembered riding over fairy tale bridges through mountains, and a name, Narz… King Narz was the one who suspended the lives beyond the walls! And the weapon that lay there had something to do with stopping him. They had to pass the dragons to get it!

Adrenaline spiked and he seized Fiona's hand and ran forwards. The haze of his peripheral vision cleared. The dragons were getting closer and a girl walked ahead of them… Linh! But he couldn't see anyone else ahead. He turned. A group of guards on his right were marching away.

"Where are you going?" he asked.

One turned to him. "There is a plot for a mass revolt in the Zaldeaan Realm, and Regent Monin knows nothing of it. We go to warn him, before our labourers and farmers are slaughtered."

Troy had wanted to leave too, to go home. "It's not real!" he yelled. "The revolt isn't real! They're trying to trick you!"

"We have to stop them," said Fiona, tugging his hand.

He met her determined blue eyes, nodded and they jogged forwards again.

They weren't far from the dragons now. Linh was closer, but she'd stopped. She was kneeling and staring at… nothing…

"It makes us hallucinate," he said, realisation hitting him so hard his peripheral vision cleared, and he glimpsed friends. Voices and yelling rose. Tor dropped to his knees. Mawana ran back, screaming Lenaris's name.

Michael raced before Linh, sword drawn. Fire gushed from the dragon's mouth, surrounding him, stopping so close that Linh should feel the heat, but she didn't seem to. She was talking to someone who wasn't there.

Dread pounded in Troy. Fiona gasped. She stared at a magical sword gleaming on the grass among smoke. The fire was gone, but *she* could see Michael's sword. Did that mean… There was only one way to be sure.

Troy drew his sword and ran forwards. Fire flared. It was going to come right at him. But Michael's sword had vanished… Troy smiled grimly, looking dead ahead. He tried to ignore the approaching flames as he'd ignored downwards views on the bridges he crossed earlier. Look straight ahead, at your destination, and hope.

Fiona ran wide of the flame, overtaking him, her freckled face flushed with exertion. The smallest, gentlest member of their party was going to reach a dragon first. Her face was set with determination, her eyes pained. She wanted to kill it to protect everyone from the visions it was inflicting on them. The girl who hated violence. He'd never loved her so much.

"Yes, we suffered!" Michael's voice yelled.

Troy frowned and turned slowly. Michael was a silhouette, masked by the shadow spell, and both his fists were clenched. Troy suspected his friend had got as far as he could on his own, and ran back for him.

"I understand inequality, abuse and trauma. But they were kids and you were supposed to look after them! Not leave Grandma to do *everything*! Has it ever occurred to you that maybe dad turned to drink because that's the only example *you* set him? How are we supposed to get anywhere when people like you can't even help themselves?!"

Michael's face was flushed with anger. Troy had never seen him so upset. "Mic! Come back to us mate!"

Michael frowned, then squinted towards him.

"They're using the shadow spell to hide us from each other," Troy added.

"Troy?" Michael asked.

"I told you I'd stop you from being distracted by the mysteries of the universe and I'll add solving the world's problems to it. We're almost there!"

Michael's lips twitched, but he eyed Troy suspiciously.

Troy paused. "You're worried *I'm* not real? The last 'you' I saw ran into dragon fire then vanished!"

Michael poked him in the arm.

Troy grinned and rubbed the sore spot with his other hand. "We need to get back. Fiona's almost reached a dragon and she's on her own."

Troy ran, Michael right behind him. Troy's joints ached, but he didn't slow down. Fiona had paused within reach of the dragon's paw and was looking around uncertainly.

"You've got this Fi!" he yelled. "Mic and I are right behind you!"

Fiona's expression firmed. She started at a great yellow eye. Michael was outpacing Troy. He raised his sword. Fiona stabbed the dragon's left eye. Michael stabbed its right. The dragon moaned and Michael pulled Fiona back as it fell sideways towards them. It made the ground rumble slightly as it fell, and Michael and Fiona fell behind it.

They'd done it! The dragon was dead! Now Troy could sit down and rest with Michael and Fiona. Who'd fallen asleep. His eyes were trying to close. A rest would be great.

CHAPTER 28

LOST IN THE PRESENT - MAWANA

Mawana stared. The itch to get closer, to approach those glowing yellow eyed, somehow cat-like, twin dark blue dragons gnawed at him. Contrary to what Mocco had always assumed, rushing into things wasn't Mawana's style. He always had a plan. It was always based on his knowledge and observations of a creature. Accounting for its behavioural tendencies. And building in escape routes, should something go wrong in Mawana's attempts to acquire new specimens for the Institute of Learning in Aracia.

But Mawana had no plan for this. He couldn't even begin to anticipate everything the two creatures ahead of him could do, let alone plan to counter them.

Tor and Selenia had halted on his right, with a half dozen guards. Tor was frowning and seemed unhappy. Selenia kept scanning the field before them, her face pale.

"What's wrong?" Mawana called.

"I cannot see anyone but you," Tor replied.

Mawana turned to the field, the walls towering beyond and the twin dragons flanking Tira's gates. Tor was right. The entire clearing appeared deserted.

"Lenaris was beside me just a moment ago. Where did everyone go?" Mawana asked.

"They blurred and faded front first," Tor replied. "Just like our ships when we sailed towards the mainland here. The dragons are casting the shadow spell on everyone. I was to keep soldiers back to aid the others if needed, but I cannot see if anyone needs help."

Mawana frowned. "I cannot hear anyone walking or speaking. They must be casting some spell to muffle sound, concealing it too. We won't know if anyone else needs help."

"The spell should fade as you near people," said Tor. "Can you go in and see if anyone needs to be pulled back?"

Mawana sighed. "And see if I get lost and forget you exist, as the others appear to have done, because they have no idea they've left us behind? Even my wife has wandered on without me. We *never* fight alone."

Tor inclined his head. He was determined to obey Ruarnon's orders to wait and call a retreat if needed. But it looked like the only way to make people retreat was running after them and dragging them back. Did Tor have enough soldiers for that?

"I will try to see what is happening," Mawana added.

He strode forwards, into a seemingly deserted field. Grass bent and was crushed under his feet, but he heard no other sound. Saw no other sign of movement. There was only the dragons ahead, but they weren't watching him. Each was focused on a distant point of the field. Enchanting one of Mawana's friends?

The urge to rush where either creature's gaze was fixed rose, but Mawana fought it down. Lenaris should be just ahead of him. His Australian friends should be to her left, Ruarnon to her right. He may be able to see everyone, at least in shadow, if he continued straight ahead.

"Protect the Heir!" a man's voice cried. Guards…

Mawana ran forwards. Grass blurred on his right. Shadowy forms raced across it, towards one shadowy form.

"Do we shield them from the dragons?" a woman's voice called.

"It made short work of Tor," Captain Arleath's voice answered. "We *cannot* risk Ruarnon."

Mawana halted. Tor stood behind him, with the injured guards. Yet Captain Arleath thought a dragon had killed him?

"Benevolence, we must turn back!" said Captain Arleath.

Mawana rushed forwards, and the shadowy forms resolved into the captain of Ruarnon's guards, four of his soldiers and a bemused Ruarnon.

"I am sorry Benevolence," said Captain Arleath. "Companion Tor is dead. We saw it with our own eyes."

Ruarnon gaped.

"He's not," Mawana protested. "He's not far behind me. Can't you see him?"

Mawana pointed urgently. Captain Arleath followed his finger, as did the guards. Then they stiffened and turned hostile gazes to Mawana.

"What trickery is this?" Captain Arleath demanded. "Why do you pretend someone stands behind us?"

Mawana took a deep breath and turned. He couldn't see Tor anymore.

"If you can see Tor, then why can't I?" Ruarnon asked.

"The shadow spell," Mawana replied. "I couldn't see any of you until I moved closer. Everyone this close to the dragons is concealed by the shadow spell. They're cutting us off from each other."

"To kill us one by one," said Captain Arleath. "As they did Tor. We must turn back Benevolence."

"What if what you saw wasn't real?" Ruarnon asked, gazing deeply into the captain of their guards' eyes. "What if it *was* a trick, to deter us?"

"Benevolence, I swore an oath to protect you. I cannot, in good faith, gamble that oath on the chance Mawana can see what is real, and myself and four other Tarlahns cannot. If the dragons can make us see what isn't real, it seems more likely a single Mawana is a hallucination."

"One that's urging you towards dragons who don't want you to go near them?" Mawana asked.

Arleath froze. "But it was so real! It was Tor's face. His voice. He ordered us back as he died! Ordered us to save the Heir."

"Ordered you to remove me from harm's way, so none of us would get near the dragons or the weapon," said Ruarnon. "They are using hallucinations to deceive us. Don't trust anything that prompts you to turn back, unless a Tor standing far behind us calls the retreat."

Mawana sighed. The dragons could fake that too. From Ruarnon's frown, they realised it.

"We've lost enough royals!" the woman guard objected. "Heir Ruarnon is the last. You must not endanger yourself!"

"We cannot let Tarlah fall to civil war like the Realm," said another guard.

"Our oath of protection is paramount," said the third. "Even if the heir does not wish to be protected."

Mawana gaped, as all four guards advanced, one struck Arleath, knocking him unconscious and the rest seized Ruarnon, who gaped, and seemed lost for words. Ruarnon stumbled, as the three guards marched them forcibly back towards a Tor none of them could see. Mawana took a deep breathe, trying to slow his breathing. He tried to focus on sleep, projecting rest onto two guards, three. Two guards stumbled, losing their hold on Ruarnon. Ruarnon leapt clear, staring at Mawana.

"Sleep magic," Mawana explained. "The dragons are manipulating them into an obstacle. We can wake them when it's over."

Ruarnon nodded, and magic tingled beside the two soldiers Mawana wrestled into sleep, until all three soldiers lay slumbering on the long, dried yellow grass.

Mawana tensed. Captain Arleath still stood and he'd drawn his sword. He was turning from Mawana to Ruarnon. "How am I to know you are an ally, if you would put our own people to sleep?" he asked Mawana.

"Because he didn't aim to harm them, or drive them away," said Ruarnon. "The way all three guards started thinking alike, it was as if the dragon's tampered with their minds."

"Perhaps travelling in groups was a bad idea," said Mawana. "I know you intended us to help each other, but apparently the dragons can manipulate us into hindering each other."

"I'll not have anyone approach creatures that can make us see and believe what isn't real alone," said Ruarnon. "We walk together. We keep an eye out for the others and help them if we can."

Mawana nodded and the three marched forwards.

Ruarnon slowed at a voice.

"Which of your duties does this fulfil, Ruarnon?"

Their heart-beat faltered. Mawana was right. The dragons were making people hallucinate. Because Uncle Omah was dead. Surely the dragons couldn't make... Ruarnon froze. Omah stood beside them in his iron armour. Every detail was there, down to the iron discs of the iron kilt below Omah's plate armour, and the gold regent's circlet around his head.

"You are becoming the reckless, hot-headed regent Advisor Monin feared," said Omah. "You let your passion blind you to the wisdom of his words. And now you risk your life, not to save my brother and his wife, but out of loyalty to your friends, as though you were a private person. Of all the faults I thought you may have; selfishness was not one of them. You abandoned two kingdoms to lead an expedition here, and now you have abandoned that expedition."

The words hit Ruarnon like a physical blow. It was Omah's voice. His eyes. It was even Omah's values and logic.... It wasn't real... but did Ruarnon truly need to be here? Their friends had proved their capacity. They'd made contact and all but formed an alliance with the Galvations without Ruarnon's help. They didn't need Ruarnon. They could protect Selenia. Ruarnon could return to their fleet and ensure the Tarlahns and Zaldeaans didn't get caught up in the Timbalen-Azulan war. That was where Ruarnon *should* be. It was their duty. Hundreds could die needlessly if they didn't fulfil it.

But something was wrong. They were forgetting something. Something important. And Mawana said they shouldn't trust anything that sent them back.

The apparition of Omah was gone. So were Mawana and Captain Arleath. Ruarnon had no desire to be alone in a place like this. They ran ahead, trying to catch up to their friend and captain.

They started. A shadowy figure was moving towards them. It wasn't big enough to be Mawana. Lenaris resolved out of the air.

"Ruarnon, I..." her face was pale.

"Are you injured?" they asked.

"I think I am with child," she whispered.

Ruarnon frowned, wondering how the knowledge connected to the present. But if the dragons could make people see things that weren't real... It could be the dragons deceiving her, but if she truly was pregnant...

"Are you sure?" Ruarnon asked.

Lenaris breathed heavily, then shut her eyes. "I cannot tell. They are affecting my mind. Clouding my judgement."

"We should go on together," said Ruarnon. "I cannot see Narz enchanting dragons to attack an unborn child. Not given all we know about him now. Vye unleashing all those damars in the Zaldeaan Realm, the fact children died... it must have tormented Narz. More guilt over people who died because *he* made a poor choice and put what mattered to him before others' safety. I don't think he'd use such a thing against us, even if you *are* pregnant."

Lenaris took a deep breath, meeting their gaze and inclined her head.

They were both rattled. Both their thinking was compromised. But the chance to ensure peace between the Elite Guard and Narz lay before them.

"Come on," they said to Lenaris, and they kept walking.

"Benevolence! You must turn back!"

Ruarnon turned. A Tarlahn soldier stood behind them, a letter in his hand.

"One of Lord Vye's servants delivered this. It is a letter from King Narz. He says that if you go near the dragons, he will kill your parents."

Ruarnon froze.

Lenaris gaped.

Narz had a strange obsession with their parents. He could have released them months ago. He hadn't. Even Darius said Narz was strange about them. But Queen Ziliene thought Narz wanted them hostage so Ruarnon would advise Teliph when she came to the throne. So why would Narz threaten to kill them now?

And Pamoran said Narz had a strange obsession with them as parents, that he wanted them kept safe. Logic said this was a lie. Don't trust anything that deters you.

"Why is he suddenly speaking about them now?" Ruarnon asked the messenger, who appeared puzzled, then vanished.

Ruarnon shivered, their heart still racing at the idea Narz could kill their parents.

"We really cannot trust much here," they told Lenaris. "I shouldn't have fallen behind Mawana and Captain Arleath."

"I shouldn't have got ahead of Mawana," Lenaris replied. "I didn't mean to. I just kept walking, and I became distracted, worried about the Australians. Then he was gone, and I was remembering my suspicion of pregnancy."

Which reminded Ruarnon they were leading their possibly pregnant best friend and her unborn child into gravest danger.

"Maybe you should go back," said Ruaron. "The rest of us can handle this."

Lenaris grit her teeth. "And what if that is what the dragons want everyone to think? That someone else will finish the work. That each of us has a pressing reason to turn back, and with the shadow spell, we cannot see each other retreating side by side?"

"Your reason could be real," Ruarnon objected.

"I don't like being manipulated," she replied. "I wouldn't mind a word with these dragons. And I want to know where my husband is."

"If you halt his expansion, I will take his place."

Ruarnon and Lenaris froze. Another phantom stood before them, blue eyes glinting with malice, sharp features as commanding as ever.

Lord Vye smiled. "With my brother's backing, I will make short work of Teliph. Under me, the Keepers will extend Narz's empire. We will crush the Galvation vermin, teach the Middle South a lesson, then, teach the whole continent the respect they need to show their betters. You do not have what it takes to stop me. Teliph does not. Only Narz has the power to defeat me, and once you unhinge his mind with sight of that weapon, nothing will stand in my way."

Ruarnon's breathing came hard and fast. This Vye looked almost exactly like the one who'd tried to kill them all. Though there was something wrong with the eyes. The eyes didn't meet their gaze or Lenaris's. They didn't appear able to see. But the words... They might well be the truth.

It would be foolish to think anyone could predict Narz's reaction to the weapon, even if they presented it with Keeper and Teliph's foreknowledge and Narz's and Melroth's security measures in place. And if Narz *did* lose his mind completely at sight of the weapon; how could they counter Vye? Other than Narz, only Teliph could face him... and if her teacher lost his grip on the present while she bore witness, could she ignore that, and kill Vye before he killed her?

"We are not ready for this," said Ruarnon. "The threat of Narz's mind unravelling is too great and we are not ready to counter it. There must be more we can do to ensure he does not fall apart at sight of the weapon."

"Yes," Lenaris replied, her eyes wide. "*After* we finish what we came here for," she added grimly, staring at phantom Vye.

Ruarnon took another step forwards and a man whose face silenced their every thought appeared. There was deep pain in those blue eyes. It seemed etched into every line of the middle-aged face. The dark hair atop the head wore a gold crown with a large emerald, sapphire and ruby set in it, signalling rule of three kingdoms, Ruarnon suspected.

"Do you know what they did with it?" the man's voice asked softly. "Do you know how many women and children died? I can still hear them screaming. Why would you remove it from a place only one can reach? Why do you wish to unleash it upon the world again, without any surety you or your Elite Guard allies can destroy it?

"Agents of the God Kings are already inside my walls. If you bring that weapon forth and fail to destroy it, you will invite slaughter of my subjects at God King hands."

Ruarnon stared into the pained, intelligent gaze of a face modelled on Narz's. Apparition though it was, every word was likely enough to be true. Sorcery War could obliterate all Narz's kingdoms and the Middle South in the crossfire. Maybe only one Divine Army was stirring, because after Narz and a few of his loyal leaders were assassinated, the God Kings could rule by force, assassinating any sorcerer who disapproved, evading a Sorcery War.

And if God King assassins moved into position in Narz's castle, then instead of presenting the weapon to be destroyed before Narz, Ruarnon and their friends could deliver it into the hands of agents of the God Kings.

"If we fail," Ruarnon told Lenaris, "we could hand the weapon to agents of the God kings, who will kill not only Narz, but Teliph, Captain Melroth and the First Healer. They could slaughter Keepers at Narz's Castle. We could end up aiding the God King's conquest of Narz's kingdoms, Galvatia *and* the Forest Realm. The weapon can probably kill Queen Ziliene too. How can we take such a risk?"

Lenaris stood still beside them, her mouth frozen in horror.

"You're all right!"

Mawana rushed up to Ruarnon and Lenaris. "Selenia told me you'd gone into premature labour. I was so worried!"

Mawana flung his arms around Lenaris, who stood with her mouth wide open. When they stepped apart, she said, "I didn't even tell you I suspected I was with child. Not yet."

Mawana trembled. "I... I didn't know. She just told me and I... I believed."

Ruarnon tensed. "I think we're becoming more susceptible to feel and believe what the dragon's wish as we get closer."

"We must be," said Mawana. "And I have a bad feeling our Australian friends have got ahead of us. We need to face this together. Come on."

Ruarnon nodded. But Mawana was already running ahead, Lenaris chasing after him. Ruarnon began to run, but their friends were already blurring into darkness, as they moved into the shadow spell and blurred beyond Ruarnon's sight. But wait, someone was moving ahead. Two figures, coming towards them. Thank goodness, they'd come back!

The black shapes blurred and became colour and Ruarnon froze. Corina's eyes filled with tears. Urmilian's face broke into a smile, his stern, calm, kingly exterior falling away. It *couldn't* be! But when Corina stepped forwards to hug Ruarnon, she *felt* real. So did Urmilian's grip on their shoulder, as he stepped forwards smiling. But they couldn't be here.. It didn't make sense.

"Pamoran came back for us," said Urmilian. "He really can work magic. Narz is troubled by all the prison breaks and the Middle South armies. Pamoran snuck us out while Narz turned north and south and didn't know which way to look. We sent word to my brother to take to his ships as we travelled to meet you. Tarlahns and Zaldeaans alike are all going home. You did it child. You saved us all."

The man who never thought Ruarnon was quite good enough. Ruarnon had worried Urmilian would think less of them for returning to Tarlah after assassins tried to kill them in the Zaldeaan Realm. Proclaiming Ruarnon a hero meant proclaiming them more than

Urmilian had *ever* believed Ruarnon capable of. He was praising them as only Omah had. It wasn't, it could not be... real.

Ruarnon took a step forwards.

"You've done it," said Corina. "We can collect your ships and sail home."

Her kind, earnest face was the one Ruarnon had struggled to remember of late. It was so happy. The face Ruarnon had pictured when they told her they had renewed Tarlah's relations with the Urai and been accepted by the Urai Council of Elders. That two of their closest friends now were Urai. There was just one other problem.

"And what of my Australian friends?"

Corina looked uncertain.

"What of the friends I nearly abandoned when I was going to place Tor in charge of recovering you? The ones crucial to Narz making peace with the Elite Guard? What of my chance to broker peace for this whole continent?"

Ruarnon's parents vanished. Ruarnon stepped forwards with a heavy heart.

Lenaris halted. That was a body, lying before her in the long grass. Arlian? Arlian rolled over, his face pale as death, eyes glazed, the punctures in his bronze armour leaking congealing blood.

Lenaris clutched her mouth.

"You couldn't save me," said Arlian. "But you can save him."

Lenaris shivered. What on Umarinaris did he mean?

Arlian was pointing... at Troy, who stumbled blindly ahead. Another figure lay beside Arlian, her wild features and smile dimmed by the pale of death. Ethlin, whose eyes snapped open where she lay. "And you can save her."

Ethlin was pointing at Linh. Who was walking towards a second dragon, further right. Neither Troy nor Linh held weapons. Neither had cast a protective shield. Both her proteges, her favourites, walked alone, unprotected. Both dragons' mouths opened, and fire rushed before them. Where was Mawana? Lenaris couldn't shield them both!

Linh flickered. And vanished. She wasn't real. But Troy kept moving. And someone was beside him, a shorter, dark, hazy figure… Fiona. Shielded by the shadow spell. Which suggested the fire rushing towards them was *real*.

Lenaris screamed, and a shield blossomed before Troy and Fiona. The pair kept walking, and she strained to shift her shield, keeping pace with them, enlarging it, as flames rushed forwards. The flames struck her shield and she trembled against the force of dragon magic. Strained as it clutched at hers, seeking to turn her protective wall into fire, and kill two more of her proteges.

Lenaris screamed again, her shield flared and the fire vanished. She gasped, stumbling. Troy and Fiona walked on, Fiona still a dark haze, Troy solid and real looking, each trampling blackened grass without seeing it, oblivious to the flames that had almost killed them. Lenaris smiled.

Then hands were supporting her, lowering her to the ground.

"Lenaris?" Ruarnon called. "What happened?"

Lenaris leaned back against them, as everything became fuzzy. "I think I just saved Troy and Fiona's lives," she replied, as her head slumped into Ruarnon's chest and everything went dark.

Ruarnon fought down the shakes, as they checked Lenaris's pulse. She was still breathing. She still had a pulse. But they'd seen two figures walk on. After Lenaris stopped fire flashing towards them. She really *had* saved someone. Which meant she really had fainted from magical exertion, and lost consciousness because of it. They had no idea how to treat it. And no food and water to give her.

"MAWANA!" Ruarnon yelled. "Mawana, Lenaris needs you!"

"What's wrong?"

Ruarnon heaved with relief. "Magical over-exertion. She fainted. I do not know what to do for her."

Ruarnon's breathing was ragged. Their chest hurt. They clutched at it. Why was it so hard to breathe?

A black shadow glided towards them and blurred into Mawana, who kept his distance. He gasped at sight of Lenaris, then turned to Ruarnon. "And how do I know this pair of you is real?"

Ruarnon couldn't answer. Their chest was hurting worse. They couldn't breathe properly. Their face was heating.

"What's wrong with you?" Mawana asked.

"I do not know," Ruarnon gasped. "Battle panic?"

A condition that incapacitated soldiers under pressure. It sounded about right.

Mawana hurried over and removed the pins from Ruarnon's bronze armour, then loosened their sword belt. He removed the bronze plate armour and supported Ruarnon with one arm. Ruarnon breathed deeply. Mawana pressed their chest with his other hand.

"Easy. I've never known you to panic."

Ruarnon shook their head. "I've never seen anything take Lenaris down before. She's never lost consciousness in a fight. I have. At least three times. And I didn't know what to do about magical over exertion…"

"And the bastard dragons manipulated your feelings into what our Australian friends call a panic attack," Mawana replied grimly. "Perhaps it is safer to travel solo from here? Where they cannot frighten us with what is happening to our friends?"

Ruarnon sighed, their breathing coming more easily. "If we travel alone, how will we know if the friends we meet are real, or not?"

Mawana groaned. "Curse these enchantments! Wherever did Narz think of such things?"

Ruarnon's mouth dropped open. "His own mind. The way his deepest fears rush into panic, ignoring or unheeding of information he possesses, that contradicts his fears. What if these dragons manipulate our minds and feelings, just as Narz's madness manipulates his?"

Ruarnon shuddered. How could anyone save Narz from such a thing? But how could anyone abandon him to it?

Now Ruarnon could see how irrational Narz's mind may be, spiralling him into panic and fear, into a state in which he could not perceive or else could not believe knowledge he already possessed that *ought* to reassure him…

"We have to free him from this." Ruarnon stood. "And if he cannot be freed, we cannot let a state like this rule the man who would rule this continent. I will not let anyone be subject to *this*."

They seized their armour, and Mawana helped them buckle the plates back on. They belted their sword on and met Mawana's gaze.

"I think the Australians separated," said Mawana. "You go after Michael and Linh. I'll protect Troy and Fiona."

"TOR! Come and collect Lenaris! She is unconscious!" Mawana yelled.

A blurred shadow moved towards them from far away, at surprising speed. It materialised into a pale faced Tarlahn guard gritting her teeth. "Tor ordered me to check she is indeed in trouble," said the woman.

Mawana nodded to her. She lifted Lenaris over her shoulder with Mawana's help and turned to walk back across a seemingly empty field, towards a seemingly empty stand of trees, where all their horses waited.

Ruarnon met Mawana's gaze, they inclined their heads to each other, then they both jogged forwards. Ruarnon veered right. Michael and Linh were the sensible ones. Ruarnon wasn't sure how Michael had made it so far ahead. Linh could be stubborn. She might charge down apparitions and continue to the dragons with sword lowered, but Michael…

A shadow stood before Ruarnon, unmoving. Ruarnon slowed. The figure was slender, but too tall to be Linh. Michael?

He was dark haired, though the young man standing opposite him was blond, and unfamiliar. He was smiling.

"I was starting to worry Troy had led you lot off a cliff," the blond youth said, with a flash of perfect white teeth. "Though I doubt Linh would let him. She doesn't seem to take nonsense."

"She doesn't," Michael said softly. Something was wrong with his voice…

"She's brilliant Andy. And a lose canon, but brilliant. She can even think of things as fast as I can. It's like… like having an equal. For the first time in my life. And Ruarnon… they're even smarter than me. It's like… like I belong with people here. The only thing I'm missing is you."

"Come back with me," said Andy. "I finally found the nerve to tell mum how I feel about you. I know she loves you. I thought it would be easier to tell her first. She already knew Mic! Apparently the way we look at each other is obvious. Even dad was starting to notice…"

Michael shuffled and bit his lip, with uncertainty Ruarnon had never seen from him on Umarinaris.

"How does your dad feel about us?"

Andy smiled, and tears shone in his eyes. "Said you're not quite as pretty as he thought I'd go for, but as long as I'm happy with you, he is too."

Tears were running down Michael's face. But this wasn't fear, dread or panic. Michael was as strong willed as Linh. So they'd shown him a vision he wouldn't fight. One he couldn't resist.

"Michael?" said Ruarnon.

Michael sighed.

"I am sorry my friend, but that is not your Andy and this moment is not real."

"I've always worried whether Andy's father would accept me as his boyfriend," Michael replied, tears running down his face.

Ruarnon wrapped his arms around Michael, who let his head rest on Ruarnon's shoulder.

"I am afraid you cannot have peace of mind about that just yet," said Ruarnon. "But should we help First Captain Rilmar make her peace with Narz, perhaps Narz will lend you Red Cloak to open the Gateway of Umarinaris, and you and the real Andy can talk to Andy's parents."

Michael nodded, wiping away tears. "It's probably time. My family already know. But we'd have to get home first."

Michael gasped. The Andy apparition was gone. But before them, fire blossomed, before a short, shadowy figure.

Ruarnon and Michael both reached out, magic flaring and melding as it touched in a wall before Linh. Michael grit his teeth and Ruarnon put an arm around him, as they maintained a shield wall before Linh, who was advancing unseeing towards the dragon beyond the fire.

CHAPTER 29

FUTURES - MAWANA

Mawana frowned. Was that really Troy and Fiona? Why were they lying on the ground sleeping? This was hardly the time or place for a nap! And the dragons sat not far ahead, one peering intently at the sleeping couple.

"Fiona? Troy? Michael? *Anyone*?"

Mawana frowned. That was Linh's voice, but he couldn't see her, or Ruarnon and Michael as they pursued her. He did see Troy stand shakily and stumble several steps towards the dragon. He seemed disorientated and Mawana wasn't sure what he was looking at. But when Troy froze and stood staring at nothing, Mawana was sure Troy was looking at something that wasn't real. And while Troy stood transfixed by a sight Mawana couldn't see, a long powerful tail swung towards him.

Mawana launched himself forwards. But the spiked tail was too fast. Mawana couldn't reach and knock Troy down in time. And knocking Troy over with shield magic could go terribly wrong. Which left...

Mawana roared, as his shield wrapped around one side of the tail and strained against it. The spikes weren't going to hit Troy. But the tail was big enough to at least knock him out, and if it hit his head directly, it could still kill him.

Mawana groaned, as the tail pushed closer. It slowed. Sweat broke out on Mawana's forehead. "Move Troy!" he yelled, knowing his friend probably wouldn't hear him.

Troy stood unblinking.

Without warning, the tail retreated and Mawana collapsed with relief as the pressure lifted from his shield. The nearest dragon was leaning forwards, reaching with its right paw. Only the claws could reach Troy…

"Mawana!" Lenaris's voice yelled. "Something's gone wrong. I think the baby is coming now!"

Mawana grit his teeth. She should be so far away he couldn't hear her. That wasn't Lenaris.

Mawana reformed a shield, straining against a clawed paw as it extended. The paw began a swipe, and Mawana groaned, seeing stars as he began to shake from the strain of stopping the creature clawing Troy's head off. What in Chaos was Troy looking at?

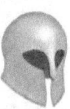

"Fiona? Troy? Michael? *Anyone*?"

Troy sat up. That was Linh and she was terrified. But Fiona and Michael had slain the dragon. It lay dead before him, while they lay sleeping.

Linh's voice cleared his mind and he remembered there was another dragon. Linh must be attacking it alone. He leapt up. And halted the run he'd intended, as the world blurred, darkened, then became clear. He stood on a steep, barren hillside which dropped away before him. At the bottom, high, dark walls and guard towers rose. Beyond were small, crudely built rock cottages and streets filled with raggedly dressed people. Black City?

He jumped. People stood on the hillside on his right, including a tall man in dark blue silks, a blonde-haired, cold-blue-eyed man, Vye.

"These are the people who would ban healing," he said. "They will riot if the Keepers go near them. Their army is gathering and seeks alliances in the Middle South. Destroy them, and you will force their army here. Destroy their army, and we shall be free to extend healing and Keepers' justice from Azula to the Middle Sea."

Did he just order those people to commit a massacre? What was going on?

Light blazed. A bolt of energy struck a guard tower in Black City. Stone exploded and rained down into crowded streets. Screams rent the air, and people fled into tiny wooden cottages, which caught fire.

Troy gaped. It *couldn't* be real. He'd been somewhere else, with people who weren't here. Whatever this was, watching and listening to it was stressful and he had to get out before he went mad.

If it wasn't real…he stepped into the hillside. Everything went dark. Slowly, the world came into focus. It was a beautiful sunny day. Children played in a dirt street, adults swept the doorsteps of farmhouses, and tended fields and picked fruit in orchards. Where was this place? Huge trees rose in the distance, framing fields along the horizon. The Forest Realm.

Screams rose. An army emerged through the trees and marched down a main road. Fields and orchards burst into flame. Cattle and flocks were blown into the sky, as fields blasted apart. People cried out and rushed towards homes that caught fire.

Troy turned back. A field lay behind him. His friends and their guards were scattered across it. Their horses were tethered at the forest edge with a few guards beyond. He could go that way. But people behind him were in trouble. Who was doing this? Who did he attack?

He turned, as sorcerers marched across grassy hillsides, Vye standing dispassionately to one side. They lined up beside the Great Forest. Troy's heart drum rolled.

"Destroy it," Vye commanded.

A wall of flame rose before the sorcerers. Trees flared into burning torches, then fire engulfed them.

"Leave them alone!" Troy yelled.

A wave of fire swept the fields. People on countryside roads ran screaming. Fire blazed towards their homes.

"STOP IT!" Troy roared.

Flames consumed farmhouses. Farmers were overrun by flames.

Troy shook with anger. He turned and raised both hands, forming a large shield bigger than a bronze one. He launched it at Vye. It shot straight through the sorcerer. He wasn't real. The whole thing might not be. But he could *see* people dying. He shuddered, as screams filled the air.

Fire roared over villages. Troy didn't know what was real and what wasn't. He didn't know how to stop it, but he tried shooting sorcerers with magic shields. The shields passed through them. Was he trapped in a waking nightmare?

Flames advanced towards Ziliene's capital. A shield formed, barring the fire. At last! Someone was fighting back! A figure in a green dress stood atop a tower near the shield, maintaining it. Flames pressed on, burning, consuming, destroying farmland, then flared against the shield. It held. Queen Ziliene was extremely powerful, surely she could save her city?

Lightning struck her tower. Her body plummeted. The shield winked out of existence.

Troy's heart pounded fit to burst. Flames struck beautiful buildings, and screams, panic and confusion spread.

"We'd never let it come to this," he said, tears running down his face. "Someone would have done *something*!"

Fire lapped against towers and spires, flowing into crowded streets of screaming civilians.

"YOU *ARE*! DO IT Troy!"

That was Mawana. Do what? But if Troy could see but not hear Mawana; none of this was real.

"*ENOUGH*!" a man's voice roared, and Troy jumped.

Everything faded. Screams quieted, then silence fell. Troy became aware of dark blue scales before him. He stood meters away from the great yellow eye of a blue dragon. He focused on it, charging and stabbed the eye with all his might.

His blade grew hot, began to smoke and he let go and backed up.

Linh's vision wavered. When it cleared, there was only one wall before her. It looked solid, as did the giant, cat-like dragons sitting before it, tails swishing and yellow eyes glowing as they stared intently at her friends.

Linh smiled and was about to run. But something lay on the ground on her right, where Fiona had been walking. She tensed. It was Fiona. Fiona lay on her back, her enchanted sword in one hand, her bronze helmet dented, her glassy eyes gazing sightlessly skyward.

Linh froze. It couldn't be. Fiona could be anywhere. Those dragons could show her anything. But when had she last seen the others? How could she be sure?

Something inside her flinched, as she scanned the unmoving body. The light brown hair was there behind the pale neck and freckled face. The form beneath bronze plate armour was short and slender. The enchanted, bronze-iron sheened sword was in the right hand, the quiver at the left hip. There was a leather kilt below the armour and leather sandals. Every detail was there.

Linh froze.

"Leave the child alone! We swore not to harm children! There must be another way!"

Linh turned, but there was no sign of the speaker. It sounded like the man was talking inside her head. But he couldn't have been. Because the image of Fiona's lifeless body that was distressing her had vanished. As if the voice had told the dragons to take it away. Linh shivered.

Only Narz and perhaps Vye knew about the dragons. And Vye sure as hell wouldn't help. …Had that been Narz? The *real* Narz?

Had he been torn between what he thought was right and what he thought was necessary, since he declared war on Galvatia? If Narz was still undecided, they had a *real* chance to convince him that war with the Elite Guard *wasn't* necessary. If they reached him while he was still arguing with himself…

Linh jogged forward. She halted abruptly, on the steps of a vast, brown, crystalline structure. Crystalline walls towered before her, barring the sky. She turned back. An open field and Captain Rilmar minding horses at the forest edge lay behind her. But before her, Lord Vye stood upon the castle front steps, a crowd flocking towards him.

"They are sorcerers," he said calmly. "Sorcerers who will aid their emperor in the conquest of the world. He wants to rule it all. They built up strength for centuries, planning to avenge kingdoms destroyed in the Sorcery War. Haven't you wondered why we have never seen such greedy, selfish, cruel sorcerers since? They live in the Timbalen Empire! They have been there all this time. And now they have come to seize what they always believed was theirs. We face a Second Sorcery War, and there are no Guardians to help us. Who will protect us?"

Anger at the blatant lies burned in Linh's gut. But people were moving forwards, rushing to sign pieces of paper held by Vye's servants. They were enlisting sorcerers to fight Elite Guard. And there were red cloaks among them. Keepers of the Peace flocked to Vye's call. Captain Melroth walked among them muttering, "It cannot happen again. We must stop them."

"No! You can't!" Linh objected.

"Yes," said a green robed healer walking beside the Captain. "We must claim lives to fight for the right to heal and save lives in future."

Healers discarded green cloaks and Keepers discarded red. They put on Vye's blue and formed a line across rocky plains in their thousands, opposite thousands of yellow cloaked Elite Guard. Panic writhed in Linh. She was supposed to *stop* this!

Emperor Yarath stood to one side, addressing the Elite Guard. "They came with stealth and speed to annihilate you! They would leave us defenceless against rogue sorcerers! They will attack until you are all dead! Destroy them! It is your only chance of survival!"

Linh's mouth dropped open, as she stood, helpless.

The sky filled with light. Lightning rained. Fire blossomed among men, women and nonbinary people. Countless yellow and blue cloaked figures were tossed into the air.

"Fiona! Troy! Michael! *Anyone*?" she yelled.

Linh took a step forward. Her friends would come. She had to keep moving. Maybe she could run ahead to make it stop?

Groups broke off to fight, spreading throughout the plains and Damaria. The city and rocky plains were gradually blasted apart in clouds of dust. Ancient Valley burned. Fire spread through the farmlands and Galvatia. Lightning rained down into Azula and coastal cities burned. They were destroying *everything*. Linh could hardly breathe.

"It's alright! I am here. You are not alone child. You will succeed and together we *will* stop this."

"Narz?" Linh asked faintly.

"I swear it," the voice in her head replied. "Come! There isn't much time!"

Images flickered and Linh frowned at a great yellow eye. She sensed Narz flinch away from his creation. Her sword was out in an instant and she hacked into the eye. Then someone was talking, but she couldn't make out their words, as they pulled her back. She let go of her hilt and the dark blue dragon toppled before her. The gust of wind it blew into her face made it feel real. But was it?

The giant body struck the ground loudly, causing it to rumble beneath her feet. Linh stared. Then she turned.

Michael and Ruarnon panted behind her, relief on their faces.

"You couldn't see the fire, could you?" Michael asked breathlessly.

Linh frowned.

Ruarnon smiled. "We did not answer you because shielding you took everything both of us had. We could not speak."

"You were behind me? For how long?" she asked.

"For your whole run," said Ruarnon. "You were running into fire the whole time. I think... I think that is what made the voice angry. The voice that was telling the dragon to stop."

Linh shivered. "But that voice was in *my* head."

Michael shook his head. "I heard it too. That dragon could have killed all three of us. It sounded like Narz was calling it off. Like he wanted ...to *save* us."

Movement on Linh's left caught her attention. The second dragon lay slain and Mawana was hugging Fiona, beside Troy, before it. Troy's sword lay in the grass, smoking, its blade melting on the edges. In the dragon's eye, her blade was sagging, smoking, also melting.

But Troy must have been listening to them, because he shivered and turned to face them. "I heard him too. He yelled *enough*, and the fire and the screams and all the awful things I was seeing... they stopped. The moment he spoke. That's when I killed the other dragon. Narz just *helped* us."

Beside Troy, Fiona shivered and Mawana stood wide eyed.

But Narz hadn't just spoken as if he wanted to protect them, he had told them to hurry, that there wasn't much time... Was he referring to the approach of war... or did he want them to reach him while he still knew his own mind?"

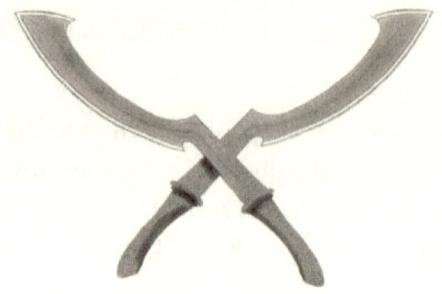

CHAPTER 30

TRA THE FROZEN CITY -RUARNON

Ruarnon and Michael stepped forward to hug Linh, who still seemed shocked. Ruarnon supposed they would be too, had they been so entranced they didn't realise they were walking through fire. Then Troy and Fiona ran to hug Linh, and Ruarnon hugged Mawana, who sagged into them.

"I don't know how I didn't faint from magical exertion," said Mawana. "I suspect the four of us won't be able to craft magic for the next few days. We shouldn't have been crafting so much magic so close to resisting Vye."

Ruarnon waved to Tor, Selenia and First Captain Rilmar, who had lain Lenaris across a horse and were leading it across the field. Captain Arleath and the guards led the other horses.

"What happened to Lenaris?" Linh asked.

"She will be all right," said Ruarnon. "She fainted from magical exertion, shielding Fiona and Troy from dragon fire."

"Before your dragon decided to try swatting you with its tail and paw alternately," said Mawana, sitting heavily. "I could do with three days sleep to recover from shielding you from that."

"You ran through *fire*!" Fiona said, turning to Troy.

"If Michael's sword wasn't real, I was hoping the fire wasn't," Troy replied, with an uncertain smile, mouthing "thanks" and giving Mawana a double thumbs up.

Linh smiled.

"The two of you were never alone," Ruarnon assured her, "even when Fiona stayed asleep and Troy walked ahead without her."

Linh inclined her head.

Tor and the others approached, and Lenaris stirred. As Tor helped her to sit upright Ruarnon said, "Four of us heard a man speaking as we walked through dragon fire. He was telling the dragons to stop. And urging us to hurry because there isn't much time. We suspect it was Narz, viewing the present via magic, wanting us to stay safe, and warning us that we must move fast. I am not sure how much he knows or guesses. Or if he is rational enough to understand our quest. But I fear he urged us to hurry because his mind is slipping, as the Middle South advances, and he worries about the God Kings.

"Lenaris, Mawana, Michael and I are in little better state than you. We will ride into Tira. But I think we must retrieve the weapon today, before nightfall if we can. And I fear our 'rest' must be riding as far as we can while daylight lasts."

Silence followed Ruarnon's words. Narz must have some idea who he was speaking to and what Ruarnon and their companions intended. If he was encouraging them, then right now, there may be no need to destroy the weapon to prove the Elite Guard worthy of his trust. But by the time they reached him, that may no longer be the case. They had to proceed as planned, swiftly and hope whatever gods or ancestors did or didn't exist were on their side.

"Do we just open them and walk in?" Troy asked, eyeing the two tall, timber gates.

"The obstacles Lord Tarz and King Narz placed lie behind us," said Captain Rilmar. "The only obstacle now is locating the weapon."

Selenia reached into her leather scrip with a shaking hand and took out the first bronze-iron sheened key and placed it in the bottom lock.

The smooth blue substance over the lock vanished, disappearing from the upper lock too, as Linh placed the second key in. They turned the keys. The gates remained glassy blue. A mechanism creaked and groaned on the far side.

Selenia raised a trembling hand. Despite the enchantment, both gates swung open at her touch. A blue-sheened fountain rose from the road within, lined by blue-sheened rectangular apartments beyond. Larger-than-life statues of stone women stood in the fountain basin, their arms curving gracefully in a dance, ice spouting from their blue sheened fingertips.

Beyond, two guards were frozen mid-stride, swords in hand, their mouths open as if shouting. Three guards stretched on the ground before them, their limbs suspended at strange angles, their glassy blue eyes registering shock. On Ruarnon's left, more guards stood mid-step with their backs to the gate tower.

Beneath the enchantment, the guards' leather vests and linen tunics appeared well preserved. Their blades seemed sharp, and shock was clear on their pale faces, fear in their wide eyes and the set of their mouths. But they were silent. Unmoving. Perfectly preserved in their moment of panic.

It made Ruarnon's instincts scream that they should turn and confront the threat behind them. The rational part of Ruarnon's mind knew Narz had walked away over six hundred years ago, but the intense fear in the frozen features before them tightened Ruarnon's muscles and had them gripping their spear in its holster on their saddle.

Beyond the guards lay empty, smooth blue pavement. Then an arc of people, their backs turned, legs stretched in great strides, arms reaching to pump for greater speed as they froze mid-flight. Every face was pale, some eyes glazed with tears and several mouths were open in silent shouts or screams.

Troy flinched at the panic before them and Ruarnon noted his eyes were red rimmed. What had the dragons shown Troy?

But the Tirans were too mesmerising for Ruarnon to keep studying Troy. Nearby, a woman suspended in mid-run clutched a baby in one arm. Beside her a man held a little girl. The little girl's tears hung in mid-air below her face. The baby's face was screwed up in a scream.

Another woman stood a few paces back, turning to a boy reaching to pick up a dog. Her mouth was open in a silent yell, desperation plain on her face. Ruarnon almost heard her shout to leave the dog and save himself.

A mother stood further down, holding the hands of two girls. Two older boys were frozen mid-stride beside her. The children looked ahead. The mother turned, the blue enchanted substance standing in lumps over tears on her face, her eyes wide with terror, as she looked back at a young boy. A man bent over the boy, half-lifting him. Beside him, a fleeing couple held hands, their knuckles white under shiny blue enchantment. Beyond, more people stood partway through doorways, running for cover.

Further down the road, a carriage turning into a side street tilted to one side, frozen partway through a high-speed turn. In the main street, people hung out of windows, pointing wide-eyed to where Narz had stood. Bells up a guard tower hung at angles, frozen while warning the city was under attack.

This was the fear that drove Galvatia to deny magic, even in the face of Narz's army. It was the fear Poran had spoken of, which drove people to evict sorcerers from their homes and towns, and to avoid magical healing, even at the cost of their lives. This was everything Narz wanted to change, yet this was of *his* making.

"It nears sunset," Tor warned. "We had best search quickly, if we are to find the weapon before nightfall."

Ruarnon inclined their head. "Please divide into pairs," they said. "Search the side streets as well as the main road and remember the weapon will not be affected by the enchantment that preserves the city. Shout if you find it."

Ruarnon heeled their horse down the main road with Selenia, but it was slow going at first, as the horses wove between frozen figures, having to circle wide of family groups. Then Ruarnon and Selenia rode past simple rectangular buildings of blue sheened mudbrick and turned down a paved side street scattered with adults in flowing linens.

Here, people were frozen mid-stride while walking or standing still. They frowned in confusion, gazing to the main road with concern, and several mouths were open, frozen mid conversation.

Narz must have crafted his enchantment just after the bells tolled; before anyone who hadn't witnessed his attack on the guards identified their danger.

"What did you see?" Selenia asked. "Among the dragons?"

Ruarnon sighed. "I'm more worried about what Troy saw. He was shaken. I thought it was for Linh that Narz told the dragons stop, but from what Troy said, Narz halted the most distressing vision Troy had.

"Narz was *so* angry. Yet when he spoke to Linh, he sounded determined, but weak, his voice softer. And that was only moments later. If his mood can alter so much, if the way our feelings leapt around during the dragon visions reflects how his mind operates, if his mind itself inspires the visions the dragon's craft…"

Ruarnon shook their head. "I have never met anyone so frail. And I have never met anyone so strong. Look around you, at the fear and uncertainty. He *caused* this. He did this to your people, your family. Yet his Keepers protect people. They make them feel safe. His Healers *save* lives. It is like his intentions for this continent aim to atone for what he did here. He can't free these people, but he would have healers ensure everyone who falls sick or is injured before their time still lives. And he uses Keepers to ensure their safety.

"For all the destruction of the Sorcery War, for all he did here and the Guardians he killed, after everyone he lost and all the proof he had that magic could destroy the world, it's like he had to prove to himself, and all Umarinaris, that magic can make life better."

"You think he feels remorse, for all of this?"

"Why else would his two greatest institutions, Keepers and Healers be its opposite? Why else would he pit his sorcery wielding damars against people he believed would attack Keepers and Healers? If either is destroyed, he can never atone for all the things he's done. Ziliene said his guilt was so great that it drives his madness. I wonder if being deprived of the chance to atone would again drive him to the pits of despair."

"Then I hope he has a plan against the God Kings. I hope the Elite Guard help him."

"So do I. Though we should hurry. Because Narz would stand a better chance against the God Kings if we can convince him to accept Elite Guard aid against them."

Selenia inclined her head, and they healed their horses forwards, weaving around the small groups of people frozen mid-chatter in the side streets, or hanging out of doors and windows, peering towards the main road, wondering what was wrong.

Ruarnon's horse followed Selenia's around a horse pulling a cart. An archway rose up, in a defensive stone wall either side of the street ahead. The paved road ended there, and a dirt road rutted with cart tracks led them on. Beyond the wall, semi-detached mudbrick apartments gave way to free-standing, single storey, mudbrick homes. Small farms, fields and pasture overcrowded with cattle and flocks lay beyond, and a second city wall with guard towers at regular intervals spanned the horizon, securing the city's food supply.

Selenia stared at the enclosed farmland. "It is hard to believe my parents lived through these times."

"It is hard to believe there was a time when city walls were needed to ensure crops could be planted and harvested and cattle raised," Ruarnon added.

Ruarnon's gaze was drawn to a hill below the city walls, stripped bare of grass and scattered with hay beneath the blue sheen of the enchantment. Cattle gathered around, their necks lowered, some tongues outstretched, bits of grass protruding from mouths. Their presence inside new city walls hinted at fear that animals would be stolen, or families who tended them were at risk of being slain or enslaved. It wasn't just Narz's attack creating an atmosphere of fear in Tira, it was the city's very design. It was the way people had lived here.

"This cannot be allowed to happen again," said Ruarnon.

"Then let's find my parents," Selenia said, healing her horse to a trot as they rode down the open track clear of frozen people.

There were people in the fields, a family squatting, hands extended to pluck weeds from a grain field. A dog stood with its mouth open to bark, its tail frozen mid-wag, before a hill lined with blue sheened apple trees.

As they crested the hill, Ruarnon gazed across a valley of grain fields. Houses on the next hill had strange crystal-like structures extending from their roofs.

"The fire!" Selenia cried.

Her horse sped into the valley and Ruarnon healed their horse after her. A man stood on a rooftop, a bucket extended before him, frozen water suspended in its arch out towards crystal shaped like flickering flames. A ladder stood behind him and people stood passing buckets down the line and up the ladder.

Selenia turned down a dirt side road. Ruarnon followed her, until dirt gave way to paved stone, a road running beneath the arch of the old city wall. There, paved roads led among mudbrick buildings, where people leaned curiously from windows. Selenia ignored them, dismounting and scanned people in the street.

Ruarnon slowed and left their horse on the roadside, following her gaze to a woman carrying a child, and a man with his arm around an elderly man who grimaced as though in pain. A hilt protruded from a scabbard at the young man's hip, a grey metallic hilt unaffected by the blue tinged enchantment.

Ruarnon stopped beside Selenia. The colour of her mother's eyes, curve of her cheeks and chin and her youthful looks made her seem like Selenia's older sister. Her father also looked too young.

Ruarnon studied the sword. The hilt was intricate, consisting of thin strands of metal twined together. But the blade was ordinary, plain, notched, though unaffected by rust or the elements. The crystal-like enchantment stopped at the sheath, not quite touching the hilt or blade.

"They must have been helping strangers," said Selenia.

She smiled and clasped the hilt, gently removing it from its scabbard. Where it scraped the enchantment, specs of blue broke away and vanished. Selenia studied it.

"I sense magic in it," she said.

Ruarnon's skin tingled. They could sense it too.

They remounted their horses and followed the paved road back into the Old City.

As Ruarnon rode past terrified eyes, pale faces, frozen tears and mouths open in mute shouts and screams, they heard the silent warning of what would come to pass if they, Captain Rilmar and their friends failed in their meeting with Narz.

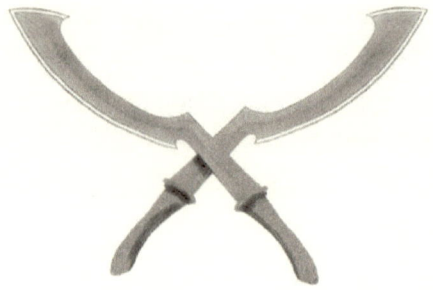

CHAPTER 31

ON THE MOVE ~RUARNON

A day and a half later, a saddle-sore, magical-exertion-weary Ruarnon sat their horse heavily and gazed into the foothills of the Forbidden Mountains. The horses were tiring from long hours riding in steep terrain. Downhill, Tarlahn soldiers and rebel guides led fresh horses from Galvatia's port city towards them.

"I can't come with you," said Selenia. "I've been thinking about what Queen Ziliene said. About Narz wanting to free Tira and fearing he'll get it wrong and kill everyone. And how he can't handle guilt. I'm a reminder of several thousand lives he suspended in time."

Ruarnon sighed. There were so many unknowns with Narz. But Selenia accompanying them could be as bad as Governor Iagl reminding Narz that Zaldeaans were massacred because he underestimated Vye. Ruarnon going when Narz had abducted their parents was risk enough.

"I will miss you. And I don't like parting with you in the wilderness. But I agree," they replied.

"We will see her safely to your people and your fleet," one of the rebels assured Ruarnon as they approached.

Ruarnon inclined their head. Then they started. "General Takanis?" they asked, as the general rode out around the fresh horses and Tarlahn and Galvation riders ahead.

"Given your Benevolence doesn't intend us to fight, and Queen Ziliene warned us battle approaches and you have an errand with Narz, I thought it appropriate for me to advise you on avoiding armies on the march."

Ruarnon inclined their head. "I would appreciate your input."

She shifted her horse beside Tor's and Ruarnon turned back to Selenia.

"I know it's tempting to focus on magic," Selenia said more loudly, addressing everyone. "But remember your hearts and heads will lead you best with Narz. From what I saw with the dragons, that's what served you well."

Everyone inclined their heads with Ruarnon, including the guards.

"I hope you get your parents out safely," she added to Ruarnon.

"I hope Queen Ziliene can help free yours, if Narz cannot," they replied.

Ruarnon hugged her, everyone said goodbye and switched to fresh mounts. Then the rebels and Tarlahns led Selenia and the tired horses along the base of the mountains at a gentle pace, into a wilderness likely safer than the one Ruarnon and their companions were entering.

"I brought two messenger birds," General Takanis informed Ruarnon, patting a box strapped to the back of her saddle. "They are Governor Iagl's. We thought they may be useful to send word to Coroth, should your path to Narz's castle be changed by shifting circumstances."

Ruarnon inclined their head, while Tor eyed the map he held, and led them east, across grassland, towards barren plains and cloud-barred skies.

"Where do you think the southerners will approach from?" Ruarnon asked Takanis.

"They are travelling by ship. But unlike most wars, they have the option of marching on Azula from a desolate wasteland, to minimise non-combatant causalities and know for sure anyone who approaches is an enemy. From what little Prince Maharl and Joharlen could tell me about the Middle South, I think they will land on Galvation shores and invade Azula from the north."

"We too will approach from north of Azula, through the plains east of these foothills along the Mountain Flow and then south along the Green Trine," said Tor. "But the southerners won't have had time to march this far inland yet. We should miss them by at least a few days, though we had best keep an eye out for their scouts."

General Takanis surveyed where he indicated on the map and nodded. Ruarnon liked that path, as it involved staying well west of Damaria, which was likely unsafe under any circumstances and may now have damars marching out of it to battle.

"The hills on the banks of the Green Trine, slightly north of Narz's castle will be the best place to hide until Coroth reaches us," said Tor.

Ruarnon inclined their head, and everyone halted while they drew a basic map and wrote Coroth a note, then attached it to the leg of the bird General Takanis held for them. The bird took flight, and with Coroth knowing where to meet them, and Narz's and the Middle South armies marching to battle, the race to reach Narz at his best began in earnest.

They healed their horses forwards, turning further south towards the gentle roar of the Mountain Flow, as it cut through foothills, on its journey to the Green Trine.

Tor and Captain Arleath scanned the plains alertly, and Ruarnon suspected Mawana's ears were pricked for southerner or Azulan scouts searching for each other's armies.

As their horse's hooves ate up dried plains beside a green carpet flanking the river, Ruarnon's mind wandered east, to Companion Karmarn's castle near the Galvation coast, the perfect location for Zaldeaans to cut off the southerner armies and bear the brunt of their invasion. Sorcerers were probably riding to escort Karmarn and his soldiers to war now. Ruarnon hoped their uncle and the Zaldeaan army had already fled.

A bird flew towards them, smaller and swifter than the one Ruarnon had sent to Coroth. Captain Rilmar raised a finger for it to land on, and removed a tiny scroll attached to its foot.

"Emperor Yarath recognises that if a Divine Army goes to war, King Narz may be too weakened to pose any threat to us," she reported. "He has ordered Octharl to remain in hiding, while our spies confirm whether a Divine Army is indeed taking advantage. Octharl is not to go to war unless it becomes clear King Narz will triumph over all armies that move against him."

Ruarnon exhaled.

"Halt!" Captain Rilmar commanded.

The urgency and quiet of her tone had everyone rein in, even Ruarnon's guards, who rarely obeyed anyone else's orders without Ruarnon's confirmation.

"At first I thought it may be just one magical creature, or a family, moving through the forest on the far side of the Mountain Flow," said Captain Rilmar. "But I fear I sense more than that. And they are moving consistently east, parallel to us, cutting us off from the hills we wish to meet Coroth in."

"But west of us is wilderness," Troy objected. "What could be moving out of the mountains?"

Ruarnon sighed. "Narz hasn't pit magic wielders against non-magic wielders before. But his damars were supposed to be a show of force against the Zaldeaans. What if he intends to use serpents from the Forbidden Mountains to deter the Middle South invasion?"

"We met few such creatures in the mountains," said Tor. "Even if Queen Ziliene has been sending her bravest subjects to hunt them, it would make sense if Narz has sorcerers rounding the creatures up, to herd them as a defensive barrier to the battlefield."

"Can we turn back west, and circle them in the wilderness?" Lenaris asked.

Tor shook his head. "The only clear landmarks in the wilderness are the bridges between the mountains. That would add days to our journey.

And if we cut across the wilderness, we risk becoming lost, which could also delay us considerably."

"Is the mountain force directly parallel with us? And are they moving at the same speed?" Ruarnon asked.

"They are slower," Captain Rilmar replied. She frowned. "Strangely slow. Perhaps the serpents are resisting the enchantment compelling them to travel east."

"Do we have time to race them east and cut across their path before they are close enough to threaten us?" Ruarnon asked.

Captain Rilmar's mouth firmed into a line. "At their current speed it is possible, though I'd want us to ride further north, to be sure we keep beyond their line of direct sight. It is too open here, and they are too close to risk riding into the trees between us and them for cover. Anyone powerful enough to control serpents may detect me if I ride much closer."

Ruarnon inclined their head and Tor steered everyone further north, following the roar of the Mountain flow at a greater distance. The plains provided no cover, only shrubs, and they petered out to grass further north, under grey clouds that became darker.

Tor eyed Ruarnon worriedly. They could ride past whoever led the serpents in plain sight, but only if Coroth caught up to them in time. If he didn't, Black City provided the best cover to hide, but it was next to Damaria and damars may also be on the move...

Did they sacrifice half a day to ride back to Galvatia? To hide and wait for Coroth, only to double back to Narz's castle?

"Is that rain?" Fiona asked, pointing across the plains.

The air shimmered over the barren plains beyond Galvatia City, where the dark heavens had opened.

"That's a deluge," said Michael. "Clouds along the edge of the barren plains right of Galvatia are moving."

"I see mist north of Galvatia," Fiona added, "before the damar infested forest. I think that might be rain in the east too, beyond the Green Trine, near the mountains hiding Damaria."

Several, simultaneous, large rainstorms…

"I suspect King Narz is releasing the enchanted sky to turn the barren plains to bog, and delay the march of the southern army," said Tor.

Ruarnon liked the sound of that. It would keep the southerner army further from them as they road for Narz's castle.

By the time everyone rode beneath dark grey clouds, rain lashed the ground on their far left, veiling Galvatia City. Mist blown on the wind obscured their view, but when they came closer to the Green Trine's banks, Ruarnon made out the dry hills of Galvatia's desolate farmland beyond the river, and a long, dark mass among it. They tensed. But if that *was* the southerner army, surely rebel scouts would have warned them?

The mass was a column, marching towards the bridge that spanned the Trine and led to Galvatia City's main gates. The column was angling away from Black City.

"It *can't* be," said Michael.

A scout climbed out of the Trine and ran towards them, her blonde hair blowing freely in the edge of the storm winds, her linen trousers soaking wet, her whole face beaming with the force of her smile.

"Greetings Regent Ruarnon. Black City has been evacuated. My people are returning to Galvatia, several thousand of them. I approached and Governor Poran himself is marching *with* them!"

Ruarnon's facial muscles slackened. Surely Narz hadn't decided to let his remaining Galvation captives go *free*? After all this time?

The scout's eyes shone, then her smile faded, and her features set more seriously. "Governor Poran says my people will be safer further west. That war may come too close to Black City."

Black City was beside Damaria, and damars had killed innocent people because Poran wasn't there to stop them once before…

"His and Narz's lack of judgment saw many non-combatants killed in the Zaldeaan Realm." said Ruarnon. "I think he is acting to save those its within his power to save this time."

Many people walked in the Galvation column. In the rear, wagons carried hunched adults and small figures, the very old and very young. Continuous sound rose from the column, voices raised in song.

As they halted on the banks of the Green Trine, Ruarnon could just make out the words, carried downriver on the wind;

"Lay down tools,

Wash yourself clean.

Wander home over fields,

And country green.

Day's work is done,

Time for home and fun.

"Gather round the fire,

Put the dinner on,

Tell us a story,

Of days long gone.

Day's work is done,

Time for home and fun."

"It's been a *long* day in Black City," Fiona said with a tearful smile, which Ruarnon returned.

The singing continued, as the Galvations began crossing the bridge, entering their no-longer abandoned capital.

"They are not the only ones marching," the scout added, frowning slightly. "King Narz's main army approaches from the south, along the Green Trine. They are two bells south of you, and their scouts will reach us within the hour. Our scouts watching them are returning, now battle is coming."

Ruarnon tensed. Hiding from the Azulan army and its scouts until Coroth joined them and led them safely across the Azulan border would be a challenge, but worse, it could delay them.

Ruarnon inclined their head. "Thank you for stopping to update us. Should you meet a band of Zaldeaan riders as you return, please tell them Ruarnon says to hurry along the river."

She bowed her head, then turned and ran along the riverbank towards the retreating Galvation column.

The Azulan army was too close. They needed to move, *now*, but where?

"How close is the force pacing us in the forest beyond the Mountain Flow?" Ruarnon asked Captain Rilmar.

"Far enough back to chance running across their path, but we cannot be sure of our safety unless we continue moving away from them."

"Past the Azulan army?" General Takanis asked and Captain Rilmar nodded.

"Can anyone see Coroth yet?" Ruarnon asked.

"Maybe," said Michael. "I think that's another group."

He was squinting into the distance across the farmland before Galvatia City.

"It is," said Mawana. "A small party moving away from the Galvation column, towards us." Mawana frowned. "They appear to be hastening further south, away from the river."

Rainwater washed across formerly dry plains, the runoff spilling in brown pools into the riverbanks, and a broader, much deeper stream than any Ruarnon had seen under the clouded sky flowed downstream to Galvatia. But the Trine wasn't close to bursting its banks. Why was Coroth avoiding the river?

"Southerners!" Mawana barked. "They aren't marching, they're sailing upriver! The storm water must be deep enough for their boats, and they are using storm winds to drive their ships this way."

The white sails were small, perhaps only one per ship. But there was no mistaking a line of tiny ships on the far side of the desolate farmland, sailing up the stormwaters through the misty rain obscuring the damar infested forest. Battle was coming, days sooner than Ruarnon had anticipated.

The Galvation column was still marching over the bridge into Galvatia, its far end marching off the plains towards the riverbank. But it was moving faster and the singing had stopped. The Galvations had seen the approaching danger and were rushing to safety.

"Long boats," said Tor. "With shallow keels that can navigate rivers. That fleet will move a lot faster than the Azulan army. We need to get out of this valley, to be well clear when those ships clash with the Azulans."

That meant traveling on the same side of the river as the damarian army...

"Can you detect where the damars are?" Ruarnon asked Captain Rilmar.

She frowned. "It is difficult, and we are not close enough for me to be sure of their numbers. But I sense a large group still in Damaria. Nothing stands between us and it. Though if you are thinking of Black City, there may be magic crafters there too."

"We can't assume anywhere is unoccupied," said Mawana. "I could not sense the magic of the pink crystal illusion wall that concealed abductions in Timbala City until it was a stone's throw away. We might not detect illusion magic concealing damars until after they see us."

Ruarnon bit their lip. By now, many of Narz's sorcerers may be trained in crafting illusion magic. And Narz may already have damars relocating to crush the southerners in a pincer, attacking the river from all sides.

"Black City is our best hope," said Tor. "Its walls will conceal us from both armies."

"What of our risk of being trapped inside?" General Takanis asked.

"The buildings are far enough apart that blocking roads wouldn't work," said Linh. "I think the only effective way to trap us is baring all the gates."

"The west gate is open," said Michael, pointing across the river.

Ruarnon stared. What they had taken for dark cliffs among hills was Black City.

"We enter from its northern gate," General Takanis advised. "Away from the Narz's army and serpents, where Coroth can see us. The southerners may see us too, but Coroth must be visible to them now, and I see no signs of them pursuing him."

Tor and Lenaris bowed their heads.

"Let's ride," said Ruarnon.

Michael healed his horse down the riverbank. Fiona followed, biting her lip. Troy rode beside her, staring at the rapidly closing distance between the southerner ships and the bridge over Galvatia. At least a third of the Galvations still rushed onto the bridge, waving tiny white flags.

"Look!" Fiona cried.

Tiny white flags waved back over the southern ships. The Middle South recognised Galvation neutrality. Ruarnon allowed themself one deep exhale, then steered their horse down the riverbank.

The water level wasn't too high upwind of the storms, but it flowed from bank to bank, and the occasional wave lapped at Ruarnon's horses' knees. The pull of the current worried Ruarnon, but their horses crossed steadily, Linh's, to her displeasure, pausing to take a drink.

"We had best let them drink," advised Captain Arleath. "This is the last known water source we are sure of."

Ruarnon inclined their head, but their heartbeat faster, urging them to hurry. Their shoulders tensed at the delay, but riding up onto plains they may share with damars moments later brought Ruarnon no relief. The guards formed a tight ring around them, as they rode for Black City's northern wall and gate. Ruarnon's heartbeat fought their steady breathing, as armies moved to clash behind them, and they fled towards a hiding place likely to conceal powerful enemies.

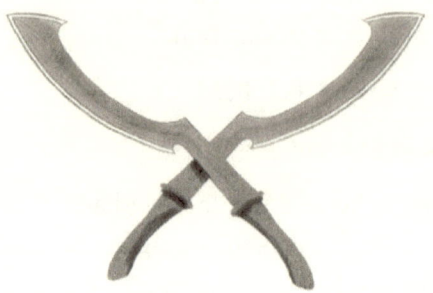

CHAPTER 32

IN BLACK CITY

W e trot ahead," Ruarnon ordered. "I want us inside Black City's north gate before those ships near this section of river."

Everyone urged their horses into a gentle trot, jolting in their saddles. The brown plains before Black City weren't too wide, but they were enough to accommodate the black mass marching beside the river on Ruarnon's right. The Azulan army was indistinct, but if it was in sight, the serpents on the far bank were likely too close for comfort.

Ruarnon turned back. The small group of riders their cousin led was moving into view on their left, dashing ahead of the small white sails of the Middle South fleet, which were lowering one by one, as the fleet sailed under the bridge before Galvatia City, onto which the last rows of Galvation wagons rolled.

Ahead, a low row of hills bordered Black City and Damaria, a crude horizontal line of rocks that appeared to be the top of Damaria City's walls rising behind them. There was no sign of damars. The dry soil beside Damaria's hills appeared still, and empty, with no flicker of illusion magic. And the thud of their companions' horses' hooves drowned out any screeching or hissing.

The guard towers rising above Black City's walls on Ruarnon's right also appeared empty, but only because they had no windows or balconies on this side. The walls were constructed from neatly cut rocks slotted together, rising to an oppressive height above Ruarnon's companions.

Pink flashed ahead. A person had appeared, their pink cloak flapping in the wind. They smiled, standing at a medium height, with a medium build and sun kissed features that were unremarkable, aside from the wildness in their eyes and confidence in their stance, as they raised a finger to their lips.

Ruarnon reined in, their companions copying.

"Are you…" Fiona said softly. "Are you one of the Dedicated?"

Captain Rilmar gasped. "The magic… you are not crafting it… yet it swirls around you."

The Dedicated smiled, their blue eyes sparkling. "Nothing about me is accustomed to being still. Why should my magic be so?"

They turned to Ruarnon. "Teliph told us you wish to save Narz from himself?"

Ruarnon inclined their head. "Do you think we can?"

They smiled. "Few among us have minds that function as most people expect. That is not only Narz's greatest weakness, but also his greatest strength. Few rational people could dream as he has without surrendering to despair.

"I will help you. But trust me when I say you do not want the damars further down aware of your presence. I am going to cast a shield around you that will prevent us from being overheard."

Mawana gaped. "You can do that?"

The Dedicated smiled again. "We can do many things most people don't think of."

Ruarnon took a deep breath. Let a stranger craft magic over them? It was too abrupt. But why appear, declare themself and state their intent, if they *were* a threat?

Tor shot them a warning look, but First Captain Rilmar didn't seem concerned, only intrigued. Ruarnon inclined their head.

Magic tingled as they and others fought the urge to craft a shield to protect themself against a stranger's magic. More magic particles shifted overhead, then moved down beside Lenaris on Ruarnon's left, and Tor on Ruarnon's right. The Australians shivered, and the guards before them tensed as an invisible dome formed around them.

The Dedicated's expression firmed, and the shifting particles stabilised and stilled, thrumming faintly with power.

"We should be going," said the Dedicated. They turned and ran at a speed that surprised Ruarnon, who heeled their horse to a trot to keep up.

The Dedicated ran with a smile fixed on their face, as if they enjoyed the steady rhythm of racing ahead of horses. Magic pulsed behind them, tugging the soundproof shield along, dragging it to keep pace with Ruarnon and their companions' horses.

Captain Rilmar rode up on Tor's other side, gazing at the dome in awe. Ruarnon caught her gaze.

"This is beyond our teaching of Elite Guard. Such complex, brilliant crafting. It is not fixed; it shifts at irregular intervals. But their discipline keeps it in place and pacing us. I would love to know more of a mind that can sustain this."

Ahead of them, Troy said with a grin, "I think I already know."

Michael clapped an arm on Troy's shoulder and said, "I think we can expect more of you."

"When you learn to work with and around your mind," the Dedicated added, turning back to smile at Troy, who flushed, then grinned sheepishly.

A steady sound became clearer and more distinct to Ruarnon's ears. It repeated rhythmically; the drumbeat timing the stroke of oars on the lead southerner ships behind them was drifting ahead on the wind. Ruarnon and their companions were likely within the fleet's sight.

"What is it?" Tor asked Captain Rilmar.

Her mouth hardened in a line. "It is difficult to tell." She frowned. "For a moment I hardly sensed anyone at all. Magic wielders, certainly. But I cannot say how many. I am not even certain where they are, or that all of them are *in* or around Black City."

She stared intently. "Precious few of my Elite Guard can conceal their powers from me. Whoever is in Black City; they are highly accomplished sorcerers."

"Narz's?" Ruarnon asked.

"I do not think so. It takes a lifetime to build the control that concealment of your presence and magic requires, to such a standard."

"Your skills run deep," said the Dedicated. "I am quite sure those you detect mean us no harm."

"They're moving behind us, on our far right," Michael called ahead, craning his neck back at the river.

A long boat rode so low in the water that its bulwarks were hidden by the riverbank. But its mainsail rose above, as did the shoulders of burly soldiers standing, presumably between the rowers. They all gazed upriver, spears or battle axes clutched at their sides, helmets and bronze armour on.

"Not far now boys!" a faint shout proclaimed. "We'll show that liar how little we're deceived by law enforcing lackeys loyal to him occupying us!"

Men roared in agreement.

"Or Healers, who will cure us of anything. Assuming we stay loyal to Narz!"

"Gah!" soldiers objected.

"Conquer them before they conquer us!" One cried.

Others took up the chant, as if it and its notion were familiar. Was that why they were so untrusting of Narz? And if conquest was so normal to these people, would they be deterred by a display of serpents?

Ruarnon's stomach sank, as the Dedicated weaved through a gully in the hills on their right.

For a few moments everyone was surrounded by high hills. Then the hills parted and the walls of Black City barred the world, dwarfing the Dedicated running towards them.

At regular intervals, guard towers rose. It was hard to tell from almost underneath them, but presumably the wall faced inwards, allowing guards to view and control the Galvation prisoners every movement. Ruarnon shivered. Was that what Tarlah had been like, when the Zaldeaans occupied and ruled it, when Ruarnon's father was young?

The northern gates stood open, the dry ground between them smoothed by the recent passage of several thousand feet. Inside, crude huts of dark stone were scattered in a rough approximation of rows, around fifteen rows deep on their right.

On their left, buckets lay abandoned throughout grain fields, and along rows of trees in an orchard beyond. Wells rose at strategic points.

Was this how the Zaldeaans occupying these lands in patrols had been fed? By slave labour and the people they occupied? Uncle Karmarn would be ashamed of that.

The Dedicated strode into the city without hesitation.

"How do we know this is not a trap?" Tor asked.

"If you would rather not follow me, go your own way," the Dedicated replied. "I have other work to be doing."

Ruarnon shook their head. They had the strangest feeling the sorcerer before them could materialise out of thin air, blow away on the wind and had a spirit to match.

"How far do our paths align?" Ruarnon asked.

"I can take you clear of combatants," the Dedicated replied, "But I will not leave the battlefield. Everyone on this continent has a vested interest in the outcome of this war, whether they know it or not. I am not the only unanticipated person who will play their part today."

Ruarnon shivered as they rode on. Entering the high gates and lifeless city was part of the reason. All it would take to trap them was the gates behind them slamming shut. But the gates stayed open, Coroth's party was drawing nearer and there was no sign of anyone else on the deserted land between window-less huts, or in the deserted fields to Ruarnon's left. Their guards scanned the guard towers, but there was no movement there either.

The Dedicated led them down the rear row of crude houses parallel to the distant western wall. The buildings were too low roofed for Ruarnon to have stood up inside and seemed barely wide enough for an adult to lie down in. The stones in the cottage's walls were haphazardly piled, leaving large gaps, not big or regular enough to be intended as windows, and the thatch in the roof wasn't tied on properly, sagging at one end. There was no door, just a gap in the walls propped by a wooden doorframe. The floor was earthen and Ruarnon spotted not a single possession inside the dark interior.

Thank the Ancestors Governor Poran had led the occupants of these buildings to safety. Danger hung in the air here.

"Coroth approaches!" Called the rear guard.

Coroth's guards nodded to Captain Arleath's guards, who fell back to ride behind Ruarnon. The Zaldeaan guards circled everyone, Coroth riding on, his posture relaxing as he recognised his cousin.

Ruarnon smiled, then their face fell. Coroth was sporting a bloody lip and a black eye.

"What happened to you?" Ruarnon asked, as Lenaris dropped back, letting Coroth ride beside them.

"I am sorry," said Coroth. "I was delayed. Captured by Governor Mandarkin and Azulan soldiers. He was searching for me because he blamed the prison break on me. He seemed to think it was a joint Zaldeaan and Galvation escape attempt *I* orchestrated. Luckily father sent loyal men looking for me and they attacked that night, freeing us and took the Governor and Azulans captive."

"Did they take the Governor's fists captive? Ungently?" Troy called back.

Coroth smiled, then flinched when it strained his split lip. "I am sorry about your face," he said quietly to Troy. "And lucky he didn't have time to do worse to mine. Demune and I took the liberty of subduing both men ourselves… with a little help."

Troy grinned at the youth who kept to Coroth's other side, while Ruarnon noted both young mens' knuckled were scabbed.

"And your father?" Ruarnon asked.

Coroth's gaze became distant, and Ruarnon frowned. Was the emotion on his cousin's face wonder?

"Father's men told me. King Narz told the sorcerers spying on us that our work was done. That beyond a show of might, the war would be fought by sorcerers. He recalled his sorcerers, after they removed an illusion over our coast, which revealed our ships anchored nearby. The sorcerers said Companion Nish and the two thousand hostages 'patrolling' his cities are being released too."

Ruarnon stared in wonder. After all Narz's fears and insecurities, now that war was finally marching against him on his own soil, he was releasing his captive army and pitting his own people against it…

Coroth's face paled. "From our last view of them, it appears the Azulan army will meet the southerners opposite this city. If all its gates are open…"

"Some fighting may spill into the city," Tor finished for him.

"Which is why we are sticking to its middle," the Dedicated called.

"And because whatever magic wielders I detect are on the walls," Captain Rilmar added tightly.

The Dedicated inclined their head.

"There's magic wielders on the walls?" Troy asked. "Right now?"

"They're not attacking us," said Michael. "Or anyone else. Are they waiting for the fighting to begin?"

"We all are," the Dedicated replied.

"Who is *we*?" Linh asked.

"I suspect every magic craft organisation has representatives here today. If a Divine Army takes advantage of the Middle South invasion, we will be ready to meet them. That is why I wished to accompany you. None of them are going to attack me. And so you are protected."

Ruarnon shivered, and scanned the walls towering over them. Every guard tower opened in a balcony on the city side, granting extensive views within the walls. But each tower contained only shadows. Yet every now and then magic tingled, not always in the same place.

Captain Rilmar was right. People were concealing their presence and demonstrating no interest in the party riding south through the city. But the idea made Ruarnon split their focus between the ground before them and the guard towers, scanning for movement, reaching to detect a flicker of magic. Their shoulders tightened and they fought to keep their breathing steady.

"Keep running! We must get to the river before the armies," an urgent voice shouted across the city.

"That came from the east gate," Mawana said quietly.

"What are humans doing near Damaria?" Troy asked.

Light flashed. Fire flared in the orchard, as a fruit tree caught alight. A small party fled into the trees around it, several crying out. A magic shield wavered above them, and flames flared again, drifting away as smoke on the wind.

"Are enemies of sorcerers friends of ours?" Troy asked tightly.

"Do not attack them," the Dedicated ordered, their face tight, all mirth gone.

A broader shield formed. It wasn't a small group of people. It was tens of them, all running as fast as they could into Black City's orchards from the east gate, fire flaring behind them.

"Whose shield is that?" one of the figures asked.

"It isn't mine!" said another.

"Is someone else here?" a third asked.

All three voices were high in pitch, their fear palpable. Gooseflesh pebbled over Ruarnon's arms. Whoever they were, they were clearly refugees.

Lights flashing around the group faded.

"They've stopped!"

"Keep running! Even if they don't pursue us now, the armies could cut us off. We must get out of these human cursed lands!" the first voice insisted.

Troy's lips mouthed the words, 'human cursed'. But those people were human height, and shaped, and they talked and seemed to feel like humans. Who else could they be?

Many figures continued running, flashing in and out of Ruarnon's sight as they passed behind trees, crashed through branches, snapped sticks and made no attempt to move quietly in their beeline across the orchards to the southern gate ahead of Ruarnon.

"Halt! That's horses. It could be a human patrol!" the first figure's voice warned.

"*No,*" said Michael, his right hand coming up to his face. "What has he *done*?"

"But the Zaldeaans always stay away from us," one of the others objected. "If it's a patrol, can't we just avoid it?"

"My apologies friends, but said group of humans can hear you," the Dedicated called loudly.

Ruarnon's breath caught, and their heart hammered against their chest as they rode into a wide gap, the intersection of the dirt road between the city's west, east, north and south gates, leaving them completely exposed to whoever was fleeing from orchard to fields on their left.

Ruarnon reined in at the Dedicated's signal, Tor's alarmed face catching their gaze.

"They will cut us off from the gate! We are too slow on foot!" a woman's voice wailed, as the figures halted on the edge of the orchard.

"I and my companions have no intention of denying your freedom," the Dedicated replied loudly. "None of us is loyal to Narz."

"Then you are his enemies, whom he means to pit us against? How do we know you will not kill us?" the first man to speak, who appeared to be their leader, demanded.

"Sorry, but who on Earth?" Troy asked, his bewilderment so clear and disarming that the leader of the fleeing group started walking towards them, out of the trees and halted in the fields. He came closer, looking perfectly human, but his face was grey and his eyes were yellow.

He stood his ground and raised his chin. Somehow Ruarnon knew, it was a defiant act. A damar looking humans in the eye. A completely self-conscious damar, who viewed humans as slave masters and killers.

"We don't want to go to war either."

Tor gasped. That was Fiona speaking.

"I am Zaldeaan," Coroth said, swallowing awkwardly. "My people were taken from our homes and forced to guard these lands. We were little better than slaves. We feared people who looked like you, because some of them slew many of our loved ones back home."

The damar's lips spasmed. His eyes filled with tears. "Because they had no choice! Because Narz made them that way!"

"But you have choice," said Coroth. "My people have been sent free. You have escaped. What will you do with your freedom?"

"Flee into the Forbidden Mountains, where humans are scared to go. Where no one will enslave us or kill us. And if any of our kin survive this war, we will come back to claim them."

"Your lessons in magic seem incomplete," said the Dedicated. "Should you ever wish to learn more, should you have children, and they need support in controlling their abilities, you will find at least one of my kin in the castle formerly belonging to Lord Tarz, in the mountains."

The damars brows furrowed and his mouth fell open, then twisted in confusion. "*You* would teach *us*?"

"How do we know they won't take our children and train them as soldiers and slaves?" a woman demanded.

"The decision is yours, to make another time," said the Dedicated. "For now, we must all move ahead of battle. And I must warn you, more of your kin march before the Azulan army, veiled by sorcery. You must stay beyond the Azulan armies' sight, lest sorcerers among them trap you with magic, and coerce you to fight."

"They are already on the river?" the damarian leader asked.

"They are nearing the south-west corner of this city."

"I will not run ahead of humans so they can hunt us!" a damarian man yelled.

"Walk behind us, if you wish," the Dedicated replied calmly.

Ruarnon heard all the words. But their thoughts spiralled chaotically. The fear. The mistrust. The terror. Everything these damars felt about humans... it was how Ruarnon had felt when they first encountered damars. And these damars felt that way about *humans*...

"What is that sound?" a damarian woman's voice called.

"It is the drums signalling the timing of the southerner oars as they row along the northwest side of this city," the Dedicated replied.

Ruarnon shivered at how close the two armies must now be. There wasn't a second to lose. Only, the damars outnumbered Ruarnon's party at least four to one. And how many of them could craft magic? They couldn't go charging past, frightening these already terrified people.

"We will ride ahead," said Ruarnon. "If you prefer. We must all get out of here before fighting along the river spills into the city."

"Why are you here?" the damar asked Ruarnon.

"To dissuade Narz from fighting a sorcerer army in a battle that could level this city, and possibly others. But should you ever seek a different home, if you seek a land war rarely visits, I know the people who guard sorcerous creations like yourselves. Creations that fought in the First Sorcery War. And the people I know are determined that such creations shall not fight any war again. I can ask if they will grant you safe haven."

"A place of humans?" another damar asked aggressively.

Ruarnon smiled. "A place of the Faeron, and Gorans, the latter of whom resemble you more than me. Some humans live there, but precious few. Most do not know either place exists."

The leader eyed Ruarnon with their mouth open. Ruarnon saw pain in those eyes. And fear. Warring against hope. Because Cauldron Island and the Island of the Guardians were exactly the Safe Haven they were seeking, and Ruarnon suspected Lylah's sisters would need no persuading to take them in. And that among Faeron, Gorans and few humans, they may learn what it is to feel safe again.

"We move together," the damar decided.

Ruarnon inclined their head. Anything to get both groups moving before death burst in after them all.

The damar gaped. Others gasped.

"A human who inclines their head to *us*?" asked a woman.

Ruarnon smiled back. "I have a habit of not being arrogant enough for my position. It is one of my quirks."

The damar considered Ruarnon, then inclined his head sideways, not subservient, but an acknowledgement. Ruarnon smiled and healed their horse forwards. The damar turned and motioned his people onwards.

"Will you fight an army with sorcerers in its midst?" a voice, magically, Ruarnon suspected, boomed before the western wall of Black City.

"We'll not open our gates to Keeper occupiers, nor Healer bribes!" a man's faint voice yelled, echoing off empty huts through the western gate.

"His Beneficence has made no attempt to occupy you. Nor disrespect your wish not to permit Healers or Keepers onto your lands."

"Only until he's ready to take us by FORCE! We would defeat him before anymore greedy fools let him encircle us by letting keepers into their walls! CHARGE!"

Ruarnon tensed. Voices roared down the gap between huts from west gate. Sails flapped over the river, as southerner ships rowed into view. Southerner infantry charged past before west gate, oblivious to the small group of riders and damars gaping back at them in horror. The battle Narz had hoped to avoid with the Middle South had begun.

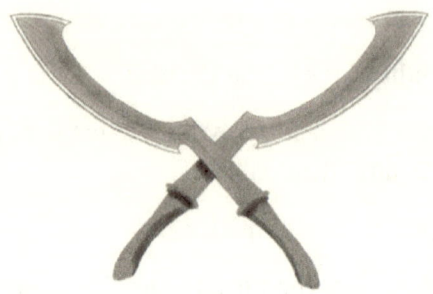

CHAPTER 33

SORCERY WAR -RUARNON

Ruarnon gasped for breath as their horse broke into a trot. They were viewing west gate from an angle, not quite opposite it yet. They anticipated Azulan cavalry or infantry to charge into view, and spears to fly among the southerner ships. But they didn't. Shadows towered before and over southern infantry. Shadowy tails flicked the air. The southerner infantry front line was smashed apart at multiple points, soldiers knocked flying. Screams and hissing filled the air. Fanged mouths rushed down over southerner infantry and ships alike.

"Infantry halt!" the southern commander yelled. "Cavalry charge!"

A thud of hooves echoed down Black City's empty streets. A scaled head shot forwards. A rider screamed as a serpent snapped him up out of his saddle. He screamed again as he was tossed up into the air. The serpent's jaws widened, and he was swallowed whole.

Ruarnon tensed. What did the southerners think they could do? Feed serpents until enough stab wounds brought the serpents down?

Light flashed through west gate. Fire erupted among serpent heads. They hissed and surged forwards. Lightning struck at them. Serpents blackened. They smoked and thrashed, dying. Horses whinnied.

A young man appeared behind the collapsing serpents, facing, not the southerners, but people Ruarnon couldn't see beyond west gate.

"What part of his Worthiness' vision of justice do these represent?" the young man asked. His voice was familiar…

"If they want to kill us badly enough to fight through monsters, so be it!" a deep voice retorted.

"This is not the way to spread Healers or Keepers. Call your monsters off, or we will fight them," the young man asserted.

"How then shall we defend ourselves?" a woman's voice asked.

"They carry weapons enchanted to pierce our defences!" another retorted.

"Yours, or those of the monsters you control?" the young man asked. "You are not our enemies," he asserted. "And the people behind us should not be. Slaying them with monsters will hardly convince them."

"That's Dargus!" Fiona cried.

"If you would negotiate, go ahead," the first man replied. "We will kill their sorcerers and protect ordinary soldiers after you are slain."

A serpent lunged at Dargus. Dargus sidestepped and plunged his sword into blue scales. The creature hissed and fell dead.

"Fall back to guard the regular army from sorcerers!" ordered the sorcerer commander, his words following Ruarnon as they rode past west gate. Their view shifted back to rearing southerner cavalry halting abruptly before Dargus fighting serpents, shouts, and confusion. Then many rows of crude stone huts lined their right again.

The damars had heard the exchange too and were now sprinting ahead through the fields on Ruarnon's left, outpacing the trotting horses. The leader leapt rows of grain, the other damars leaping after him with the same strength and dexterity. Then they were sprinting down the dirt road towards south gate.

Tor shook his head. "With such speed, strength and agility… surely Narz intended them as soldiers? Yet they are as feeling as thinking as the rest of us."

"Maybe he thought they would be ideal soldiers," Lenaris said from behind. "With strength, skill, agility *and* consciences. But in giving them thoughts and morality, they saw the immorality of their treatment."

Ruarnon shook their head. Between the damars and the attitude the southerners were displaying to war, peace was a distant daydream to this continent. Narz was its most immediate threat, but it had plenty of others.

Light continued flashing, its glow beaming above the dark western walls of Black City on their right. Dargus killing serpents, they suspected, with friends, there being too much magic for one person. Then the light display ceased, people cried out and weapons clashed.

"The southerners are fighting the Azulan army?" Troy asked. "Having seen an Azulan *annihilate* a herd of magic serpents?"

"I sense concealment magic on the other side of the western wall," said the Dedicated. "Damars march before the Azulan army. If the southerners were foolish enough to engage, they're likely fighting damarian soldiers."

Ruarnon flinched at a deafening crash and whipped around. Light flashed on the far side of the orchard on their left. Two figures stood atop the eastern battlements between guard towers. Light streaked between them. The first wore a gold mask, the second a deep red cloak.

"A divine soldier," Coroth said hollowly. "The Divine Army *is* infiltrating the southern armies."

The Dedicated stiffened. "Others are coming. Keep up the pace. I am shielding us against magic for now, but I may need your help soon," they added to Captain Rilmar.

Mist shimmered, then vanished overhead. Ruarnon's shoulders tensed. It was too soon for any of them to be crafting magic against sorcerers. They weren't well enough rested.

Thunder cracked, and light flashed.

"Some of that is coming from *inside* Damaria," Mawana reported.

Fire blossomed and shield magic shone all along the eastern battlements of Black City. People wearing gold masks battled men in dark red cloaks. Lenaris's horse whinnied as a stray bolt hit fruit trees an arrow shot away, which caught alight.

"They are not aiming at us," the Dedicated said calmly. "Only stray magic threatens us. And something ahead."

"That won't stop it setting the orchard, then the fields alight," Michael warned, as a second tree glowed like a torch and fire from the first magic bolt spread. "Even if they don't do it on purpose, they'll burn the city down."

"The southern gate isn't too far ahead," said Lenaris. "The damars are already racing through it."

Hissing sounded ahead. A shorter, feral damar pack was charging around the southern wall into the southern gate.

"*NO!*" the damar leader roared.

"We cannot save them all!" one of the women yelled.

"Then we take the ones we can," the leader replied.

Ruarnon stared, as short, savage damars paused their charge in the gateway. Their arms lowered. Their postures relaxed. Then they turned, following the human-damars calmly out the gate.

"What's he going to do after he saves them?" Troy asked. "If the Galvations or southerners or anyone whose fought damars knows savage ones are in the mountains, they'll go hunting them! He's putting his people in danger!"

"No," said Fiona. "He's saving his own kind, even if they aren't self-aware or don't have nearly the same IQ. It's not *their* fault they're savage. Or killers. Its Narz's. Just because he made them that way doesn't mean they have to live that way. Not if those people can calm them."

Ruarnon stared as the two groups, human-height damars in human clothes, and short savages in loin cloths, sprinted across the plains beyond the city side by side.

Under whatever magic the human-damars wielded, the savage ones were no longer savage. They were placid. Like the reptiles on Cauldron Island when it wasn't at war…

Damars had been born into and for violence. But the damarian leader was right; it *didn't* have to be that way. And the human-damars could stop it. But they would need Flariah, Desriah and Sryah's help. Ruarnon vowed to write to them as soon as possible; when the end of the world wasn't so near at hand.

Screeches began to rise over the western wall of Black City. Hisses and cries of soldiers and the clash of weapons became a cacophony, counterpoint to booms and flashes of light from the eastern walls. As if Ruarnon rode through a corridor of calm, while the armies of Chaos himself warred either side of it.

Troy groaned.

"Are you ok?" Linh asked.

"It's *too* bright. *Too* loud. I won't be able to tell the difference between where we're riding and the battle when we get through that gate. It's a solid mass of too much sensory input. Thank god the horse knows where its walking; I can't see shit with all those colours."

Michael said nothing, but he rode hunched in himself, his head down, as if the sights and sounds were assaulting him physically. Ruarnon was tensed against both. But they needed to see and hear it all. It was the only way to keep everyone safe. Even if was overwhelming.

The booms, shouts and clash of weapons either side of Ruarnon faded and the flashes of light dimmed.

"How did you *do* that?" Troy asked the Dedicated.

"Many of our number find bright lights or loud noises painful. Others, like myself find them distracting. This filter shield helps us focus at times like this."

"Sorcery catering for sensory issues?" Michael asked. "That's brilliant!"

His posture had relaxed and he was sitting up straight again.

The clashes of weapons were more like taps now. Shouts and cries had become soft moans. But there was a deeper sound, steadier than the battle noises.

The Dedicated flung up their fist and everyone reined in.

"But we're not far from the gate," Troy objected.

"We do not want to go through if that force marches on Black City's southern side."

"What force?" Troy asked. "Another army?

The deeper sound was getting gradually, slightly louder, as if coming closer. It wasn't constant, but it was repetitive. A chant.

"Kill the scum. For the Master, kill the scum."

The voices were dull, but guttural. And the flashes of light above the eastern wall hadn't just faded, they'd stopped. The red cloaked sorcerers turned side-on to Ruarnon's party. More deep red cloaked sorcerers stood along the northern wall behind them, with their backs to Ruarnon's party.

"Tell me we didn't ride *under them*?" Troy asked.

The Dedicated shook their head, their face ashen. "They arrived after us."

"But we didn't see them get here!" Troy objected.

"What are they focusing on?" Michael asked the Dedicated, whose posture had turned rigid, facing the eastern wall.

"An army I'd hoped the damars I want to teach wouldn't have to meet. An army with their ability to speak, their strength, speed and magical skill, warped by Vye's sorcery."

Captain Rilmar shivered. A moment later, Ruarnon did too. It wasn't just magic tingling beyond the northern wall behind them. It was more like a pulse, one that raised every hair on Ruarnon's arms. It was so strong Ruarnon half expected to hear it crackle.

"Your horses are too slow with you on their backs. Dismount and run!" The Dedicated yelled. "We do not want them to see us!"

"As they say!" Ruarnon ordered, swinging themself out of their saddle and running forwards, leading their horse to trot behind them.

The Dedicated led at an impressive speed given they'd run three quarters of the way across the city already. Black huts flashed by on the right. Fruit trees, some burning, flashed by in the distance on Ruarnon's left.

"Kill the scum! For the Master, kill the scum!"

More magic tingled. Figures stood on the western battlements now, their backs to Ruarnon, as they peered down at the battle. They too wore red cloaks, ready to command damars to attack the southerners.

"Kill the scum! For the Master, Kill the scum!"

A new red cloaked figure appeared ahead on Ruarnon's right. His blonde hair and deep red cloak flapped in the wind. Ruarnon couldn't see his face, but they could imagine the arrogant smile it likely wore. And those cold blue eyes filled with pride.

"Pity attacking him would draw his attention," Lenaris said quietly.

"Kill the scum! For the Master, Kill the scum!"

"They're *behind* us!" Mawana warned.

Ruarnon shot a glance back. Figures obscured the open space between the northern gate, but they moved along the northern walls at a rapid pace, rushing towards the quiet screeches, incessant weapon taps and moans that were muted shouts beyond the western wall. Rushing to a battle Ruarnon feared would become a slaughter.

"Soldiers!" Vye commanded, his magically amplified voice carrying across Black City. "Destroy them!"

A gentle roar of weapon taps and low moans that were likely desperate cries rose behind Ruarnon, echoing quietly across the empty city. More frequent, muted weapon taps suggested the damarian soldiers could breach a southerner bronze shield wall with Zaldeaan berserker-like efficiency.

"Kill them all," Vye ordered. "I need no human infantry."

Ruarnon fought down the temptation to put an arrow in his back. He was right there! But he also had the power to blast everyone apart simultaneously, perhaps through the Dedicated's shield.

Vye turned to watch his soldiers' attack southerners across the riverbank, revealing a smile that made Ruarnon sick to their stomach.

"Fire the monsters! All archers, fire the monsters!"

A line of flaming arrows flashed at the peak of their arc, then dipped below view. Damars screeched, a quiet, half-muted chorus. But the relentless tap of muted weapon blows and low moans of soldiers beyond the walls neither slowed, nor ceased.

"How could Narz let Vye breed those things?" Linh panted.

"He probably intended to pit this lot against the Divine Army," Michael replied. "But Vye's commandeered them."

Colour flashed on the edge of Ruarnon's peripheral vision. They turned. Dull lights were flashing behind them, where purple and blue robed figures appeared on the battlements of the eastern wall, between deep red cloaked sorcerers; *real* Luvaras Priestesses and Priests.

Vye vanished. Ruarnon trembled at a pulse of magic. The red cloaks had vanished, and lightning was raining from the eastern walls of Black City, down below view, into Damaria.

Men cried out behind Ruarnon. Deep red cloaks on the northern wall were punching their own faces. Pink cloaked figures stood on the ground across the gap between black huts before the northern wall, their arms waving about at deep red cloaked figures, who toppled from the walls. Ruarnon gasped. A fall from that height would be fatal.

Fire glowed, raining from the northern walls onto damarian soldiers marching to battle. A chorus of screeches rose and Dedicated shielded the open north gate. Damarian fists pummelled their shield, then collapsed before it.

Ruarnon faced forward, resting their neck.

"Whose side are *they* are on?" Troy asked nervously.

"Anyone who cannot wield magic who gets attacked by monsters or sorcerers, I suspect," Captain Rilmar replied.

Light flashed, and Ruarnon craned their neck again. The Dedicated were retreating, and damarian soldiers were pouring into the northern gate behind them.

"Shit!" Troy yelled.

"We're almost at south gate!" Michael assured him.

Several people cried out and everyone slowed as the ground rocked beneath them. Cracking roared through the city. The ground and walls either side of north gate were cracking, rocks and earth beneath them crumbling, damarian soldiers toppling.

Purple cloaked figures had joined the Dedicated. Lightning blasted damarian soldiers in the pit opening up at the northern end of the city. The front lines of damarian soldiers before the pit wobbled, then tumbled into it, as if an invisible line of people pushed them.

"Retreat to the far bank! Retreat to the far bank!" the southern commander screamed.

A loud crack echoed across the city.

Ruarnon halted to survey huts, in case any were about to collapse on them. The huts vibrated in tune with the cracking, but it was the eastern wall of Black City crumbling and raining outwards into hundreds of damarian soldiers marching behind it, deep-red cloaked figures toppling with the rubble.

The booms of rubble and screeches of damars roared loudly, the Dedicated's sound-shield faltering against the strain.

Explosions boomed behind Ruarnon. Beyond debris and dust from the wall collapse, stone buildings burst apart. Debris crashed into damars rushing over the rubble of the eastern wall into the city. The ground shook again. The northern end of the western wall was cracking now, its guard towers falling outwards, its walls crumbling after it, damarian soldiers screeching as rubble crushed them from the northern end to the western gate.

Dust cleared, revealing more damars running into the city to attack Luvaras Priestesses and Dedicated, who were nowhere in sight, though stone huts were exploding into and felling charging soldiers, bursting stone huts tracking the damars progress into the city.

On Ruarnon's left, further back, fire flared, and winds whipped fires across grain fields and through the orchard, barring the path of and incinerating damars trying to enter the city from the east. The damarian screams were muted, but almost human, and they made Ruarnon flinch.

They tensed as a tall group of damars built like Zaldeaan berserkers tried to charge towards their rear guard. The damars fragmented, collapsing into dust and drifted away on the breeze behind them

"My kin will help protect us," said the Dedicated.

Pink robed figures stood atop the southern city walls ahead, focusing their attention on the road behind Ruarnon's party. Ruarnon tensed as they ran beneath the figures, ducking instinctively beneath the southern gate arch, flinching away from such power. Then Tor was telling everyone to mount their horses. Savage damars were battling advancing southerners on their right. Azulans stood with rigid postures beyond the damars ahead, not yet engaged in the fighting.

"What's moving behind us?" Mawana shouted to Captain Rilmar, as everyone healed their horses forwards, alongside embattled damars and southerners.

Captain Rilmar grimaced. "Damarian sorcerers."

Ruarnon whipped around in their saddle. A storm of lightning was raining inside Black City's northern section, dark figures silhouetted behind it marching into the city. Tens of damars hurtled lightning bolts at stone huts and the eastern city wall's rubble alike, destroying anything that moved, including surviving soldier-damars. More damars marched into the city, a wave of fire burning through the field before them.

More light shone as lightning from purple and blue cloaked figures on the southern walls blasted damars with lightning, winds driving the fire back into shrieks and screeches. Ruarnon shuddered, as sorcerer armies fought, and pandemonium reined in Black City.

Chapter 34

Across the Battlefield. -Ruarnon

Coroth moved ahead of the Dedicated, his guards flanking everyone. But Ruarnon hardly noticed. On their right, desperate southerners were pushing the damars back into the Azulans, trying escape sorcery chaos. Only a few hundred southerners fought together, taller damars attacking them from behind, having apparently cut off their army. Their whole fleet had turned and was retreating downriver. Some cavalry were swimming across the river behind the ships, while more fled along the far banks.

The entire southerner army was in disarray, but the Azulan lines held. The Azulan rear marched in an orderly retreat. The front lines backed up from embattled damars and southerners. Their shields were raised, but not their spears. And the Azulans weren't losing arrows. They made no attempt to disrupt the southerner retreat.

There was something odd about the damarian battle. Damars not engaged were… standing their ground. Waiting for southerners to approach, then attacking. Instead of hunting prey. This was Narz's defensive battle. Azulans *and* damars letting surrounded southerners escape downriver. Taking no prisoners. This part of the army was acting *only* to defend.

But the chaos and aggression behind Ruarnon… was that Vye's doing? If the battle, and accepted retreat of enemies on Ruarnon's right was how Narz wished to fight, how had he let Vye unleash pandemonium in Black City *and* Damaria?

Southerners and damars alike were falling, not wounded, but tripping over the fallen. Green flashed among them. A pair of green cloaked women appeared beside a fallen southerner at the edge of the battlefield, then all three vanished.

"They're healing the *enemy*?" Troy asked. "And protecting the wounded?"

"Their creed forbids them to take sides," Fiona explained. "Their purpose is to heal and cure all who can be saved."

"And the regular soldiers do not engage," said Ruarnon. "Narz doesn't fear the Middle South. Or want to rule them."

"Teliph says he never did," Coroth called back.

Ruarnon frowned. Colour appeared among green hills behind Narz's armies and beside the Green Trine. Healers materialised before wagons, and an enclosure with armed soldiers around it. The healers were indeed healing both sides, keeping the enemy captive to ensure their safety while they worked.

Ruarnon stared, their grip on their reins slackening. Were Healers trying to minimise casualties in a war Narz hadn't wanted? Or was this how he had trained Healers to operate?

"There are too many damars for the Priests and Priestesses," Mawana reported behind them. "Sorcerer-damars are still flowing out of Damaria's ruins. The Priests and Priestesses are fighting back-to-back behind the city. The Dedicated are reducing more to dust, but not fast enough."

"There's nothing we can do against those damars," said Ruarnon.

"No, but they can," the Dedicated replied, pointing to a group of red cloaks riding around the rear of the Azulan infantry. The Keepers rode diagonally across Ruarnon's companions' path, their gazes' intent on the sorcery battle in the ruined city beyond.

The leader wore a circlet with a red ruby at its centre, Captain Melroth. His gaze flickered to Coroth, and Ruarnon, his eyes widening in surprise. Then he bowed his head in acknowledgement and turned his gaze beyond.

The Dedicated slowed to a brisk walk, motioning everyone to slow.

"Damars are definitely fighting Captain," a man shouted over the beat of Keeper's horse's hooves.

"Lord Vye's betrayal has begun," Captain Melroth yelled. "Kill them all! They must not reach the battlefield!"

A shield formed over the Keepers as they charged.

Damars shrieked further back and light flashed behind Ruarnon. They whipped around. Sorcerer-damars weren't just fighting Priests, Priestesses and Dedicated. Some were charging around Black City's ruins, two arrow's shots behind Mawana, fire erupting among them.

Fire blossomed above the Keeper shield. An explosion rumbled, shaking the ground around them. Half a dozen damars blasted into the air. The rest were obscured by dust.

"How many?" Ruarnon asked.

"Hundreds," Mawana replied faintly, as Coroth and his guards lead them around the Azulan lines, infantry frowning at them, but not otherwise responding.

"The sorcery wielding ones must have hidden inside Damaria while the soldiers attacked," Mawana added. "They are still exiting Damaria to attack Priests and Priestesses around Black City. I suspect Vye unleashed them when he fled."

"Does he control them?" Lenaris asked.

"Not if he wishes to live," Tor replied. "The Keepers will gladly kill him, and he clearly fears the Priests and Priestesses. I suspect he has fled to hide."

The ground shook. Ruarnon turned their neck as far as it would go. A large section of Damaria's southern wall exploded outwards, raining before Captain Melroth and his Keepers. The clearing dust cloud and collapsed walls revealed hills scattered with crude stick huts and higher up, utilitarian stone apartments. Earthen streets were crowded with damars.

Keepers targeted damars on the eastern side, pulling stone walls down, while flashes of fire and exploding buildings signalled Priest or Priestess attacks, the purple and blue cloaked figures having moved to the eastern end, where bright lights flashed back and forth and sections of city wall crumbled. Cracks, shrieks, crashes and roars echoed louder than before, the Dedicated's sound shield failing entirely to filter the cacophony of destruction.

Damars tried to march onto the rubble of Black City, towards flanks of southerner army caught between sorcery and soldier damars along the riverbank. Dedicated appeared before them. They slowed and collapsed, one after another. Landing on rubble didn't wake them.

"Who are they?" Troy asked, also craning his neck.

"They are dead," said the Dedicated. "Death doesn't have to be noisy, or flashy. It can be silent, simple and killing that way requires less of the magic crafter."

Ruarnon noted the bitterness in their voice. They suspected slaughter; perhaps even magical combat was far from whatever work the Dedicated usually undertook.

"You are tiring," said Captain Rilmar. "Allow us to shield ourselves. Spare your magic for sudden and urgent usage."

They inclined their head.

Cries of southerner soldiers, screeches of damars and the clash of weapons became louder on their right and behind them, as did the more distant booms of magic.

"I sense more sorcerers in the fighting behind us," said Captain Rilmar. "Along the riverbank."

Tor frowned at her.

"Divine Soldiers have infiltrated the southerner army, I am sure of it," she added.

Cries of fear or anger intensified, and behind them orders were shouted over it.

Fires smoked among Azulan front line soldiers, who carried rectangular, white misty shields, now raised before them. But they weren't the target.

"THE TRAITORS ARE AT THE REAR! SLAY THEM!" a man's voice boomed.

"Slow down!" Coroth commanded, reining in.

"Something nears our right!" Captain Rilmar warned, her mouth opening in surprise at Coroth scanning the area, his face pale and taut with tension.

Ruarnon tensed. The ground beside retreating Azulan soldiers rippled, the soldiers and damars before them rippling too. Then a dozen horses materialized on Ruarnon's right, bearing gold masked riders circling Azulan infantry, to charge lines of bright red cloaked Keepers at their rear... who had lined up before the Healer camp, likely protecting their colleagues as they tended the wounded.

"Left!" Ruarnon warned, as a gold mask tilted to one side, assessing them.

They barely slowed before lightning flashed towards them. The Dedicated groaned and the light flashed, redirecting skywards. Ruarnon reinforced Captain Rilmar's shield and sensed Mawana's expanding, as fire blossomed on their friends' right.

Ruarnon strained against lightning. Their head began to ache. Their vision blurred. Then the pressure eased. Three Divine Soldiers turned to Keepers running around Azulans to confront them, while deep red cloaked sorcerers pushed through Azulan infantry to aid the Keepers.

"They may assume there is a general among us," Tor cautioned.

"But they don't care enough for a sustained attack," Captain Rilmar replied, as light streaked between Divine Soldiers, Healers and Azulan sorcerers ahead.

Coroth led them further left, putting the river in Ruarnon's peripheral vision and Narz's castle on their right. But Divine Soldiers weren't the only threat. Great winged shapes were taking flight in the hills around Narz's castle

"Black dragons!" Ruarnon warned.

The creatures grew rapidly larger, swooping lower. Wings spread over the Healer camp. Lightning bolts deflected from them. Fire blossomed and turned to smoke. Dragons glided gracefully out of smoke; their large yellow eyes fixed on sorcerers below.

A Divine Soldier wheeled his horse around, shielding himself as he crossed Coroth's path and charged south-east, away from the battlefield, wide of sorcery battered Damaria.

"What's he doing?" Troy asked.

More shouts rose. The Azulan infantry by the riverbank were backing up. Keepers and deep red cloaks moved around them, between regular soldiers and charging, gold masked riders.

Giant wings flapped overhead. Shouts among infantry increased. Azulans retreated in earnest, moving between the Healers and the river, as a dragon landed beside them, facing gold masked riders.

Bright light flashed. A horse screamed. A gold masked rider toppled off his mount. Ruarnon sensed Mawana's shield flair.

"What are you doing fools! Kill the dragon!" a Divine Commander bellowed, as his soldiers halted their horses before the nearest dragon.

Fire flared between two gold masked soldiers. A shield flashed between them. Three masked riders wheeled their horses around and followed the first deserter.

"Fuck me," Troy exclaimed.

"Not now, Troy," Fiona quipped, and despite every danger around them, Troy laughed.

"The dragons are only defending," said General Takanis. "They are no threat to us."

"We stay wide of the Divine Soldiers," Ruarnon added and Coroth bowed their head.

The Dedicated said nothing. Sweat beaded down their face.

Ruarnon sensed their friends shields form, as the three gold masked riders approached on their right. Ruarnon braced to meet their attacks, but one divine soldier waved a white flag, then all three passed by close enough to make Ruarnon shiver.

More light flashed on their right, as two more dragons landed beside the retreating Azulan army, before gold masked riders. Southerners cried out, flinging themselves into the river. The damars stilled as one, then stepped as one, sideways from the river.

"*Retreat*! All units retreat!" a commander screamed.

"Why are Divine soldiers attacking each other?" Troy asked.

"It's the enchantment we met before Tira," said Michael. "It's trying to protect Keepers by turning Divine Soldiers against each other."

Fire flared behind the dragons and Azulan soldiers screamed. Keeper shields expanded to protect soldiers. Then bright light flashed at Keepers, who shielded themselves.

A dragon roared, and gold masked soldiers were bathed in fire by three new dragons swooping low, one after another. Warmth washed over Ruarnon, and the horses whinnied. Troy swore.

The fighting on their right, the west, was too close. But the battle in Black City was worse, the riverbank in the north was a disaster zone, and the sorcery battle spilling out of Damaria to bar the east was deadliest of all. Narz's castle and the south was the only direction to run without fleeing through sorcery war.

Ruarnon grit their teeth and clutched their reins for dear life. A fourth swooping dragon ignored a bolt of lightning flashing against its side, snapped a gold masked rider out of his saddle, soared up above the plains, then dropped him.

Light flashed in the corner of Ruarnon's eye. Captain Rilmar's dome shield obscured Ruarnon's view slightly, protecting everyone as three gold masked deserters charged behind them, yelling war cries. Fire bathed the masked riders. One shrieked and fell to the ground, but the others rode on.

Wind gusted into Ruarnon's head as flapping sounded above. Two dragons flew overhead, ignoring whinnying horses and dived, snapping at gold masked soldiers. A third of the Divine Soldiers were down, but the last pair stopped fighting each other when one man screamed, "ENOUGH! KILL THE TRAITORS!"

The remaining masked riders turned their mounts and fire blossomed along the Keeper shield. Masked riders ducked and weaved, dodging two dragons swooping them, shielding themselves against Keepers.

"Reinforcements!"

Captain Melroth's Keepers had divided, huddling under dome shields, retreating onto the plains east of Damaria. Bright flashes of light preceded damars crowding through Damaria's southern gates. Two dragons swooped overhead, bathing damar-sorcerers in flame.

A dome shield formed beside the Keepers. The cloaks beneath it were blue. The Luvaras Priest's shield dome shifted, then shot towards the damarian hoard. The front two lines were vaporised, but the third line shrieked, smoked and charged on.

A dome of purple cloaked figures appeared on the Keepers' other side, and earth cracked and rumbled before them. Lightning flashed and damars smoked, while damarian sorcery bathed the human shields in fire and smoke.

Not all damars charged the humans. Pink cloaks flashed in and out of existence between them. Where pink disappeared, damars punched at each other, or tackled each other to brawl on the ground. The Dedicated were turning them against each other, but the damarian sorcery battle was shifting in full force onto the plains.

On Ruarnon's right, Healers and pink cloaked figures were vanishing with the wounded. Their wagons lay empty. The wounded in enclosures were vanishing too, the Dedicated aiding their retreat.

"Mijora have mercy!" Captain Rilmar cried. "There is a second sorcerer force, advancing behind Damaria. I could not be sure before, but it is dropping its concealment. A whole Divine Army is taking the field."

Ruarnon shuddered, and nearly sprained their neck trying to see how far back the Divine Army marched.

A large section of plain behind the damarian-Priest, Priestess and Keeper battle rippled, then became a mounted host of over a hundred gold masked figures. It was skirting the fighting, riding alongside the hills east of Narz's castle, fires flaring ahead of it toward Captain Melroth and his Keepers.

"They waited in safety till *now*?" Troy asked.

"They used the Middle South like Narz used the damars," Michael replied heavily, "as a vanguard."

Ruarnon sighed, as the dry plains beneath their horse's hooves gave way to small rises, and Coroth led them into foothills before the larger hill on which Narz's castle lay. The screams, roars and booms of battle behind them were fading, not because of magic, but blessed distance.

"Thank the Ancestors," said Lenaris, as they rounded a hill, obscuring the battles behind them.

"Or the Sky Gods," Mawana added with a wink and Ruarnon smiled.

Lenaris was never one for religion, and nor was he, but they whole heartedly appreciated the sentiment, not that the height or dirt of these hills provided much protection. But it was better than having only air between you and a sorcerer army that could incidentally wipe everyone out.

Captain Rilmar shivered.

"What is it?" Ruarnon asked.

"I warned my Second the moment I suspected Divine Soldiers were marching. Octharl's spies have convinced him that Lord Vye and the Divine armies are the enemy we mistook King Narz's forces for. My Second is mobilising the Elite Guard. They are coming."

"What is their objective?" Ruarnon asked.

"To ensure the Divine Army does not survive."

Ruarnon shivered. Should Narz panic and tell the Keepers to attack the Elite Guard, pinning them between Keepers and Divine Soldiers…

It was almost a relief to cross the next hilltop and be distracted by view of the battle again. The gold masked column advanced under a magical shield. Earth cracked and Keepers and deep red cloaked sorcerers protecting their retreating infantry dived for cover, as deadly shrapnel of loose rocks and hard earth hurled among them.

A dragon reared, its wings expanding to block the barrage of earth and stones. Lightning bolts struck the dragon. Something slender struck its eyes. Bronze-iron sheened powerbow bolts, Ruarnon suspected. The creature roared and crashed into the plains.

Dedicated appeared in force, forming lines before the Keepers and deep red cloaked soldiers, who gaped, as the Dedicated deflected lightning, tearing a hole in the Divine column's shield, turning soldiers beneath the tear to dust.

"I have done what I can for you," the Dedicated leading them said suddenly. "I must aid my kin."

"Thank you," said Ruarnon. "We wouldn't have made it here safely without you."

The Dedicated inclined their head, winked out of existence and reappeared at the front of the Dedicated line. "Friends, take a nap!" they shouted.

"They're the *leader* of the Dedicated?" Troy asked.

Ruarnon stared as the Dedicated lay down. Some were shaking. Others stood with the support of crutches. At least three sat in chairs on wheels. Others used sticks to navigate the ground around them as they lay.

"Disabled sorcerers fighting a sorcery battle *lying down*?" Troy asked. "Now I've seen *everything*!" his grin was infectious, despite everyone's tension.

Divine soldiers began to collapse, *beneath* their magic shield. Yet Ruarnon suspected half the Dedicated had their eyes shut. They lay in total relaxation, as if their magical senses detected and targeted Divine Soldiers.

Screams rose. Keeper shields behind the Dedicated were failing. Keepers were catching alight. Captain Melroth and his Keepers were riding to their aid, but more shields failed before Melroth reached them, their occupants screaming as they fell to lightning.

Keepers weren't trained soldiers. Their opponents were. They were going to lose.

"Can't we do something?" Fiona asked.

"Not without provoking them to attack us and at great strain from this distance," Captain Rilmar replied.

"Who's that?" Linh asked, pointing to a man on a hill beside them.

Tor motioned a halt, and everyone reined in.

Dargus addressed the hills beside them, where people in plain linens stood. "The Keepers are outnumbered," he said loudly. "I know not all of you agree with them. I know many of you doubt King Narz. But they are dying. Will you let Azula fall to the God Kings?"

A roar of protest rose.

"Then fight!" Dargus shouted.

People leapt up from the cover of long grass. A human tide rose and swept down the hillside, bellowing war cries, Dargus at their head, flanked by a dozen people wielding bronze-sheen-iron weapons.

Fire flared towards them and several screamed or panicked and fled before it hit. They weren't soldiers. They were ordinary people, some little older than children, in linen tunics and grubby pants. They advanced without formation, some armed with spears or bows and arrows, even pitch forks.

A woman raised a large magical shield above them, and fire flared harmlessly against it. A whirl wind rose, whipping up dust and stones, growing until it hit the gold masked vanguard with such force that clothing and weapons flapped out of control, magical shields warped. A volley of arrows shot up from Dargus' followers. Wind moved aside and a half-dozen masked figures fell to arrows.

"They're commoners," said Michael. "All of them. And they're going to fight. Here," he said, calling to two young women running nearby, who approached him hesitantly. "It can pierce magical shields," he said offering them the hilt of his bronze-iron sheen blade. "And cut through magic. Take it."

Ruarnon drew their sword and offered its hilt to the other young woman. Both women accepted the weapons with silent bows of thanks. Then they turned and ran to battle.

Mawana and Lenaris handed their swords to grateful young men, on whose faces hope flared, as they took up the blades, before they too turned to battle. Troy, Fiona and Linh handed theirs to people Ruarnon would have thought too old to fight, but all three silver haired people smiled their thanks and ran on at a speed defying their age.

"Benevolence, do you need my advice further?" General Takanis asked.

"What would you do?" Ruarnon asked.

"Lead them," she replied, nodding towards Dargus' rag tag army. "And ensure as many of them survive this as possible. Dargus is a natural leader, but not a commander."

Ruarnon bowed their head. "Ensure you survive too."

She smiled, inclined her head and healed her horse around the rag tag army.

"You lot! With the bows! Follow me. We're guarding the infantry flanks."

"What?" someone called.

"You three, with the spears, you approach on our right. You with the swords! Charge in front of the archers."

Under Takanis' relentless orders, people regrouped. Confusion gave way to obeying confident orders and they repositioned their shields at her instruction and charged with straighter postures.

"Veer right!" Takanis boomed.

Ruarnon gaped, as Dargus' entire army shifted wide of a lightning bolt.

"Who is that?" Dargus called back.

"Raise shields!" Takanis commanded.

Magical shields streaked before front line shields, and fires smoked before them.

Ruarnon smiled. If any of these people lacked military training, their chances of survival had just multiplied.

"I hope we see her again," Tor said fervently.

Ruarnon inclined their head. "But it's past time to be out of here."

"I don't think our horses can go any faster," Troy said worriedly.

That was what had made it easier to watch the fighting; the horses had slowed.

"The road is just ahead," said Coroth. "Can you keep up with my guards and I on foot?"

"I'd rather not dawdle with the Second Sorcery War at my back," Troy replied with a hint of his usual smile.

"Everyone dismount," Ruarnon ordered. "Let the horses follow at their own pace. We move at a jog."

Mawana set the pace on foot at a steady jog, as booms, bright flashes and pandemonium spread behind them, and their horses wandered across the grassy hillside and sought ditches to lie in.

The physical effort of running helped Ruarnon's breathing steady and their mind to clear. With clarity came the realisation they were now racing King Narz's guilt about casualties of a battle he had never wanted and Vye's treachery. He had received the letter Darius asked Ruarnon to send, with Darius' signet ring, clearly outlining Vye's betrayal. His failure to stop Vye made no sense.

But it didn't matter now. What mattered was they doubted the Dedicated could fight with such power for long. The Divine army outnumbered everyone, Vye's damars were helping it and the one force that may contain both, the Elite Guard, could be ambushed by Keepers, if Narz panicked when they arrived. The risk may not be Elite Guard and Keepers fighting. It could be the Divine Army winning the war.

Ruarnon barely registered light flashing ahead, until Coroth spoke. "The God Kings have sent another force."

"The castle isn't going to be much safer, is it?" Troy asked hollowly.

"You'd get bored if it wasn't," Michael replied, his face pale, his eyes gleaming.

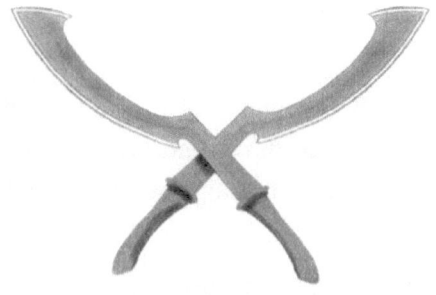

CҺAPϿЄR 35

IN KING NARZ'S CASϿLЄ -RUARNON

Ruarnon jogged beside Companion Tor, following Coroth and their mounted companions on a zig zagging, narrow road uphill, towards a crystalline structure glazed with a faint rainbow sheen Ruarnon suspected was protective enchantments.

The hillside trembled. Rocks and scree tumbled down slopes and bounced across the road. Coroth's guards grimaced. But delaying at signs of danger would make little difference to what they faced ahead, and everyone knew it. They kept moving.

Ruarnon's shoulders tightened, as the road curved around a bend, revealing shadows of people. Or were those shadowy statues flanking the road? Whatever it was, they were surrounded by magic. At first it tingled, then it pulsed gently. More magic tingled around the next bend, higher up. The hillside obscured Ruarnon's view, but they could point directly at where magic washed off more statues in gentle waves.

As they jogged to the nearest pair of statues, the figures sharpened. Ruarnon tensed. Two men stood opposite each other, the shadow spell no longer concealing them. They showed no awareness of Ruarnon's companions' footsteps thudding up the road. Of everyone panting for breath or running towards them. Instead, they stood still, staring across the road. It was hard to tell if they were breathing.

They wore deep brown silks blending into the rocky hillside. One's tawny and the other's tan face was almost emotionless, making Ruarnon shiver. Their dark eyes were open wide. They moved no more than statues as Coroth jogged past.

The hair on the back of Ruarnon's neck stood up as they passed the figures. There was something unnatural about their stillness. The calm, determination and alertness os those features was surely enhanced or distorted by sorcery. The frozen occupants of Tira had seemed more alive.

Ruarnon shivered again. At the next bend, the next pair of figures stood like statues. They were slightly older, with emotionless, focused, all-seeing, all-hearing faces. One man suddenly turned towards them and Ruarnon flinched. The eyes were alert, showing no recognition of a fellow human, boring into Ruarnon's skull, making them freeze with tension under that unnatural gaze, until it flicked away. The head turned to its former position and the man became a statue again.

Ruarnon's breathing came in rapid gasps as they resumed running.

"What happened to them?" Mawana asked Coroth.

"I don't know. Captain Melroth doesn't know where they came from. He says the enchantment upon them is exceptionally powerful, more than any of the Keepers could compete with."

"Why enchant them to spy for him?" Fiona asked.

Coroth sighed. "He didn't. Teliph said he was furious about the enchantment when he brought them here, but he couldn't break it. So he set them as lookouts."

"Why would the God Kings make anyone like that?" Michael asked.

Coroth shivered. "As a form of torture. Making them watch something awful. Narz wouldn't tell Teliph what."

Ruarnon grimaced. The God Kings enchanted people as a form of torture? Whatever held the watchers so still, surely it prevented them from living? It even seemed to mute their feelings. Why would anyone want to dominate another so utterly?

They were nearing the third bend, which doubled steeply above itself and was flanked by another pair of watchers. Both turned suddenly, examining Mawana. For what? They stared as if they saw into Mawana's mind, magic washing off them, as it did the pair below.

The next pair studied Captain Rilmar and everyone froze. The watchers stared unnaturally long without blinking. Captain Rilmar gazed calmly back and Ruarnon admired her composure. One of the watchers frowned and Ruarnon tensed. Then both watchers turned to gaze glassy eyed back to the road.

Several people exhaled deeply. But Fiona's face was draining of colour, and she walked on tight lipped, a sword belted at her right hip, its iron-bronze sheened hilt sitting more than halfway up her waist. As the gentlest person among them, everyone had agreed she should carry the weapon, until Captain Rilmar and quite possibly Teliph herself said it was safe to present and destroy before Narz.

The next pair of watchers studied Troy, who was chewing his lip. They turned swiftly to pin Fiona with their stare and Ruarnon held their breath. Just as swiftly, both watchers turned their glassy eyed gazes back to the road. Ruarnon exhaled deeply.

As everyone climbed higher, around more bends, the watchers studied Michael, Linh, Tor and Lenaris. They studied Captain Arleath and Ruarnon's guards. But not Coroth, Demune or the Zaldeaan guards.

With their glazed-eye intensity, Ruarnon doubted the watchers knew or cared that Coroth supposedly served Narz. They expected these enchanted men to search everyone, for whatever they sought. So the fact the next pair of watchers stared unseeing through the Zaldeaan guards walking past them, the people who couldn't craft magic, made Ruarnon's chest tighten and breathing difficult, as they rounded the last sharp bend and climbed the final slope.

Another dozen paces and a level hilltop stretched before them, ringed by watchers. Every second watcher gazed down, while every first watcher gazed up at different angles. Each face was as focused and emotionless as the next.

It sent chills down Ruarnon's spine. Had that white flash earlier been an attack up here? Surely the enchantment on these men would give a God King pause, not to mention whatever defensive capabilities they and the castle walls possessed.

Ruarnon flinched, as the air before them resolved into a wall of shadow. The shadow arched high above and obscured Narz's castle.

Coroth's mouth firmed into a line, and he kept walking. Ruarnon followed reluctantly. Troy swore behind them. Magic particles danced in the air ahead.

The shadow spell lightened. Then it dissolved into an enormous opaque shield dome, surrounding the watchers and the entire hilltop.

Coroth halted and the dome split, folding outwards into a small door for him to walk through. Ruarnon's chest tightened as magic pulsated around the doorway before them. They stepped towards it, dwarfed by its power, fighting the irrational fear that the archway would collapse and crush them. They held their breath and stepped quickly through.

On the other side, the watchers stood staring through the shield, down at the hillside or up at the sky. There was no sign of who parted the shield. As if the shield had opened itself.

"Who's letting us in?" Troy asked tightly, as he stepped through.

Coroth opened his mouth but didn't answer immediately. Ruarnon scanned the hilltop again. There was no one else to be seen. No footsteps apart from their companions.

"It's like Red Cloak," Troy continued, as Linh and Fiona followed him through the shield. "Doors open for us. Showing us the way."

Linh gasped. "You don't think Red Cloak's here?"

"Though why let us in?" Michael asked, rushing behind her through the shield. "In the middle of a war in which lots of people want Narz dead? Why trust us?"

"Is it wise to talk in front of them?" Lenaris asked behind Michael, inclining her head at the watchers.

"I am not sure they can hear us," Mawana replied, shivering as he stepped through the shield.

Lenaris's eyes widened in concern.

"It's more powerful than the Elite Guard shields in battle," Mawana explained. "This is what I've always imagined Guardians had the power to do. I never wanted to see or feel it for myself. No one should have this much power."

Ruarnon swallowed awkwardly, noting Coroth and the guards waiting for them. "We'd best press on."

The last guard stepped through, and the shield dome folded together again and vanished. Perhaps it was better not to see who was opening and closing it. Perhaps that would be more frightening.

Ruarnon followed Coroth towards the shiny brown crystalline walls. Many towers, spires and balconies rose before them, on which stood more silent watchers. The shine wasn't tingling magic. It was more like a burn. An intensity Ruarnon's magical senses flinched away from. As if the walls radiated power.

Ruarnon had to remind themself this terrible power was being used for protection. But they couldn't help wondering, if these were the defences Narz commanded, what did his offensive magic look like?

The road ended at a flight of glazed steps, where two watchers flanked the castle double doors. Coroth climbed the steps.

"Whom do you bring to King Narz's castle?" the watcher on the right intoned, his gaze fixed on the hilltop.

"I bring First Captain Rilmar of the Elite Guard, Heir Ruarnon, Regent of Tarlah and King of the Zaldeaan Realm, Mawana of the Urai Jungle and their friends."

"Why do you bring them?" the watcher on the right intoned, staring ahead as though Coroth didn't exist.

"They wish to negotiate peace with His Worthiness, on behalf of the Timbalen Empire."

"The Peace Ambassadors may pass," said the watcher on the left.

"The Peace Ambassadors may pass," the watcher on the right echoed.

Ruarnon took a deep breath and climbed steps as shiny and slippery as glass, between the watchers and under the high, unadorned crystalline arch into King Narz's castle. The interior walls were crystal, and the high ceiling was clear, daylight shining down through it. There was no sign of watchers inside, nor anyone else.

The high, narrow doors of the entrance closed loudly in the silence. They left no crack of light. Instead, they crystallised, becoming indistinct from the walls. Ruarnon shivered. Getting in here was one thing. Maybe they should have given more thought to getting out.

"This way," Coroth said reluctantly, taking the lead, his shoulders slumped.

"Are you all right?" Ruarnon asked him quietly.

Coroth bit his lip. "I know it's silly. It's just Teliph thinks so well of him and he thinks well of me. I don't want to disappoint him. He's like a father to Teliph and part of me... part of me wants his approval for us to marry.

"I know —it doesn't matter. It's not important now. I just, I never thought I'd be leading my cousin to persuade my future father-by-law not to have his Keepers ambush the Elite Guard. To persuade him not to destroy the people he *should* be allied with. And not to let the Divine Realms run riot across the *entire* continent. I know he's failing and Teliph's worried. I just... I never imagined things could be this bad."

"Teliph will do everything she can," said Demune.

"So will we," said Linh.

"It was easier on the other side of the war," Ruarnon said, placing a hand on their cousin's shoulder. "You got used to the other side having all the power. And you still found ways to get round it and counter them. I think we can do that here."

Coroth inclined his head. "It's this way," he told them and led everyone on.

The Zaldeaan guards walked in a loose circle around them. Ruarnon's guards instinctively formed a circle between the Zaldeaans and Ruarnon's companions.

It didn't feel like a safe place. The walls likely had eyes, ears or worse. There could be defensive enchantments, or sorcerers anywhere. Ruarnon was alert for both, listening carefully as they walked.

Suddenly, another hallway crossed theirs. It stretched endlessly on either side, with no sign of doors.

"Where did that come from?" Troy asked.

"The far side of a concealment spell probably," Michael replied.

Lenaris and Mawana scanned the new corridor carefully, but Ruarnon couldn't hear anyone down it and their friends moved on without a word.

The main corridor continued, silent beyond their footsteps, as empty as before. The ceiling continued to loom high above them, daylight shining through it, onto sparkling crystal interior walls. In another place and time it would be beautiful, awe inspiring even. But now, it was a vast empty space allowing enemies to attack them from many directions.

Yet there was no sign of enemies. It was so quiet that the rapid beating of Ruarnon's heart echoed in their ears.

Torches began to burn on brackets at regular intervals either side of them, making everyone jump. Crystalline walls cast strange rainbow reflections onto a stone floor in the firelight. They walked past more hallways branching off the main corridor, and each appeared only when Ruarnon's companions stepped beside it, and each was identical to the one before. This wasn't a home. It was a purpose-built labyrinth.

A horrid sound made everyone stop.

"What was that?" Linh asked.

"Lord Vye has released damars," Coroth replied, staring grimly ahead.

"He's going to try and kill us and take the weapon from our dead hands?" Troy asked.

Coroth drew his sword. Ruarnon drew the sword Omah had given them, missing their enchanted blade already. The Australians wore similar looks of regret as they drew plain swords from Myleth Island from their sheaths.

Tarlahn and Zaldeaan bodyguards shifted their defensive circle with swords or spears in hand, scanning the corridor for the creature that made the cry. The ground shook faintly under pounding footsteps.

"*Giant* damars?" Troy asked, as his friends formed a line beside Ruarnon. "Tell me they can't wield sorcery."

"And aren't protect by it," Michael added darkly.

"They cannot be," Coroth replied. "Any damars held back from the battle will be reserved to pit against Guardians. These creatures won't be soldiers. I suspect they are King Narz's mistakes."

A large shadow appeared a hundred paces down the corridor, warping before their eyes. It solidified and Ruarnon gasped. It had three heads and ran with a limp, its left leg a sixth shorter than its right. Another brute pushed ahead, bent almost double, with arms the length of a gorilla compared to its short legs and body.

"They're deformed," said Linh.

"I doubt just physically," Coroth replied.

Ruarnon wished they had more archers. And spear men. Five of each wasn't enough.

Linh stepped in front of everyone.

"What are you doing?" said Troy. "Where's your sword?"

She waved him off and bellowed, "STOP. *No* running inside!"

Ruarnon gaped at the demand in her tone. The charging mass slowed.

"I SAID *STOP.*"

The damars halted. A damar with a single giant leg leant against the wall for balance. The giant in the lead cocked all three heads at Linh.

"Walking *only* inside. No running. Walk!" she pointed forcefully around her companions.

Three giant heads nodded, and the lead giant led others, large and small, one, two or three legged around their companions. Ruarnon gaped and everyone moved aside from the grey hided creatures towering over them and thumping noisily past.

A one-legged giant hoped along, running its hand against the wall. Another almost walked into Linh.

"Around!" she commanded, and it stepped aside, frowning, shifting awkwardly. Was it blind?

A third, medium sized damar walked directly at Linh. "*Around*," she commanded, motioning with her finger. It watched her finger, nodded, then circled her.

"There's no magic tingling round them," said Ruarnon. "You noticed the absence of magic and assumed they were charging in response to verbal commands?"

"And lack the intelligence to distinguish between boss and enemy, if you command them well enough," Coroth added. "Well guessed."

She smiled; her posture still rigid.

"That last one was deaf?" Troy asked. "And the one holding the wall, was blind?"

"And they were all scared," said Fiona.

"More damars scared of people," said Troy, shaking his head. "*And* able to understand human speech, though that lot didn't seem able to talk. This continent is going to need to do a LOT of reconciliation when this war's over."

"Let's ensure it ends with the least amount of death and destruction possible," Ruarnon added. "Onward."

Ruarnon's back tensed at the idea of presenting itself to giant damars, who, for all they had listened to Linh, could attack again. But they started walking anyway.

"We leave those things behind us?" Troy asked.

"Would you rather butcher them? Or exhaust ourselves putting them to sleep?" Mawana asked.

Troy shook his head and the others fell in behind Ruarnon, along the now eerily quiet, deserted-seeming corridor.

"You cannot waste your ability to wield magic," Captain Rilmar asserted. "Others are already fighting with it. I sense magic shifting ahead."

Coroth tensed. "Then Vye knows I am here, and sent a lesser force to kill me, while sorcerer-soldiers fight the God King's assassins."

"Why would Vye try to kill you?" Ruarnon asked.

"To demoralise Teliph," Coroth replied, pale faced. "If he wants King Narz's throne; he will have to kill her first. I may endanger you."

"We wouldn't have made it this far without you," said Ruarnon. "And your presence may not endanger us more than our own."

"Is Vye watching us?" Linh asked. "Does he know he hasn't harmed Coroth?"

"I doubt he would bother checking," Coroth replied. "He knows Zaldeaans cannot wield magic and if I am the only one he spotted, he will assume we are dead, while he focuses on battles he hopes will help him seize his crown."

Ruarnon tensed. "He *let* the Divine Assassins enter the castle? The invading God King is his ally?"

"He must be. Divine Assassins had no hope of penetrating the building undetected. King Narz threatens their authority, and if Vye gives them the chance to kill him; being made king of lands they deem unworthy of conquering would be a logical reward for Vye."

"Will Vye let us approach Narz?" Michael asked.

"I think he genuinely believes you have come to kill King Narz with the weapon," Coroth replied. "That is how he would free my father's army were he me, and my family, if he were Ruarnon. He will think allowing you to enter the throne room is in his interest. That you are noble, brave and fools, as he thinks of me."

Ruarnon bowed their head, as they continued down the silent, magic sparkling corridor.

A loud cracking echoed behind them.

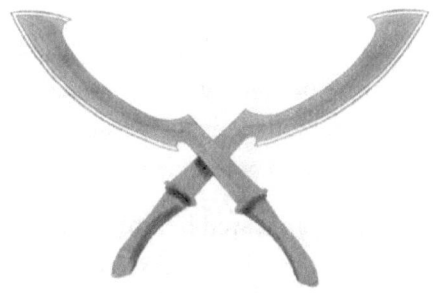

CHAPTER 36

KING NARZ'S DEFENCES - RUARNON

R uarnon spun around. Two crack lines shot across the stone floor. The floor collapsed behind the cracks and fire shot into the air it had occupied.

"RUN!" Ruarnon ordered.

They rushed forwards, as cracking echoing towards them.

"It is only the perimeter," Coroth shouted. "Someone is forcing their way through the outer walls."

The corridor rumbled. Ruarnon turned back. Behind their friends, rear guards and the cracked hole, ice solidified from floor to walls, to ceiling. Blue flames danced beyond the ice wall. Both enchantments seemed defensive, blocking sorcerers' access to the inner castle. Raw power radiated behind Ruarnon, making their head spin and their heart race.

Mawana slumped against the wall on their left. Fiona leant against Troy, who supported her, gaping with worry.

"The magic's too strong," said Ruarnon. "We've got to get away from here."

Lenaris wrapped an arm around Mawana, dragging him forwards. Tor supported Ruarnon, and Troy supported Fiona.

Ruarnon started to straighten, feeling less dizzy, though very much distracted by magic tingling. In their peripheral vision, blinding white light flashed.

Ruarnon spun, wrenching Tor around. Light shone down behind them, blasting away stone floor and heating crystal walls until they oozed and melted. Heat radiated against Ruarnon's skin, making them flush and sweat. Magic crackled and their whole body tingled with it.

An intersecting corridor appeared before them. A corridor in which something black blocked the illusion of sky above and moved downwards.

"RUN FASTER!" Coroth bellowed, charging ahead.

The ground Ruarnon stood on began to lift, as they, Tor, Captain Rilmar and half their bodyguards ran. They leapt over its edge, falling several feet down to stable corridor and turned back. Mawana and Lenaris landed behind them. The floor was above Ruarnon's height and rising.

The other half of Ruarnon's bodyguards leapt from so heigh it made them stagger, rolling to lessen the impact. The floor had risen over a storey high. The ceiling was moving down to meet it. Michael, Fiona, Linh and Troy weren't far across.

"Turn back!" Lenaris cried.

Troy gaped, aghast.

"Now!" Lenaris cried, her voice cracking.

Michael nodded, spinning a staring Fiona around. Troy and Linh ran back. They leapt. Ruarnon's knuckles dug into their palms.

Troy swore loudly.

"Roll to spread out the impact!" Linh demanded.

Then floor and ceiling rushed to meet each other, crashed together, and Mawana's shouts to their friends went unanswered, as if the enchantments on the walls barred sound as well as magic.

"We must move on," Coroth insisted. "There are more defences. If we slow down the rest of us may be separated."

"We can't leave them!" said Lenaris.

"We can't help them either," Coroth replied. "There's nothing we can do."

Mawana stared at the wall. Lenaris called out, but the Australians didn't answer.

"We can't risk being cut off from Narz," Ruarnon asserted.

"But they're part of Lylah's prophecy," Mawana objected. "The five of you make all futures better."

"Maybe we can ask Teliph's help," Ruarnon replied, "But we need to reach her first."

"Strategic retreat," Tor told Mawana. "That is all you can do now. Help for them must wait."

Ruarnon noted how Tor stared at the wall as he said it. He was also fond of the Australians.

Ruarnon took a deep breath, feeling like they'd left half of themself behind, and led everyone onwards at a brisk walk.

"Ah!" Troy cried. "I think its broken!"

Linh gripped his shoulder firmly. "Try to keep it still. Move your leg with your hands if you need to reposition it."

Opposite Linh, Fiona's eyes were filling with tears. Michael stood beside them, his hands shoved in his pockets, his eyes darting around. He didn't seem to know what to say but was clearly upset.

"Let me help!"

Linh started at the new voice. A youth was running towards them. He was slender, with brown hair and vague blue eyes that seemed unfocused.

"Who are you?" Michael asked.

"Someone who knows healing magic," the young man replied.

He stopped and knelt beside Troy, without really looking at him. There was something off about his voice too. It was friendly but had a dreamy quality to it. Like the boy was relaxed, and content, despite the castle's defences crashing down and Divine Assassins roaming the castle.

"Keep it nice and still," the boy told Troy, looking past him.

Troy groaned. Then his face relaxed and his mouth opened in wonder. Linh gaped, as he wiggled his foot. Troy smiled. "How's a healer so young so good?"

The boy smiled but still didn't meet Troy's gaze. "I'm older than I look."

He stood. "We shouldn't be here. There's assassins about."

The words were serious and demanded action. But he spoke slowly, and there was no fear or concern in his voice. He was calmly stating a fact, as if the danger didn't bother him.

"This way," he added.

He reached out. Linh gaped as his hand went into a seemingly solid crystal wall, took hold of something and the wall transformed to door, which opened at his touch.

"Who *are* you?" Michael asked.

The youth paused, gazing unseeing at the walls. "I don't matter. Not nearly as much as they think I do. Not in the end. They'll see."

He shook himself. "Are you coming?"

"Am I accompanying a total stranger into a wall in the most dangerous building I've ever entered?" Troy asked with a grin. "Sure? Why not?"

Linh weighed what she knew. This boy had appeared out of nowhere, in the most suspicious of places. But he'd healed Troy. And his magic craft was incredible. He was young, but surely he was a Healer?

Michael was watching her. She nodded and she and Michael followed Fiona and Troy into a brown crystal corridor that was much narrower but had an equally high ceiling to the one they'd left. The door swung shut behind them, and melded into crystal and solid wall, just like the castle front door. Seeing it a second time was no less eerie.

Linh forced herself to concentrate on their path ahead and stared as the boy reached into the wall and opened another door, leading into a corridor taking them parallel to the one they'd just left.

"Where are you headed?" Troy asked as he followed.

The youth paused, then continued walking. "Nowhere really. I just… needed a break. There's so much-"

He trembled. Fiona stepped forward to place a hand on his shoulder. The bronze-iron sheen weapon buckled to her waist jolted. The boy flinched and his gaze darted away. Linh gaped as illusion magic tingled, and the weapon vanished, blending seamlessly with Fiona's side.

"I can't help you?" Fiona asked, not noticing what had upset him.

The boy shook his head. "It's not my body. It's my mind. I'm sick. Very sick. There's just so much to do…"

"Can't the other Healers help?" Fiona asked.

He smiled, gazing at the floor. "They will. With my work. They can't do anything for my mind."

"What's wrong with it?" Linh asked. "In our world, there's counselling. It doesn't need magic. There must be people here who can help with that sort of thing."

He smiled, leaning against the wall in a way that made Linh worry he was also physically ill. "Your world? I would like to see that."

"It *does* have more in the medical and psychological fields, and generally better plumbing," said Troy. "But at least people here don't tell each other outright lies and deny science."

"But you have democracy," said the boy.

Linh shivered.

"And, Med-i-care?" he pronounced the word carefully, like someone saying something they'd only seen in writing.

Linh shivered more violently.

He surprised her, standing again, though he swayed as he walked. But he moved quickly.

"Your friends will be in here. You'll have to run before the next defence hits."

"Thanks for your help," said Troy.

"Will you be ok?" Fiona asked.

The boy eyed her, not quite meeting her gaze. "I will never be ok. But other people will. That's what matters."

He reached into the wall and opened a door. But no one hurried through it. Because he was fading. And that odd feeling, it wasn't goosebumps about him knowing things he couldn't, it was the tingle of magic. It was humming all around him.

"It's all right," he said, noting Linh's gaze. "I'm waking up. This was only a short break. A little nap. I've been dreaming myself into reality when I sleep of late. Living other lives with other people. It's wonderful magic. But I cannot go on this way."

He smiled at the first, as though gazing into a beautiful world beyond Linh's sight, and comprehension. But the smile vanished, and his expression darkened at the end.

Send his *subconsciousness* into an illusory *second body* and 'dream' in the real world? The Dedicated said they could do things other people couldn't think of, but surely this *wasn't* possible?

"I am sorry I took you away. There was just so much to learn. And so many people needed the knowledge, the vision, to fix this world. But I am sorry."

Linh stumbled. How could this *boy* be Narz? Though his mind *was* only half present. And what *did* happen when a mind as damaged as his from PTSD could craft vast amounts of magic?

Troy frowned. "If you mean Red Cloak's sorry, tell him…"

"We've seen some fucked up shit, made amazing friends and wouldn't have it any other way," Michael finished for him, and Linh gaped.

Michael smiled at her. He meant that. Sincerely. He must know what she suspected, but he didn't seem to be trying to placate… a boy who *couldn't* be Narz… but *was* fading away before them.

The figure spoke more sharply, more confidently. More man than boy. "I will be more dangerous when I wake. Please do not come near me when I am dangerous. I remember everything thing awake. I feel *everything*. And my mind is *so much* worse."

"Take care," Fiona called.

"You must go now. The door will close when I leave."

It was already starting to swing slowly forwards, into and *through* his arm. Troy jumped, then rushed past, leading a worried Fiona by the hand.

"Don't trust Vye," Linh warned, meeting the fading gaze.

"I don't. I will kill him when the time is right."

Linh shivered. Michael steered her out. For a moment the faded form slumped against a door closing into it. It looked longingly at Linh and her friends. Then it vanished. The door melted into the wall and closed.

"He *dreams* himself *out of his body*?" Michael said softly, shaking his head.

"Like the state of his mind crafting magic can blur the lines of reality itself," Linh said faintly, with a shiver.

But Narz had spoken to them before, at Tira. He had *Seen* and responded to the vision the dragons were giving her. But no one had answered him then. They hadn't had a conversation with a Narz they could see, one who could work magic, *out* of his body.

"We better hurry," Troy called. "We've got to catch the others before the next enchantment blasts this corridor apart, or whatever its going to do!"

Linh nodded and she and Michael ran alongside Fiona and Troy. Fiona gazed back over her shoulder. She still looked worried the ill healer was completely mad. But he was far more rational than she thought. Narz had been all along. They just hadn't understood what drove him.

Linh wondered what 'the right time' to kill Vye meant.

Ruarnon didn't like this. They'd run for what felt like some time, pounding footsteps echoing off walls. But no more corridors flashed into existence before them. Brown, rainbow sheened crystal walls stretched on, as did the stone floor. Then people stood before them. A crowd of young men backed up.

"We mean no harm!" one called. "We are here to liberate, not enslave them."

"What do you mean liberate?" Lenaris asked. "Few people are imprisoned here."

Ruarnon motioned the others to slow. They turned to Coroth, who was frowning and shook his head. These men didn't wear red cloaks, or green, or bronze armour. They wore ordinary linens, suggesting they weren't soldiers. But why were they claiming to be here to liberate?

The man breathed heavily, eyeing Lenaris with… fear.

"Not all of us mean to conquer," another young man pressed. "I know that's what our powers are known for, but they can be used to protect. To *save*."

Ruarnon shivered. It was the same thinking that galvanised Narz's soldier-sorcerers and Keepers. Yet these men spoke it as if the idea was new. As if it were revolutionary.

"We know of Healers and Keepers," Lenaris replied uncertainly.

The young men frowned. They were standing *inside* Narz's castle and neither name was familiar?

"We do not object to sorcerers," Mawana offered.

The first man breathed a sigh of relief. The others breathed more freely, their postures relaxing where they stood.

"You have come to join us?" one asked.

"Only sorcerers wouldn't object to sorcerers," another answered him with a smile.

"I am sorry," said Ruarnon, "But where in Umarinaris are you from?"

The men frowned.

"I don't know that country," one said.

Ruarnon forced their mouth to stay closed, as others gave their origins, none of which Ruarnon recognised, until one said, "And I'm from Tira. They've been so lucky. It's one of few places where the walls are holding, and everything isn't falling apart to the war. I was reluctant to leave it, but not everyone's so lucky."

"Tira?" asked Tor.

"You mean the *Sorcery War*?" Ruarnon asked.

"Well, no one remembers any other," the young man replied amicably. "It's been going on so long. But we're going to free other city's now. With Narz leading us, we could do anything."

Lenaris and Mawana cried out. All of the men had vanished. Instantaneously.

"They believed they were *in* the First Sorcery War? That it is currently happening and Tira has not fallen?" Tor asked.

Ruarnon's mind was racing. "They were Narz's followers. His friends who died in the war. How can ghosts of his friends haunt these walls?"

"We can explain that."

"Michael!" Mawana cried.

"But now's not a good time," Michael added, as he and the Australians ran towards everyone from… ahead.

"How are you ahead of us?" Lenaris asked.

Troy gaped, turning back and Linh and Michael eyed each other uneasily, as if they weren't running in the direction they thought.

"A Healer led us through the walls," Troy replied uncertainly. "He healed my broken ankle. Then he just… disappeared."

"We just met young men who spoke as if they were Narz's friends and the First Sorcery War is still happening," Ruarnon explained.

"And they hadn't all been murdered by Guardians yet," Lenaris added darkly.

"His dreams," said Linh. "The boy we met said he was dreaming, and when he started fading, that he was waking up. It's like he can magically project appearances and voices when he dreams. Like he projects himself into the real world and speaks to real people while he sleeps. It's like, somehow all of us were in Narz's dream."

"That was *NARZ*?" Troy asked, staggering beside Linh.

Michael dived sideways, catching Fiona as she swayed.

"And if he's dreaming his murdered friends and projecting them into reality too…" Linh continued. "He *healed* Troy's leg. If he can project his dreams onto reality and wield magic while he's asleep and half out of it… what would happen if he had a *nightmare* in reality?"

Linh's head was spinning. She was confusing Fiona and Troy, though Fiona was shivering and likely making connections. Troy was too shocked, but if Narz had just appeared to her as a teenage boy and healed her broken ankle, she supposed she would be in shock too. It was a lot to take in.

Part of Linh was angry with Narz for not stopping Vye. Part of her saw how tired he was. Part of her was blown away by someone declaring they didn't matter at all, and *everyone else* did. He *meant* that. As if everything he did was spreading magic for *other people's* benefit. Because they were *worth* saving.

"More magic," Captain Rilmar warned.

The stone floor ahead cracked and crumbled, as thick vines forced their way through and snaked up towards the ceiling. One vine touched a large burning torch, wrapping swiftly around it and snapping it into kindling. More torches burst in the grip of vines, which snuffed out flames.

Within moments the floor was covered in vines, which rose and snaked around each other, tangling together until they blocked daylight far above. Almost as suddenly as they appeared, they stopped growing, and stilled, into a solid barrier of entwined vines.

Troy punched the air.

Michael growled. But Linh wondered. The shield barricading the whole castle had opened when Coroth approached it and admitted everyone. And they hadn't seen the sorcerer who did that. It *was* like how Red Cloak led them to Myleth Island from Oval Island, as if someone *wanted* them in the castle. And there was only one way to check how far in that person wanted them to go.

Linh strode towards the vines.

"Linh!" Troy objected.

But the vines didn't stir. Not until she got close. Then some of them shifted, parting wide enough to let her through and high enough to admit people a good deal taller than her.

"It's ok," she called. "Someone wants us to get through. It might *actually* be Red Cloak."

"Hiding as usual," said Troy. "Let's get out of here."

They both turned, anticipating Lenaris objecting.

"We're no good here," Lenaris said. "Let's be swift."

Linh and Troy nodded, and Linh led the way into the vines. They were multiple steps deep, but none shifted as she passed. Troy hurried after her. Linh's heart beat rapidly and didn't slow until everyone was through and the vines snaked, closing up behind the last guard.

Someone *did* want them here. A little voice in her head said *two* someone's. Narz, who'd helped her, Troy, Michael and Linh around the previous defence, and Red Cloak opening this one from afar, as he preferred to act. Maybe she'd meet them both in the flesh, at last.

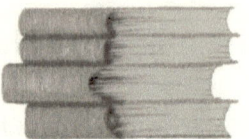

CHAPTER 37

LINH

A brown stone floor spread before Linh, from which multihued brown crystal walls rose, apparent daylight shining high above. There was neither sight nor sound of the next enchantment, though the floor was vibrating slightly.

"Sounds like assassins are still fighting," said Troy.

"I suspect it is Divine Soldier attack parties," said Captain Rilmar, "diverting attention from quieter, concealed assassins. But we have passed the most destructive enchantments. I sense nothing comparable ahead, only the general hum of magic from the walls and smaller shifting's of magic."

"Why stop trying to kill us?" Troy asked.

"I think the enchantments were designed to delay," Captain Rilmar replied. "Holding Divine agents until Keepers reached them, so Keepers aren't spread thin throughout the castle."

"You think we were lucky to stay ahead as they activated?" Michael asked, and she nodded.

Linh eyed Michael meaningfully. Was it coincidence Narz had dreamed himself to them the moment they got stuck on the wrong side? Had Red Cloak told Narz they were in trouble?

Ruarnon led everyone forwards, and Linh followed reluctantly. It was different, now she had come face to face with Narz. She still couldn't except it, not fully. And perhaps he'd been calm and emotionally distant because he was exhausted and asleep. Perhaps the awake Narz was, as he'd warned, more alert and more dangerous. But it was clear Narz meant them no ill will.

The longing in his gaze before he faded… Coroth said he'd kept the young Zaldeaans back from the war with Galvatia. He'd become a father to Teliph and he'd just dreamed his dead young friends from the Sorcery War into the castle. Had it been Narz who ordered Red Cloak to lead them to Myleth Island, to keep them safe while Narz cherry picked democratic legal practices and the welfare state from Linh's mind?

The enormous, enchanted crystal walls rising around her spoke of fear. As did the labyrinth and traps behind her. But it was like… Narz was drawn to young people. And so many of his followers, of the people he was trying to protect *were* young. Dargus, Melroth, Jaygoff.

If Narz was going to trust anyone as his fears materialised, it was going to be young people. And he was fascinated with Earth. Lylah was right. Narz needed them.

Everyone slowed, as a corridor crossing theirs came into view, identical to those that had caught fire, turned to ice, been blasted by lightning, smashed themselves together or become overgrown with vines. No one dared speak and their soft footsteps on stone floor echoed loudly against the silence.

Faint shouts echoed on Linh's right. Mawana motioned everyone to stop. Faint crashes and shouting rose.

Captain Rilmar frowned. "Divine assassins. Keepers are fighting a group of them."

Linh's stomach clenched.

They waited until Captain Rilmar was sure the Keepers were far away, then continued their silent march. The illusion of daylight was deceptive, and the colourful sheen of the walls seemed to go on forever.

"There *are* sorcerers nearby," Captain Rilmar cautioned. "I cannot be certain where," she added, frowning.

A cross section of hallway appeared left and right.

"FORWARD!"

A roar echoed from Linh's far right and the floor and walls rocked.

"I see light down there," Michael warned.

"GET DOWN!" Captain Rilmar shouted.

Mawana leapt, pulling Lenaris forwards. Linh tugged Fiona forwards. Something crackled. The hair on Linh's neck stood up. The corridor brightened, as a bolt of lightning arched overhead and crashed into a distant wall.

"INTRUDERS BEYOND THE VINE WALL! INTRU…"

Fire and lights blazed, as the voice cut off. Fire shifted before red cloaked Keepers on Linh's right. The flames met resistance in thin air, human shaped resistance.

Linh leapt clear behind Mawana. They ran a short distance, then Ruarnon motioned them to wait for the others. The glow of fire shone from the intersecting corridor, someone groaned, then the glow vanished.

"All of the enchantments have been activated. Someone is forcing their way through the walls," a voice reported.

"We may need Lord Vye's help," another voice advised.

"He has no intention of that. He might let them take King Narz. Lord Vye's in this for himself."

"Who did the assassin attack?"

"Coroth; leading a party of soldiers."

"He will be aiding Teliph. Leave them be. We will deal with the Divine Soldiers."

Ruarnon motioned everyone forwards, and Linh happily obliged, shaking slightly about Divine Assassins attacking *them* and Keepers having come to defend them. They needed to get ahead of the assassins for their own safety. She had a feeling Keepers and Narz himself would defend them from Divine attack parties, but they had to make it to the throne room for that.

The staggering height and unnecessary width of the hallways became eerie. Everything was too quiet, too still. Faint shouts or echoes of blasts from corridors far away made her aware of the rest of the world, but the world was shrinking to the deceptively still, shimmering walls around her, and the deep quiet of endless corridors.

She walked carefully, straining to detect the next obstacle. There was no sign of danger at the next intersection, or of anything but endless corridor ahead.

Linh cried out, as everything blurred around her. She kicked, but her legs didn't touch the ground. Then she stumbled, as the corridor cleared, and her feet hit stone floor unevenly.

Her heart pounded at a bright red cloaked figure ahead, but no sign of Mawana, Lenaris, Ruarnon or their guards. There was no sign of anyone but Fiona, Michael and Troy, who staggered past.

"What's this?" Troy asked Jaygoff.

"I am sorry to pluck you from the air without warning," Jaygoff replied. "But his Beneficence has changed his mind. Those Keepers barely arrived in time to protect you. Other Divine Assassins could kill you. And he cannot keep watching you. The easiest way to ensure your safety, is to send you home."

Troy's protest died, as his features slackened.

"Home?" Fiona asked, as if it were a foreign word.

"After all this time?" Michael asked.

"It is too dangerous for you now," said Jaygoff. "And the other Keepers are protecting our trainees. He can spare no more for you."

Linh's heartbeat hummed in her ears.

"So he *does* care about us," said Michael. "He must know a lot more than we think. But then, he knows more about everything else."

"But the way he spoke in his dream…" Linh protested.

Jaygoff's mouth twisted in distaste.

"He was giving us advice on when not to approach him," Linh continued. "Why the sudden change of heart?"

"It is not your war," Jaygoff explained. "I did not understand who you were when we met in Queen Ziline's palace. I believed you were friends of Heir Ruarnon. You probably knew and wanted to help them recover their parents. But you *aren't* from Umarinaris. He told me. He explained about the inspirations for his reforms."

Jaygoff's voice wavered. "It wasn't just his wishes or ideas. He has learnt so much from you. But at great cost to your safety. And now you are in more danger than ever."

"He's not going to let anyone hurt us, is he?" Troy asked.

Joygoff sighed and his shoulders heaved. "An attack party approaches the throne room. Should his mind crack at the wrong time… He does not want to risk you. You have done so much already. He says he has robbed you for long enough. That I must send you home."

"Robbed?" Troy asked.

"Our families," Michael said slowly. "Narz has only one living blood relative. But we've all got quite a few. And they haven't seen us for over a year and won't know if we're alive or dead."

"But," said Fiona, "if he can care about four lost teenagers, when everyone he loves and everything he cares about could be moments from total destruction by the God Kings…" Tears shone in Fiona's eyes. "He cares *too* much. Don't you see that could destroy him? That's *why* Queen Ziliene said he can't handle his guilt. He does what he believes is necessary to protect everyone, but he *cares* about people. All the people his actions have harmed… it must be tearing him apart!"

Troy gaped. "A villain who has hurt *hundreds* of people because they're so scared they can't tell enemies and bystanders apart, then feels guilty about it? He's going to lose it, isn't he? Completely? *That's* why he wants to send us away."

Linh agreed.

Jaygoff's face was draining of colour. "My brother is by his side. I will return to him. Teliph will come if he needs her. This is our struggle. Everyone who follows him, who believes in his vision, will support him to deal with his guilt at those he has wronged. He is our leader. He is building our future. And we *will* stand by him to whatever end. But you have given enough. He does not want to take more from you."

"How can he send us home?" Troy asked.

Jaygoff gestured. The air behind him rippled. The empty corridor teamed with magic, revealing a stone archway, carved with a familiar script. A dozen young Keepers stood around it, their faces pale, but determined. Men, women and gender ambiguous people, they all seemed to accept Jaygoff's words, and were committed to following Narz.

"But you don't know how to… did Red Cloak teach you?" Michael asked.

Jaygoff grimaced and turned to the archway. The other Keepers held hands and magic pulsated around them in waves. The script in the archway glowed golden. It didn't lead to more vast, brown crystal corridors. Waves washed onto a deserted beach. Silver backed banksia leaves rustled in the wind. A voice that made Michael stumble, and his eyes fill with tears called, "Mi-chael! Where did Troy lead you lot?"

Troy gaped between Michael and the archway. "Is that really…?"

A tear ran down Michael's face. Troy wrapped an arm around him.

"Narz has his followers and supporters. Go back to your lives," Jaygoff said quietly.

The smell of salt and faint scent of eucalypt gums blew through the archway on the sea breeze. Nostalgia crashed over Linh, as the smell, feel, sights and sounds of home washed over her. A powerful longing to return to everything so familiar, so comfortable, to everyone she was missing rose in her.

But she had heard words like 'it isn't your fight' before. Lenaris had said it when they wanted to accompany Ruarnon to the Zaldeaan Realm. But Linh and her friends had gone. Not just because Linh feared Ruarnon's advisors would prioritise Tarlah over the lives of defenceless Zaldeaans under siege by damars, but because her friends could be true friends to Ruarnon. Not subjects, nor Tarlahns. They could impartially speak about what they thought was right. No one could do that for Narz.

"He needs someone to tell him exactly what they see, as a friend," she said. "Not subjects, not part of his vision, not people he fears for and is straining under the burden of protecting. People who can say to him what they think is right, and that's all he'll hear or perceive from them.

"His mind is falling apart. He needs clarity. Clarity free of worry, fear and guilt. The kind of clarity he had when he dreamed himself to us. If he doesn't have that when he meets Elite Guard, or the Divine Army, he could destroy himself. And if he falls, everyone depending upon him falls with him. I won't let that happen."

Michael wiped his eyes. "This means he *can* send us back. And he can do it after we stop him from destroying everything he's built. We're staying."

Fiona smiled sadly at him.

Michael smiled through his tears. "Andy won't love me any less for making him wait. It's not like I didn't wait forever before he realised he wasn't just interested in girls."

"We're staying," Troy told Jaygoff.

The Keepers around the archway, most of whom had broken into a sweat or were pale from the strain of keeping the Gateway of Umarinaris open, turned to each other in worry. Then they turned to Jaygoff.

Jaygoff drew a deep breath. "I will not tell him now if I can help it. He will be upset, if he remembers where he sent me and why. He may be confused when you meet him. I will try to signal whether to approach him or not. Or Teliph will do so. May the Old Gods return with you."

Linh wasn't sure of the exact meaning of that last, but its general one was clear.

"Look after your brother, and the Keepers," said Fiona.

Jaygoff bowed his head. Then everything blurred, Linh's stomach lurched, and she shut her eyes. When she opened them, Mawana cried out.

"Thank the Ancestors," Lenaris breathed.

"Are you four ok?" Ruarnon asked.

Her friends, Tor, Coroth and Captain Rilmar stood before them, while Tarlahn and Zaldeaan guards tightened ranks around them.

"Narz just tried to send us home," Michael announced. "He thinks he's about to crack big time and didn't want us killed by Divine Soldiers while he lost it. We're staying to help him keep it together."

Ruarnon eyed Michael. Michael's bottom lip trembled. "Andy can wait a little longer."

Ruarnon smiled sadly, then inclined their head. "Thank you. I never thought there would be a question of me acting as catalyst for peace on my own. But there wasn't really, because of your choice. I appreciate you all more than you know."

Linh's features softened and she smiled.

Then Ruarnon's face firmed, as they became the indomitable regent again and said, "Let's make haste."

It was time to save Narz from himself.

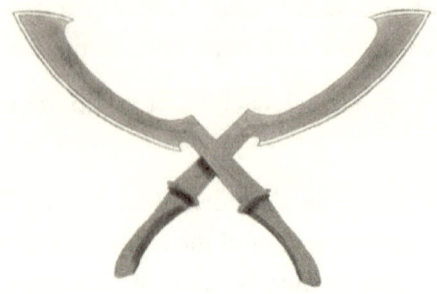

CHAPTER 38

THE MAN WHO WAITED SIX HUNDRED YEARS - RUARNON

Ruarnon's bodyguards positioned themselves in front, but Ruarnon strode around them. The guards magic craft wasn't strong enough to bear the brunt of what lay ahead.

"Stay back Benevolence," said Tor. "If all goes wrong; you are all to flee. I would have you go with them, Captain," he added to Captain Arleath, whose eyes widened, but who bowed his head.

It was Ruarnon's duty… but Tor's face was closed. He was mutely asking Ruarnon to respect his right to buy everyone a moment to save them from unforeseeable magical attack if they were struck first on entering the throne room. Captain Rilmar –but she had been overcome once already.

A lump rose in Ruarnon's throat. They inclined their head and Tor took the lead as everyone marched on. Faint cries sounded in the distance. The ground rocked as they crossed the next intersection of corridors. But from ahead came silence. An endless corridor stretched before them. It flickered, and for a second the wall on the left was crooked. Then the flicker stabilised, and the wall was straight.

"This is the heart of the castle," said Captain Rilmar. "I cannot tell the empty hallway illusion apart from shifting magic around us, but great power lies beyond that illusion, such as I have never felt before."

"The throne room?" Ruarnon asked quietly and Captain Rilmar inclined her head.

Tor strode forwards and disappeared. Ruarnon's stomach lurched, and they halted, trying not to track how long Tor was absent by the beat of the heart, because it was many beats already.

Tor stepped back into sight. Ruarnon exhaled deeply.

"The hallway ends shortly after the illusion," Tor reported. "King Narz sits atop a dais on the left-hand side, watching a struggle against a magical shield blocking a corridor opposite his throne. He is surrounded by Keepers and Lord Vye stands at his left side. One of the Keepers saw me, but merely bowed his head as I walked away."

"Teliph?" Coroth asked anxiously.

Tor shook his head and Coroth paled.

"Jaygoff said he or Teliph would signal when to enter," said Linh. "And Narz warned us. He's much more dangerous when he's awake. He said not to approach him then."

Lenaris tensed. Ruarnon scanned the corridor for the threat. A red cloaked Keeper walked towards them.

"Lord Coroth," the man said with a bow. "Lady Teliph sent this for you."

He offered Coroth a papyrus scroll, which Coroth took, saying, "Thank you Mayard. She is hidden?"

The man bowed his head. Coroth bowed back and Mayard turned and disappeared through the illusion.

Coroth read the note aloud; "Act now. Only Mayard will see you until you enter. I have prepared for you."

Ruarnon frowned.

"Mayard is a personal bodyguard of Teliph and King Narz," Coroth explained. "Teliph trusts him. I suspect she has crafted an illusion of empty corridor at the bottom of the steps. No one in the throne room will see us unless we step off the stairs, in case his mood changes and we need to retreat in a hurry."

"Won't the sorcerers sense her illusion?" Michael asked.

"They are preoccupied maintaining the shield preventing a Divine Soldier attack party from entering the throne room," said Tor. "Though something tells me Narz will detect the shield. But what if that message is fake?"

"Lord Vye would have sent an imposter with a misleading verbal message, being disdainful of non-magical means, like letters," Coroth replied.

Ruarnon straightened their back, thought of calm, measured control and became it, as Omah had once done, and followed Tor and their guards' forwards. They kept their breathing steady and tried to ignore the nervous tingling all over their body. Or was that magic? It grew stronger as they moved forwards; magic, but more subtle than they anticipated.

Tor and their guards disappeared before them. Then Ruarnon stood before a wide archway and a flight of steps leading down into a large, round room, the walls of which shone pearlescent, as though constructed from dense shield magic. Multiple archways lay at different heights around the room's pearlescent walls, stairs leading up or down to them from the throne room floor. Light flashed behind a section of wall on their right, lightning striking the far side of a shield; Divine Soldiers trying to get in.

Opposite the flashes rose a broad marble dais. On its every step stood five Keepers on both sides of a blue carpet, standing to attention, a pale faced Jaygoff among them. The blue carpet climbed up to a throne of blues, blacks and whites, carved and polished from solid opal. Solid silver emanated from the back of the throne, like rays of power.

King Narz sat beneath those rays, wearing a coronet constructed of sapphires, bound by silver into multiple swirling lines gracefully entwining his dark-haired head. His posture beneath his dark blue silks was still, his figure tall and proud. His face was ageless, the weathered skin soft, yet deeply lined round the eyes, the brow etched with frown lines, the mouth and edge of the eyes containing hints of smile lines. The blue eyes were dull whirlpools of pain and control, the posture regal enough to take Ruarnon's breath away.

"That's Red Cloak," Fiona whispered.

Her three friends stared. Narz had brought them here *personally*... and abandoned them without a word... because he was the greatest and most terrible sorcerer on Umarinaris. In those whirlpools-of-pain-eyes was a suppressed edge of awareness; Narz knew it. He hadn't wanted to frighten them.

Lord Vye stood tall and proud on King Narz's left, the hard edges of his face reflecting faint flashes of sorcery. His lips hinted at a smile as he eyed attacks on the shield, anticipating a battle that would see the Keepers around him and King Narz slain. From his gaze, it was impossible to gauge whether Narz saw treachery written across his Second's face.

Footsteps sounded in the quiet room, as Captain Melroth ascended stairs opposite Ruarnon, and looked right through them until he reached the dais, then turned to King Narz.

"Your Keepers have served bravely Captain Melroth," King Narz observed. "Stand them down."

"But Sire; the Divine Assassins!" Captain Melroth protested, his face tightening with worry.

"Will have insufficient time to realise what fools they are," King Narz replied.

"Keepers, down shields," Captain Melroth ordered, his voice steady, fingers trembling at his sides, his right hand reaching for a bronze sheened iron sword at his right hip, Jaygoff nodding reassuringly at his brother.

The shield opposite the dais fell.

Ruarnon froze.

Shards of ice flashed towards the dais. They flipped, reversed and sped back, plunging into gold masked, gold silk clad figures standing in the hallway, piercing pearly white shields of their clothes. It happened so swiftly that not one assassin made a sound. They went limp, like puppets whose strings had been cut, then collapsed, lying dead on the floor; all twenty or so of them.

Ruarnon gaped. Lord Vye's knees buckled. Then he moaned. Wind rippled Keeper's red silks and cloaks, blowing back and forth across the dais, as Vye floated off it towards the floor, his limbs splayed. The tinniest movement of his mouth and wrists hinted that he was trying to struggle, and his face paled in horror, when his struggles accomplished nothing. Vye had demonstrated his power to kill all Ruarnon's companions in an instant in the Forbidden Mountains, but in King Narz's grip; *he* was powerless.

"Five hundred and twenty-four Zaldeaans," Narz said slowly, as Lord Vye cried out. "Men. Women. Midluns. Children. How silly do you believe I am?"

The parts of Lord Vye that could move began to tremble.

"Why doesn't he use magic?" Troy whispered.

Michael's mouth opened in surprise. "He thinks he can't. Look at him; he's trying. That's not just pain on his face; its fear."

Several Keepers shuddered, as Vye cried out, his limbs twitched and jerked, sweat pouring down his agonised face. Then his cries cut off. Vye gasped for breath and the parts of him that could move continued to tremble.

"They were stubborn Greatness," Vye said weakly. "Too preoccupied with their war on Tarlah too -Aahh!"

Lord Vye's jaw snapped.

"Do not lie to me. For hundreds of years I have watched worms like you lie to themselves, claiming to be gods, using and abusing their subjects without mercy."

Vye cried out again, as an invisible force pulsated against him and he tensed in a futile struggle against it. Ruarnon gaped. If anyone deserved to suffer like that; Vye did. But witnessing it wasn't pleasant.

"You are in no way more intelligent or worthy of life, than a peacock," Narz continued. "Your family live lives that span centuries, yet you failed to recognise that I am far older than all of you. I was first to discover the enchantment that runs in your bloodline. I watched from afar, as your ancestors withdrew their invasion from the north, hiding behind gold leaf gates in kingdoms they would transform into slave empires. And I vowed that I would not rest until I obliterated their dynasties."

"What could you have accomplished?" Vye whispered, with a weak, sarcastic smile, his voice amplified by the acoustics of the strangely shaped throne room.

"Not very fertile are they; your family?" King Narz replied.

Vye paled.

"No full blooded, so-called divine arrivals for two centuries, I believe?"

"You *sterilised* the royal line?" Vye asked, gaping.

"I spent my third century of life in your slave empire and half of my forth. It took much time to meet and befriend your dear aunt Tirisium. Her sympathies for ordinary folk were known even then. And when I told her of my aunt's kingdom, of sorcerers and non-magic wielders living with equal status, of merit and ability determining rank, not a perverse sense of entitlement, she saw her family more clearly than ever.

"She saw beyond the injustice of a woman banished to her chambers and kept out of public life for however many centuries she lived because of her gender, beyond the casual cruelty the guards and servants she came across encountered so regularly, and so began our alliance; with the sterilisation of the misnamed Divine Royal Family.

"But the next stage of our alliance took far longer than either of us hoped. The best way to kill the God Kings was treachery from within. It took Tirisium and I many years to cultivate allies; sorcerers and commoners alike, and to commence our work killing off your family. The delay allowed us to spread our beliefs and cultivate followers far and wide. It also, unfortunately, perpetuated your life to this moment."

Vye flinched, his eyes wide and confused.

"Tirisium told me not quarter of a bell ago that your Uncle's Dugarth, Chyramun, Kasikus and Dramoor hide amidst the illusion magic that conceals the Sun Chamber. My four greatest enemies on this continent have gathered to discuss how best to counter me, when your treachery fails. They are meeting in the one place they feel safe and confident, because none of their enemies possess the knowledge of how to locate them. The best place to kill them all. Tirisium is waiting."

Vye shivered, as light shone beside the dais, revealing a woman in blue silks, whose iron hair was softened by kind blue eyes and whose posture hinted at command, standing amid a large, open, polished rock cut room.

"Tell her how to enter the chamber," King Narz demanded.

"Aunt," Vye said faintly, his neck bent to see her better, his gaze horrified and neck twitching, but Narz wasn't letting him turn away.

"I have no use for your hands Vye," King Narz continued calmly. "Nor for your feet, arms or legs. I require only your capacity for speech and yes; I despise you that much. Tell her."

Vye cowered. "A sorcerer's touch on the First King's crown in the throne room opens the main passage," Vye whispered.

He started, as Tirisium turned, and the portal through which they viewed her moved up an ornate golden dais as she climbed, then reached for the gold leaf crown in a fresco behind the throne. The wall vanished. Tirisium beckoned, and a group of servants in grey bowed low, then hurried ahead of her, carrying trays of meats, fruits and a silver wine jug.

Ruarnon frowned, as the group moved down a narrow mud-brick passageway, which split into six different passages opening off a central point.

"Turn back the way you came," Vye rasped.

King Narz's mouth fell open and Ruarnon wondered if that secret had thwarted another attempt to reach the Sun Chamber.

Tirisium frowned, then walked backwards. Male voices drifted down the hallway. An arched entrance rose on the right and flickered, a spell or illusion. Tirisium halted before it. The servants walked on, and Ruarnon's heart began to pound.

Tirisium stepped into the arch. For a moment, time froze. Ruarnon stared at four shocked, heavily bearded faces turning to Tirisium, then blanching at King Narz sitting in his throne behind her. Their gold-plated armour shone with the sheen of defensive magic, as did their glittering, jewel studded crowns. Which availed them not at all, as serving trays and a wine jug crashed to the ground, and bronze-iron sheened weapons in the hands of supposed servants slit their throats.

Lord Vye wailed and whimpered, as fake-servants lifted four limp, ostentatiously dressed forms and carried them before Tirisium, back out the secret passage, across the throne room, then down a colonnaded approach to a large courtyard. Silk clad figures froze under colonnaded, sheltered walkways around the courtyard, staring, as blue clad servants ran forwards and set up four camp tables, on which the four bodies were laid.

The air before Tirisium thrummed with a deep horn, and silk and linen-clad figures alike rushed into the courtyard, some abandoning shoes or scarves that fell off in their haste. On three sides of the courtyard, a line of shocked figures froze mid-step, staring.

"The God Kings are not Gods," Tirisium announced, her voice clear and carrying. "They are men. Look upon them. Touch them if you dare. Four of them are dead. The fifth marches to his doom. The reign of the God Kings is ended."

The courtiers parted, as men in bronze armour pushed through the crowd. At least a dozen courtiers didn't look shocked, but were beaming at Tirisium with barely contained joy; her followers.

One of the guards halted before the dead kings, drew a deep breath, then rammed his spear point into the neck of the nearest king. Thickened blood oozed out and the body didn't otherwise move. The guard smiled.

"Try the others!" he ordered.

Three more guards, each armed with spears, stepped forwards, each stabbing a king forcefully in the neck.

"They're not taking chances," Troy whispered.

"The TYRANTS ARE DEAD!" the lead guard screamed.

Ruarnon waited for the crowd to react. But many stared in disbelief or stood numb with shock. The dozen who had smiled at Tirisium began to cheer, and more and more faces became wonderstruck, others coming forwards by ones and twos and poking the king's hesitantly, to prove it to themselves. Then the cheering slowly spread, until almost everyone was shouting.

A few richly dressed people didn't look pleased, particularly the ones wearing vests constructed from jewels and precious metals. Tirisium nodded to them, and guards seized them, presumably arresting the God Kings' supporters.

When the prisoners had been carried away, and many surprised people looked through the portal at King Narz, silence fell and Tirisium spoke. "The reign of the God Kings is ended. I am a mortal Queen, if a long lived one."

"The Mortal Queen! Long live the Mortal Queen!"

The crowd took up the chant, and Tirisium used the interim to give orders to the guards, "Release every political prisoner. Free all Divine Soldiers who do wish to serve me as such, and have the Divine Assassins meet me in the Chamber of the Moon."

"Who is behind her Grace?" a voice cried. "Those men and women wear red Keeper's cloaks!"

Tirisium turned back to smile at King Narz, then replied, "My first act as Empress of the South will be to invite Healers to attend the areas ravaged by plague, and to welcome Keepers to train my City Guard. There will be peace and open relations with the North."

Ruarnon stared. This time it was the grey cloaked servants in the crowd who cheered the loudest.

"I shall travel north to meet with King King Narz after my coronation."

She bowed her head to Narz and then the portal through which they had viewed her vanished.

Tears welled in Narz's eyes and began to run down his cheeks. "Peace," he said. "At last. The worst of the God Kings dead; their tyranny ended. I have waited so long!" and his smile widened, as more tears ran down his face.

Mawana flinched. Narz was no longer restraining Vye, who slowly stood, his face burning with hatred as he raised his right hand, and Narz continued to smile at a distant happy sight only he could see.

Captain Melroth stepped behind Narz's throne. He thrust his bronze-iron sheened sword upwards, through Vye's chest. Vye froze, the lightning forming above his hand vanishing. Melroth twisted the blade and Vye gurgled, blood running down his chin. Captain Melroth withdrew the blade and Vye crumpled, blood pooling around his mouth and chest.

Narz did not seem to notice. He was still smiling, tears of joy shinning in his eyes, his face looking impossibly youthful, as he gazed into the distance.

"Captain Melroth," Narz said softly.

Captain Melroth cleaned his blade on Vye's tunic, then knelt before his king, saying; "Yes Beneficence?"

"Where is Teliph? She must know our good news!"

"I shall fetch her Sire," Captain Melroth replied, his tone softened, as though someone had knocked the wind out of him. His gaze lingered on King Narz for a moment before he turned and walked towards a passageway where Teliph stood, motioning Ruarnon to stay where they were.

Narz sniffed, blinking away more tears and sat up a little straighter. The effect made him look ten years older, a young man now, instead of the youth he had been only a moment ago. All the while the Keepers, including Jaygoff, focused on the entranceway the Divine Assassins had been slain in, or the one on its right, standing rigidly, their gazes concerned or unreadable.

"Teliph!" King Narz cried, his voice high pitched with joy, as Teliph entered the room with Captain Melroth and both stepped before him. "Our plan worked! The one I was too worried to tell you about in case it failed! The God Kings are all but defeated!"

"Beneficence, Lord Vye planned treachery," Captain Melroth warned.

"Yes," King Narz replied, his voice still unnaturally high. Then he took a deep breath, straightening, composing himself, and said more deeply, "His brother, the last God King will he here soon. Send every Keeper in the castle to the throne room. Lord Vye's traitors will have let the Divine Army into our castle by now. I will destroy them."

His face hardened, his eyes grew cold, focused on a distant point no one else could see, and Ruarnon shivered, fearing Narz's outburst against Vye was only the beginning of his temper.

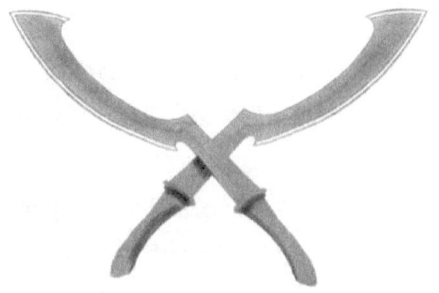

CHAPTER 39

WAR IN THE HEART OF THE CASTLE -RUARNON

We can't wait until the Divine Army arrives," Linh insisted.

"He will not hear you while he prepares to defend against them," said Coroth. "And should he take your arrival poorly, it may leave him defenceless against the Divine Army. We must wait."

Cold raked its way through Ruarnon's core. It was a terrible gamble. From what Ruarnon had seen, the Divine Army could kill everyone in the room before them, if Narz didn't aid his Keepers. They couldn't risk incapacitating him.

"Coroth is right," said Ruarnon. "You saw his outburst about the Zaldeaans. Sight of me as their king could destabilize him. And with his magic, we cannot force him to listen. And he has already changed his mind about your four and shown an interest in your safety. Your rushing into danger could distract him while he is killed."

"And then the Divine Army could kill us all," Troy said dully, his gaze on the ground. "Why did the most powerful person in that room have to be the frailest?"

"Because everyone he's lost is what drives him to protect everyone he now has," Fiona replied. "Everything he saw broken in the Sorcery War is what made him want to fix the world. And surviving that war taught him to survive anything and made him unstoppable, as well as the deeply scarred, flawed person he is."

Ruarnon sighed. Narz was impossibly strong, and incredibly weak. He teetered precariously between the two. Ruarnon fiercely hoped they balanced Narz the right way, at the right time. Not doing so would be catastrophic.

The scene before them had changed. The Keepers on the dais and King Narz stared at a section of magic shield barring a corridor right of the passage Ruarnon and their friends hid in. The shield vanished, revealing deep red cloaked sorcerers who halted suddenly, on sighting Captain Melroth and Jaygoff removing Vye's body from the dais.

"You were trained to *defend* this kingdom!" King Narz accused.

Small specks of light appeared around him. They crackled.

"NOT TO SET A TYRANT ON MY THRONE!" Narz roared.

Wind ruffled Keeper clothing on the dais. Storm clouds built above King Narz's head, small bolts of lightning crackling between them. Narz seemed oblivious to it.

"My Lord, that is our intent!" a man cried, descending the steps and kneeling. A dozen others followed him and knelt, but the corridor was crowded, and many sorcerers hesitated.

Captain Melroth nodded to Jaygoff. They deposited Vye's body unceremoniously against the wall and the captain ran to the dais, climbing the blue carpeted steps, while Jaygoof resumed his place among a row of Keepers.

King Narz raised a hand and Captain Melroth halted suddenly. Narz's gaze cut above the frightened sorcerers, piercing the corridor. Sorcerers jumped and flinched as though he had touched them.

"A Divine Army marches on this throne room," King Narz announced. "Their king would take control of this entire continent. Will you allow them to do so?"

"But Lord Vye said-"

"The TRAITOR IS *DEAD*! Captain Melroth was more merciful than I would have been. Will you defend your people?"

Several tens of men hurried down the steps, kneeling behind their comrades. A dozen hesitated. Greed curved their smiles and ambition glowed in their eyes. They intended to join forces with Divine Soldiers, in exchange for rich rewards.

Light flared before King Narz and the kneeling sorcerers bent low. Sorcerers in the corridor were incinerated, walls beside them melted, the stone floor that caught their ashes cracking from the heat.

Captain Melroth shivered and Teliph stared, motionless, her gaze troubled and calculating. Coroth took a step forward, then stopped, his face creased in frustration that he couldn't risk exposing everyone else's presence by approaching her.

"So treason is purged from our midst," said King Narz, anger burning in his eyes. But there was something darker there, something wilder. Those were *his* sorcerer-soldiers. He had counted on them to protect ordinary people from the slavery of a God King, and they had betrayed him. Twitches of his face hinted at his pain, but anger had taken him over and the dark wildness in his eyes remained.

Captain Melroth stirred, but Narz looked past him and the Keeper Captain seemed unable to step any closer.

"Why do you keep looking to the corridor Teliph?" Narz asked, his tone level, his gaze full of suspicion.

Ruarnon shivered at the speed with which he had snapped back to alert perception.

"If Coroth is hiding there," Narz deduced, "it is not safe for him, and he should go."

Teliph closed her mouth and said nothing.

"He is not alone?" Narz asked, his eyes widening. "Who else have you brought here? Why?"

"I don't like this," whispered Fiona. "He *knows* all of us are here. He *helped* four of us get here. Why doesn't he remember?"

"His suspicion will only increase if we delay," Coroth replied.

"Father, I would introduce you to my lover's cousin," Teliph announced.

Narz's features softened. "The youth has come to claim their parents!" he said softly. "And they are safe, but Ruarnon is in danger here. I shall see them later, after the battle. Tell them."

Ruarnon shivered. Narz spoke warmly of them, and knew and used their pronouns with ease, as if he *knew* Ruarnon.

Teliph climbed the steps before Ruarnon, her features strained, while Captain Melroth advanced to King Narz's right side, the spell that had restrained him broken.

"And Teliph," Narz added, gazing at air across his throne room, "keep yourself safe. If we lose you; everything will be lost."

The hardness was gone from his face. His features were stern, except his eyes, which softened, looking almost sad, hinting at worry.

Captain Melroth eyed Narz with concern. The wildness behind Narz's eyes came to the fore and he clenched his jaw and hands, breathing deeply. The wildness retreated, but his face hardened again.

"We're going to watch Narz fight a *God King*?" Troy whispered.

"The safest place in the castle is where we now stand," said Teliph. "The protective enchantments upon me are such that I might survive being thrown off a cliff, onto a rocky shore. And they extend to anyone near me, for whom I have any regard; which is all of you.

"He has some fixation with your parents," she added, turning to Ruarnon. "Family is more precious to him than life itself. As am I, I suspect. But the fact he has deprived you of your parents for so long, and his guilt in doing so for selfish reasons may destabilise him. Be prepared to walk away if your presence upsets him, to leave the negotiations to your friends."

She turned, her features twisting with worry. "Captain Rilmar, I do not know if it will be safe for you to meet him. It is too late to show him the weapon."

Fiona's eyes widened.

"He saw it," Linh told her. "When he was dreaming. He concealed it from himself with illusion magic. I forgot."

Teliph trembled, then frowned. "He *dreamt* himself to you?"

"To four of us," Linh replied. "He healed Troy's broken ankle and helped us get around the corridor defence we fell behind, when the floor and ceiling crushed together."

Ruarnon could almost hear calculations clicking together in Teliph's mind. "Then it must be you who speaks to him. Give that to me."

Fiona bit her lip, but at Linh's nod, and Ruarnon's, she unbuckled the weapon and passed it to Teliph.

Teliph reached towards the wall, and it peeled away, allowing her to deposit the weapon inside, then crystal resolidified, concealing the weapon.

"How did you do that?" Ruarnon asked.

"The walls contain more magic particles than most substances on Umarinaris. They are not as difficult to shape as solid objects."

"Could Narz's enemies retrieve it from there?" Ruarnon wondered.

"The enchantment on the weapon is weaker than defensive enchantments in these walls. Only in peace time, under no pressure, could a powerful and talented sorcerer locate it."

Ruarnon inclined their head. So the weapon couldn't undermine Narz and it wouldn't help. But Narz himself had confirmed he would speak to Linh, Fiona, Michael and Troy.

White shield wall flashed and vanished, diagonally right of the corridor in which Ruarnon and their companions hid.

A Keeper ran forwards. "They are coming Sire! The Dedicated evacuated the Keepers and Protectors. The Priests and Priestesses are overwhelmed trying to contain the damars. The whole Divine Army marches freely up the hillside."

Narz sighed, but his reply was firm. "Tell the High Priest the traitor Vye is dead. Ask him to take control of the damars."

The Keeper bowed and ran back down the corridor.

"Target only individuals who break away," Narz ordered the Keepers around him. "Target their main force," he ordered the sorcerers-soldiers, who bowed, then moved against the wall beside the dais.

"I shall make it easy for you, and expose the vermin," Narz added.

He focused on the melted walls and ashes of the traitorous sorcerers in the corridor opposite, making Ruarnon wonder if those were the traitors who had let the Divine Army in.

Crystal walls gleamed brightly, in unnatural rainbows. A deep cracking gave way to high-pitched tinkling as walls exploded. The floor and walls across the throne room shook, as did the corridor Ruarnon stood in. Exploding walls burst into glittering dust along a semicircle edge of throne room wider than the corridor.

When the dust settled, a vast stretch of brown stone floor was exposed, at multiple levels. Brown crystal walls cut off abruptly, exposing a long column of figures in silver robes and gold masks, marching down the far end of the ruined corridor.

"The enemy have come!"

The cry came from above.

Brown silk-clothed watchers lined a floor level ending abruptly above the destroyed corridor, down which the Divine Army halted. The watchers' faces were no longer devoid of emotion. Wild happiness flared on some, while others' features twisted, and their eyes burned with hatred. More features set in grim determination.

"You will fight, soldiers?" Narz asked, his voice projected across the room and up into the air.

"Aye Liberator!" a man yelled. "What fortune that you could steal us here to take our revenge the moment the enchantment broke. Did you kill the God Kings?"

"I arranged their deaths," King Narz replied.

"Some of our comrades remain trapped."

"There is one God King yet alive. If Fortune smiles upon us; he approaches in that column."

"And will your Beneficence hold it against us if we claim the pleasure of killing him ourselves?"

King Narz smiled grimly. "I shall not. May Fortune smile upon you soldier."

"And on you Sire!" the man replied, as the former watchers pushed powerbows to the edge of their floors, cranking back ratchets and loading iron bolts.

"Who *are* those people?" Troy asked.

Teliph sighed. "Rebels against the Divine Order. The God Kings slew their families before them, then cursed them to watch the murders over and over, and made those men like statues, unable to express their feelings as they watched their families die."

Coroth frowned at her. "How do you know?"

"I have looked into their minds. They told me. When Tirisium had her assassins kill the God Kings, the enchantments binding them broke."

"They're not sorcerers, are they?" Michael asked.

Teliph shook her head. "They have suffered decades of torture. Now they seek revenge. They will kill as many Divine Soldiers as they can and find freedom in death."

"In death?" Coroth asked.

Teliph sighed. "Most of their minds are irreparably broken. Revenge is the only reason they are responding to what is happening here and now. I suspect a few would have thrown themselves off the castle cliff if the chance to avenge their loved ones hadn't instantly presented itself."

Ruarnon shivered. A small army of mad power bow operators bent on selling their lives dearly, killing as many Divine Soldiers as they could… What monstrosity were the Divine Realms, to produce men like these?

"Let's kill the bastards! Fire!" the watcher Captain cried gleefully.

Iron power bow bolts hurtled down from the split upper floor, punching through shield magic and bronze armour, staggering or toppling the front line of the Divine Army. Magical shields materialised before the former watchers as they reloaded their power bows, but their captain called, "Save your magic and give your kiddies a hug and your wives a kiss from us!"

"Respect his wishes," Narz ordered, and the shields vanished.

Fire flared around several power bows. Burning men continued cranking bolts, hammering triggers and released a second volley of power bow bolts, as if they couldn't feel the bite of the flames.

A dome shield flared before the Divine Army. Bolts bristled against it.

"Down the end burning lads!" the watcher captain cried.

Ruarnon stared. Human torches seized spears and sprinted along the top floor of the castle. They thrust their spears forwards and hurled themselves at the dome shield. Several men struck the shield with distant thuds, sliding down it, but three groups hit together and crashed through.

Above and before them, power bows adjusted and reloaded, taking aim at holes in the shields. Watchers cranked bows back along ratchets, loaded bolts, pounded triggers and cackled as their bolts shot into holes in the shield.

"Narz trained them to use power bows? Despite their curse?" Ruarnon asked.

Teliph sighed. "His skill with magic surpasses any sorcerer I have studied, including those about whom histories survive from the Sorcery War."

Lightning flashed upwards. Some former watchers hurled themselves at the dome shield, others were too far away.

"Take them out for me Liberator!" their captain cried.

"I will Captain," Narz promised.

Tens of lightning bolts struck the top floor, which shattered into shards and sprays of crystal, throwing power bows, cracked stone floor and bodies to the level below. Some bodies flew towards ground level and Keepers appeared, the bodies drifting towards them and vanishing.

The former watchers were dead, and the Divine Army wasn't yet within magical range of the throne room. Ruarnon's heart pounded out of control

Narz's face twitched, his eyes alight with rage and a vein pulsed in his neck. The storm clouds above him grew darker than ever, building until they filled the ceiling and crackled with lightning.

Ruarnon's body tingled as if magic within them was having a fit. Their friends clenched jaws, or hugged themselves and Keepers shivered, Captain Melroth gazing nervously from Keepers to king.

Narz screamed. A bright bolt blinded Ruarnon as it shot towards the Divine Army.

When spots of colour before Ruarnon's eyes cleared, a pile of ashes, half-melted masks and charred armour lay before a reduced, shield-less Divine Army.

The scene froze. Keepers stared in awe. Deep red cloaked sorcerers positioned to attack the silver column. Silver cloaked soldiers stood exposed.

Sections of shield flared. Commands were shouted along the silver column and its dome shield reformed. More silver cloaked squads ran around the main column, crafting separate dome shields and advancing, filling space created by Narz's destruction of the walls.

"Now!" the deep red cloaked captain cried.

The throne room's edge, destroyed walls either side and the corridor dazzled with lightning. Bright bursts pelted the silver column. Its dome was showered in sparks.

Three lightning bolts soared out and rose toward Narz. They arced mid-flight, striking small silver shields in the corridor, penetrating them instantly, leaving only charred dents in the floor.

Lightning flashed and struck sorcerer-soldier shields, as more Divine Squads entered the throne room. Silver moved upwards, and lightning flashed down from on high.

Ruarnon gaped. Silver cloaked figures relinquished dome shields in the gaping corridor and took flight. Gold-masked figures soared above and looped around sorcerer-soldiers. They twitched aside from lightning bolts and bursts of fire. Then they hurled lightning that produced screams as it penetrated sorcerer-soldier shields.

So they did resemble gods, in more than one way…

"Shields!" Captain Melroth barked, the line of his mouth set in grim determination.

Keepers tensed, and sorcerer-soldier shields were reinforced. But the flying figures moved with speed and grace, dodging attacks. Lightning flashed at silver figures soaring overhead and rained back down to burst against Keeper shields. Multiple bolts lanced out from King Narz, striking a dozen flying silver figures sideways, but King Narz's gaze was fixed on three larger dome shields thirty paces away.

A large lightning bolt soared over the sorcerer-soldiers, towards the silver column. When the spots blinding Ruarnon faded, dust rained from where divine soldiers had flown into its path, and dust and melted armour scattered the floor at the head of the silver column. This time; the damage was limited to the middle. Soldiers either side shifted to close ranks, reformed their shield and came on.

King Narz's power had limits and the God King was content sacrificing his soldiers …

"There's a God King inside that, isn't there?" asked Troy. "And he's using his soldiers as human shields, the bastard."

"Why don't they use the invisibility spell?" Fiona asked. "Or an illusion? Why advance in plain sight, where Narz can pick them off?"

"They were," Teliph replied. "When King Narz destroyed the walls; the enchanted wall fragments shredded their illusion. They probably can't sustain it *and* their shields against such attacks."

The dome shield above the silver column warped and moved forwards as one. Shouts rose. Soldiers beneath it were running.

"Benevolence, we should retreat," Tor advised.

"Our best defence is Teliph's defence," said Ruarnon. "And she is not going anywhere."

Mawana stepped protectively beside their four friends and Lenaris shifted to Ruarnon's other side. Their magic stirred around them, shields ready to form if needed, as they braced to reinforce Teliph's enchantment against chaos.

Lightning surged towards King Narz from all directions. Bolts turned back, blasting flying silver clad figures into the air, or redirected to shower the oncoming Divine Army's shield with sparks.

Captain Melroth and his Keepers looked on in awe. It was all Narz, with sorcerer-soldiers fighting two small attack parties.

A crash rent the room. Narz struck the silver column with a second, brilliant white bolt. Men screamed. White blinded everyone. Dust and shards of glittering brown wall gusted. Bolts of lightning shot out.

Footsteps thudded. Divine soldiers still approached.

Narz's depleted sorcerer-soldiers, down at least a dozen men, were in trouble.

"Shield wall!" Captain Melroth commanded, and Keepers began to sweat as a shield wall formed before the sorcerer-soldiers. Bolts of lightning glanced off at odd angles, some striking screaming figures overhead. Shield flashed before Teliph, deflecting a stray bolt.

Silver-clad figures emerged from the glittery rain. Several were blasted into the air. The rest formed two groups. Lightning rebounded off shield domes over each. Many charred figures were exposed on the ground as they advanced, but more soldiers rushed down the gaping hallway.

Ruarnon tensed, as stray rubble bounced harmlessly off the invisible shield before Teliph. Keepers on their left cried out and leapt aside, as chunks of marble blasted outwards from the dais.

The remaining sorcerer-soldiers huddled under one shield dome. Keepers screamed and leapt, as the far side of the marble dais exploded.

King Narz's eyes blazed, oblivious to flying figures assaulting shields of his people around the throne room. Fire balls and lightning hurled towards him. They turned to smoke and empty air, ten paces away. But if Narz lost control and stopped fighting rationally; his remaining sorcerers were going to die. They were outnumbered, and outmatched.

The left Divine Soldier dome advanced, trading bolts of lightning with sorcerer-soldiers and Keepers. But Narz was intent on the right dome. It turned blue, filling with water. Sorcerers thrashed, air bubbles forming around others. The shield released at several points, divine soldiers gasping for air as they shot out on flows of water.

Lightning streaked through water. Water glowed eerie blue. The shield collapsed. Water washed across the dirty floor, draining away down cracks, leaving motionless bodies where a shield had stood.

Lightning raced along groundwater to Divine Soldiers panting at the edges. They jerked and screamed in its grip, then it dissipated and the last figures from the right dome fell dead.

Ruarnon stared. Was this the hatred and desperation Sorcery War spurned? Images imprinted themselves on Ruarnon's mind, brutal killings, shouts and cries they wouldn't unsee or unhear. This was why Mawana's people hadn't aided Ruarnon's against the Realm... ...why the Northlanders shut themselves off from the world... ...why the Elite Guard Creed was crucial. King Narz had no restraint and Captain Melroth stood rigid while Teliph wept silently on Ruarnon's left.

"He will not recover from this," Teliph said softly. "He will remind himself of his worst nightmares now. He cannot be saved."

Coroth held her, but his gaze was on Narz. Narz tore the left group's shield dome apart, letting Keeper bolts of light fell everyone within it.

No shield dome lay behind the fallen soldiers. The rest of the silver-clad column was spreading out and charging forwards, screaming incoherently with fear and desperation. They were human after all.

Keepers flocked into the throne room behind the dais. Healers ran around them, crouching over Keeper and sorcerer-soldier fallen. New Keepers formed shield domes before the oncoming silver caped figures, fending off fire, some directed at them, some bursting over their heads, aimed at Narz.

Lightning lanced down from overhead, and the edge of the Keeper shield broke. Half a dozen Keepers and a Healer flew backwards, striking the ground, lifeless.

"Eligar!" Captain Melroth screamed. He leapt off the destroyed dais, running to the fallen Healer.

King Narz flinched at Melroth's cry and stared after him. His voice was soft, yet Ruarnon made out the words over the scattered fighting of silver figures and sorcerer-soldiers; "Why do they die? I try *so hard* to protect them. But they keep dying. The enemy won't stop. They keep killing. So much death. We were all so *young*..."

Ruarnon shivered, not at the explosion of temper that made the ceiling burn overhead, causing the last flying soldiers to drop like fireflies, but because King Narz was speaking not of Healers, but the deaths of his comrades in the First Sorcery War, his mind wandering back in time.

There was a scuffle before Ruarnon. Teliph wrenched herself out of Coroth's arms and ran down the steps. Several bolts of lightning struck towards her and were redirected.

"Father!" she cried. "You can still protect them! There are over a hundred Keepers here, and they need you!"

"But... The Southerners were not meant to fight! So many *dead*!" Narz cried, his features twisted in anguish.

Then his eyes widened, and his features stilled. "The damars are *dead*?" he whispered. "All of them? *Why* do the Priests attack my creations! Why have they betrayed me? Even Aunt Ziliene thought they would be...

"Where is Aunt Ziliene?" he asked, his features softening, making him looking much younger, and more afraid. "I need her. She always calms me when... are they back? Did I find them? They're coming again!"

"Your Beneficence," Melroth interrupted, stepping before Narz, while the other Keepers trembled and directed their frightened gazes at the bolts of lightning they were straining to protect themselves against from the advancing Divine Army. "You have almost defeated the enemy, but we need your help Sire."

"But there are such terrible battles, and you would have me look at *small* things, like Coroth and Poran and those Galvations. I CANNOT deal with EVERYTHING! DOES *NO ONE* UNDERSTAND?!"

"That is clear."

Narz's eyes narrowed in suspicion, and Ruarnon trembled. Captain Rilmar stepped before the throne. Lightning from Divine Soldiers glanced away from her, striking those casting it, felling them.

"You need not stand alone," Captain Rilmar added. "We too have identified the God Kings as enemies."

"Who are…"

The wild spark in King Narz's eyes blazed to the fore. If Narz killed her; the Elite Guard would avenge her, and the Third Sorcery War would unfold in all its terror...

Ruarnon took a deep breath, craft their shield and ignored Tor's cries as they sprinted down the steps. They flung themself before Captain Rilmar, meeting Narz's gaze directly, ignoring the pounding of their heart.

Narz gasped. The wildness in his eyes retreated, the hardened anger of his features softening, but he still quivered with not-quite-acknowledged terror of the Guardians.

"Oh," he said softly, and pain pierced his gaze. "You've come to… it's almost time. I *Saw*… They are safe. I have always kept them safe."

His tone was earnest and his eyes pleading, but he struggled to look Ruarnon in the eye, and Ruarnon realised the effect they had on Narz was guilt. Guilt could cripple him.

"May I see them?" Ruarnon asked, focusing on damage that could be rectified.

Narz smiled. "Of course! Why, they shall be free to rule! And you…" joy flared on his face, then was blown clear by doubt.

Sorcery crackled against the Keeper shield. Sorcerer-soldiers hurled daggers at a shield dome advancing on Ruarnon's right. A gold leaf armoured and helmed man marched with them, flanked by gold caped bodyguards. More silver cloaked soldiers marched behind him.

"We must go," Captain Rilmar tugged Ruarnon's arm, and they ran back up the steps.

"Lord Vye's brother," King Narz said behind them. "The man who would take the North!"

Ruarnon whipped around atop the stairs. Narz shivered and frowned in confusion at the silver cloaked mass advancing before him.

Someone rushed past Ruarnon.

"This will *never* be your land!" Teliph cried, as she positioned herself between King Narz and the God King. Coroth spluttered, but Ruarnon held him back with one arm, knowing he would only get himself killed. Coroth glanced tensely at Ruarnon, not resisting them.

Blue lightning shone forwards from the God King, his guards adding their own thin beams to it. Teliph reached forwards, tears on her face, anger blazing in her eyes.

White light shone forth. It halted halfway across the throne room from Teliph. Bolts shot chaotically sideways, vaporising silver cloaked soldiers parallel to it. The wall on Ruarnon's right cracked and the floor shook. Every Keeper and sorcerer-soldier ducked.

Teliph grit her teeth, face straining and sweating. The gold cloaked bodyguards shivered. Teliph screamed.

A shield pulsed out from Narz, between the divine column and his sorcerers. The white divine soldier bolt struck the ground beneath it. Debris shot through the air. Chunks of floor smashed up through silver cloaked figures, tossing them around. Rock hit walls, which exploded in glittering showers. Chunks of stone and shards of wall rebounded off Narz's shield above Keepers, Teliph and himself, raining down on the silver and gold cloaked mass.

The world flashed opaque before Ruarnon. Chunks of masonry were deflected. Bolts too. Narz's shield extended before the throne room entrance before them. Beyond his shield before the dais, Keepers and sorcerer soldiers still crouched, unharmed. Narz had saved them all.

When stray magic burnt out and debris stilled, a charred crater was all that remained of the God King and his bodyguards. Behind them, more silver cloaked soldiers froze.

Coroth ran past as Teliph swayed, and she collapsed into his arms, her face pale and clothes botchy with sweat patches. He scooped her up and carried her up the stairs.

Ruarnon sensed eyes on them as they approached. Gold masked gazes swept from the incapacitated Teliph to Narz, who gaped at Teliph, horror-struck.

"What have I done?" he asked. "I was to protect you! No more young generations to suffer Sorcery War!"

His features twitched, torn between rage and grief. Gold masked gazes noted it, as a cry of triumph rose from the silent throne room floor. Ruarnon followed it, to a silver cape, silver armour and helm that turned gold. "Their leaders are overpowered! Let's finish this! Kill the traitors!" the man roared.

Silver cloaks turned to the Keepers, who stood protectively before Healers and tensed as one. Lightning flared. A silver cloak cried out. Vines lashed down the ruined corridor, seizing silver cloaked figures and knocking them into each other. The crack of masonry roared, followed by rumbles echoing down the corridor.

Silver cloaks cried out, some falling into the crack opening down the corridor. Others leaped aside, into crystal shards raining from the ceiling. Enough silver cloaks fell to make yellow cloaked figures advancing behind them visible. The Elite Guard had entered the war.

CHAPTER 40

RED CLOAK -LINH

Time slowed for Linh. Narz gaped. His magic was still. He cast no shield to protect his Keepers, who strained against stray bolts from silver cloaked figures. He didn't even defend himself, a bolt flashing by his right. He was too shocked by the Elite Guard's appearance. But if his rage overpowered his fear… This was the moment.

Linh hurtled down the stone steps.

"*NO!*" Lenaris's voice screamed.

Sound stopped. A white shield corridor formed around Linh, and Fiona, who ran beside her. The shield corridor ended by Narz's side, where he stood, eyes wide with defeat. It was the same face that had looked over his shoulder and waved in acknowledgement, before luring them to what turned out to be the safest place in the world, unaffected by every war since. Red Cloak was protecting them one more time, as he had intended from the moment he snatched them from their world.

Narz *was* Red Cloak. It was Narz who had been watching them. And despite that for all appearances he was defeated, he was still protecting her, and Fiona, and Troy and Michael, whose footsteps thumped behind her.

But Linh only was halfway when Narz's face turned ghostly pale and he shivered in terror. Yellow-cloaked figures advanced down the hallway, shielded against silver cloak's lightning. Rage flared in Narz's eyes, annihilating his fear. Light burned bright above him. Its heat waves pulsed down the shield tunnel.

"YOU *WILL NOT* TAKE THEM FROM ME!"

Linh sprinted towards him.

Narz's hand raised. Terrible power crackled above him. His fist clenched, his biceps tightened to hurl that power. Fiona sprinted towards too, tears of sympathy in her eyes. Fiona would know what to say. She always knew. But Fiona tripped. She was falling. It was up to Linh.

What did she say to the man who'd wrenched her from her home, and suffered more than anyone she knew? Who'd done terrible things and saved countless strangers? How did she pierce his delusions?

Linh pushed past startled Keepers up the dais. She halted before the throne, reaching for Narz's shoulder, then squeezed it. It felt just like any other human's shoulder. It was also sticky with blood. A wound he hadn't noticed. But he noticed her.

"I cannot turn from them. They will-"

She couldn't let him talk himself into anything. "You told me we would stop it," she said, ignoring the way her voice shook. "And we will. It's time to stop Narz."

He's eyes widened. Confusion clouded his expression.

"The war is ending. It ends here. It ends now. It ends with *us*."

His mouth opened. His features softened and his eyes glazed over. He didn't seem to see the Elite Guard anymore.

"Linh?"

He frowned, his expression still soft, as he gazed past her, unseeing. Still not looking at her, or the others, as he had when he dreamt himself beside them.

"Are you going to kick me?"

She had said that a lifetime ago, on Myleth Island. He *had* been watching them all along, and the idea that a five-foot teenage girl with a temper wanted to kick the most powerful sorcerer in the world gave *him* pause. But the set of his mouth and vagueness of his eyes still showed confusion. She'd need to steer him, before his mind wandered back to a destructive path.

"I forgave you for that a while back," she said. "That was before I realised you were taking everything I knew about health care and our legal system, applying it to your world, and making it better."

Narz's eyes glazed with tears. "You think *I* did well?"

Linh's eyes filled with tears too. Yes, he'd caused a lot of harm. People were dead because of his choices. But he'd also liberated every person in the Divine Realms. And how many thousands would the Healers he had trained and funded save? How could he doubt he'd also done good?

"Just because you fucked up, doesn't mean you didn't *also* do good. Who knows how many people will live, who would have died without your Healers?"

Narz smiled, another tear running down his face. He was looking at her now. Not into her eyes, but *at* her, though his eyes weren't in focus, as if his mind was partly somewhere else. And he was breathing more freely, his posture relaxing a little.

"Such wonderful ideas," he said. "Do you think, my version, will live on, after me?"

Linh nodded, and a tear escaped her eye. "Can you imagine Teliph's reign?"

"But... without me... and Darius lost..."

Narz startled. Ruarnon stepped up beside Linh, clasping Narz's other shoulder.

"I will advise Teliph. I swear to you. We will give this continent a peace only you, she and I can dream of."

Ruarnon's tears were mirrored by Narz's own.

"But your parents..."

Guilt pulled at Narz's bottom lip, but Ruarnon cut it off.

"I will spend some time with them, but I will stay here, to advise Teliph as she rebuilds this continent."

"As you have done before," Narz said, smiling sadly, his gaze becoming distant.

Narz's features tightened, as though he was in pain. "But are lives saved equal to lives taken?"

Linh gasped. Those were Monin's words, from when Ruarnon's council advised them on how to sentence Poran and Dargus.

"How do *I* atone?" Narz asked, echoing Dargus, when Ruarnon pronounced his sentence.

Narz *had* been watching. Everyone. More than anyone thought. It *was* how he knew so much. And perhaps it was why he was so conflicted with guilt. His ability to *See* let him understand the impact of his actions more than perhaps any other human.

"You send Poran and Dargus to the Zaldeaan Realm as Healers," said Ruarnon. "Let them and any who wish to atone live out their lives in service to Zaldeaans. Grant them the opportunity to *save* Zaldeaan lives."

Narz smiled through tears. "I would like that. Can someone see that they do? Can that chance be granted to... anyone else?"

Linh heard the unspoken words. *Anyone else I have wronged. The Galvations. The Timbalens.*

"I will see to it," Ruarnon promised.

But they were talking as if... A heavy footstep thudded on Linh's other side. Troy reached them, supporting Fiona, who clutched a bloody knee.

A youthful smile lit Narz's face. His posture relaxed. And an aura of power around him vanished, revealing burns and bloodstains on his blue silks, wounds he had sustained while shielding others, but perhaps not himself. His knees buckled, and Troy rushed forwards, shocked into compassion by his sudden vulnerability. Troy and Michael caught Narz and sat him carefully atop his throne.

He turned to the boys, bemused.

"Friendship!" he smiled at Troy, whose mouth opened in wonder.

"He *has* been watching," Michael said quietly.

"Had to keep you safe; cleverness," Narz replied, his eyes glinting, and starting to glaze over.

Linh stepped closer, still holding his shoulder. The man who had brought them there, the man behind everything, who greeted them with a warmth they had once not believed him capable of, was dying.

Narz smiled and a tear of joy ran down his face.

"I wish I had such friendship." He trembled. "I wish my family were here."

"What were they like?" Fiona asked.

Narz looked up, smiling sadly into Fiona's gentle eyes.

His lips fumbled, as if losing the ability to form words. But he managed two; "Show you."

Everything went dark, then hazy. It became clearer. A little boy and a little girl stood talking to each other before Linh, who gasped at them.

"I fink, yowr it!" the little girl cried.

"No! Yoo are!" the little boy replied.

"Yoo are, yoo are, yoo are!" the little girl chanted.

There was a third person, running towards them. Linh was watching the scene through that person's eyes. "I believe you are both it and as I am the oldest; that settles it!" a young man's familiar voice called.

"No fair!" the little girl replied, both hands on her hips.

"You're supposed to take my side Narz! That's what brothers are for!" the boy protested.

"Children, dinner!"

The two younger siblings smiled, Narz replying, "Yes mother."

The little boy claimed he was fastest and ran ahead, the little girl pouting, then squealing with delight as Narz scooped her up and ran with long strides to catch the boy. They burst through the door of a wooden cottage side by side, stopping suddenly before a large table of rough wood.

"Sit down," their mother insisted with a smile, laying a dish of duck, which Linh somehow knew was a special treat, on the table.

The siblings rushed to their seats, hearing the door opening behind them. All three turned to their father. Why was father coming in the back door and wearing that mysterious look about his face? The little girl smiled and clapped her hands, the little boy asking excitedly, "What's the surprise?"

"We have a special guest for dinner," father declared, stepping aside to reveal a smiling young woman.

"Auntie Ziliene!" the boy cried, the little girl clapping her hands again and smiling.

Linh knew her friends were crying. Because the young Ziliene didn't turn to her niece and nephews. She looked right at where Linh and her friends must be standing. Tears ran down her face, as she smiled and bowed her head in acknowledgement.

"She can see us!" Troy whispered. "That's really…"

Then the children were speaking to Ziliene and the tears had gone from her face as she smiled and answered, her smile focused on Narz. But the words were becoming muffled, and Linh couldn't understand. Ziliene reached to hug Narz, and everyone's view was obscured by Narz's tears as his head moved over her shoulder.

Something was wrong. Everything became dark, and then white light shone, a dome shield. It surrounded Linh and her friends, Troy holding Fiona tightly as they wept, Fiona reaching for Linh with one arm and Troy reaching for Michael with the other. Even Michael was crying, another boy who'd lost his parents. Ruarnon's arm wrapped around Michael's other side, and Michael smiled at them.

Linh hugged her friends tightly, her head against Troy's chest, beside Fiona's, knowing that Narz; Red Cloak, lay dead on the dais before them.

Linh lost track of time. She looked up when the shield around the top of the dais shifted, as Teliph knelt beside Narz's body. Coroth jogged up behind her, kneeling to place an arm around her back as sobs wracked her body and tears slid silently down his face.

Fiona lifted her head from Troy's chest and turned her red, puffy face to Teliph. "He was thinking of his family when he died," she said softly, her voice cracked.

"He let you *See* into his mind?" Teliph asked.

"He was having dinner with his parents and siblings, and he was young again and his aunt was their guest," Fiona added, another tear trickling down her cheek as she smiled.

"She could see us," Michael added.

Teliph's eyes widened and several more tears spilled down her face. "He let her see into his mind! In his final moments, you made him feel safe enough to let her *See*. They were reconciled..."

More tears ran down her face. Troy sobbed and it occurred to Linh that Queen Ziliene must also be dead.

"You did more," Teliph said, her voice broken, tears spilling down her face. "The enchantment on Tira has broken. We all felt it break. Everyone stopped fighting. It happened *before* —when he was speaking to you. Tira lives, again!"

Ruarnon smiled through their tears, likely picturing the look on Selenia's face when they told her.

The conversation paused just long enough for Linh to notice that everything beyond them was silent. The fighting had indeed ceased.

Then Teliph drew a deep breath, resting her hands on Coroth's, which held her gently.

"He found you by opening the gateway seeking safe haven for sorcerers," she said. "I'm going to build it. Here. The City of Safe Haven. Healers will heal there, Keepers will patrol it, and Luvaras Priests and Priestesses, Dedicated and non-magic wielders and Galvations and southerners; everyone will be welcome. And I will found a school of magic, that anyone who wishes to learn to heal can do so."

"I will help you," said Coroth and she smiled at him.

"I will stay as you long as you need my advice," Ruarnon offered, "if you wish. I promised Narz I would, and I mean to keep that promise."

Teliph smiled, more tears running down her face and she bowed her head. Ruarnon bowed back, teary-eyed. Linh and her friends had fulfilled their role in Lylah's better futures, but Ruarnon's was just beginning.

"I shall also help," a voice called from a passageway near the dais.

Everyone turned.

"Uncle Daxius!" Teliph cried.

Daxius stood in blue silks, his gaze as sharply intelligent as ever. As Teliph stood, he shivered at sight of King Narz's body, tears gleaming in his eyes, then he pushed them away to hold Teliph. Warmth and kindness that had not been so obvious when he was their prisoner in Imperial City blazed in his smile.

"How are you here?" Teliph asked.

"Lylah believed I was needed," Daxius replied. "She took it upon herself to order the Urai to transport me here without the emperor's permission."

"It may be best if we do not tell him you are missing," Ruarnon said.

Daxius met their gaze and they smiled at each other. There was a darkness in Daxius' eyes, but Linh suspected meeting Ruarnon reminded him he had innocent blood on his hands, from Imperial City.

Troy loosened his grip and Linh stepped back. Lenaris and Mawana stood before the dais. The dome shield protecting them had vanished. The remaining silver cloaked figures were unconscious and shielded, drifting towards fifty odd yellow-cloaked Elite Guard in the corridor opposite the dais. Two familiar faces rushed to embrace Captain Rilmar. Beyond, a silent tension froze the room.

Keepers stood protectively before Healers, and they and the sorcerer-soldiers stood tensely, opposite Elite Guard. The Elite Guard halted behind dead and captive silver cloaked figures. Their uncertain gazes shifting between nervous sorcerers.

Captain Melroth stepped between the Keeper line and fallen silver cloaks. Captain Rilmar smiled as she strode to meet him. The Elite Guard turned to her, while Narz's sorcerers focused on Melroth.

"On behalf of the Elite Guard," Captain Rilmar said clearly, pitching her voice to carry, "I would like to offer not merely peace, but friendship, to the Keepers and Healers of the Northwest."

"And I," Captain Melroth said, his sooty face tear tracked, "on behalf of King Narz's sorcerers, accept. There is much we can learn from one another."

Captain Rilmar smiled and bowed her head. Captain Melroth returned the gesture. As if it were a signal, the atmosphere eased, sorcerers on both sides breathing with relief, sorcerer-soldiers frowning at Elite Guard, Keepers and Healers eyeing an established sorcerer organisation with awe.

"How goes the battle?" Captain Rilmar asked her squad.

"The Priests took control of the damars," the woman replied. "Some damars wished to surrender. Others wanted only to fight. The latter have been put to permanent sleep, and the former taken captive. The Dedicated aid the Healers with the wounded, guarded by nervous Keepers. Priests and Priestesses keep their distance. All await the outcome of the battle here."

Yellow cloaked Elite Guard parted with looks of surprise, even awe. Two figures advanced between them, two serene, wizened faces, one framed by a silk hood of midnight blue, the other of purple. Both faces showed a kindness that reminded Linh of Nuard. The pink cloaked figure who walked behind them greeted Linh and her companions with a smile, little sparks of magic tingling in the air around them.

"Queen Ziliene was mistaken to be so mistrusting of us," the Luvaras Priest announced, as they approached Captain Melroth and Captain Rilmar. "Some of us are not so much younger than she, descendants of those protected by similar enchantments to the one King Narz unknowingly craft upon himself and his aunt."

There was something about their openness. Linh couldn't help asking, "Did you know Amina and the others were pretending to be Luvaras Priestesses?"

The Luvaras Priestess smiled. "Naturally. We might have helped them, had we not feared it would scare them half to death."

The same warmth and confidence Amina radiated smiled at Linh, and she smiled back.

Then the Priestess' expression turned more serious. "We shall not bow to any ruler," she said, "but should a threat like the Divine Army ever arise again Empress," she addressed Teliph, "you shall have our aid."

She smiled at Teliph and Teliph returned her smile.

"And ours," said the Dedicated.

"And ours," the High Priest added.

"But on this day," said the Dedicated, "when all main sorcerer forces, save the distant North Landers, are in the same room, I propose more. Captain Melroth speaks of learning. King Narz was a superb teacher. And Teliph intends to found a school of sorcery. We Dedicated should like to register our interest as teachers. If all sorcerers work together in learning, we hope wars like those that have marred our world this past year can be avoided in future."

"I will found a school, in time," Teliph replied. "And I welcome any of your ranks who wish to teach there."

The Dedicated, High Priest and High Priestess inclined their heads sideways, an acknowledgement that evaded submission.

"There is one thing more that must be done now," said Captain Melroth. "Fulfil King Narz's final order." His voice cracked, as he directed a pair of Keepers.

Everyone waited, and Linh wondered, until two Keepers entered the throne with two other people. The man wore his blonde hair in a Tarlahn braid, while the woman's dark hair was in many braids, like Mawana's.

Tor and Lenaris bowed. Ruarnon's eyes filled with tears. They ran silently into their parents' waiting arms.

"Captain Melroth tells us you have been redefining Tarlahn kingship," King Urmilian said, his voice rich and warm, his eyes older than his young, slightly too thin face, when they finally stepped apart. "And I see Companion Tor approves strongly of it, as I am sure I shall."

Ruarnon smiled through their tears.

"Congratulations Lenaris!" Corina called. "A girl I think!"

The way Mawana held Lenaris's stomach showed the rounding of early pregnancy. Mawana beamed and Lenaris smiled.

"You *are* married?" Corina asked.

Lenaris laughed. "Yes, Benevolence."

"Speaking of which," Daxius said with a smile, turning to Coroth and Teliph, "I hope my blessing is sufficient, not that you truly need it now, Empress."

He bowed. Keepers, Healers and sorcerer-soldiers knelt and bowed to Teliph as one, Captain Melroth smiling as he bowed beside Daxius.

Teliph took a deep breath and cast a sad gaze at King Narz's still form. She gently propped his head on the folded red cloak Captain Melroth handed her, then stood and saluted her subjects with her fist in the air and a watery smile on her face.

"Long live the Empress! Long live the Empress!" Red and green cloaked sorcerers chanted.

Then many people gasped. A portal opened on the dais, its far side opening over sorcery blasted plains, where Keepers stirred, taking up the chant, alongside more Healers and sorcerer-soldiers. Dargus joined the chant, General Takanis smiling beside him.

A second portal opened beside the first, over a courtyard packed with Azulan soldiers, who stared, then began to smile and take up the chant. A third portal opened above a crowded city, with a distant view of King Narz's castle, its streets packed with frightened faces, who gazed into the throne room with awe.

More portals opened, one over the deserted streets of Galvatia City, where Governor Poran smiled with tears in his eyes, another over the farmlands, where Princes Maharl and Joharlen stepped out of their farmhouse and hope flared in their eyes.

The next opened over ship decks crowded with uncertain Zaldeaans and Tarlahns. Companion Karmarn waved to Coroth and Urmilian, while Governor Iagl looked on with a fierce smile. Then the Zaldeaans noticed Coroth at Teliph's right side while she saluted her subjects. Understanding dawned on their faces, and they too took up the chant; "Long live the Empress!"

The last portal opened on a sombre mood; a green carpeted throne room, its walls painted with forest frescoes, its floor crowded with weeping figures, Queen Ziliene's still form laid upon its dais. Confused women in purple silks stood by the dais, smiling when they spotted Fiona and she waved at them.

A woman in green silks bowed before Amina and said, "King Narz's empire has an Empress. We need a leader to make peace with them, and her Brightness appointed you as heir, My Lady."

Amina turned to Queen Ziliene's stately body and smiled. She straightened, facing Teliph through the portal and raised her left hand to acknowledge Teliph, with a motherly smile. Teliph raised her left hand in reply, returning the kindly stranger's smile.

"All the insanity *was* worth it!" said Troy, shaking his head and grinning from ear to ear.

Linh punched him in the arm.

"Ow!" he replied, rubbing it with his other hand.

"You threw yourself into everything when you weren't sure?" she asked.

"I was," he said. "I was following you. And Fi and Mic. I trust you lot."

Fiona beamed, Michael smiled and Linh's pretence at annoyance melted into a blazing smile.

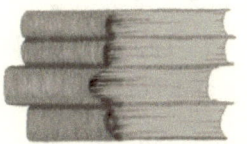

CHAPTER 41

The Luvaras Priestess' Gift -Linh

A day later, after a quiet dinner celebrating peace with the Tarlahns and Mawana, Linh stood with Fiona, Michael and Troy, paused part way down a familiar corridor of Narz's Castle. This time no one stood around the Gateway of Umarinaris ahead, and Ruarnon, Lenaris, Mawana, Tor, Captain Arleath and Ruarnon's faithful guards approached not far behind them.

"It feels too soon," said Troy. "We haven't even told the others."

"They know we'll be leaving soon," said Fiona.

"I doubt they expect it yet," said Troy.

"But you don't want to keep your younger siblings waiting, or your mother worrying any longer?" Michael asked.

Troy shook his head and Fiona squeezed his hand.

Linh sighed. It was never going to be easy to say goodbye. She didn't want to. But she missed Ba. And her parents. Now that everything she'd been trying to achieve was done, or as much as she could do if it, and after all the fear and doubt and time spent trying to get home, the way back lay before them, and it loomed largest in her thoughts.

"It's time," Michael said solemnly. "But I don't want to go home. This place and the lives we lived here had so much more meaning."

"It was wonderful to make a difference," said Fiona.

"I wanted to see what happened to everyone!" Linh stamped her foot in frustration. "Galvatia's still drought-stricken and Captain Rilmar and Commander Octharl are signing treaties without Emperor Yarath's permission!"

"We've seen a few signs it will turn out right," said Troy.

"We're getting ready to take Selenia to Tira to meet her parents," Ruarnon said, as they, Mawana, Lenaris and Tor stopped beside Fiona.

"Are you coming with us?" Ruarnon added hopefully.

"I'm afraid we're ready to leave to," Michael replied and Ruarnon's face fell.

A group of Luvaras Priestesses strode towards them from the other side of the Gateway of Umarinaris, Teliph walking beside the High Priestess.

"You have more than earnt your passage," said the High Priestess. "It will please us to send you."

Mawana's gaze lowered and Lenaris smiled sadly. They, Ruarnon and Tor stepped up beside Linh, Fiona, Troy and Michael, followed by Ruarnon's guards. Everyone approached the Gateway of the Umarinaris together, but the distance was too short and they crossed it too swiftly.

Yet Linh knew they had been there for King Narz when he needed them most, and their quest in his world was finished. It was time to go home.

"You are half of the first group of friends I truly had," Ruarnon said. "Drake, Lenaris and I were always friends, but the other children in the palace didn't have our interest in learning, or politics. Or fighting. Everyone else I knew, save Lenaris, always saw me as Heir. Always treated me differently. But you treated me like one of you.

"Your tendency to speak your minds and show your feelings went beyond Tarlahn propriety, and it was more than refreshing. You helped me to focus on what mattered most. And you taught me to see the funny side of things. And Troy, you taught me to find reasons to smile in even the darkest situations. I will miss you always."

Fiona teared up and hugged them first.

Troy was just as teary, and surprised Linh by not only hugging Ruarnon, but giving them a peck on the cheek, which for some reason made Michael smile.

"I'll miss having conversations with you in them," said Michael. "Linh's great, but I don't know anyone quite like you."

Ruarnon hugged him and Michael smiled sadly as he hugged them back.

"We always doubted everything Nuard said about us being another Myth of the Strangers," said Linh, "or heroes sent to save the world. And of course we're us, but *you* made space for us. You gave us the chance to make a difference by listening, trusting us and letting us tag along. Thank you."

Linh tried to blink back tears as she hugged Ruarnon. They were such a calm, measured, steady presence. Like the earth you stood on, or the structural features that held the ceiling overhead. It would be so strange living without them.

"Don't do anything I wouldn't do at home," Mawana said with a smile.

"Do everything I *would* do here," Troy replied.

Fiona hugged Mawana first, then Michael. Linh hugged him next. Troy's eyes welled with tears and Mawana hugged him like he had no intention of letting go. Linh gave Fiona a one-armed hug because Fiona was crying too. Eventually, Michael put an arm around Troy and peeled him off Mawana.

Fiona stepped forward to hug Lenaris.

"Remember the confidence you built here," Lenaris told her. "Take it home."

"I will," Fiona replied.

Michael hugged Lenaris.

Troy turned a tear-streaked face to her and Lenaris swept him into her arms. Lenaris was crying too.

"I am not worried about you," Lenaris whispered. "You have Fiona to love you and Linh to rescue your arse when you get into trouble, assuming she didn't have the chance to stop you getting into it first."

Troy chuckled and Linh laughed.

Then Troy and Lenaris stepped apart and Lenaris turned to Linh.

Linh sighed. "Most of the *really* strong-willed women I know are on Umarinaris. I don't know who to look up to at home."

Lenaris smiled. "I'm sure you're strong willed enough to find us in your world."

Linh smiled back and Lenaris held her tight.

"Say goodbye to Mocco for us," Fiona added to Mawana, as Linh and Lenaris stepped apart. "And to your family."

"Tell him we'd ask him to keep you and Lenaris out of trouble, but we also want him to have time to be an Elder and don't want to subject him to unreasonable amounts of strain," Troy added with a grin.

Lenaris and Mawana responded with watery smiles.

Troy gripped Fiona's hand and Michael's. Fiona gripped Linh's. They needed something to hold on to, given everyone they were about to walk away from.

"I'd wish you well on advising Teliph," Michael said to Ruarnon, "and reconciling with the damars, and the Middle South and Galvatia. But I'm sure you've got it well in hand. I'm also confident Lenaris and Mawana will settle down in a safe, stable, boring environment to raise their baby."

He flashed a wicked grin, Ruarnon laughed and Lenaris and Mawana laughed wetly.

Troy shook his head. "I'm going to have to apologise *so* hard to Andy for ruining you."

Michael smiled at Troy. "I suspect he'll think he owes you one. Are we ready?"

He turned to Fiona, who nodded. Linh sighed and nodded too. Troy smiled sadly, another tear running down his face as he turned back to the people, they had lived every day with for over a year, and the faithful guards who had watched their backs, all of whom smiled and waved. Linh and her three friends waved back, then turned to the Priestesses, Teliph and the Gateway of Umarinaris.

Linh sighed again, sharing her friends' reluctance to leave.

Why was a smile playing about the High Priestess' face?

"I think you have earnt another reward," said the High Priestess. "Would you like to *See*?"

Linh's face split in a smile. "Yes please!"

"Look to the wall."

Linh turned to the brown crystalline wall beside the archway. Its rainbow gleam swirled in a mix of colours. There was a burst of colour and they *Saw* Coroth, now with smile lines on his face, walking down a crowded street of tall, elegant stone buildings, many domed with glass, holding the hand of a young girl, with a little boy riding his shoulders.

"But I don't want to go to school!" the little girl protested. "I want to stay at home with you and Sar!"

"Do not tell your mother that," Coroth replied wryly. "She founded this school. If she has her way; children, your age will be attending Sythe Schools all across the empire. Empress Tirisium is founding them in the South too."

"It's beautiful, Teliph," said Fiona.

Teliph smiled, her eyes glazing with tears.

The domed buildings, spires, balconies, and happy chatter of people walking down the paved street… they were *Seeing* the as-yet-unbuilt City of Safe Haven.

Colours swirled together, then separated again.

"Are you sure you are ready for this brother?" Joharlen asked Prince Maharl, as they stood before a stone building with a great glass dome, among the rich red-brown buildings of Galvatia City. The streets were crowded with people on foot, riders, carts and dogs, and beyond the open city gates, green and yellow grain fields extended below a vast, clear blue sky.

Linh exhaled deeply.

People stood along the street, staring. Some were wringing their hands, many stood with eyes open wide, others shaking their heads slowly. Fiona smiled and pointed out an older man and a young couple, their faces full, their hair clean. Linh's old cellmates from the Forest prison stood in the front line of the street, Tayku squeezing Sharma's hand, Captain Shafar eyeing the road with anticipation.

"Amina insists I get used to this," Prince Maharl replied to Joharlen.

He stepped forwards. Before him, the crowd were parting to admit the passage of green cloaked figures. Healers in *Galvatia*...

"Welcome," Prince Maharl said with a smile, as he strode forwards to meet them.

Colours swirled again, as smiles spread on Linh's friends faces and they waited eagerly to see who was next.

A crowded, unfamiliar throne room formed, with far too many weapons on its walls. A familiar high priestess, carrying a familiar diamond studded helm walked towards the dais, where she handed the crown to Governor Iagl. Governor's Iomar and Kia stood by and Linh gaped. Syenne sat in the throne.

Governor Iagl took a deep breath, whispering in Syenne's ear, "Don't tell the others, but I acknowledge you were always going to be better at this."

Queen Syenne smiled, as he placed the crown upon her head.

The room was crowded with men around the edges, who smiled with little enthusiasm, or clapped with stern faces or politely. But the ladies smiled and clapped with enthusiasm, including a woman who bore a resemblance to Ruarnon's father, who looked very pleased. Companion Karmarn smiled openly and clapped freely beside her.

Another swirl of colour. A gasp of excitement as bright colours and tropical plants of the jungle spread before them. Lenaris sat on a wooden chair on the jungle floor, heavily pregnant, while Kahorn, Tither and Mirata stood by, watching Mocco toss a toddler in the air, who giggled with delight, demanding, "Again Uncle Mocco!"

As Mocco obliged his nephew, Mawana ran around a gnarled tree trunk, screaming a mock scream, as a laughing blond child craft a shield on his left, and he dodged a tree trying to grab him on his right.

"Are you certain accepting immigrants from the west was wise?" Mirata asked Kahorn.

"It was until we set our nephew lose among them," Kahorn replied with a chuckle.

"I'll have you know my students are quite well behaved, when not under the corrupting influence of my boisterous husband," Lenaris replied imperiously, and Troy chuckled, while Linh smiled.

On Linh's right, Lenaris's eyes opened in wonder, and a very broad smile spread across Mawana's face, likely as many mischievous possibilities crossed his mind. Ruarnon smiled too.

Then the colours swirled, and Linh breathed deeply when, as she expected, a Tarlahn scene opened before them. Ruarnon's face looked older, more defined, and they wore no circlet on their head, because their father was king now. They led a little girl with deep brown eyes, tan skin and brown finely braided hair into a room that made everyone smile.

Sunlight streamed into the Golden Meeting Hall between pillars on the right and the child pointed enthusiastically at silver busts.

"Mother says that's where the spirits of the companions and advisors are," the little girl said. "And the gold ones; that's where the old rulers are."

Ruarnon smiled. "So Lenaris began your education early?"

"Of course she did. She said I needed to be ready to be your heir," the little girl replied with her mother's confidence. Linh smiled, suspecting the girl was the baby Lenaris was pregnant with now, adopted as Ruarnon's heir.

The girl frowned. "But who are they?"

She pointed to four bronze busts on new pillars Linh and her friends didn't recognise.

"Those do not contain spirits," Ruarnon explained. "I had them made from memory in the west, to help me advise Empress Teliph, and to remind me to make wise decisions when I become ruler here, one day. They are old friends of mine."

"No way!" Troy exclaimed, eyeing a curly haired bust.

Fiona smiled at a kind face, Michael smiled at a sharply intelligent one which was mostly unreadable, but had gleaming eyes and Linh blinked at a determined face which smiled. Did she really look like that? She must —to Ruarnon.

Troy smiled at Ruarnon, who gave a rare grin in reply, as if they had already planned this instalment in the Golden Meeting Hall.

Colours swirled, and the Empress of the Timbalen Empire set down her embroidery on her silver couch and turned to Emperor Yarath, who sat too straight in his gold leaf chair, his wrinkled hands rigidly clasped, in a Timbalen reception room Linh didn't recognise.

Empress and Emperor were grey-haired now, their faces lined, his more than hers; deep frown lines over his forehead. A silver-haired Captain Rilmar entered the room, wearing the gold silk cape of the Emperor's Elite Bodyguards and a smile.

"My kin would not have been able to cure the plague without First Healer Darius and his Healers, your Greatness," Captain Rilmar said. "This alliance is necessary to extend our knowledge of healing."

Emperor Yarath's hands loosened. "I am glad," he said quietly, addressing the carpet. "I am glad that you and Octharl defied me all those years ago. I was… …afraid… I could have crushed something wonderful, but you stopped me. Thank you."

Captain Rilmar smiled and inclined her head.

"The Second Sorcery War ended long ago. I know that Rilmar. Show Empress Teliph in. It is time our relations with the Far West begin anew."

Linh gaped. From how much he had aged, this would be at least twenty years into the future. But he *would* get there.

The colours swirled and Linh's nerves tingled at the prospect of going home. Then she froze, as the wall darkened. There was a rectangular image in the middle. A photo of a slightly older Linh, and underneath, a caption that read: Vote One, Linh Mai, Australians of the World Party.

Linh's mouth opened slowly. The Priestess could *See* the future beyond the Gateway of the World?

"There's no such party!" Troy objected.

"Not yet," Linh replied, smiling determinedly.

Troy's mouth fell open.

"Did you really think I'd let all we've learnt and my stubbornness go to waste at home?"

Her conversation with Narz, how much better his healthcare and prosecutions in his legal system were working... things could be better at home. Ideas were already drafting themselves in her mind.

Troy smiled fiercely.

They fell silent and everyone held their breaths as colours swirled again. The world rocked, as if falling away before Linh. It was dizzying, standing in King Narz's castle, before a flight arrivals board and the railing outside customs, where a small crowd gathered to meet their loved ones.

"That's Tullamarine Airport," she said.

"But what the hell could..." Troy objected. He stopped when new arrivals passed through the gate, all carrying the same bags, with the same logos, not a suitcase in sight.

"Why are they carrying charity bags?" Troy asked. "Where's the rest of their possessions?"

Linh held her breath.

"New students!" a man in the crowd holding a sign called. His sign had logos of every major Victorian university and some Melbourne high school logos on it... "New students over here please!"

A nervous group of young people filed through the gate and strode towards him.

"Rural Professionals Programme!" another voice cried. "Rural professionals over here! Ah, doctor Avuri and doctor Avuri," the woman said, greeting an approaching couple.

"*Refugees*," Linh breathed, her eyes full of tears. "Arriving by *plane*, straight from overseas camps. To programs to set them up in their new lives."

Troy's mouth dropped open. "The government *flew* them in?!" he asked.

Their view was over a young woman's shoulder, who walked forwards as a charity worker approached, leading a little girl by the hand and a group of otherwise unaccompanied children. The young woman crouched before the children, who clustered together, eyeing the high ceiling and strange building around them uncertainly. The woman said in Fiona's voice, "Welcome home. Would you like to meet your new families?"

The children met her gaze and smiled as they nodded.

"And don't worry about the wildlife," said an older, wild curly haired as ever Troy, grinning as he approached. "I'll protect you from the crocodiles, snakes, spiders etc."

"Can we see snakes?" a little girl piped up, her eyes lit with enthusiasm.

Troy's grin broadened. "How about I take you on a trip to the zoo?"

The children cheered, and Troy laughed and began exchanging fist pumps with them.

Colours swirled.

"Troy let loose with refugee orphans," said Michel, shaking his head. Then he smiled. "I'm sure you'll make them happy mate. And Fiona won't let anything bad happen to them."

Michael went very still as the colours cleared again. An older Michael stood before them, at a podium, before a microphone, wearing a suit. The press swarmed around him.

"Is it true you are working with the Australians of the World Party?" a reporter asked.

Older Michael smiled. "Linh Mai is a dear friend. She's consulting with us on our policies for Truth and Treaty, which we hope to make agreeable to *every* state. There's a lot of work to be done. And we will help her party help Australia rise to the challenge."

Colours swirled and resolved back into brown, crystallised wall, as Troy staggered. "It's not over at home!" he asserted, sounding energized. "And you two look set to take on the world," he added, his awed gaze and smile taking in Linh and Michael.

Linh smiled. They could never return to an ordinary life after this. They would have to keep living boldly, taking risks and daring to hope against the odds to carve new, extraordinary lives for themselves at home.

Linh turned to Teliph. "Good luck, with everything."

Teliph smiled.

"And thank, very much," Fiona added to the Priestesses', who tilted their heads sideways in acknowledgement.

Linh beamed, as the engraved symbols around the stone archway glowed bright. She gazed across wet sand, and a beach on which she and Troy had sighted strangely tall rainforest trees that vanished suddenly.

Waves washed against a peaceful shore. A hot sun beamed down, and gum leaves rustled in the wind atop shady hills covered in wildflowers. The smell of salt, sea and home blew on the wind. And this time she was returning to it.

Linh breathed it in, smiling. She and her friends turned to back to exchange final smiles and to wave to Ruarnon, Mawana and Lenaris one last time. Then they stepped forwards, still holding hands, and traded smiles as they moved between the stone arch up which a glowing golden script spiralled, onto dry sand. Linh looked down at her pale blue school dress and runners and sighed at being back in school uniform. Troy frowned at how loosely his polo shirt fit.

Linh turned back, across wet sand circling Noriyong Island, blue waves foaming onto the shore, then deep green sea, all the way to the bright blue sky above the horizon. She sighed, sadness welling within her at new friends and Umarinaris gone.

"We'll hit our destination if we stay on the beach," said Michael. "We can avoid people searching for us in the trees a bit longer."

Linh, Fiona and Troy smiled at that.

"I'm not sure I can go back to immature, naïve, superficial classmates," Linh said firmly.

"I'm not going back," Michael said quietly. "It's not too late to apply for second round places at Uni for next year. I can't wait to study something pitched at my level. You should come Linh; you'll eat those idiots at school who give you a hard time alive otherwise. You'll probably give them nightmares, not that they don't deserve it," he added with a smile.

Linh frowned, seriously considering. She smiled and nodded.

Troy looked crestfallen. "School won't be the same without you two," he said, his gaze lingering on her.

"How am I supposed to manage Troy without you Linh?" Fiona asked, smiling sweetly.

Linh and Troy smiled.

"You won't have us, but you may have someone else," said Michael, his face splitting into the greatest smile Linh had seen on it.

A tall, blonde haired, surfer-type looking boy stepped out from the trees and his face also split in a smile when he spotted Michael. "Mic! I've been worried sick! I thought Troy got you lot abducted or something!"

Troy laughed. "Andy! You, me, Fiona and Mic are going on a double date this weekend!"

Andrew turned to Michael, who smiled shyly at having told three people, none of whom Linh suspected, knew Andrew very well, that they were a couple.

Andrew beamed.

"Actually," Troy added with a sly smile, "a triple date. Linh can take a book."

Linh punched him in the arm, then ruined it by laughing. Troy beamed and laughed with her.

Seriousness fell on her again. It had all begun with a book. The one she was reading on the bus ride to this excursion, that had inspired Narz to revolutionise Umarinaris with legal and health reforms. One that would serve as a nice, thorough introduction into Earth and Australian politics. She suspected mastering that wouldn't be as easy as crafting shield magic.

Michael was running into Andrew's arms. Fiona and Troy smiled and held hands, as the two boys kissed. Then Andrew cupped Michael's face in his hands and smiled so widely Linh wondered how she'd ever written him off as a bit of a dick.

"There's something I've been meaning to tell you all day," Andrew said breathlessly. "And if they already know about us…"

Michael frowned.

"You know how its my grandmother's eightieth the weekend after next?" Andrew asked in a rush.

"Yeah," said Michael.

"Mum said I should invite you."

Michael's hand went to his mouth and his eyes filled with tears. "You told your parents?"

Andrew smiled.

"But that's your dad's mother. How did your dad take it?"

It was strange, seeing the Michael who had been adamant about sailing to Tarlah look nervous about his boyfriend's father's reaction to anything.

"That you're not quite as pretty as my ex-girlfriends but he's always liked you."

Michael smiled through his tears and Andrew bent to kiss him again.

It seemed their friendship group had a new addition. Hopefully one whose heart and love of life was as big as Mawana's, with Lenaris's courage and Ruarnon's patience and brains. Not that Linh wanted to put pressure on her new friend to replace the friends she and the others had left on Umarinaris. But Linh would need her friends help. Why not ensure Narz's legacy lived on in two worlds?

True, many politicians here were a bunch of dicks, and there was so much red tape, and social media and a certain media empire filling people's minds with nonsense. But if anyone was stubborn enough to cut through Earth's bullshit, Linh was equal to the task. Fiona would ensure she didn't become too hard-headed. Troy would help her smile. Michael would be the brains she picked. Only time could tell what Andrew would contribute, to the many possible futures that lay before them, hopefully brighter ones, definitely involving all five of them.

Acknowledgements

This trilogy having been shelved because I was studying/ working/ chronically unwell means it has taken FOR-EVER (let's just say I count it in decades). So as in book one, I'd like to thank everyone who's taken an interest or encouraged me in any way over that time. From people who've asked about my writing and listened patiently while I talk in perhaps a little too much detail, to everyone who's given feedback, be it blurb critiques, beta reading or reviewing book one or two.

More specifically, thanks to Judah Lamey for tirelessly listening to my vision for three book covers, taking on feedback, tweaking and updating maps and covers alike and producing great chapter heading art for this trilogy.

Thanks to Gillian and Rebecca for your general feedback on this book. Thanks to Will for giving feedback on the final version of all 160k words, about characters from nine different civilisations (not counting absent creator gods or the Aussie off-worlders).

And thanks to my housemates for putting up with all my talk of writing, publishing, marketing and for giving thoughtful advice (even when I agree it's good yet don't quite manage to take it, like the incomplete battle diagram for the battle in Black City, Damaria and surrounds, which now exists on my desk courtesy of Susan).

Lastly dear reader, thanks to you, whether you unorthodoxly joined this trilogy part way through, or enjoyed book one enough to follow Ruarnon and Linh to the conclusion of their journey's. I hope you've enjoyed the ride!

Please leave a review!

A few sentences of your overall impressions of War in Sorcery's Shadow can indicate to other readers whether or not it's their cup of tea, so I'd appreciate you leaving a review on;

Goodreads/ BookBub/ StoryGraph/ and or a bookstore.
(Trilogy links via my books page and QR code)

About the Author

Elise Carlson's love of adventure began with a childhood diet of Narnia and teenage years spent playing Final Fantasy. Fascinated with the ancient world, Elise majored in Archaeology and History at University. Then it was time to travel (Europe, Egypt and Turkey).

Their need to earn a living and a desire to work alongside enthusiastic and imaginative counterparts –children— resulted in a teaching career. They taught in Australia, moved to England for exploration of castles, ruins and stately homes and then New Zealand to explore volcanic areas, mountains and to visit Hobbiton. They are now living, teaching and writing in their native Australia.

To stay in touch with Elise and get *Rebellion is Due,* about a turbulent night in Tarlah in Ruarnon's father's youth, sign up Elise's newsletter.

You can connect with Elise to discuss life, books and or writing on:

Bsky

@eliseswritings.bsky.social

Mastodon

@ElisesWritings@wandering.shop

Sythe Series

3,000 years after Teliph I founds sorcery schools, Sythe has become a global peace keeping, law enforcing, monster containing, search and rescuing and healing organisation. Sythe Series is told in first person by a teenage tough from the wrong side of town, Rarkin, who seeks qualifications at Sythe School and Monster Containment employment to escape his abusive father.

But it's a dangerous time to work for Sythe. In the centuries following a Nuclear War that destroyed a continent, and drove modern Umarinaris to abandon modern tech and retreat into city-states, one other organisation remained global in its reach; organised crime. And Organised Crime is entering a bold new era, where it moves against Sythe directly, leaving Rarkin and Sythe's newest students and employees most vulnerable of all.

Selfless and brave, with a strong sense of right and wrong and a thrill for adventure and recklessness, Rarkin must overcome personal trauma, compounded but ultimately assisted by his autism, to make friends at Sythe, trust them and let them in. The days are coming when his own and his team's lives will depend upon it.

You'll find the latest series info at: elisecarlson.com/sythe-series/

www.ingramcontent.com/pod-product-compliance
Lightning Source LLC
Chambersburg PA
CBHW020823030726
47496CB00001B/60